The Deadliest of Intentions

By

Marc Stevens

This book is dedicated to all those who protect this country and all we hold dear. You shall forever be my heroes.

Contents

1..7

2...20

3...35

4...49

5...64

6...81

7...96

8..114

9..131

10...149

11...168

12...187

13...203

14...222

15...234

16...251

17...265

18...283

19...301

20...317

21...337

22...357

23...377

24...397

25...417

26...437

27...456

28...474

29...494

30...516

31...536

1

Any thoughts I might have had on taking a little personal time were kicked out the air lock. The blood-chilling call from the Chaalt people's Principal Investigator and Senior Operative, Sael Nalen, filled me with dread.

We had recently discovered and captured a Prule Hivemind. The information we had on the Prule suggested they were galaxy destroyers. We had no desire to try to secure such a threat, so we turned it over to the Chaalt. They have a secret research facility set up to specifically contain and study the Prule. Sael Nalen contacted Justice, the AI of my ship, the Legacy, and alerted us the facility went dark.

"Justice, put me through to Sael."

"Channel open, Commander."

Sael came on immediately and cut me off before I could jump to any conclusions. "Nathan, before you assume incompetence is the reason I am calling, I must tell you we have been caught off guard by treasonous treachery."

Justice was broadcasting my comms so my mixed-race crew could hear all that was being said. My first officer, Tria, who was a Chaalt as well, gave Sael Nalen no time to explain herself before yelling out, "You speak madness! Who would betray our people to the Prule?"

I gave my Tibor Troop Master, Klutch, and my two Grawl crew members, Coonts and Xul, looks of apprehension. The silence that followed Tria's outburst showed Sael's displeasure with the interruption. Sael finally found her tongue and said, "All indications point to the ex–council member, Commander Gredda Porsha."

Tria looked surprised. "You told us she was relieved of command."

"Yes, she was cast out for her handling of our botched negotiations with Nathan and your followers. She was the council member responsible for ordering the use of the spyware you found on the data cubes we gave you."

Tria had a scowl on her pretty face that had no right to be there. "Are you sure? I know she was not well-liked, but I find it hard to believe she would betray her own people to the Prule."

"No, at this point, we are not completely sure of anything. What we do know is the facility's day-to-day communications have ceased, and all of the defensive measures we installed to prevent the possibility of the base's capture have been activated."

I threw my two cents worth into the ring. "How can you say Commander Porsha had something to do with what is happening if you are not sure of the facts?"

Sael exhaled loudly. "Everything I have told you and are about to reveal are secret communications to select military commanders. Charleze Krimov, the shuttle pilot for the elder council, was found dead in Gredda's residence. She was mutilated, and all of her military ID chips cut from her body. It is normally impossible to keep the chips from dissolving upon death of the host, but Charleze was connected to some very sophisticated life-support systems that kept her alive while she was being butchered. This also implies that Gredda had help from a senior AI chip specialist to maintain the harvested chips' functionality. I suspect that part of my briefing has yet to come."

Coonts and Xul were having a quiet discussion. Coonts finally asked the question that was forming on all our lips.

"Principal Investigator, what does the pilot for the council have to do with the research facility going dark?"

"Because the shuttle she normally piloted and twenty-one members of the senior council were at the facility when it went dark!"

We were shocked. Klutch put his thoughts to words as only a plainspoken Troop Master can. "What does this steaming pile of scat you are serving up have to do with us? You have had the Hivemind for seventeen rotations and still have yet to allow our science team to step foot on that base. Now I am glad they are not there, because your next step better be to destroy that place before the Hivemind starts making use of your precious tech."

I was surprised by Sael's next curt comment. "That was my assessment as well, Troop Master. The remaining members of the council are willing to do whatever it takes to rescue the missing senior leadership."

Tria turned and embraced me crazy hard and whispered in my ear, "We must help if we are able."

"Sael, are the members of the council asking for our help?"

"No, Nathan, I am the only one asking for your help. The remaining elders have turned over all aspects of the rescue operation to the military council, many of which are the newly elected replacements for those who were dismissed. They are young and brash and have already squandered the lives of several thousand troops and two warships trying to make a direct assault on the base. The systems protecting the facility are the very best we have."

"Why would so many of your leadership council want to go to the research center at the same time? Surely, they could have received intelligence reports that would have avoided any unnecessary travel to the facility."

"Obviously, only the leadership council can answer those questions. I am giving you the limited amount of intelligence I have received."

"Sael, what could we possibly do that your military has not already tried?"

"I don't know, Nathan. I have seen you and your people do many things others would have thought impossible. I am hoping you can come up with a plan that will spare the lives of thousands if the council continues to throw our people against those defenses."

Xul had a look of dismay on his face, and it was not a sight most normal people could handle. "Principal Investigator, surely your scientists would have had several fail-safe devices to destroy the facility as a contingency in such a scenario."

"You are correct, Xul, the devices you speak of are present throughout the facility. They are yet another piece of evidence that points to Gredda being the person responsible for this criminal act. She was on the team of designers that developed the emergency destruct systems."

Tria could not keep silent and again cut Sael off. "If all this evidence points to Gredda, why do you say that the military is still unsure?"

"Because, Captain Burlor, several of Gredda's closest allies have been found slain! The times of death do not fit the timeline established for the Prule facility takeover or the departure of the council's shuttle. They were killed after the facility went dark. This points to a much broader conspiracy that might involve several accomplices. For all we know, the deaths may have nothing to do with the research lab, or they may have everything to do with it. What we don't have is rock solid data, so I came to you hoping that you could in some way help unravel what has been happening."

The twist and turns of this were making me dizzy. Sael using Tria's former military rank in her retort was an eye-

12

opener. I wondered if it was to put Tria in her place or to alert us she was being recalled to duty. Then my thoughts went in a new direction, and it was my turn to interrupt.

"Senior Operative, where were you when all of this was going on? Surely you would have been updated from the second these events started taking place."

"Since I have already violated security protocols by revealing what has taken place, there is no point in stopping now. I was sent to verify the intelligence that you had gathered on Eiger's whereabouts."

"And?"

"I had to pull the insertion team off Jurlaw before they entered the Crisbarry Mountains due to the current emergency response orders."

Tria was scowling and blurted out what was on her mind. "Principal Investigator, am I being recalled to duty?"

"Your rank is reinstated, and you will serve at your current location until I receive orders stating otherwise. All military personnel have been recalled during this crisis."

I was still digesting the Eiger intel and couldn't decide which was the bigger irritation, Tria being back under the command of the Chaalt or Sael going after Eiger without giving me a heads-up. In the past, intel of that nature was a two-way street. I suspected it was somehow the senior council's wishes to rid me of that distraction. It wasn't hard guessing their end game. They wanted me to concentrate on discovering new technology so they could bargain with me to get their hands on it. They obviously were still choking on the bitter pill they had to swallow

13

when I stripped the Prule salvage ship of its most valuable secrets and then pawned the scrap off on them. I was now wondering if reinstating Tria was some sort of stab at me for not giving them a larger share in the tech I recovered.

Before I could pop my cork at the surmised subterfuge, Justice pinged my implants with a private message. "Commander, I am aware of your concerns for Tria being used by her superiors to control your actions. I have formulated contingencies to prevent such manipulations in the future. I also believe I can secure Tria's permanent posting with the Legacy without further interference from the Chaalt council. I suggest you inform the Principal Investigator we will get back with her with a plan to retake the research facility."

I frowned and shook my head, wondering what the hell we could do that the Chaalt hadn't already attempted.

"Sael, we will get back with you once we have a plan of action."

I heard a partial comment that sounded like a less than friendly epithet, but Justice killed the connection. My crew members were looking at me with dismay on their faces.

"Justice, please enlighten the rest of the crew on your plans before they have me committed to a thought reprocessing institute."

My crew looked relieved that it was Justice behind my comments to Sael and not one of my half-baked, seat-of-my-pants, almost-get-us-all-fragged schemes.

"Commander, we have the means to breach the Chaalt shield dome and enter the facility."

Now we all had skepticism stamped on our faces. We have yet to get a rundown from Sael on the exact nature of the defenses.

"Okay Justice, just how are we going to do that without getting shot to pieces? I know you heard Sael say that they have lost two warships already."

"The Daggers are capable of phase shifting through the shield dome."

That statement had more than a few mouths gaping open, including mine. Justice sounded a little off when he made his declaration. I also noted that he did not say *safely* phase shift through the shield.

"I take it there are some hazards to this exploit that you have yet to mention."

"Yes, the Dagger must be phasing at close to maximum power, and I must cycle the shift at exactly point five milliseconds before the Dagger strikes the shield or it will disintegrate into a burst of atoms."

The engineer in Coonts could no longer hold his tongue. "Justice, I was not aware the Daggers were now operational. If they are indeed ready, we must formulate tests to determine if what you say can be safely achieved."

"Engineer Coonts, I have been using my subsystems at Alpha Base to test the performance of the Daggers. I have just completed the twenty-second test flight on four of the Daggers. I have yet to thoroughly test the weapons systems, but all are functioning."

Coonts nodded and scratched his head, then asked the next logical question. "How much testing have you conducted on the Daggers' shield penetrating capabilities?"

"One test."

As a group we blurted out, "ONE!"

"Yes, further testing would have increased the possibility of damage to Alpha Base's shield systems. The penetration caused an unexpected feedback spike to the shield generators. A luminous discharge was also recorded that could cause permanent retina damage to an observer without proper protection. The Grawl scientists were quite adamant that I discontinue testing until I cleared it with command personnel."

I was just about speechless but had to know. "Is there anything else?"

"Yes, stopping the Dagger before it can pass through the target area taxes the inertial dampening systems beyond their design capabilities."

I expected a little more, but when Justice did not elaborate, I again had to ask, "Justice, I would appreciate it if you were to explain ALL of the apparent dangers of phasing through a shield. When you say beyond the design capabilities, how far are we talking about?"

"The pilot might experience sixteen or more gravities for a short period of time, depending on the angle of penetration and the circumference of the shield."

Coonts possessed the least sturdy skeletal system of my crew. He stood wide-eyed and staring at me. Xul was shaking his head negative then said, "Surely the inertial dampeners in the battle suits would offset the additional G load!"

Justice's voice was deadpan. "The gravity measurements were taken from the second-generation Zaen battle armor. The Troop Master's dense body structure will be the most resistant to high G trauma. The Commander's and Tria's enhanced muscle and skeletal systems have a resiliency that should offset the probability of incapacitating damage, but the experience will most certainly be unpleasant."

I cringed because I had done "unpleasant" so many times it seemed to be part of my regular routine. As far as securing Tria's permanent freedom from the long arm of the council, it was a no-brainer. If we do this and survive, we get what we want.

Coonts surprised me with a request.

"Commander, since my participation in the shield breach operation will most assuredly lead to permanent damage or death, I request permission to undergo the Oolaran weaponization procedure."

That got the little Grawl looks from everyone. He was well-aware of the procedure and the painful recovery period. Coonts continued to surprise me with his drive and determination to become everything that his race, as a rule, was currently not. He was going to show the other members of his people that they should also strive to be something other than the corrupt manipulators they are known to be.

"Coonts, until we have an actual plan, I cannot preclude your participation. If it turns out that you will not have an active role in the operation, you will be free to make that decision."

Coonts nodded. Xul just stood shaking his head at his fellow Grawl.

"Justice, what is the status of the energy matrix?"

"Commander, we will have sufficient energy to transition to Alpha Base in eleven minutes. I have alerted the scientists to our new mission profile and have them preparing a nanite missile loadout for the Daggers."

Tria just about freaked at Justice's weapon selection. "Justice, we cannot release weaponized nanites within my home world exclusion zone. It is forbidden!"

"Tria, using your DNA model, I can program the nanites to ignore your people's biological traits. I will program a finite time code into the nanites that will be irreversible. Once they have performed their assigned missions, they will be consumed by a corrosive payload of molecular acid. My programming will cause the nanites to swarm onto any remains of the Prule or their infected systems before they self-terminate. Depending on what technology the Hivemind has assimilated, it may be necessary to inundate the facility with weaponized nanites to prevent any probability of escape."

"We will destroy the entire facility if we do this!"

"Tria, I recommend that the asteroid the facility resides on be obliterated if you succeed in rescuing your senior council members. It is the only way to ensure the Prule machine infection cannot spread to your home worlds. If any of your senior scientists have somehow survived, they will confirm my evaluation."

Tria's anger boiled out in an unnatural display of emotion.

"How could the fools let this happen!"

I embraced her and said, "I am convinced that the Oolaran and Sentinel races are the only ones who truly know what the Prule are capable of. It would only take a small mistake for the Hivemind to have the advantage, especially if it had outside help."

Klutch, walked up to Tria and put his hand on her shoulder. "Tria, there is an easy way to ensure something like this never happens again. We destroy every Prule piece of scat we encounter; it leaves nothing to chance!"

I could see the resolve in Tria's eyes when she nodded to the Troop Master. She turned to me and I nodded to her as well. If we hadn't turned over the Hivemind to Sael and her science team none of this would be happening. I now knew why Sael came to us for help. She was blaming herself as well and knew we would not make the same mistake twice.

"Justice, take us home!"

"Acknowledged, Commander!"

2

I sat silently cursing in sentences. My first officer, Tria, had chosen me as her life mate, and I willingly accepted her claim. We have been in so many terrible situations together that there was no way I could not love her. I was all set to give her the million-credit tour on how humans interact with their life mates. Tria's physiology was almost human in every way, except for her extra set of arms. Other than that, she was amazingly similar to a human female. Justice had on many occasions pointed out we would be unable to produce offspring, but we were fully compatible. Every time it seemed like we had a real moment to consummate our relationship, some freaking calamity inserted itself into the equation. This would turn out to be another of those moments. Our feelings of want and desire were going to take a backseat to the nonstop horrors our galaxy seemed to have an overabundance of.

"Justice, what is your assessment of the Oolaran power source we recovered?"

"My tests have shown that it is fully functional. I have been studying the possibilities of using the Oolaran power plant to power the Legacy's beam weapons as well as the anomaly weapon. If my theories prove correct, we can increase the destructive output of our main weapons by forty-two percent. With engineer Coonts assistance and Felix's manufacturing skills, we can design and build a transfer switch capable of shunting the power source's considerable output to the beam weapons."

"Was the anomaly weapon Sael gave us functional?"

"My subsystems, along with the aid of the Grawl scientists, have assembled the weapon. Static testing has shown that it is complete. It only requires a power source and AI integration."

Coonts held up a finger.

"Yes Coonts, do you have something to add?"

"Commander, we could possibly modify the Sentinel-designed power transfer switches that Alpha Base uses to power the defensive beam weapons. If they prove to be inadequate, we can base a more robust transfer switch on their design."

"Engineer Coonts, my subsystems have already tested Alpha Base's power transfer systems, and they are incapable of handling the output capacity of the Oolaran power generator," Justice said.

Coonts frowned and gave me a curt nod. "Justice, I will need a specification rating before I can design a transfer switch."

Justice fired right back. "My findings have been downloaded to the science lab computer and are available for your research."

Our current situation had us all on edge. Coonts and Justice sniping at each other was the usual manifestation of the crew's mission anxiety. Even I was not immune to pre-mission jitters, but Tria always had a way of easing my fears. The thought of losing a crew member weighed heavily on my mind. Tria gave me confidence that no matter what, we would pull through as a team. We never planned for failure, only the unexpected. Tria embraced me once more as my surroundings glared a brilliant white and my reality faded away.

As we returned to normal space-time, Justice gave me a sitrep. "Commander, I have no anomalous activity to report, and we will make a straight-in approach to Alpha Base. The scientists are prepared to start work on rearming the Legacy. Felix has been briefed on the damage to your armor and has begun manufacturing new armor suits with modifications based on my battle damage assessments."

"Thank you, Justice. Do you have an estimate on the time it will take to install the Oolaran power generator and anomaly weapon? You know as well as I how impatient Sael is. I am going to have to tell her something soon, or she will come knocking on our door."

"I estimate thirty-seven hours with the scientists working in shifts around the clock. It will take longer to remove the Sentinel power generator and our modifications than to install the original weapons system."

"Has Coonts started on a workable transfer switch?"

"Yes, I have been monitoring his progress. He is close to a solution that will allow the Oolaran power source to share power with our beam weapons. The switch design was not a problem for him since we have the Sentinel switch as a blueprint. He is currently working on the power chokes necessary to keep from overcharging our beam weapons. I surmise it will take him several hours to formulate the correct metering devices that will meet or exceed my duty rating specifications."

"I have been wanting to talk to you about the way you and Coonts pick at each other. Of all the traits you seem to have adopted from me, that particular one is not one of my more flattering."

"Commander, while you and Coonts interpret my wordings as petty bickering, I can assure you it is just the opposite."

"Oh really? Please explain to me my misunderstanding of your intention."

"Commander, my words are a carefully calculated manipulation. I observe everyone in my charge to better understand interactions between them. I have found that if I interject a small slight into my collaborations with Coonts, it tends to bring out the best in him. Coonts is a gifted engineer whose talents were never fully utilized under Drayen's rule. He only needs to be prodded in the right direction to get the very best of what his

23

considerable IQ has to offer. There are several things that Coonts excels in that my programming cannot compete with. Coonts's ability to design complex systems from scratch is not one of my better programmed capabilities. I have to disassemble most complex devices to determine how they work before I can have a better understanding of how to improve on a specific manufacturing design. Coonts is able to take a specification and design it from its base materials. His knowledge of hardware and systems acquired from other races is an invaluable commodity. I only have what little Oolaran systems information was left in my memory cores. Each system Coonts develops is a wealth of information for me to add to my files. Coonts is in fact teaching me as he exhibits his engineering skills."

I closed my eyes, shaking my head. I should have known better; the AI soaked up knowledge 24/7. While it did explain some of the bickering, it did not cover all of it. It was probably best to just let it go unless it got to the point of affecting crew performance, but still, I needed to say something.

"Couldn't you just ask him nicely to teach you rather than irritate him?"

"Negative! Coonts practicing the human trait known as one-upmanship is a far better leaning tool than the trait normally exhibited by him, which is known as a superiority complex."

Well, at least we agreed on something.

"You said the Daggers were ready to go. Can you get four in the cargo bay? I still want to take an Eagle with us."

24

"I can accommodate four in the hold now that the modified tiedowns are in place. The shuttle can remain in the hangar. It will be close quarters, but I foresee no problems with the arrangement."

The thought of taking untested equipment into combat no longer bothered me as much as it used to. Most all of our loadout was tested in combat conditions. What was eating at me was the shield penetration itself. The possibility of Tria or I being mashed into scat weighed on me. Klutch was built for that kind of abuse, and I had no doubt about him going through the insertion without a scratch.

"During flight testing I want the missile loadout for the Daggers to be something other than nanite weapons."

"Since my initial assessments, I have added additional scenarios to the testing profile. The rotary launchers on each Dagger will be loaded with variable yield antimatter missiles. I will have the nanite weapons available for loading after system familiarity testing is complete."

Justice made a high-speed approach to Alpha Base and landed in the hangar. It had become a ritual with the scientists to greet us upon our return to Alpha Base. When we debarked the Legacy, we received a warm welcome and the Grawl gathered around us to make hand contact. The crew and I made it a point to touch each of their hands. My Zaen replicator engineer, Felix, stood with a small smile on his face, and he too made hand contact with each of us. The Grawl were not known to be a touchy-feely race. Those who followed me felt the need on some level to touch the warriors of their adopted clan.

The Grawl dispersed; some boarded the Legacy, and some were doing a walk-around inspection of the exterior hull. Graf, Jaren, and Felix quietly waited for everyone to start on their assigned duties and then came forward to give me their reports. Graf and Jaren turned to Felix, and he nodded.

"Commander, I have already completed fabrication of the new exterior armor shells for Tria and the Troop Master. The replacement weapons and parts for all the battle suits is queued into the replicator and should be manufactured within the next two hours. Some of the enhancements recommended by Justice will take a little longer while we work on the proper engineering specifications."

"Thank you, Felix. Is there anything you require from me or the crew?"

"No sir. Justice has foreseen my needs and has assured me a very busy schedule. If you need me, I will be in the replicator building."

I waved the young Zaen on, and he quickly departed to finish work on our suit repairs. Felix continued to impress me. The responsibilities we heaped on the Zaen had made a mature young man out of the spoiled brat we initially had to put up with. As Felix walked away, Graf stepped forward.

"Commander, Justice has briefed us via the Chaalt real-time data link. Jaran and I have already come up with a timetable and work shifts that will not degrade the scientists' acuity and ensure a twenty-four-work schedule. The only hindrances I foresee will be replicator delays due to priority materials manufacturing. Felix has assured me the replicator will be run at maximum capacity. We have stockpiled the raw materials necessary for all repairs and new systems requirements. With your permission, we shall immediately implement the new work cycles."

I could only smile. The efficiency of the Grawl was once again on display. If the Grawl race would only give up their greedy and power-hungry ways, they could be a shining example to other developing species. The smiled faded from my face. A great many humans suffered from those very sins, and changing that was never likely to happen.

The crew and I pitched in, and we worked nonstop shifts for two days straight. On the third day, Justice alerted us the Daggers were ready to test fly. I looked around and saw my crew was nowhere to be seen. It did not take a genius to figure out they were probably checking out the Daggers. I headed for the artifact building and saw I had guessed correctly. Sitting out front of the building were four of the shiny black missile-shaped spacecraft. The cockpits were open, and Tria, Coonts, and Klutch were sitting inside. We were wondering what the performance capabilities of the spacecraft would be. Any apprehension we had concerning our upcoming mission was nullified for the thrill of testing unknown alien technology.

As I walked by each of my crew members, they made eye contact with me. Their looks of determination helped settle my jittery nerves. I gave them a small smile and a nod. They each gave me a thumbs up, broadening the smile on my face as I climbed into November One. If I was going to be smashed into scat, I would be doing so in good company. As far as I was concerned, my crewmates were some of the finest this galaxy had to offer.

I settled into the protective tub, and Justice swelled the cushioned surround to fit my torso. A floating holograph appeared in front of my face, and the cockpit closed.

"Commander, all Daggers are optimized and ready in all aspects."

"Thanks, Justice, take us for a lap around our star system so we can get an idea of the Daggers' flight characteristics."

"Roger that, Commander!"

Justice took us out of Alpha Base and accelerated us to just under the speed of light. The ride was smooth and uneventful. I could see our progress as we moved at what I perceived as a snail's pace away from base. After several minutes, I finally realized that sub-light was not all that fast when you consider the vastness of space.

"Okay, Justice, I have had enough of slow. Give us some gas."

"Minimum phase drive cycle engaging now."

My vision momentarily blurred, and I revisited my first encounters with jump sickness. While it wasn't debilitating, it was noticeable. My morning rations stirred in irritation. Exclamations came over my comms and made me notice our movement on the holograph. Justice highlighted Alpha Base, and it was a small pulsating dot well behind us and rapidly fading away. I was sure the Legacy was easily this fast but never had a display like this one to show us.

"Let's see what a sudden stop is like. I want to know what we can expect on the combat drop. Tango Two, Charlie Three, Kilo Four, did you copy that?"

I heard a quick reply.

"Two."

"Three."

"Four."

Justice called out, "Sixty percent phase drive!"

My stomach started doing some unwelcome mood swings and my cockpit surround swelled even tighter around me. The holographic display went blank. I was guessing it could no longer keep track of our velocity. I gritted my teeth in anticipation only to have my stomach kick its gyrations up a few more notches.

Justice called out once more. "Seventy-five percent phase drive acceleration. Due to the design limitations of your recon armor, I will forgo maximum phase drive testing!"

I felt a vibration that wasn't present before, and my breathing was coming a little faster now. It was a toss-up whether it was a little bit of fear or just adrenaline adding a spike in my respiratory system. All at once, I let out an involuntary grunt. The cockpit liner and my light armor felt like they were both trying to crush the life out of me. I was starting to panic when my vision blacked out. I knew my eyes were open, but I could not see. Relief flooded in as I started seeing the holographic display slowly come into view in front of my face. I ached all over and felt the cockpit and my armor ease off.

I groaned out, "Tango, Charlie, Kilo, give me a sitrep!"

Klutch called back first. He sounded like he might have just run a few laps around the hangar, but other than that he was clear as a bell.

"Kilo Four is optimal and ready for additional maneuvers!"

Tria's voice was slightly hoarse, and she sounded as rattled as I was. "Tango Two is NOT optimal. I was blinded by the deceleration but am slowly recovering my vision."

"Charlie Three, give me a sitrep!"

Justice answered instead of Coonts. "Commander, Coonts is unconscious, and his telemetry shows he has sustained several minor stress related fractures to his skeletal system. The Grawl equivalent of retinas have both detached, and he has minor brain swelling. Before our stop maneuver, I informed Coonts I would not accelerate his Dagger beyond sixty percent of phase capacity. He protested vigorously and insisted he should go higher. While I did accelerate you, Tria, and Klutch, to seventy-five percent of maximum, I did not do the same for Coonts. My suspicions proved correct in that he would sustain minor bodily harm at sixty percent capacity and a full reverse phase stop."

"None of that sounds like minor damage. Is he stable enough for a maximum velocity return trip to base?"

"Yes, Commander, I can assure you the damage Coonts sustained can be easily repaired during the weaponization procedure."

"Turn us around and get us back to base."

I felt like I had been body-slammed by Klutch and wondered if there was any other way to carry out our mission. The insane stop maneuver from full acceleration could leave us incapacitated and vulnerable. I knew Justice would protect us, but I really did not want to go up against the Prule in a diminished capacity. Coonts demanding Justice push the envelope had me wondering if he intentionally wanted to inflict damage upon himself. I also wondered if it might just be a plan cooked up by the two of them all along. It would be a surefire way to get the Oolaran weaponization procedure sooner rather than later. He got his wish if that was the case. I'll bet he didn't factor in the pain during the recovery time. He was going to learn the hard way. I let a small smile crease my lips. Ballsy little bastard!

I was abruptly jerked back to the now of our excursion.

"Commander! I have detected the signatures of multiple Quill star drives. I now confirm sixteen separate tracks!"

Oh shit! Something deep down inside of me hated the crits worse than the Prule because they were cannibals. Their menu even included the deceased members of their own race. It may just be the way things go in the galaxy,

31

but it totally repulsed me in a large assortment of ways. I was going to ask Tria what she thought but didn't have to; Tango Two's icon lit up on my holographic display, and her voice filled my cockpit.

"Commander, I request permission to reconnoiter the hostile's location."

Before I could give her a response, Klutch chimed in.

"Kilo Four will cover Tango Two!"

I rolled my eyes and shook my head.

"Justice, evac Charlie Three back to base and go ahead with the Oolaran procedure. Set the rest of us on a course that will take us to an observation point where we can see what the Crits are up to."

"Affirmative, Commander. I would like to first brief you on the stealth characteristics of the Dagger spacecraft. The Dagger has a very low detection threshold while using the sub-light drive. When it is coasting or stationary, it is almost invisible to most all of the scanning systems I am familiar with."

"And when we are using the phase drive?"

"I have found no current method to mask the unique distortion waves emitted by the drives. I theorize Sentinel Race thirteen relied on the extraordinary speed of the drive and the anomaly weapon to make slashing attacks through hostile ship formations. Any combatant that is capable of targeting the Daggers and actually hitting one with a weapon would find that the phase field would absorb the return fire harmlessly into interdimensional space. I surmise that any enemy commanders who found

32

themselves in that unenviable position lost their lives shortly after the encounter."

Before I could comment any further, Klutch came over the comms, and he sounded less than happy.

"Justice, just to be absolutely clear on what you are telling us. The Daggers are very hard to detect while they are NOT phasing."

"Yes, Troop Master."

"But doesn't that mean we are defenseless to incoming fire!"

"Troop Master, I never claimed the technology was perfect. I am briefing you on my observations. If incoming fire is imminent, the phase field can be activated at any time."

The garbled grunt I heard just before Klutch terminated his comms could have been a new Tibor curse I had never heard before. Tria came over the comms again.

"Can the phase field be overpowered by intense enemy fire?"

"Unknown at this time. I have no data concerning the limitations of the phase field."

3

Maybe using the Daggers to investigate the Quill contacts wasn't such a great idea after all. Before I could put a voice to my concerns, my stomach went into nonstop turmoil. I could feel a small amount of positive G load and surmised that Justice had the Daggers operating at maximum phase. My holographic display was blank except for the three icons representing our formation. Apparently, Justice would be the only one to know what was going on in the galaxy until he slowed us down. I closed my eyes and took a deep breath to try to calm my urge to upchuck. I became aware of a low frequency drumming vibration that suddenly ceased.

Opening my eyes, I saw the display was back online and filled with a solar system complete with a central star and four planets. The first three were way too close to the star, but the fourth was in the habitable zone. It was slightly smaller than a Mars-sized planet and had twelve red markers in low orbit. There were four more further out that looked like they were moving in the direction of our formation. Justice decided it was time to enlighten us on the current situation.

"Commander, we are coasting in toward the targets. The Quill have detected our entrance into the system but cannot pinpoint the source of the interdimensional disturbance."

"How do you know that?"

The four red icons that were moving toward us lit up with large pulsating circles. They overlapped each other and covered a large portion of the solar system. They seemed to be directed well to our left and would miss us on our current heading. Justice could see their sensors as they searched for our location. As we coasted in closer to the fourth planet, our sensors started giving us usable information. The planet had an oxygen atmosphere and water that covered a third of its landmass. What was really interesting was the crude radio waves Justice was recording.

"Commander, the radio waves are primitive, and I currently have no way to translate them, but the urgency in the unknown language is unmistakable. The inhabitants of the planet are under siege."

Damned crits! I already knew what the Quill do when they take up a low orbit over a planet. They strip the planet of its resources, and in this case, it probably included the harvesting of the biologicals as well.

Tria's voice filled my cockpit, and she sounded almost panicked. "Commander, you know what they will do with the inhabitants!"

I closed my eyes and shook my head. This would be a good way to get us all killed. The thought of letting the Quill use the people of the planet as a food source made me grit my teeth.

"Justice, I want a no-shitter on our chances of taking out the Quill harvesters in the planet's orbit!"

"Commander, the picket ships will have to be dealt with if you want to successfully remove the Quill from orbit. I can make additional assessments once I determine the full capabilities of our weapons systems. I have a maximum velocity attack vector on the ships currently searching for us. Once I engage the phase drives, all of the hostile combatants will be aware of our presence. Depending on the results of our attack, the harvesters may decide to retreat from their current mission."

I already knew what the answer would be, but I was going to ask anyway, just in case it was the last time I would ever be able too.

"Tria, Klutch, do you have any reservations about sticking it to the Quill?"

"Tango Two is ready!"

"Kilo Four is a go, Commander!"

"Okay, Justice, let's get on with it."

"Increasing forward velocity to maximum and anomaly weapon power generator to one hundred percent!"

I felt a small amount of positive G and a hum I never heard before. The holo display showed our course correction then blanked to just our three-ship formation. The noticeable hum stopped almost immediately, but I heard it start to build in volume again. The holo display blinked and there were three red triangles blinking from red to yellow on the very edge of my display. One of the hostile ship indicators was making a turn toward the planet, and Justice showed us it was accelerating hard in that direction.

"Commander, three of the targets are drifting and are heavily damaged. The fourth is sending out continuous signals that I surmise are warnings or distress messages to the rest of their fleet. The anomaly weapon power source requires twenty-two seconds to build to one hundred percent discharge capacity. We will reengage the hostiles in ten seconds."

The constant churning of my stomach was slightly diminished by the excitement of knowing the Daggers were able to inflict catastrophic damage to ships more than a thousand times their size. The humming stopped once again, and Justice confirmed what my mind was comprehending.

"Target destroyed! Disengaging phase drive and switching to manual pilot control."

A joystick raised up out of my right-hand arm rest. The holo display lit up with detailed targeting information and put a large blinking red triangle on the closest harvester ship in orbit. Tria's and Klutch's Daggers had green lines extending from them to different targets on either side of mine. They peeled out of formation on intercept courses. "Missiles: 24" blinked in the lower right corner of my display. A switch cover on the top of my joystick blinked at me. It left no doubt that the trigger in front of my index finger was the main weapon. I felt a bump on my left hand as a lever extended next to it. The words "sub-light drive" appeared to one side of it, and in the center middle above it, combat maneuvering. The far forward position blinked phase drive. I pushed the lever to combat maneuvering, and a green line appeared on my display to the right of my current heading. I rolled the joystick right and lined up with the target heading indicator. Justice was making this as easy as possible without actually doing it himself. The action managed to take several of the twists out of my guts while I concentrated on my attack vector.

The Quill were not idly waiting to be pounced; they were retracting their harvester tunnels and attempting to get underway. My target was rapidly growing in my display. I squeezed the trigger as the word "fire" flashed across my display. I immediately felt G load and glanced to my left to see Justice had engaged the phase drive. It was a heads-up to the incoming counterfire. If Justice did not intervene, I may have got my ass shot to pieces. Several red lines narrowly missed my escape maneuver but suddenly stopped when the enemy ship looked like it was being pinched in half amidships. A new attack vector appeared on my display, and I pulled the drive lever back to combat maneuvering to make a course correction. Apparently, the Quill had no luck detecting us until we opened fire on them. Justice made it more than clear that once we did, phasing was the only way to keep from getting the favor returned to us. Justice quickly answered the question forming in my mind.

"Commander, the phase drive will automatically engage if your detection level reaches a certain threshold or you fire the Dagger's weapons."

I should have known that Justice had my back at all times. My display showed two additional hostile indicators disappear from the target list. The anomaly weapon was amazingly deadly. I could only guess what the much larger version on the Legacy was capable of.

"Commander, the anomaly weapon rapidly siphons off the Quill energy fields protecting their ships. It appears the anomaly projected from the weapon somehow feeds on the barrier's energy and grows in strength and intensity just before it strikes the target's hull. When the anomaly contacts the target, it consumes all it touches before dissipating."

A grim smile crossed my face. It sucks to be them! I lined up on my next target as it tried to leave the planet's atmosphere. It went down in two large pieces. The inhabitants of the planet would have the remains of their foes raining down on them. They might be able to salvage some very advanced new tech if they have the right scientific capabilities. My phase drive activated, and I flew directly at my next victim. It was firing nonstop at my Dagger, and the red lines appearing on my display were intersecting with my approach vector with no apparent affect. I squeezed the trigger, and the hum began to cycle in pitch once more. The Quill ship disappeared from my screen. Klutch and Tria made quick work of the remaining Quill harvesters. I pulled back on the drive lever and made a coasting pass through the fringe of the planet's atmosphere. The fiery passage and sonic shockwaves would further scare the inhabitants, but for now their nightmare would be over. I wanted to get some data on the locals before we left the system.

"Justice, get us some video and as much comms as you can record, then get us out of here."

"Actively recording, Commander."

"Tango Two, Kilo Four, form on me and let's go home!"

It was becoming a regular occurrence: whenever I felt things were going to be alright, they turned to shit.

"Commander! I am detecting a very large transition wave on the far side of this solar system."

"Roger that. Justice, give us an intercept vector."

"Commander, I now have an unknown contact, and the target is massive. The drive characteristics are similar to recorded Quill pulse drives. The readings I am observing indicate a power curve that dwarfs any previously recorded Quill star drive telemetry. I will put you on a course that will give us data on the new target but will ensure maximum safety."

That information kicked my respiration up a notch or two. I felt the phase drive engage, and we made a sweeping turn. A new heading showed up on my display as being well below the large red diamond. The drive disengaged when the target made a turn in our direction. We were now coasting full stealth, and Justice further corrected our course to what I assumed was an escape vector. Our formation tightened up, and I could see on my display that Justice had us about a foot apart. I was relieved to see the massive spacecraft did not align itself on an intercept with our new heading. My holo display flickered, and a close-up of the target appeared. Holy crap! The damn thing looked like an oblong paper wasp nest and it was freaking big!

"Commander, I am detecting an enormous power spike that is still growing in intensity within the target. It also appears to have shut down its star drives."

As a backward-thinking Earth boy, I could only guess what they were up to. My experience, on the other hand, told me they were up to some mean-spirited crap if they could get a lock on us. All at once, our phase drives activated, and we turned away at full power as a tremendous beam of energy shot out from the hostile ship. The shot was well behind us, but it had a warning alarm beeping in my cockpit. Justice cut our drives and made a tight turn to the right of our previous course. He sent us hurtling away and defenseless against incoming fire. The massive alien ship fired its main weapon once again down our last course, and the alarm in my cockpit stepped up an octave. I felt positive Gs when my phase drive went to full power once more. We were in trouble, and Justice was trying to escape the reach of the hostile's main weapon.

"Justice! Please tell me we are not going to get incinerated before we get the hell out of here!"

"Commander, the ship is of Quill origin, and I surmise it is a habitat vessel. Its main weapon is more powerful and has better range than any previous enemies we have encountered. This would include the energy weapons used against us by the Prule, as well as the beam weapons aboard the Legacy. It appears the Quill shunt the energy from all shipboard sources to fire the weapon. The vessel has reengaged its star drive and is altering its course to align with our last phase drive heading. We are now out of the effective range of its weapon. I will make additional sprint and maneuver adjustments to our course to ensure they cannot follow."

Tria came on over the comms. "Justice, it appears they are able to track us while coasting. I thought we were invisible to Quill tracking technology."

"Tria, I hypothesize that the discharge from their main weapon ionizes the space around the beam in all directions for a considerable distance. It apparently makes us visible by the shadow we cast when in close proximity to the beam discharge. My sprint and maneuver tactics gave us the time we needed to put a safe distance between us and the hostiles."

"I'm surprised they gave up that easily."

"They have not. I am detecting more than a thousand faster than light missiles attempting to track our last known course. I also detected more than two hundred small fighter class vessels of unknown capabilities. None of the weapons or spacecraft have the ability to catch or track us at our current distance. We will have no choice but to concede the battlespace to the Quill."

Klutch could no longer remain quiet. "What do you think is going to happen to the planet when we leave this system? You know what the crits are going to do to the inhabitants. We cannot stand by and let it happen!"

"Justice, I thought the Daggers were immune to incoming fire?"

"Commander, I will not risk your lives to prove my theory. The Quill weapon is unlike any previously encountered."

This was not the outcome I had hoped for. The power of the Quill's main weapon system could decimate the world we were hoping to protect. "Justice, you say it appears that the Quill shunt all available power to the weapon? Would that include their shields?"

"Commander, the ship's shields remained in place, but I did notice a considerable decline in its power levels when the main weapon prepared to fire. I can follow your logic and would like to point out that even at the shield's lowest attenuation, it was still magnitudes more powerful than a fully-shielded harvester ship. I do not have enough data to determine if the anomaly weapons aboard the Daggers can inflict enough damage to bring down the capital ship's shields."

The Troop Master didn't seem to care either way. "Commander, I volunteer to draw the habitat ship's fire so you and Tria can make a coordinated attack. If we can inflict enough damage, they might decide to seek a softer target elsewhere."

Tria quickly added. "Nathan, we must try for the sake of the people on the planet, we cannot let them be harvested by the Quill without a fight."

"Justice, I know you haven't installed the IST equipment aboard the Daggers. Is there another way we can communicate with Alpha Base or the Operative?"

"Negative, Commander. The Daggers lack comm buoys as well."

"I know our shakedown cruise has us a great distance from base. How long will it take us to make a full-power return?"

"Forty-nine minutes."

I cringed. That would be more than enough time for the Quill to get revenge for the bloody nose we gave them. There was a good chance they would blame the local inhabitants for our sins and decide to lay waste to the planet.

"Justice, what are our odds of inflicting enough damage to discourage the crits from attacking the planet?"

"Unknown, Commander."

"Don't give me that crap! I want the numbers!"

"Twenty-two percent."

I closed my eyes and shook my head. At least it wasn't a single digit. "What about the missiles and fighters?"

"They will be a distraction but should not be a major threat to the Daggers. The point defense weapons are more than capable of defeating the weak shield readings I am detecting on the Quill fighters. The missiles are loitering out front of the fighter screen and have powered down their drives to conserve energy. They will be incapable of targeting the Daggers while making a maximum power attack run."

"Okay, this is how it's going to play out. I want you to turn us around and make a full-power approach at the target then shut down the phase drives. Make enough maneuvers while we are coasting to take us off our original heading. I want Tria and Klutch to come in at an optimal attack vector while I go to full power and drive through the missile and fighter screen. I will go weapons hot and shoot up everything in my path. That should get me noticed by the capital ship and draw its fire. When its shields drop to minimum, Tria, you and Klutch hit them at the weakest shield readings Justice can find. Fire as fast as the main weapon will cycle. If the shield comes down, give them all of your antimatter missiles and then get the hell out of there."

Klutch would have none of it. "Commander, it was my idea to make a diversionary frontal attack! You wish to claim all the glory for your clan and I must protest!"

The Troop Master was full of it. There would be no glory in being vaporized if the Quill managed to hit me with their main weapon.

"Klutch, this is not the time to question my authority. I am giving you and Tria a direct order! Now do your duty, Troop Master!"

I could only imagine what it smelled like in the Tibor's Dagger. Tria had nothing to say and probably knew she could not change my mind. She chose to remain silent. There was no other logical course of action. What needed to be done needed to be done now, before the capital ship got any closer to the planet.

"Justice, turn us back now!"

"Affirmative, Commander. I have formulated a best-scenario battle plan and I am ready to execute on your order."

"Execute!"

I felt positive Gs as my phase drive went to maximum output. The trepidation I was feeling cancelled out the rotations my gut was making. With all of my heart, I wanted to think that everything would be fine and this would be the end of the Quill capital ship. Even the beast within me was silent. What will be, will be. My holo displayed filled with targets ranging from two hundred small ones to a single freaking big one. I was closing with them at incredible velocity and then the drive went silent as Justice made course corrections to confuse their targeting.

"Commander, the Quill capital ship has changed course away from the planet and is transferring power to its main weapon. The star drive has cut power, and its shields attenuation is increasing."

My hands started sweating and I gritted my teeth, then a sudden calm came over me. I cranked my neck to the side, popping the kink out of it. Screw the Quill! I will drive this ship right down their throat if I have to!

My point defense weapons opened fire nonstop. The phase drive went back to full power, and I plunged headlong to my destiny.

4

The drive suddenly shut down, and Justice made a hard turn from my current heading just as the Quill fired their main weapon. An alarm sounded in the cockpit, and I was pushed back into my seat once more. We made another looping turn as the nose of the Dagger passed across the target. I squeezed the trigger on my joystick, sending a return gift in the direction of my foes. I saw the blue triangles of my crewmates making hard turns away from the Quill capital ship. They were blazing away at any ship within range. My point defense systems were doing the same. The shield indicator around the massive ship was blinking on my display then returned to normal. Our weapons were pulling the shields down but not penetrating. I cursed and was getting ready to waste a few antimatter missiles.

"Commander, I have detected the transition signature of the Legacy sixty-two light-years from our location!" Justice suddenly called out. "I am turning on an intercept course to get us in communication range."

My maker must have been watching out for us after all. Another massive burst of energy passed well to our rear as I pushed the phase drive to maximum. The Legacy must have detected our drive signatures because it made a small jump that put it squarely in our sensor range. Xul came up on our comms.

"Commander, I am detecting extremely large energy spikes and thousands of unknown drive signatures. Do you require assistance?"

"That would be an understatement, Xul! Prepare to take us aboard!"

We coasted in and braked hard as Justice pulled each of us into the Legacy. Justice's primary system took over and pulled the combat data from our Daggers. The Legacy went full stealth as we turned back toward the Quill with the deadliest of intentions. As we exited the Daggers, I went to Tria and hugged her, then turned to Klutch and put my arm around his big, wide shoulders. He had a very unpleasant odor about him, but at the moment, it made no difference to Tria and I.

"Armor up. We are going to be bait one more time."

The crew gave me a questioning look, but did not hesitate to run to the ready room. Xul joined me, and I inquired as to Coonts's condition.

"Commander, he has undergone the carbon fiber bone enhancement and is currently sedated. Justice said he should remain that way for twenty-four hours minimum."

I nodded, then told him to get current on the data we collected and get suited up for combat operations. He

49

turned and followed me to the ready room. Tria and Klutch had already shed their uniforms and were putting on suit liners. I sat next to Tria and quickly did the same. Justice came up on the comms net.

"Commander, the Daggers have suffered no combat damage, and I am reloading the missile launchers. You will be ready to depart in ten minutes."

I stepped up into my armor, and it snugged in around me. The beast within me stirred at what I was contemplating.

Xul walked up to us in his older generation armor and stood waiting for a briefing on my battle plan.

"Justice, is the Legacy's anomaly weapon ready to be tested?"

"Yes, Commander. The power source and weapon show no faults in my startup test. I have integrated myself with the targeting system, and all indicators show that it should function as designed."

"All right, let's go test it on a worthy target! Tria, Klutch, we are going back in the Daggers and letting the Quill shoot at us again. Xul, when their shield power drops off prior to firing their main weapon, I want you to jump the Legacy in close and shoot them in the ass. If the shields fail, we are going to give them everything we got aboard the Daggers. Once we turn away, I want every target of opportunity turned to scrap on our way back out. We will do a quick battle damage assessment and coordinate through Justice for a follow-on attack. If everybody is ready, let's get on with it!"

50

I got three thumbs up, and we ran to the Daggers. The padding inside the protective cockpits reconfigured itself to fit our much larger armored bodies. Justice quickly pushed us out into the void, and we went to full power on the phase drives. We joined up in our close combat formation. Data started streaming in to my display, and we saw what we had feared all along, the Quill's ship had turned back toward the planet and was accelerating.

"Justice, can we catch them before the fire on the planet?"

"Yes, Commander, but be advised they are launching additional missiles and fighters."

"You think they would have learned by now that their fighters are only an inconvenience and not a viable threat."

"Commander, the missiles and fighters are heading toward the planet and not in our direction."

That statement got my blood to boiling. "Justice, start launching our Chaalt interdimensional missiles and have them jump ahead of the Quill. When the Quill are in point-blank range, have them go active and take down as many of the fighters as you can. I can only hope the inhabitants of the planet are still hunkered down because I know we can't stop all the missiles."

"Launching now, Commander!"

We finally got the Quills' attention, and they were turning back to a heading that would intercept us. We flew straight at them and were rapidly closing the distance between us. Justice's subsystem alerted us that the Quill

51

were shutting down their star drive in preparation to fire on us. The Legacy disappeared from my display, and our phase drives shut down so we could make a course change to take us out of the Quill weapon's targeting envelope. We nosed steeply down and then turned back toward the target. The Legacy reappeared behind the Quill ship and then jumped away. The shield indicator around the capital ship disappeared, and the monstrous vessel started a slow sideways drift that told me it was mortally wounded.

"YES! Tango Two, Kilo Four, let's finish the job! You are weapons free!"

"Two!"

"Four!"

We were close enough to the target that Justice gave us real-time video of the capital ship. It looked like a small sun was burning in the aft section. What was truly amazing was watching the back of the ship as it was being sucked into the star-bright anomaly. The anomaly suddenly disappeared, and a huge cloud of debris started trailing out the massive cavity. Justice gave us a sitrep.

"Commander, our stealth missile attack destroyed two hundred and forty Quill fighters and shot down more than two hundred missiles. The Legacy took out an additional one hundred and seventy missiles after attacking the capital ship. Do you want the Legacy to reengage the target?"

"No, Justice. Take out as many missiles as you can!"

"Commander, unfortunately the remaining missiles reached their intended targets. I have recorded more than three hundred high-yield nuclear detonations on the planet's surface. It appears that the largest continent was the intended target. I am no longer detecting any radio traffic or life signs at that location."

I closed my eyes and said a prayer to my maker. This was not the outcome I had hoped for. It was a very small consolation knowing the people on the planet would not be a food source for the Quill. A burning rage filled me, and the beast was calling to me for revenge. It would get its wish.

"Xul, you are weapons free, reengage the habitat ship. Tango Two, Kilo Four, destroy all Quill you encounter. No survivors!"

"Two."

"Four."

I took manual control of my Dagger and made a low pass over the devasted continent. When I could stomach no more, I climbed out of the now-toxic atmosphere. I headed for the nearest hostile ship and turned the fighter into whirling pieces of scrap. I looked back at the fragments that were once the Quill capital ship. My face contorted into a mask of rage, and I screamed out to no one but myself, "This is just the beginning!"

It took us just over an hour to chase down every Quill ship that had an active power source. For good measure, I used the last of my antimatter missiles on several of the largest pieces of the Quill capital ship. I was so worked up by what the Quill had done that I had Justice launch a comm buoy into the debris field. It would broadcast indefinitely in the Quill dialect. The message stated, "This is the price you will pay for preying upon the weak and defenseless."

When we returned to the Legacy, my dark mood was still haunting me. It was difficult for me to decide whether or not the fate that befell the inhabitants of the planet was better or worse after we intervened. I was trying my best to put it behind me because the perpetrators of the heinous act were all burning in hell. My crew and I stepped out of our armor in silence. We could not find words that would not have something to do with what we had just witnessed, so we kept quiet. One by one my crewmates walked away, save for Tria, who stood momentarily at the ready room door.

"Nathan, do not anguish over the outcome of our battle. It was the will of our maker."

Tria's words, while somewhat comforting, did little to change my feelings. I could not sit and think about it another minute and decided to move on to other matters. The first would be to go to the med bay and check on Coonts. At some point he would want to see all the video and data we collected from our encounter with the Quill. The recovery period he would be forced to endure might be lengthy due to the fact he had such a frail bone structure and physique. It was not a good foundation to build on. He would need things to occupy his mind other than the pain of healing.

When I entered the med bay, I shook my head. I had a feeling the little Grawl had gone overboard on the enhancements. He proved my suspicions correct. Before I could say a word, Justice called to me.

"Commander, Coonts was quite adamant that he should receive many of the same muscle enhancements that you underwent. I cautioned him it would also require the subdermal lamination as well. He insisted I go forward with both."

I rolled my eyes. One thing was quite noticeable: his head no longer dwarfed his body. Coonts now had broad shoulders and large muscular legs. Once he finally healed, it would take us all an adjustment period to get used to him as he is now. His once-burgeoning ego would most assuredly be inflated to epic proportions. He was sedated, and it was pointless to attempt to talk to him.

I decided to head to the command deck and compose an intelligence report to send to Sael. The massive Quill starship would need to be discussed in detail. There was always the chance she or her people had encountered one before. Tria had no data on it. As I entered the bridge, I saw that only Tria was present. She was standing in the corridor leading to the living quarters with her arms crossed.

"Justice, I want to collate and condense our video and current intelligence so I can prepare a briefing for the Principal Investigator."

I was slightly surprised that he did not answer me. What was even more surprising was the look on Tria's face when she stalked across the bridge in my direction. I did not know what to make of it, and it gave me an uneasy feeling. I started backing up.

"Tria, is there a problem that I should—"

She hit me! The totally unexpected shot nailed me right in the gut, purging the words from my mouth. I threw up my hands, in a sign of surrender. I was shocked stupid when she leaned down and heaved me up on her shoulder. She turned and carried me to my cabin, where Justice was courteous enough to open the door for her. We entered, and the door quickly closed. She threw me on my bed and pounced on me like a cat.

It was more than a day and a half before I was able to leave my cabin. I felt weak from lack of food, slightly battered, and lightly bruised, everywhere! The mating habits of the Chaalt entail total domination by the females over their male counterparts. They are, after all, the alphas in their race. I, on the other hand, am like the other sixty-nine percent of males in my species. I like to be in the driver's seat. This attitude netted me a good portion of my bruises—not all of them, mind you—but a good many of them. Chaalt foreplay amounted to an onslaught of Sha'Leen, and it took tremendous effort to shrug it off. At times she was genuinely shocked by certain human interactions but quickly embraced them all. If it were not for my carbon fiber reinforced skeletal system, I might have suffered a fracture skull and a broken neck. I now have a great deal of respect for the muscular enhancements to her legs. The Chaalt having an extra set of arms also puts the advantage squarely in her corner.

The consummation of our relationship was going to be something I would remember the rest of my life. I can say without reservation that the experience was definitely fifty shades of WWE!

I was getting worried. Justice had not said a single word for more than two days. You could address him if you needed something done and he would oblige you, but you would get no verbal response. The AI was eager to analyze what had taken place, but now his speechlessness was beginning to trouble me. I went back to my cabin to privately confront him on my concerns but was unceremoniously ambushed by Tria. Talking to the AI was not going to be possible.

On the fourth day, Justice finally spoke, and it startled me and my concerned crew. Klutch and Xul were trying their best to pretend nothing had happened and everything was business as usual. Poor Coonts had awoken in such agony Justice put him under until his body could heal and adapt to the very unnatural things done to it. All in all, I was just happy to hear the AI speak and really didn't care what the subject was.

"Commander, I have restored power to the IST as instructed by Tria. The Principal Investigator has twelve attempted communications queued in the system. I took the liberty of sending her the data package from our last engagement."

I turned and raised an eyebrow at Tria. She just shrugged and walked off the bridge.

"Justice, open a secure IST channel to Sael."

"Channel open, Commander."

Sael came right to the point, and I didn't have a chance to get a word in edgewise.

"Nathan Myers! I see no evidence that the Legacy sustained battle damage in your engagement with the Quill. Why has our line of communications been disrupted?"

Looking back to where Tria had walked off, I just shook my head.

"Sael, there are days I don't want to hear any scat from you! I told you I would get back with you when we have a solid plan of action. Unless you have data on the research facility that you are willing to share, we are still working on a plan. I felt you should know what we stumbled into when we were testing the Daggers. Do you have information pertaining to our engagement?"

"I have not thoroughly examined the data but can say that we do not have any intelligence on that class of Quill ship. The size of the new vessel and the power of the main weapon are certainly troubling. I must commend you on your victory; it was an impressive display of courage and valor. While your tactics could have been more sophisticated, the outcome proves their viability. We all mourn the loss of life on the unprotected planet. If I have your permission, I would like to pass the battle data and coordinates of the planet to my superiors. We would like to show the Galactic Union what the Crits have been doing while they attempt to peacefully negotiate with them."

"You can share the intelligence with your superiors but not with the Galactic Union. Not all members of the Galactic Union council are trustworthy. I am sure several are tied to the illegal artifact trade. Any data shared with them must be completely sterilized of our complicity."

"Nathan, if we can involve the Galactic Union, they will go to the planet to search for evidence. If there are survivors, they will most assuredly give the planet protected status and possibly help with decontamination."

"I tell you what, Sael, you can claim whatever you like and invite the Union to see, but none of our involvement can be revealed! Are we clear?"

"Yes. I will transfer the data to my council with another recommendation to allow me to contact you concerning the research station. When the council finally comes to their senses and asks for your help, I will give you a complete briefing to disclose the nature of the research center defenses."

The signal ended. I was fairly sure I could trust Sael but still had doubts about her council. At some point in time, the Legacy will be in close approximation to Sael's flagship, the Fury. Justice had covertly infected the ship's AI with one of his subsystems, and we would secretly get a data dump of all pertinent information recorded by said subsystem. I knew Sael suspected Justice was aboard. I didn't think it would be a healthy idea to confirm that fact, at least not for the foreseeable future.

I used my implants to try to locate Tria. For some strange reason, I could locate my other crewmates but not the Chaalt warrior. Evil robot! I needed to have a private talk with Justice but would avoid my personal cabin to do it. I instead headed for the hangar bay.

"Justice, jump us back to Alpha Base," I called out to the conniving AI.

He gave me no response, which was really starting to get on my nerves. "Justice, I believe you should now have a fairly complete library of my interactions. I really need you to get back to business!"

The evil robot decided it would be a good time to make a DEHD core jump. Everything went still and started glowing brilliant white. It was a surefire way to put a halt to the rant that was forming on my lips. When my awareness returned to normal space-time, my mood was taking a turn for the worst. I continued toward the hangar.

"Justice, I have had just about enough __"

Suddenly I felt my legs getting rubbery and tried to steady myself by leaning on the bulkhead next to the science lab hatch. I was grabbed from behind and dragged inside.

"Tria!"

Forty-five minutes later, I was adjusting my uniform and trying to gather my wits. I moved to the hatch with a frown on my face. I was still determined to confront Justice for his speechless shenanigans, but now it would be difficult to be angry. Looking back over my shoulder at Justice's coconspirator laying naked on the lab table, the frown melted from my face. I began wondering why Tria seemed so carefree. A lot of lousy crap was going on, and

60

we were about to be up to our eyeballs in it. It didn't take but a few more steps for reality to sink in: She had doubts about the outcome of the upcoming mission, and to tell the truth, I did as well. The thought of possibly being incapacitated before our boots hit the ground put the frown firmly back on my face.

I accessed my implants and found that Justice had already landed at Alpha Base. Klutch and Xul had departed more than thirty minutes ago and were in the base cafeteria. Graf and Jaran sat outside the Legacy, apparently waiting to talk to me. I didn't know if Klutch or Xul briefed them on my possible whereabouts, and I had no intention of explaining my tardiness. A shower was in order, but I thought it would be best to at least find out what the two Grawl wished to speak with me about. I heard something behind me and whirled around in a defensive stance. Tria walked by with her uniform in one of her hands and nothing else on. I felt just the smallest touch of her Sha'Leen, and I backed up a couple of steps. I heard her giggle, but she never turned around.

5

I went to the boarding hatch, and both Graf and Jaran stood to meet me. I apologized for making them wait, but the little smiles they gave me suggested they might have got a thorough briefing on the nature of my activities. The cringe that crossed my face sobered their expressions.

Graf stepped forward. "Commander, we have come to ask permission to check on engineer Coonts. We have been told he has volunteered to undergo the Oolaran weaponization procedure and you granted him permission."

"Yes, I allowed it, but the engineer chose the extent of the modifications. As far as we know, he is the first of your race to undergo the procedure. I personally believe he should have limited some of his selections. Coonts exercised his right of free choice and will now have to live with the outcome. Due to the extent of his modifications, Coonts will have an extended recovery time. Justice found it necessary to sedate him because of his inability to cope with the discomfort associated with the recovery process.

He is in the med bay, and I am sure Justice will answer any questions you might have."

I turned toward the hatch and called out louder than was necessary, "Won't you, Justice!"

His answer was elevated in volume as well. "Affirmative, Commander!"

The Grawl looked somewhat mystified by my exchange with the AI. Waving the Grawl on, I stalked back through the hatch to what I hoped would be an uneventful shower. As I made my way to the command deck, the big security doors opened, and I cautiously peeked around. I queried my implants, which seemed to be working properly, and noticed that Tria was in her quarters. I hurried down the corridor to my cabin and entered. I kicked off my uniform and treated myself to a hot shower that soothed most of the aches inflicted upon me. When I was done and dried off, I stepped out to get a fresh uniform and found Tria sitting on my bed. I thanked my maker she was clothed because I could really use some recuperation time and a hot meal. She fixed me with a smile that made it a toss-up whether I would get either. When she got up, I stepped back and she just laughed.

"Nathan, I am starved. Shall we go see what Tam Lin sent us in the way of human and Chaalt rations?"

I was famished and quickly offered an arm. She looped one of hers in mine, and we went down tube and out the boarding ramp. We met several of the Grawl on our way the cafeteria. They reached out and touched our hands in passing. When we stepped out of the lift, we could hear what sounded like a party going on. We were going to go in and see what the ruckus was about, but Tria and I stopped in our tracks at the entrance. Klutch was standing with his back to us and flailing around with one of his fists. The Grawl took notice of us and immediately went quiet. That's when we heard what the big lummox was saying.

"Then Tria punched him and threw him up on her____"

The short, wide buffoon finally noticed the silence and ceased his theatrics. He slowly turned around to face us, then promptly sat down and commenced eating like nothing had happened. To say the least, we were slightly embarrassed and a tad irritated. If it were not for the fact we had grown used to the Tibor's antics, I would have probably given him a black eye. Tria, on the other hand, didn't take it as well as I did. As we walked by him toward the food dispenser, she shoved him face-first into the large pile of rations on his tray. This brought a roar of laughter from the Grawl and a big toothy smile from the Tibor. He just shrugged his big shoulders and went right back to eating. I don't think I have ever heard the Grawl more joyous and happier. I was genuinely surprised that everyone was ignoring the upcoming mission and the perils that it would entail. It was as if Tria could read my mind.

"Nathan, our clan has seen us persevere against impossible odds. We have walked through the place you refer to as hell and we have always returned. They now refuse to accept any other outcome. All believe we will succeed."

I had considered more than a few times to ask the quirky AI what our odds of success would be but quickly cast the thought aside. I knew they were questionable and didn't want negative apprehension creeping into our mindsets when it was go time. Looking around at my people, I decided I would never try to change that mentality.

Tria and I finished our meal and went to the fabricator building to check on Felix. The young fabricator operator was consulting with several Grawl scientists and engineers. The word among the Grawl was that Justice, along with the help of the scientists and engineers, had a breakthrough in reverse engineering the IST system. It was something that the Chaalt would not take kindly to if it became general knowledge that we had managed such a feat. The Chaalt had made it an extremely difficult process, but Justice was relentless when it came to new tech. Felix was putting the final touches on the new comms equipment so it could be installed on the Daggers. It would fill the gap that the Backscatter transmitter left in our comms array. For now, what the Chaalt didn't know would not hurt them.

As we entered the building, Felix was all smiles and met us at the production line. Sitting on a table were four basketball-sized globes.

"Commander, Tria, the devices are complete and ready to be installed. Justice is waiting for me to bring them to the hangar on the Legacy."

"We will save you the trip so you can continue your work schedule," I said. "Thank you for your hard work and dedication."

The young Zaen bowed to us and turned to other pressing matters. Tria and I gathered up the transmitters and headed to the Legacy. Justice had the hangar doors open, and we could see he had the pilot modules pulled out of all four Daggers. He extruded two long arms from the bay, and we placed the devices in them.

"Commander, I will have the communication devices installed and tested in the next three hours. It will take an additional four hours to reassemble the Daggers. Once complete, they will be ready for the upcoming mission."

"What is Coonts's current status?"

"It is unfortunate that the Grawl cannot embrace the Oolaran weaponization as well as human and Chaalt physiologies. Coonts's body is attempting to reject the enhancements. I am actively suppressing his immune system, which will lead to an extension of my previously estimated recovery time. He is slowly stabilizing, but I do not think he will be capable of participating in the strike on the research station. I will be forced to keep him in a medically induced coma until his body accepts the modifications and begins to properly heal."

Damn! Coonts was unable to go before, and now that he had undergone the weaponization procedure, he was incapacitated. The little Grawl was an intricate part of our team and was our dedicated tail gunner. He had grown adept at covering our backs, and it made me nervous to not have the additional eyes going into the research complex. I didn't know how much longer we could afford to wait. If the Prule Hivemind was indeed in control of the facility, it would not be sitting idle waiting for someone to figure out a way to bring in the troops. We could not continue pushing off the mission. Our plan of action needed to be enacted sooner rather than later. The only good thing I could think would come out of this predicament was that if we did not return, Coonts would be able to carry on our primary mission.

Again, Tria seemed to know what I was thinking. The Chaalt warrior was now more than ever attuned to the emanations of my aura. She took me by the arm, and we walked out of the fabricator building.

"Nathan, we must not give the Hivemind the time it needs to assimilate the research station's systems. When the Daggers are ready, we must be prepared to go, whether we are invited or not. The council is foolishly wasting precious time and resources. We must set a deadline for our actions and let the Operative know we will go with or without clearance from the council. We are already at a huge disadvantage, and waiting only makes it worse."

Tria was right. We would be putting ourselves at great risk as it was. I would not throw away our lives because of the indecision of her people's leadership. Out of the corner of my eye, I saw Xul hastily moving in our direction, a look of deep concern on his face.

"Commander, I have just checked on Coonts's status and ask permission to speak freely."

"Xul, you do not have to ask permission to speak freely. I want all my clan to give me their honest opinions, no matter the circumstances. What is on your mind?"

"Commander, I believe Coonts may have erred in his quest to be mission capable. While he may have had the best of intentions, the extent of his choices may prove to be detrimental. His condition is fragile, and without Justice's continuous monitoring and interaction, there is a possibility that Coonts might permanently be disabled."

Apparently, Justice was giving me a best-case scenario. Xul, on the other hand, saw Coonts's condition from a different perspective. Either way, I had already determined he was a no-go for our mission.

I nodded to Xul. "You are correct, Xul. It will not be possible for Coonts to recover in time to accompany us. We are currently changing our mission parameters to account for his absence. He will remain here during the mission."

Xul looked me in the eyes and swallowed. He then puffed his chest out like Coonts was quite fond of doing.

"Commander, I volunteer to stand in engineer Coonts's place, no matter the outcome!"

I was surprised by what the little Grawl just said. It had already been determined a Grawl of normal physique would most assuredly perish during the insertion. This was not normal Grawl behavior. It's a known fact the Grawl prefer to leave the dying to someone else. As long as it was up to me, I had no intention of letting anyone die needlessly. It warmed my heart to know this little alien was offering up his life to try to protect ours. I could not help but smile and wonder what part of interaction with humans caused such an inordinate amount of testicle growth.

"No, Xul. You honor us all with your bravery, but I must decline the offer. We need your scientific expertise, and you would have to step up into a leadership position if the insertion goes badly."

The Grawl's chest deflated, and his shoulders slumped slightly. He gave me a dejected nod and then turned away. As Tria and I started toward the Legacy, Xul's face brightened and he suddenly looked determined once more.

"Commander! What if I assembled a scientific team to explore the possibility of finding something in our Prule salvage that might give us an advantage? We have a tremendous number of unknown devices that the Prule decided was valuable enough not to destroy. Perhaps we could spend our remaining time before you execute the mission researching the salvage with a focus on new weaponry?"

Tria and I stopped in our tracks. With everything that had been going on, I hadn't given any thought to messing with the salvage. We looked at each other in surprise. It was an option we were overlooking. Since we did not have a firm mission plan other than to get inside the facility and shut down the shield, it would be a good idea to let Xul run with his idea.

I grabbed the little Grawl and embraced him. He was a surprised but returned the gesture.

"Xul, assemble your team and get them to the Legacy as soon as possible. We will immediately DEHD core jump to the Sig's new base of operations. I want you and your team to begin searching for useful items. I know we only have a limited time to search and can only investigate a small fraction of our finds. If you can come up with anything useful, I will take any advantage we can get."

Xul took off at a dead run. He had renewed purpose and was delighted he was able to do something to help prepare us. The uncertain future that awaited us all didn't seem as bleak as before.

Justice broadcast on the PA system so all would hear. As usual he was always listening. His normal deadpan voice had an edge of urgency to it.

"I have commenced charging the matrix, Commander. We can depart for the Sig base in fifty-seven minutes."

To the last Grawl, they all volunteered. I did not want to be the bad guy and decide who needed to stay behind. Felix would need help with materials handling so he could keep the replicator running at capacity. I would have to decide between Graf and Jaran who had to stay and keep the base running smoothly. They would have the unenviable task of telling the other Grawl who stayed and who could go. Twenty minutes later, Graf and twenty very excited Grawl were boarding the Legacy. As Tria, Klutch, and I boarded, I waved to Jaran and the skeleton crew he had selected. While Jaran kept up the act that he was indifferent to his orders, the other Grawl looked dejected. Depending on the outcome of our mission, we were all overdue for a break. I pushed the thought from my head that every time I let pleasantries like that cross my mind, the universe always took a turn for the worst. I pulled Tria close, and she smiled; it erased my pessimism.

Justice took us out of our base at high speed and jumped us to the star system of the once-secret Scrun slaver base. Signaling the base with our access codes, I verified our identities. I was surprised when Sushi commed us back and insisted on giving us a fleet escort in honor of our return. It was impressive to see the ten gigantic Sig battle cruisers move into a spearhead formation as Justice tucked us neatly aft of the lead ship. As we crossed over the horizon of the planet, we dropped from the formation and went into low orbit. When we boarded Eagle One, I told the Grawl they were not to discuss our mission or reveal any intel once they stepped off the shuttle. If any should ask, we were cataloging our salvage; say nothing more. All inquiries were to be directed to me.

Justice launched the shuttle with the tow beam. Klutch was in the captain's seat and let the shuttle continue falling nose down through the caustic atmosphere. I don't think the Grawl scientists were used to such actions. The once chatty cargo hold was now quiet save for a few groans of discomfort. Klutch seemed to be having fun gliding the big combat shuttle sans the gravity thrusters.

The steep, spiraling descent for the entrance tunnel brought the moaning from the cargo bay up several notches. Tria was in the other pilot's seat giving the Tibor a sideways glance. I felt a slight thump when our dive went supersonic. I was standing behind him with an iron grip on the back of his seat, trying to keep my feet glued to the deck. The tunnel raced up to meet us at a deathly pace. The Troop Master nonchalantly reached out and engaged the gravity drives, arresting our fall and nullifying the negative gravity. This put a stop to the wail coming from the hold, and Tria's stern look of disapproval softened. Once inside the complex, Klutch put us down in the large landing area. The noise now coming from the cargo bay did not sound like blandishments. It was more of a racket that one might hear from a lynch mob. The Grawl quieted as they debarked but all gave the Tibor a withering stare. He just gave them his usual goofy-looking toothy smile.

We were greeted by a Sig military color guard and were escorted past rank after rank of Sig soldiers standing at attention. We were led to Sushi, who bowed.

"Welcome home, clan members of the Sig people. You honor us with your presence."

I gave him a warm smile and attempted to shake his large hand. It was awkward, but he played along anyway.

"Sushi, it is good to see you again, but the parade was unnecessary."

"On the contrary, Mr. Myers, the exploits of you and your people are held in the highest regard by all of the members of the Sig race. You are quickly becoming the

72

favorite subject matter in many of our training classes. You are proof that overwhelming odds are an inconvenience and not a legitimate reason to retreat."

I winced at his statement. I did not want my insane exploits to be the reason someone would spit in the eye of certain death. Luck can be a very fickle ally. In our line of business, sooner or later, you will get yourself mired in a large, steamy one only to find that your last resort has run out on you. Instead of me spewing what I believed should have been the proper cautionary words of discouragement, I changed the subject.

"Sushi, we are here to catalog some of our salvage. We are going to take items of interest back to our base for my scientists to study. We would like to get started as soon as possible with the items we stored in the former slave-holding area."

"Of course, Mr. Myers. This facility is at your disposal; our home is your home. If you need our assistance in any way, please let me know. I will let the security station in that sector know that you are on your way. Gravity sleds will be made available to you. If the number is insufficient, let me know, and I will arrange for additional sleds."

I thanked Sushi and looked around for my science team. Everywhere I looked, there was huge piles of salvage with corridors disappearing out into them in all directions. The salvage was piled about head high for a Sig but was more than four feet over me. That made it at least eight feet over the Grawl's heads. The corridors were just wide enough for two of the eight feet by sixteen feet gravity sleds to pass each other. The corridors went in all directions and my scientists were scattered among them all. A lone Sig walked up to me, and I could see by his wrinkled appearance he was much older than any Sig I had met previously. He had what turned out to be a translator slung over the shoulder of his long, dark coat.

"Greetings, Mr. Myers, my name is Dumaturamatsumer. I am the Sig scientific scholar in charge of this facility and the head cartographer. If you would kindly gather your people, I have gravity sleds waiting to transport us to section one-twenty-four."

I tried to let the scholar's name roll off my tongue in such a way it might be properly pronounced with a certain amount of regularity. He finally held up his hands.

"Mr. Myers, unless one is adept at speaking our language, even a translator will have difficulty adjusting to the subtleties of the Sig dialect. Pasta has long ago informed us that your species would rather label us with a title of endearment that is easily pronounced and memorized. So please feel free to do so now."

It was nice of him to make it easy for me, but try as I might, I could only look at my surroundings and come up with "dumpster." There was no way I was going to pin a name on him that would insinuate the elderly Sig scientist was a container for discarded waste. My awkward silence alerted Tria to my conundrum, and she pulled me close.

"Nathan, he is a senior scholar, and we should show him respect. Please choose wisely, because I believe all our future visits will involve interaction with him. Perhaps just senior scientist for the time being."

While Tria's suggestion was appropriate, another even more so, finally came to mind. I squeezed her arm in acknowledgment, but she could tell I had made my decision. She smiled but was looking at me out of the corner of her eye.

"Sir, I would like to bestow upon you an honorific from my home world. 'Chief' is a title used by the natives of my planet to show the proper respect to the most skilled and learned of our many tribes."

The elderly Sig stared toward the ceiling for more than thirty seconds before a big smile lit up his face.

"I accept your title of seniority and leadership!"

Turning to Klutch, I called out. "Troop Master! Get the scientists on the sleds. We are ready to go!"

Klutch took off barking orders, and in no time, he had gathered our flock on the sleds. He took the controls of the second gravity sled and pointed forward. Chief took the controls on the lead sled, and Tria and I stood at his side. We quickly moved off into the maze of corridors at an alarmingly brisk pace that widened my eyes. He would occasionally press a button on the T-handle, and the sled would emit a piercingly loud beep. The security teams on the paths would quickly move to the side as we swiftly passed them by. Five minutes later we arrived in front of the pressure door that we had once blasted from its hinges. It was back in its proper place but showed the battle scars we had inflicted upon it. It also showed where the Sig had made multiple welds and repairs to get it back in place.

We slowed to a stop well in front of the doors because a security squad of twelve Sig blocked our path. Chief spoke to them in his language, and they immediately stepped six to a side and came to attention. The giant door creaked and groaned as it opened. We moved to the front of the old security station and unloaded from the sleds. Chief approached me.

"Mr. Myers, I will remain here. If I can be of any assistance to you for any reason, please do not hesitate to ask."

Going over to Graf, I leaned down to the senior Grawl. "Graf, divide your team up between five of the sleds. Tria, Klutch, and I will take the sixth. Meet me back here in two hours so we can determine if we will need more time or more sleds."

Graf turned away and called to his group to get them organized. I waved to the Troop Master to get on the lead sled. When I attempted to take the controls, he gave me a not-so-subtle nudge to the side. When I frowned at him, he gave me a big, goofy grin as an apology. I rolled my eyes and took Tria by the hand and pulled her next to me. She put two of her arms around me and another on the Troop Master's shoulder. She looked at me and nodded her head toward the Tibor, urging me to do the same. I sighed and reached toward the Tibor's wide shoulder. I should not have procrastinated. The sled suddenly jerked forward, dumping me on my ass. If it were not for Tria righting me, I would have fallen off into the path of the trailing sled. The freaking Tibor never even turned around. The big oaf just went barreling down one of the paths to I don't know where.

6

When I could see the back wall of the storage area looming in front of us, I turned and noticed there was no longer any sleds behind us. Klutch must have decided we were wherever he determined we needed to be and stopped. He looked at two of us and then pointed to a fork in the path.

"Commander, I will search in this direction. Just yell out if you need me."

Tria and I stepped off the sled. Klutch took off, letting out a low, rhythmic croaking sound that I knew was the Tibor humming to himself. Tria and I took the opposite fork. Looking around at the endless piles of equipment, a feeling of hopelessness swept over me. Even if we found something useful, how could we possibly study it and verify its capabilities in the short amount of time we had left. I was second-guessing myself and thought we might be wasting our time fruitlessly digging in the trash of our greatest foe. That was when I heard a faint beeping noise. I turned around, looking at Tria, and she reached into her recon armor storage and pulled out a Guardian transponder. It was slowly, faintly beeping, and she looked at me quizzically.

"Justice insisted I take the transponder with us. I suspected it was so he could keep track of us, but now I am unsure of his motivations. I do not know what to make of the signal it is emitting."

Tria started walking in my direction, and the beep grew louder. The repetitious cycle of the device slightly increased a well. As she got closer and held it out to me, the beep slowed. The volume also diminished to its previous output. A small frown crossed Tria's face, and she stopped. She slowly turned around and retraced her steps. The transponder went up in pitch and frequency once again. Tria stopped when she determined the signal had peaked. I moved to her side, and she again held it out to me. I shook my head, and she smiled. She turned to the salvage on her left side and the transponder quieted ever so slightly. Turning to the right, the volume increased. Her eyes widened, and as she touched the transponder to the pile of junk, the beep increased. We started digging and throwing the collapsing pile of debris aside. The volume and cycle frequency increased as we dug. We were soon surrounded by salvage, and our path to the sled was blocked.

We had uncovered several items that had to be weapons, but most were old and tarnished. None had any effect on the transponder signal, so we tossed them aside and methodically pulled items from the pile until at last the signal was a nonstop beep. There in the pile at our feet was a rectangular device one foot wide and twice that long. It was about eight inches thick and tapered on both ends. The unknown device had a ten-inch diameter megaphone shaped protrusion in the middle of it. Inside had what appeared to be a glass lens at the base. On its side was an indentation with three buttons. It had large heavy straps made of an unknown material. There were four of the same configuration equal distances down its length. It was obviously meant to be wrapped around something or someone.

Tria reached down and touched it with the transponder. The beep promptly stopped. Whatever this thing was, it had to be of Guardian design or manufacture. I could think of no other reason for the transponder to specifically respond to it. Reaching down I tried to pick it up, but it took both hands because it must have weighted over two hundred pounds. Tucking it under my arm, Tria and I crawled up out of the mess we had made out of the pathway. As we reached the top, we saw Klutch making his way toward us, smiling.

"Commander, I have found what I believe is a Kashuga plasma caster and three intact power supplies," Klutch said, pointing back to his contributions on the sled. "The weapon and rechargeable power packs are much larger than I remember, but I am familiar with its operation and unique capabilities. As long as the projection tube is not damaged from overuse, it is a very formidable weapon."

Tria nodded to me then inspected Klutch's find.

"This is somewhat similar to a Kashuga weapon but appears to be of much better quality than the products they usually sell. There were several Kashuga on the last ship I served on. They are not like the Zaens, who sell the best they have. They are a mid-level advanced race that go out of their way to make as many credits as possible from any species they encounter. They built their reputation by manufacturing budget-oriented weapons for the open market. The plasma caster is one of their best sellers. The Coram buy it in quantity, then rebrand it to avoid the infringement laws. They make considerable profits selling it on the black market. Nothing they sell has ever been of this quality."

Klutch gave Tria a dismissive look and then turned his attention to the device we had found. "What is that, Commander?"

I looked around to make sure none of the Sig security teams were on the same path with us. I leaned in close to the Tibor.

"We are not sure. Tria brought one of our Guardian transponders, and it led us to the device's location."

I handed it over to him, and he hefted it up and down a few times.

"We could possibly bludgeon our enemies to death with it!"

Shaking my head at the Tibor's goofy smile, I told him to put it on the cart so we could continue our search. In the process of doing so, he inadvertently pushed one of the buttons. The device emitted a barely audible hum. Tria and I stared at the machine and started backing away from Klutch.

"Klutch! What the hell are you doing? Turn that damn thing off!"

The Troop Master's lizard eyes were now the size of silver dollars, and his smile disappeared. He turned away looking like he was going to throw it. He apparently must have pushed another of the buttons in his attempt to disable it. There was a flash like a good old-fashioned camera would make, but the results of the discharge in no way encouraged me to say "Cheese" for a follow-up shot. On the pile of junk in front of us was a ten-foot-wide shimmering gray circle. Before Tria and I could say a word, Klutch dropped the device like it was a hot potato then dove headfirst into us, knocking us to the ground in an attempt to cover us with his body. Tibor weight in excess of six hundred pounds due to their unique body density. Tria and I groaned in pain as we bore the weight of the Tibor on top of us. That in itself would not have been so bad, but the tackle was accompanied by his warrior's scent. Unfortunately for us, he had knocked the air from our lungs. Our next breath of air was vilely contaminated.

We heaved the Troop Master off of us and crawled, retching for more than twenty feet before we collapsed into puking fits of anger. Man, oh man, when I was done puking, I was going to put my foot so far up the Tibor's ass he would belch smart boot technology for at least a week! Tria recovered first and stalked toward the Tibor with all four of her fists clenched. Klutch held his hands up at her.

"Tria! I think I know what the device is!"

Wiping my mouth off, I stood to join Tria for the Tibor ass-kicking contest I was about to preside over. Klutch was pointing to where the bizarre circle had once been. It was now gone. I was still mad but now curious. My testy looks belayed just how hairy the trigger was on my right boot, and Klutch came right to the point.

"Commander! The device is a transporter!"

That put the brakes on the party I was getting ready to start. But I was still in no mood for bullshit.

"How the hell would you know that?"

"Commander, I have spent a great many years jumping in and out of hyperspace! That opening looked like interdimensional space!"

Tria looked at me. "He is correct, Nathan. I concur with his hypothesis."

My anger quickly subsided, and common sense was firmly back in control. "If it is a hyperspace portal, how can we be sure where it leads to?"

Tria picked up the device and examined it carefully. "The portal was very short-lived."

"I have an idea," she said, handing it back to Klutch." "Point it back at the same spot as before. Wait until Nathan and I are ready, then repeat what you did before to activate it."

Tria took me by the hand and pulled me to the edge of the junk pile. She pointed upward, and we both carefully climbed up. We stood looking down at the Troop Master. Tria led me about twenty-five feet to the far side of the pile. We could now see the backside and an adjoining pathway. Tria told me to wait where I was and made several careful hops back toward Klutch's side. I heard her call to Klutch to activate the device. She came bounding back to me and stood staring over the side. My interest peaked, and I held her hand and watched eagerly. Nothing was happening. I frowned and was going to tell Tria we needed to continue searching and we could play with it later. Suddenly the circle of shimmering gray appeared below us. Tria gripped my hand tightly and grinned.

"I think I have it figured out now," Klutch called to us. "It is a sequence, but I am not sure about the third button. I will push it now!"

The portal promptly disappeared. Klutch let out a whoop.

"I know how it works! Wait where you are, and I will activate it again."

The portal reappeared on the opposite side once again. I held my finger up to Tria, and she shook her head. I ran as carefully as possible back to a point I could see Klutch.

"Throw something into the opening!"

When I turned to look at Tria, she was going down over the opposite edge. Klutch picked up an oblong piece of unknown equipment and tossed it in. It disappeared. The Troop Master and I stood staring with big smiles on our faces. Tria stepped out of the portal with the piece of scrap in her hands and we were shocked she would do such a thing. I wanted to be mad as hell at her for pulling such a stunt, but it was the obvious next step. I decided it was my turn. Tria stopped me when we saw a red band around the edge of the opening start blinking. She gripped my arm tight and for good reason. The band blinked faster, and then the portal disappeared.

Klutch had been timing the event. "Commander, the portal was active for three minutes unless I push the third button, then it terminates immediately."

I wasn't sure what would happen if the portal closed while someone was in it but figured it couldn't be a good thing. Red seemed like it was pretty much universal for a no-no. We needed time to study this thing, so I decided we should go back to the shuttle and get back to Alpha Base as soon as possible. The idea struck me that next time we came to look around, we would do so slowly and bring both transponders. We had spent about an hour and a half digging in the salvage, so by the time we got back, the Grawl should be gathering. Hopefully they had some luck finding items of interest.

We pulled up in front of the security station, and the Grawl were already loading the shuttle with their finds. Sushi walked up to me.

"Mr. Myers, several of the security teams reported unusual flashes of light emanating from the back of the storage area. Is all well?" Sushi inquired.

Sushi was being politely nosey. I knew the security station had excellent surveillance coverage of the storage area. There was no doubt in my mind he saw some or all of what transpired. But he and his people were solid allies. Even though I would have liked to keep the device a secret, I was not willing to deteriorate the trust we had built between our races. Telling petty lies when faced with certain knowledge of the truth was something that was practiced more often than not on the planet of my birth. As one of the very few examples of my race running loose in the galaxy, I was not going to be known to my allies for exhibiting that characteristic.

"We found some very interesting tech among our salvage," I explained. "We are going to take it back to our base and run extensive tests. Once we have determined it is safe to operate without fear of dangerous repercussions, we will disclose the nature of our studies with our allies."

My statement netted me the desired effect. Sushi smiled.

"Mr. Myers, all our interactions will be kept in the utmost of confidence. I look forward to hearing from you."

Rather than try to shake his oversized hand, I bowed. Sushi's smile grew larger, and he returned the gesture. We boarded Eagle One, and I took the controls for the flight back to the Legacy. This made my passengers exceptionally happy; Klutch not so much. We exited the Sig base and made a high-speed vertical ascent toward the Legacy. When we were within tow beam range, I killed the gravity drive, quickly arresting our forward velocity. Justice locked on to us and pulled the shuttle into the hangar bay.

"Justice, are you going over the data we have on the portal device?"

"Yes, Commander. The interdimensional gateway device is an amazing piece of technology. It creates a tear in normal space-time that is so miniscule I did not detect its use. The short-term duration of the portal suggests a very limited range. We need to study it in real-time lab testing. I hypothesize it is only able to access cavities closest to the field emitter. While the device can give us a distinct advantage over our adversaries, it can also be dangerous to the users. We need to determine if opening a portal to the void could decompress ship spaces."

That very same thought had crossed my mind.

"Is the DEHD core charged?"

"Yes, Commander. We are ready to jump on your order."

"Take us home, Justice!"

I was relieved that Justice was back to his old self. Having a new toy to occupy his processors could deflect some of his scrutiny to more useful pastimes. I found his interest and close observation of my sexual interactions with Tria very annoying. I still did not know what to think about his extended period of speechlessness. The thought slid from my mind when my surroundings turned brilliant white.

When the Legacy returned to normal space-time, Justice had nothing unusual to report, so we made a beeline for home. I made a cursory inspection of the Grawl's finds. They reported loading several different pieces of equipment onto the sleds. Graf abandoned them all when one of the science teams discovered parts of what appeared to be a large missile or torpedo. What made it unique was that it was exactly the right diameter to fit the Legacy's torpedo launcher tube. The Grawl had to use gravity jacks to load the pieces on all the remaining sleds. It partially filled the cargo bay, which was another reason the Grawl were happy I was pilot in command for the return trip to the Legacy. A large number had to give up the relative safety of their seats to accommodate the parts of the weapon. The scientists had asked the nature of our find, and when Tria told them, they lost all interest in the missile and sat wide-eyed and gawking at the compact portal device. Klutch was not only disappointed he was not piloting the shuttle, but he was a little miffed that no one made a single inquiry concerning his discovery. He sat on the cargo bay deck with his arms crossed, brooding and giving off the unsavory odor of his displeasure.

Everyone was more than happy to debark the shuttle. All found someplace to be other than in proximity to the Troop Master. I shook my head and decided I would bolster his dinged ego.

"Klutch, I want that weapon ready to go. Give it a thorough inspection to make sure it is still safe and in proper operating condition. You will be bringing it on the upcoming mission!"

That seemed to snap the Tibor out of his glum mood and would undoubtedly bring the air quality on the Legacy up a notch or two. He gathered up the weapon and the power packs, then headed to the science lab. This made the Grawl much happier as they unloaded the collected salvage and moved it at Graf's direction to the inspection area of the artifact building. We had a large number of artifacts collected from the Prule ship in a makeshift lab. The new finds would join the rest in what was getting to be an overly crowded storage area.

The need to build a larger lab was looming on the horizon. I could also foresee the need for additional scientists and engineers. My science teams had been divided several times already, and it was probably degrading their capabilities. We had the credits to easily make those future goals a reality; our next mission would determine whether we needed to. I frowned in frustration because I was once again letting doubt creep into my mind. Justice picked up on it and pinged my implants.

"Commander, perhaps another round of sexual combat with Tria would allay any misgivings about your upcoming mission. I have noted with great interest that it does not matter if you win or lose; it still elevates your sense of well-being to levels previously never recorded."

I flinched and gritted my teeth. If the evil robot was trying to get me to think about something positive, he succeeded. I was now wondering if I should continue my goal of finding the proper orifice on the Legacy to shove my combat boot into.

"Justice! The only thing I want from you at the moment is your assessment of the portal device. We need to know its capabilities and limitations!"

"Commander, the device is indeed of Guardian origins. Its construction closely matches that of the transponders. It has no obvious openings to access and appears to be made of the same unknown materials. The operation of the machine is straightforward as exhibited by the Troop Master. I believe it was intentionally designed that way to accommodate various levels of intelligence. Our available data suggests the Sentinel races had a large number of allies."

I could not help but prickle at Justice's intended or possibly unintended swipe at my primitive background. I was, after all, the product of a backward-thinking world from a lonely backwater in the galaxy.

"Justice, could you please just give me the facts and leave out the speculation!"

"Of course, Commander. A flashing luminous band around the portal indicates its duration is about to expire. Operators have thirty seconds to make use of or evacuate the portal after the device alerts you to imminent closure. My observations have also revealed its limitations. The crimson fluorescence also alerts the user when it is unable to complete a portal. It rapidly flashes, then the portal quickly closes. Testing indicated it was able to access voids in all directions out to one hundred feet. The device is also a choke point, able to check the environmental conditions that are present around the operator. You will be capable of entering the void through the device without fear of decompressing your location. Attempts to span greater distances through solids failed one hundred percent of the times tested. In overhead applications, my transferred sensor device was deposited directly to the side of the portal. Unfortunately, using it for downward access, you are subjected to whatever fall might be waiting on the opposite side of the portal. The wearer of the device is capable of terminating the portal at any time by pushing the lower control button. I have made several attempts to recover sensors that I purposely terminated portals on, and all attempts have failed. All telemetry ceases upon closer of the portal. I speculate they are stranded in one of the infinite dimensions of interdimensional space. The device is an extremely valuable military asset, but as with any alien machinery, it should be used with considerable caution."

I snorted in derision, thinking I should have practiced that tidbit of brilliant logic right after coming into contact with Justice. That thought also presented me with the very real scenario of an ornery one-eared wolf, teaching his whelps how to clean their teeth on my bleached white bones. I looked around and saw Tria leaving the artifact lab. The irritating AI was not one hundred percent correct on one point: I was not a good loser. For whatever reason, Tria seemed to pick up on the vibes I was giving off. She turned and walked directly at me. A silly smile planted itself on my face, and my stride quickened. I had no intention of losing for a third time in a row.

7

I was reaching for Tria's outstretched hand when Justice tipped over the ever-present bucket of piss that must be perpetually hanging over my head.

"Commander, I have an IST transmission from the Operative. She is demanding to speak with you now. I have twice informed her you are unavailable, but she continues to send transmissions. If it were not for the growing urgency and volume of her requests, I would have gladly shut down the devices."

The look on my face went from one of anticipation to that of finding out the flavor of fecal matter. The reaction was the result of the evil robot's comments and the Operative's knack for calling at just the wrong time. At one time, the IST and Backscatter comms devices seemed like they were must-have tech. I have since learned they are actually a curse perpetrated on me by the Operative to punish me for my primitive Earth boy sensibilities. She could now, on a whim, verbally abuse me like a Throgg from anywhere in the galaxy. While this probably did not start out as that type of communication, Justice most assuredly made it one.

"Nathan! If that defective machine cannot follow command directives when it comes to our communications, my people have the capability of permanently disabling the devices!" Sael barked.

So, it was going to be one of those conversations. If she would have practiced a small amount of diplomacy, it might not have pushed my buttons in all the wrong order. The comms devices really benefited the Operative and her people more than us. I was sure it was just another way for her to keep tabs on our movements throughout the galaxy. Why she would spout such scat when we were actively trying to find ways to help her people left me bewildered and more than a little pissed off. Tria was squeezing my arm as I took a slow, deep breath. The rest of my crew was eyeballing me, probably thinking that I was just trying to calm myself. They were going to be wrong. I was in fact putting a chronological order to the curse words swiftly stacking up on my tongue. Tria made it a waste of time.

"Principal Investigator, we do not care if you shut down the devices, nor do we need you again trying to exert your authority," Tria said. "At your request, we have been working on ways to get inside the research facility. Something I might add that our trusted leadership on the council has not been able to do! Your careless disrespect and the endless scat you constantly spew at us is undermining our efforts to help you. I suggest you start looking for someone else willing to yield to your command and selflessly put their lives on the line. Justice! Shut down the IST!"

"Affirmative, Tria. All BS and IST communications equipment have been disabled."

I stood staring slack-jawed at Tria. My intended harangue would have been a cool glass of water compared to the fire she had just shoved up Sael's ass. Everyone within earshot quickly found a reason to be elsewhere. I was going to step away myself, because I was considering calling the old witch back and giving her another chance to rephrase her last statements. Tria grabbed me by the back of my uniform.

"With all that is going on, my patience has run out! I now more than ever find it is extremely difficult dealing with Sael's constant meddling. She is becoming insufferable!"

Tria had a point. Sael was back to being a real pain. The way she was picking at Justice was only exacerbating the problem. He was now openly retaliating by blocking her comms, even though I knew he had more than a single reason to do so. I decided to keep my mouth shut rather than say something that might be misinterpreted. Maybe a bite to eat would be the judicious choice given the elevated tensions. I kept a neutral face and invited Tria to join me in the galley.

"I am sorry, Nathan," Tria said. "I should have remained silent. Knowing Sael, she will take her anger out on you when she has finished dealing with me. She will no doubt be here shortly and will either overlook my indiscretion or bring me up on charges of insubordination."

"What makes you think she will come here after the ass chewing you just gave her? I know I wouldn't!"

Trying to lighten the mood helped a little. She now had the smallest of smiles on her face and stood with arms crossed, giving me the stink eye.

"Yeah, I suppose you're right. Sael isn't going to take verbal abuse from anyone, regardless of rank, and not have something to say about it."

Tria frowned at my conclusion. "Sael Nalen is no longer the calm and calculating manipulator she once was. Her emotions seem to be more irrational than ever, and to tell you the truth, I cannot figure out why she continually turns her ire on us. She praises us one minute, then dumps a load of scat on us the next."

I had to agree. "Could it have something to do with her new rank as Principal Investigator?"

"I have no idea. It wasn't that long ago she was nothing more than an assassin for the military. Kala Mor Dee never had to worry about anything other than completing her assigned mission goals. Now she has to deal with the demands of our leadership as well as the military council. I suspect when she was told she would be given her freedom to do as she wished with the Fury and her crew, it was at the behest of the leadership council and not the military council. We could be witnessing a power struggle between what remains of the Chaalt leadership and the newly elected military commanders. Sael is caught in the middle."

I chewed slowly on Tria's words. That would explain some of Sael's mood swings but not all of them. I knew she was up against a brick wall when it came to ordering us around. She should be well-aware that would never happen anyway. Something else was going on, and it was proving to be a weight the Principal Investigator could not bear. If Sael did indeed show up here, I was going to get to the bottom of it one way or the other. Tria looked at me with those big green eyes, and I could tell she was worried.

"Nathan, I have a bad feeling something is very wrong. We must be prepared to do what others are not willing to do. I sense we are quickly running out of time, and the future of my people is at stake."

Tria had an uncanny ability to know when things were going to shit. She had me thinking the Prule takeover at the research facility was only part of the equation.

"Commander!" Justice interrupted. "The Fury has just jumped into the very edge of our star system."

There was only one way to get to the bottom of what was happening. I was determined to get a real no-shitter from Sael, whether she liked it or not.

"Commander, the Fury made a hard about turn and jumped away using its exact entrance coordinates. I am now detecting the telltale drive emissions of a cloaked Chaalt combat shuttle. I have taken the precaution of bringing the shield and weapons generators online and await further orders."

"Justice, turn the BS and IST systems back on. What is the status of the shuttle?"

"It has increased its velocity to maximum. The shuttle could jump closer in system to greatly decrease its travel time. It appears that is not the pilot's intentions. ETA forty-seven minutes."

I took Tria by the hand and pulled her along till she was running with me toward the Legacy. "Justice, is the crew aboard?"

"Yes Commander, I have alerted them of our imminent departure!"

Justice was reading me like a book, and that was a good thing for a change. He now seemed like he was back to business as usual, and it helped calm my growing anxiety. We hit the boarding ramp, and it closed behind us. Justice launched before we could make it to the lift tubes. When we stepped onto the bridge, Klutch and Xul were sitting at their stations looking puzzled.

"Justice, what is Coonts's status?"

"His overall condition is slowly improving but he will remain in an induced coma for the immediate future."

I was going to revisit my decision to let members of my clan have access to the Oolaran weaponization programs. It has caused us more than a few unnecessary delays at inopportune times. Up on the view dome I could see a small blue triangle that was rapidly growing in size.

"Justice, give me a sitrep!"

"Commander, the shuttle has ceased accelerating and is now retro braking to diminish its forward velocity. I will recover the shuttle with the tow beam. The matrix is charged and optimized. I will take us to the Fury's jump point and transition us to our last recorded DEHD core destination. I will plot a course through the system that will allow the matrix to recharge and then jump back to Alpha Base."

I frowned, wondering what the hell we needed to jump out of system for. Tria answered my unasked question.

"Justice is attempting to mask the Fury's jump into our star system. By using the Fury's exit coordinates, we will be overlapping the transition distortions waves created by its passage. It will greatly complicate any attempts to track the Fury. Our actions and those of the captain piloting the Fury are intended to mask the ship's whereabouts and transition points."

I just nodded because I was still at a loss why it should even matter. The perceived cloak-and-dagger routine had me worried. Something stinky was up, and it had nothing to do with Klutch. Looking at the view dome, I could see Justice slowed our intercept course. We were fortunate our shuttles and the Daggers were at Alpha Base. The large Chaalt assault shuttle was going to be a tight fit in the hangar. We headed back to the down tube. It had to be Sael piloting the shuttle, but with all the skullduggery going on, I couldn't be sure of anything.

We entered the hangar bay as the boarding ramp extended from the shuttle. Sael Nalen stepped out of the air lock and started in our direction even before it touched the ground. Her final step perfectly timed with the ramp making contact with the Legacy's deck. She looked mad but not furious. I looked at Tria as she stood rigid and stared straight at Sael. Not knowing what to think or, for that matter, what to say, I did the same.

"At ease, Captain Burlor. I find your military demeanor distasteful after the childish tantrum you broadcast for all to hear! You have no idea what you have just done!"

Sael looked at me and knitted her eyebrows. "Stop that nonsense! Are you not the ranking officer on this relic?"

Sael threw up her hands and stalked away from us only to suddenly turn and come back.

"If you would have spouted that scat at any other time during the current crisis, I would have been within my rights to bring you up on charges and send you back to our home worlds to await a military trial," Sael said, waving a finger in Tria's face. "You instead played the part I expected from Nathan so perfectly, it was as if it had been scripted. I now fear you may have done more harm than was necessary. By declaring to one and all you will no longer help me attempt a rescue of the council, you have temporarily removed the targets from our backs. When the ruling council members are finally disposed of, we will be labeled as traitors and dealt with accordingly!"

Tria and I glanced at each other incredulously, then turned back to Sael. Consternation would be an understatement right at the moment.

"Sael, what the hell are you talking about, or should the real question be, what the hell have you got us into now?"

"No more secrets or political scat, Nathan. I have uncovered a plot that can change how my people are governed, and not for the better. My methods for discovering the truth have exposed my intentions. I am now a target for execution."

She was going to say more, but everything went mute and our surroundings started turning brilliant white. When we returned to normal space-time, I called to Justice.

"Call a crew meeting in the conference room."

I waved Sael on, and we went to the lifts that would take us to the bridge level. As we entered the conference room, the crew was just getting seated. Justice had arranged the seating so Sael would be at the opposite end of the table from me.

"Why is engineer Coonts not present?" Sael asked.

"He exercised his right of free choice to undergo Oolaran modifications. Unfortunately, his Grawl anatomy did not respond well to some of his choices," I explained. "Justice is confident he will pull through, but for now he is recuperating in the med bay at Alpha Base for an undetermined period of time. Before you start ranting about the devil that haunts me, he did not receive any of the imprinting protocols."

Sael's mouth opened then snapped shut. She mumbled under her breath loud enough for us to hear, "Your madness must be contagious."

"Okay, Sael, give us everything you got, and for all of our sakes do not leave anything important intentionally or unintentionally out."

My statement garnered me a frown, but she let it go with a clearing of her throat.

"The new military council has no interest in saving the legitimate leaders of my people," Sael began. "They are in fact planning to destroy the research facility and all inside of it. It will later be divulged as a last-ditch effort to save the Chaalt race from the Prule. All military vessels including the Fury have been recalled in preparation for the assault. Those of us who are not one hundred percent behind the current leadership will be ordered to stand down. The current administration wants no confusion or the appearance that not all stand with them. As you already know, all information on the lab and any knowledge of its existence is classified. As the Principal Investigator of my people, I have stretched those rules to the breaking point. Some may assume I am within my authority, but I can assure you the conspirators now serving on the council will see it as treason. I was attempting to reach you on an open IST channel to say that the meeting you requested with me would have to be put on hold due to an undisclosed military crisis. IST transmissions are monitored, and it would have given several in our intelligence community information they previously did not have access to. It would have instigated a large number of inquiries. I did not expect Tria to reveal that I have already alerted you with highly restricted information."

I looked over at Tria, and she was staring holes through Sael. We knew one thing for sure: this was not just Sael being the pain in the ass she had proven to be in the past.

"Sael, start at the very beginning so we can wrap our heads around what you are telling us. Are you saying that the Prule Hivemind is nothing more than a pawn in a much bigger game?"

"Not necessarily a pawn, Nathan. It was an enabler! Its takeover of the research facility has allowed certain military council members an opportunity to change the course of the Chaalt people's future. They intend to return my people back to the militarized society we once were with the military council firmly in charge of the government."

"Sael, how exactly did you come to this conclusion?"

She didn't like the interruption. But I didn't care for the drama without some background facts.

"I started getting a bad feeling about who was being ordered to make a direct assault on the facility. Most were seasoned veterans, and I personally knew many of them. Several were close to retirement and would have undoubtedly been elected to leadership positions. They were ardent supporters of civilian governance. My network of trusted allies alerted me the commanders in charge of the breach teams were getting almost no information. They were being sent in blind against our very best defensive weaponry! To me, it made no sense, so I made a visit to the fool who was placed in charge of the operation. She was an officer with considerable rank, but it came from her service in strategic supplies. Her combat experience was running munitions freighters into combat zones. She was so far out of her depth she just sat wringing her hands at my inquiries. That is when she revealed her orders did not come from her normal chain of command. They came directly from the new military council. It did not take me long to determine that the council member responsible for the orders was Gredda Porsha's commanding officer before being asked to join the council. I knew then things were not as they seemed."

I could tell Tria was getting pissed. She finally put words to her piercing stare.

"If Gredda Porsha was in on this, she will die when they destroy the facility."

"If Gredda is at the lab. We only have circumstantial evidence suggesting she is there. I believe at some point when the true conspirators come to light as our saviors, Gredda will somehow be reincarnated as a hero of the people."

I sat looking up at the ceiling shaking my head.

"I have been collecting the evidence, Nathan," Sael said. "I found out that Gredda and her elite strike team were the first to enter the Prule lifeboat. They spent several days on the wreck before they allowed anyone else aboard. They claimed they were making a detailed security inspection. In fact, they did, but I believe that a lot of the conspiracy was planned during that time. My covert sources have informed me that Gredda's strike team medic is also an advanced AI specialist with extensive military chip knowledge. I believe she made it possible to gain access to the ID chips and codes necessary to commandeer the council's shuttle."

Klutch was rubbing his bullet head. He squinted at Sael. "Someone would still have to convince the council members to willingly board the shuttle and tour the facility. Who has the power to persuade so many of your leadership to visit the lab?"

"There is only one person on the leadership council with the power to sway so many to her will: Corra Galvic. A great many solar rotations ago she was an Operative in the military. During my investigation I found that many of her records seem to have vanished. When you have been a Senior Operative as long as me, you know where to look for intentionally buried and obscured records. I found data that indicates she was Gredda's regimental commander when she was inducted into the services."

The look of disbelief was slowly disappearing from Tria's face. It was being replaced by shock at the revelations Sael had uncovered.

"Why would Gredda kill personnel thought to be her allies?"

"I believe she tried to recruit them to her cause. Some may have voiced doubt; it is obvious the council's shuttle pilot did. Three of the five slain were also next in line should something happen to seated council members. At the time of the assassinations, several of Gredda's strike team members had orders and transfer records indicating they were training on the frontier of the exclusion zone.

My sources could find no records at any military barracks on any of the frontier worlds documenting their presence or training schedules. I believe they were committing the executions necessary to ensure no interference with their plans. It would be foolish of me to think they are not actively pursuing me."

"Please correct me if my interpretation of your data is faulty," Xul said, taking his turn at deciphering Sael's conspiracy theory. "You are saying that ousted members of your military council are attempting to perpetrate a coup using the very real threat of an imminent Prule machine infection?"

"While that is an oversimplified explanation, you are essentially correct. We are not talking about just any former members, but ones specifically cast out for the unsanctioned espionage against you and the rest of Nathan's clan."

The more I heard, the more I didn't like it. Now I wondered what Sael meant by Tria playing my part. Were we being used as well?

"What the hell were you saying about Tria playing my part?"

We were all scowling at Sael. This was quickly turning into a Throgg hump of epic proportions with each new revelation.

"Nathan, Tria's IST transmission was undoubtedly recorded," Sael said. "While I would have preferred to have you be the one to vent your anger at me, Tria did it for you and unwittingly revealed my complicity. There is the real possibility that the two of us will now be known as the traitors who turned their backs on our people in the face of a military crisis. I am sure the new powers to be will broadcast it far and wide that we have chosen an alliance with you over our own people. Once the research lab and everyone in it is destroyed, military law will inevitably be put into place for an indefinite period of time. The conspirators will move quickly to fill the void left in the governing body. A select few members of the ruling cast will remain, but the military council will be firmly in control. When the dust finally settles, they will come for Tria and me. Once I have been judged and executed, they will enact their revenge upon you by taking what you cherish most, or kill you all trying."

The scent in the room was horrific and eyewatering, but no one said a word.

"Why haven't they destroyed it yet?" I said through clenched teeth.

"Because, Nathan, the Hivemind broadcast a message that was picked up by military and a small number of civilian networks. It is wanting to bargain the lives of the council members for its freedom. We have legitimate video showing that most still live. I know for a fact the council will never give the Prule its freedom. The wasted lives of my allies, was to give the appearance: the new council would exhaust all options before terminating the facility. I personally believe it was also a message to me to forgo interference if I wished to survive. I chose to ignore the warning. I have collected what I believe is enough evidence to convict them all of treason. It will have been in vain unless we have lawful leaders willing to listen."

I had great hopes that we would one day find a race not tainted by corruption. It was chipping away at my faith to find that even the most advanced races were not immune to its poisonous touch. It took more than a few deep breaths to calm myself and the beast within me. Justice would make it a waste of time.

"Commander, sensors at Alpha Base have detected the faint transition signatures of Chaalt dark energy drives. I now have a solid lock on a cloaked three-ship formation. They are skirting the edge of our star system very close to the exit transition coordinates of both the Fury and the Legacy."

If Sael didn't think we could track her people's warships while cloaked, she for sure knew it now. Judging by her reaction to Justice's alert, she obviously had doubts.

"Justice, give me some options!"

"Seven minutes till minimum DEHD core charge. Alpha Base defensive shields and weaponry are in standby mode awaiting your orders, Commander."

Sael's eyes widened. I saw a look on her face I had never seen before: sheer panic.

"Nathan, you must not attack my people! That is exactly what the conspirators want to happen. You will become an enemy of the Chaalt if you do this!"

8

Tria gripped my arm but said nothing. My crew sat stoned-faced and ready to follow orders no matter the outcome.

"Sael, I have no intention of firing the first shot," I said. "However, I will not give them an opportunity to attack my base of operations."

I did not like the limited number of choices available to me. If I was going to force their hands, I would have to reveal some of our capabilities to do it. The captains of those ships needed to know they did not have a marked advantage.

"Justice, bring Alpha Base's shields online but do not open the weapons silos."

"Shield dome active, Commander!"

Sael looked at me, then cast her eyes to the floor. She knew I just gave away a secret to her people that I would not have done were it not for her being here.

"Commander, the Chaalt ships have ceased cloaking and have transitioned. They have entered a high geosynchronous orbit above Alpha Base and are requesting they be allowed access."

"Tell them it is well-documented: the only Chaalt emissary allowed to enter Alpha Base is the Principal Investigator."

"Message relayed, Commander. DEHD core matrix charged and ready for transition on your order."

Sael looked up at me with a small smile on her face. It quickly vanished because there was the possibility her counterparts might have orders to start shooting.

"Commander, they are now demanding we turn Sael Nalen over to them and have brought their shields online."

That got a rise out of the beast in me, but I pushed it back to its hiding place. Sael must have sensed the change in my aura and did the unexpected: she grasped my other arm.

"Nathan, I will turn myself over to them rather than have you shed Chaalt blood!"

Having my favorite Chaalt warrior on one arm and another that I have felt the need to strangle on a number of occasions was conflicting the hell out of me.

"Justice, how close to their coordinates can we jump without hitting them?"

"They have cut their drives, and I have a destination transition plotted. We can get close, Commander."

"Okay, Justice, jump when I give the word, then I want you to make a hard turn and go full stealth."

"Affirmative, Commander. Vectors locked and coordinates verified!"

"Relay my comms please."

"Alpha Base comm channel open and ready to broadcast."

"You Throggs must be pleasuring yourselves with stim sticks. It should be more than obvious the Fury is not at this location. Clear my orbitals now, or I will pay you a visit so we can discuss the matter face to face!"

I wondered if I would get a response. Justice alerted me that my statement must have caused more than a little excitement.

"Commander, I am detecting a spike in the encrypted IST traffic between the Chaalt vessels. I have now identified an out-system IST data stream. I speculate you have sown confusion as to whether or not the Senior Operative is indeed at our location."

"Let's stir the pot a little more. Jump now, Justice!"

The familiar silence and whiting out of normal space-time usually brought a grin to my face upon return. The use of the magic-like tech gave me a rush of excitement that would make it difficult to hide the emotional display. This transition was an exception. Everyone on the bridge physically ducked when the view dome came back online with the three massive Chaalt warships filling its totality. My sphincter started sending some very mixed signals as to its reliability in holding back the riot that had suddenly gathered in the lower half of my body.

A shudder rumbled throughout the Legacy as our warp bubble shouldered aside the ships that were more than twice our size. Their shields flared brightly in protest of our proximity. Justice cloaked and went full stealth as we made a crazy hard turn leaving the reeling monstrosities in our wake.

"Justice, I said close, not ram them!"

"Commander, all three ships have got underway and appear to be preparing to jump out of our star system."

Sael stared at me in disbelief. She looked like a bunch of unpleasant things were about to spew out of her mouth, and I was in no mood for it. I gritted my teeth and stuck a finger in her face.

"Not a single word, Sael!"

To her credit, she bit down on the comments she was on the verge of making. She instead stomped over to Coonts's unoccupied console and sat down with her back to me.

"Commander, the Chaalt warships have transitioned, and I have no anomalous contacts to report."

"Take us back to base, Justice."

"ETA two minutes."

Tria was still a little wide-eyed but gave me a nod of her head to let me know she was okay with the outcome. To tell the truth, now that my heart rate was back to normal (as well as my intestinal fortitude), I could also live with what had just transpired. The message to the Chaalt council should be loud and clear: don't come pissing on my turf and expect me to be good with it. I decided I was going to find out how they feel about me defecating in their backyard.

"Justice, I want Sael's shuttle offloaded as soon as we land. I want Eagle One and our Daggers ready to go in as soon as their weapons magazines are reloaded. Prep everything for the research facility breach scenario. Mission is now a go. Sael, you need to give Justice detailed coordinates on the base's location. We need to get as close as possible so your people will have very little time to react to our intrusion."

"I will give you the information on one condition."

"And what might that be, Sael?"

"I am going with you!"

"That's not possible. We have to use the Daggers to phase through the base's shield. A shuttle would be shot to pieces long before we could recover from the insertion and figure out how to get the shield shut down. Now that your people seem to be turning on us, I'd rather leave the shield in place until we have saved your leadership council or abandoned the mission."

Sael's face reddened as anger built up inside of her. I really didn't have time for any of her scat. With the beast rattling the bars to its cage, the mood I was quickly getting into made me feel that my chances were better than average that I could beat the information out of Sael, in a matter of minutes.

"Commander, our fifth Dagger is combat-ready," Justice said, dashing my hopes of getting a little recreation in before we got down to business. "It would be a simple matter to install Tria's backup cockpit module into it. Since I will be piloting the Daggers during the insertion, no input from the Operative will be required. While she might not be as attuned to our combat operations as engineer Coonts, she is still a viable asset. If she has knowledge on the zone of operations, it will further increase our odds of a successful mission outcome."

Sael and I were both speechless. We stared at each other for an awkward amount of time. Try as I might to downplay the idea, I still had the urge to pop her in the kisser for the crap we were unwittingly being dragged into. I couldn't help but think she was directly responsible for the majority of it. If I would have heeded the Troop Master's advice and fried the Hivemind, we would be off doing other things that were a lot healthier than tangling with the Prule. Apparently, the information lag finally caught up with her because she was now frowning.

"What exactly did you mean by recover from the insertion?"

"Justice has determined that the Dagger's phase drives have to be operating at maximum. He also has to time the phase perfectly when we hit the shield, or our atoms will be scattered throughout your home worlds."

She was still frowning and then her eyes opened wide. "How are we going to keep from overshooting the target area?"

With a big smile on my face, I just shrugged. "No problem. Justice said he can do a reverse phase stop."

"Is it possible to do such a thing?"

"Yes, he has proven it is possible."

"How many times?"

113

"Once. Well, technically, twice; the second time we were actually in the Daggers and only traveling at seventy-five percent of drive capacity."

"What was the result of the maneuver?" Sael whispered. I had to lean forward to catch what she said.

"It was kind of like having Klutch fall on you from about forty feet, only worse. It is how Coonts ended up getting Oolaran weaponized. Justice accelerated his Dagger to sixty percent of maximum and refused to go higher. Coonts sustained several injuries during the stop. He insisted he undergo the Oolaran procedure when he finally awoke two days later. I relented to his demands only to have his Grawl anatomy reject the enhancements. He is slowly making progress but has been in an induced coma for more than a week."

Sael went back to Coonts's station and sat down. She no longer had anything to say. Justice set us down in the base's hangar and unloaded Sael's shuttle. Sael went aboard, and I wondered what was going through her mind. I knew she would not back out, but we also did not see her while Justice loaded our Daggers and then Eagle One. All the members of my clan gathered outside of the Legacy. They were making a fair attempt at hiding their anxiety. The closer it got to go time, the more their looks of optimism changed to that of concern. Tria stood at my side, and we were ready to board. One by one, the gathering each touched our hands. Young Felix was the last and gave us a solemn nod.

"Commander, Tria, I will be standing by ready to repair your battle damage when you return. Until then, the scientists and I will be researching the large missile they recovered from your salvage. It appears to be a complete weapon that was disassembled for study. Justice's subsystem has confirmed its Oolaran origins. With the help of the scientists and engineers, I will have a manufacturing specification and design schematic in the very near future. We will need to gather additional materials, but I foresee no problems adding it to your offensive arsenal."

I smiled at the Zaen, thinking he was just trying to occupy my mind with something other than our mission. He touched our hands and stepped back with the gathered Grawl. Out of the corner of my eye, I saw the hatch to Sael's shuttle open. She stepped out wearing her heavy battle armor. The combat suit was adorned with a considerable amount of deadly looking hardware. She had a large long barreled rifle, two pistols, and an array of thrown devices, not to mention her swords.

"Nice rifle, is that some kind of sniper weapon?"

"It is a light anti-transport weapon, and no, you cannot have one!"

She had her helmet in the down position, giving me a stern look. The tension in the air was palpable. Not wanting to start the mission on such a heavy note, I smiled and blew her a kiss. She shook her head and cringed.

"Primate!"

"Old witch!"

Tria shoved me up the ramp. Smiling, I stopped at the hatch and took one last look at the members of my clan. Each held up an arm. I did the same, then took Tria by the hand and entered the Legacy. I was trying my best to leave any doubts I had about the mission outside the hatch. My mind was swirling with the low growls of the predator that would soon attempt to possess me. I'm sure it somehow resented the fact that it was no longer in complete control during combat. It was a battle of wills that I was starting to win.

"Justice! We are ready to roll!"

"Affirmative, Commander. The Senior Operative has transferred our destination coordinates from her shuttle's nav computer. She is waiting in the cargo bay to speak with you before she boards Sierra Five."

"Roger that. Tria and I will be there after we armor up."

We headed to the ready room, and as I walked through the hatch, I heard it close behind me. We normally left it open. One glance over my shoulder explained why. Tria shed her uniform and gave me a look that I was quickly recognizing as a precursor to a shot of her Sha'Leen. My legs almost gave out, and she caught me in her arms. If I managed to get myself killed on the mission, I would have a damn good reason to die with a smile on my face.

We made it to the cargo bay almost an hour later. Xul was standing at the hatch patiently waiting as if he had nothing better to do.

"Commander, Justice and I have been going over many of the possible scenarios. We are as ready as we can be, considering how little data we have. The Senior Operative could only supply marginal details about the base's layout. I suspect she has intentionally done so to ensure she has a place on the strike team. I could be wrong, but it may also be a way for her to assert her authority once you enter the facility."

"Tria and I have already discussed that issue. We can handle Sael as long as you and Justice can keep the Chaalt military off our backs."

"We have a contingency plan that has better-than-average odds of keeping the military council from attempting to destroy the complex while you are inside. I know you will do everything in your power to rescue the rightful rulers of the Chaalt people. If it comes down to your life or theirs, please remember you have chosen to stand for the good of all. Those held by the Prule have shown us they are allies of opportunity and would not burden themselves with such a task."

I had to give it to Xul: he didn't beat around the bush when it came to formalities. He left no doubt about whose corner he was in. He touched both of our hands.

"Our maker stands with us, Commander. I look forward to seeing you when you have completed your mission."

Tria and I entered the cargo bay and heard a heated discussion between Sael and Justice. Why they would choose to verbally spar before we started the mission was beyond me. Justice had all four Daggers in the cargo hold to lessen our launch detection. The first Dagger on this side of the cargo bay was Kilo Four. Klutch was sitting in the cockpit, and I was going to have a word with him before we launched. As I stepped up to the open canopy, the first thing I noticed was the portal device strapped onto the front of his armor. Justice must have decided it would not hinder the Tibor's movement. I was more than a little skeptical as to his selection for the machine's operator, but it was too late to change the evil robot's strategy this close to launch. I could hear a familiar low croaking groan: the big lug was snoring. Rather than take the risk of startling him awake and suffering the consequences, we moved on to find out what Sael was bitching about. When she saw us coming, she turned her ire on Tria and me. She stalked toward us ranting something about Justice. She suddenly stopped her blustering and stood with a look of disbelief on her face. I guess the satisfaction we were radiating made our auras a billboard declaring our activities.

"Are the two of you insane?" she shouted. "Could you not find something better to do with the short amount of time we might have left in our lives?"

To my surprise, Tria let out a barking laugh and shouldered past Sael, but not before commenting, "You should try it sometime. It just might make you less of a Throgg!"

I slapped my hand to my forehead. "Thanks, Tria!"

She laughed again, throwing up two of her arms, and climbed into her Dagger. I turned back to the Senior Operative. Her face was a mask of rage, and her language some of the more colorful I had ever heard from her. I had been in a pretty good mood, but it was quickly souring. I was just going to turn my back on her and jump into my Dagger but thought better of it. I didn't want to hear any scat from her if we actually lived through the insertion.

"Sael, if you calm yourself and speak civilly, I will be more than happy to hear you out. If you continue to yell and curse, I will have Justice call your people, and we will jettison you out the air lock."

I was surprised that did the trick, because she shut up. Her eyes, on the other hand, gave away the fact she was trying to figure out a way to barbeque me.

"We are ready to launch. What is bothering you so much that you feel the need to rain scat on what was the start of a wonderful day?"

"That defective agent of the Oolaran has somehow hacked into my nav computer and stolen highly restricted data!" she hissed through clenched teeth.

I almost laughed and let slip she had no idea how much Justice had already stolen but canned the idea.

"Why would you think that, Sael?"

"Have you gone over that machine's plan to dissuade the traitors from killing us if we manage to breach the shield dome?"

She had me there. I must have missed that briefing because I was trying my best not to lose another wrestling match with Tria that didn't involve wearing uniforms. Reliving the experience made it hard to concentrate on the crap Sael was spewing at me. We needed to move on.

"Justice, would you please enlighten me as to why the Senior Operative is having a meltdown?"

"Our numerous contacts with Chaalt military spacecraft have divulged a wealth of information on their detection and scanning capabilities. I have made several calibrations to enhance our cloaking equipment based on those observations. The warships sent to collect the Senior Operative were forced to retreat because they were unable to track the Legacy and feared we might engage them. We were swept multiple times at full military power in close proximity to the emitters. I am now convinced the Legacy is immune to detection from all current Chaalt scanning devices."

I was pretty sure that was for Sael's benefit and not mine. I asked what I thought was a simple question and was not expecting a dissertation on the Legacy's stealth capabilities. It did manage to render Sael speechless but not close her mouth, because it was now gaping.

"That is not what I asked."

"Commander, I have changed the mission parameters to ensure the Chaalt council will think twice before attacking the research facility while we attempt rescue operations. Recently acquired data has convinced the Overseer and me that there is a more viable way to draw the Chaalt warships away from the area of operations."

Sael could no longer hold her tongue. "The crazed machine is going to overfly the council chambers on the Chaalt home world of Athella! That would not be possible unless the Legacy gained access to restricted information,

information that only Tria or I would possess. Who do you think they will blame for the breach of security?"

I had no doubt that Sael was right and Justice managed to burgle the data from her shuttle's computer systems. Why he would jab Sael in the ass with that information was beyond me and hinted at the AI's use of his less desirable human traits. While the evil robot's intended plan was a bit startling and I'm sure my reaction might have given that away, the surprise quickly passed. Since we were going to enter the Chaalt exclusion zone uninvited anyway, what difference did it make how many laws we broke. If Justice could cover our backs long enough to rescue the Chaalt people's rightful government, we should be able to talk our way out of just about anything. I was ready to start the mission, and Sael's endless bitching was the straw that broke the camel's back. My give-a-shit was officially busted!

"Sael, did you or did you not come here to be part of the rescue mission? I don't want any more out of you, just a yes or a no!"

I could tell she wanted to explode, but my piercing stare stifled her rebuke.

"Yes."

"You have already turned over classified information identifying your council members and the location of the research station. At this point, it will not matter how many of your laws we choose to break. What's done is done. Quit sweating the details, and let's get on with the mission!"

121

"The research center is located on the fringe of the exclusion zone and nowhere near our governing home world. Justice's perceived threat to the council will mark your clan for termination if we do not succeed."

She had a point, but I had no intention of failing. I looked back at Tria and Klutch. They both were standing up in the cockpits of their Daggers with arms crossed. Neither looked worried, just annoyed that I would be standing here arguing with Sael when we had a mission to complete.

"Justice! Take us to the jump point!"

"Affirmative, Commander. Launching now!"

"Senior Operative, I am ordering you to get your ass in the Dagger or the air lock. I don't care which you choose, but do it now!" I barked.

Sael stiffened. The look of anger seemed to melt from her face, and then she nodded. Without another word, she climbed in Sierra Five, and Justice closed the cockpit and canopy. I got a thumbs up from Tria and Klutch and returned it. The beast was snickering in the back of my mind; the jubilant dark echoes brought a grim smile to my lips. We were going into the fire once more, and I embraced the thought of killing the enemies of all. It was as if it was all that I was ever meant to do. Maybe there was something to what many aliens were whispering. Perhaps I am the sword of my maker.

9

The ruminations on my destiny were interrupted by my reality fading away. When I became aware of my surroundings once more, I heard Justice calling to me.

"Commander, launch is in thirty seconds. I have eight hundred and forty Chaalt warships in this sector of the exclusion zone. One hundred and twenty-two are in close proximity to the area of operation. Our transition has been detected, and all vessels have commenced scanning at full military power. The Legacy will be visible to Chaalt scanning systems during the Dagger launch sequence. Once you are away, I will make several short transitions to draw as many of the warships away from the target as possible. When the ships are a predetermined distance from the research center, I will activate your phase drives and align you with the optimal insertion vector. The Legacy will be back in the area of operation in approximately fifty-one minutes. My ETA could be sooner or later depending on any number of unknown factors. Good luck and good hunting!"

The Legacy was cloaked and accelerating in the general direction of the lab complex. Justice made a hard turn and spit our Daggers out into the void with the tow beam. The reaction from the Chaalt warships was instantaneous. My holo display showed that all but a few made a rapid turn in our direction. We were coasting in toward the target several degrees off of our insertion vector. The Legacy's icon disappeared from my display and reappeared a blink later and uncloaked in the midst of several Chaalt ships. The icon turned to a blue circle when Justice cloaked. The Legacy made another hard turn and transitioned away. The warships continued toward the Legacy's transition point, but Justice was already gone. His theory that they could no longer track the Legacy was proving accurate. Many of the Chaalt ships were now spread out and broad-spectrum scanning in all directions of the exclusion zone. The Legacy was moving through multiple scan fields with no reaction from the Chaalt.

Justice moved further away from the warships and uncloaked once again. This time he got a response from all the ships in our detection zone. All were turning in the Legacy's direction, with several making jumps directly to the location. Again, Justice jumped away, and this time it was followed by my phase drive activating. The Legacy never reappeared on my display, so I assumed it was going to do a little showing off somewhere over Athella. I was intently watching my HUD as our Daggers closed up to a tight four-ship formation. We were moving rapidly at a large asteroid that had an orange blinking box around it.

My pulse kicked up a notch as did my respiration when every ship on my holo display turned and accelerated in our direction. I felt the telltale positive G load of maximum phase, and my display blanked out. An alarm sounded and quickly increased in pitch and intensity. My holo display was blinking on and off, and I was sure it didn't mean my popcorn was done! Last time I had the displeasure of hearing that clamor, the Quill were trying their best to incinerated me and spread my molecules about the universe. Closing my eyes, I pushed back hard against the cockpit as it suddenly expanded. The interior of my battle armor followed suit and started squeezing the hell out of me. I thought it would crush the air from my lungs. It was the last thing going through my head when I blacked out.

I awoke to Klutch rapping on my helmet with his armored fist and calling to me. I almost freaked because I knew my eyes were open but I could not see. I hurt everywhere and wondered if my skeleton still resided in my body.

"Commander! Tria and the Operative are unresponsive, and we need to move now!" the Tibor said urgently. "There is something below us, and whatever it is, it wants up here awful bad!"

My vision became a small white dot that progressively got bigger. I groaned out loud and attempted to pull myself upright, but my arms felt like dead weights. I felt my head being pulled forward, and then my eyes could make out Klutch. He had his helmet pushed up against my faceplate.

"I hear something digging below us, and that can't be a good thing!" he reiterated.

I grabbed the edges of my cockpit module and pulled myself up. I was wobblily, but Klutch kept me upright. My eyes were getting their act together, but I was having a hell of a time deciphering the information they were pumping to my G-mashed brain. I was inside some kind of structure that had collapsed on the interior.

"Where are we? Are we inside the complex?"

"We made it through the shield and crashed into the side of a defensive weapons tower. The phase drives were still active for a few seconds after impact. The wreckage of the tower was siphoned into the phase field. The inside of the structure has collapsed onto the levels below us."

My eyes were back on duty, and I could see Tria's Dagger sitting in a hollow that was perfectly round. She was slumped forward in her open cockpit module. Looking over my shoulder at the exterior wall, I saw two large round holes and two that were touching each other in a pattern that resembled bullet holes on a target. Just below us was the Operative's open Dagger. I pulled away from Klutch and face-planted next to my Dagger. He helped me up, and we trudged through the debris toward Tria. Relief washed over me as she jerked back into her cockpit module. She was cursing a blue streak and then called my name. I made it to the side of her Dagger and grabbed her by her arms.

"I am here. Tria, can you see me?"

"Just barely, Nathan. My eyesight is impaired but getting better."

I pulled her out of the cockpit module and embraced her till she could stand on her own. We started hearing a string of expletives that told us the Operative was now coherent. Tria and I slowly made our way over to Klutch, who was trying his best to get Sael out of her Dagger. She was slapping at the Tibor's hands and cursing me in a case of mistaken identity. Klutch had enough of that crap and unceremoniously jerked her out of the Dagger and let her fall into the wreckage. She was now cursing me harder. I shook my head, and we stood her up. That was when I noticed the loud crunching and grinding noises coming from below us. Klutch was not kidding: something was working overtime under our feet. Sael was still cursing me pretty good and now repeating herself. Taking a lesson from Klutch's playbook, I rapped her upside the helmet.

"Sael! Shut up and listen! Something is digging its way in here!"

That got me a murderous look that quickly faded. The sound was progressively getting louder, and the Operative in Sael finally took over. She turned and reached into her Dagger and pulled her rifle and swords from it.

"We must find defensible cover!"

I wanted to tell her "no shit," but decided to recover my weapons before whatever was tunneling its way toward us made an appearance. We armed ourselves, and I called to Justice's subsystem.

"Lock the Daggers and activate the point defense systems!"

The canopies slammed shut and the upper weapons turrets popped out. The projectors swiveled around, pointing at a mound of debris that started to shake and settle. My suit AI called out a warning.

"Commander, it is advisable to seek shelter!"

That was all the heads-up I needed. I pointed to an outcropping that was the remains of a floor well above us. We hit our gravity thrusters and flew up through the massive cavity and landed on the ledge. We went prone, and I called out, "Weapons free!"

Justice's subsystem never heard the command "Don't fire until you see the whites of their eyes" because the turrets fired point-blank into what remained of the floor. The blinding flashes of energy sent a storm of pulverized debris upward at us as we recoiled from the edge of our perch. We could plainly hear a warbling screech as the raining wreckage finally quit falling around us. We didn't have to guess as to what would make such a hellish racket. There was a really pissed off Prule Hunter somewhere below us. Looking into the huge glowing hole that was once a floor, I didn't know how anything could have survived the inferno unleashed by the Daggers. If nothing else, we now had a way to stay in cover and exfiltrate the area. I had every intention of pointing at the hole and telling Klutch to take the lead but was interrupted by a loud crunching noise. A large weapons turret and the remains of the upper floors came crashing down on us, burying the Daggers and leaving us sprawled among the wreckage.

I was hoping this goat rope was not a premonition of things to come. I pushed a piece of roof beam off me and looked around for Tria. Hearing movement to my right, I started digging until I saw an armored hand doing the same. I grabbed on and pulled, getting several croaking oaths as my reward. Klutch burrowed out of the fallen mess. Seeing debris shifting to his right, Klutch moved in that direction.

"Commander, I think I am on the level below you," Tria called to us. "One of the Daggers and possibly the weapons turret have me pinned. When I attempt to move, more rubble settles in on me."

"Hold where you are and do not move! We will come to you."

I waded over to where Klutch was helping the Operative climb out of the fragments. He pulled her up to her feet. She gave the Troop Master a strange look.

"What sort of device do you have strapped to yourself?"

She reached out to touch it, and Klutch batted her hand aside.

"It is something you should not concern yourself with!"

She glared at the Tibor but kept her mouth shut. She moved past him and pulled her rifle from the trash. I could see an opening downward through the wreckage. It was the hole the Daggers had made with their point defense weapons. Pulling my shotgun from its clip, I waved in that direction.

"Klutch, Tria is somewhere below us. Let's move out!"

The Troop Master grabbed his plasma caster and armed the projector. The Operative quickly stepped behind him.

"You fool! That is not a close-quarters weapon!"

Klutch gave her an evil grin. "I do not tell you how to use your weapons, so don't tell me how to use mine!"

He moved out, leaving the Operative staring at me in disbelief. I pushed past her and threw a thumb over my shoulder.

"Cover our flank!"

The disparaging oath was under her breath but still loud enough to hear. My concern for Tria made Sael's bullshit intolerable. I turned on her and gave her a stiff arm.

"If you spout anymore of that scat, you are on your own. You got that?"

She looked shocked at my anger but nodded.

"I said, have you got that?"

"Yes!"

I turned and closed with the Troop Master. He had a grenade in his hand and was peering down the hole we were getting ready to descend into.

"It is suspiciously quiet below us, Commander. We already know a Hunter would not give up so easily."

He tossed the grenade to the bottom and nothing happened. He called to his suit AI, "I need a vector to the Dagger at Tria's location."

Justice's subsystem put a directional marker in our HUDs and Klutch jumped in. He started sliding downward and threw his hand out, snagging a beam to arrest his fall. He pulled himself to the side and held an arm out. I jumped next and caught his outstretched hand, and he hoisted me to his side. I stuck a hand out for Sael, and she jumped. She made no attempt to reach for my hand and slid right by me. It pissed me off, but I was not going after her until I had Tria extracted. Several seconds later, she called up to us.

"I have no movement and will set up a defensive position."

Technically she should have stayed with us as our tail gunner. When we freed Tria, we would be going down to reconnoiter our surroundings. I would let it slide for now but if she did it again, she would find out what it feels like to have my foot in her ass. Klutch took the lead and started pulling pieces of the upper floors out of our way. We quickly uncovered the drive end of a Dagger, and I called to Tria on a private comm channel.

"Tria, Klutch and I are close. What is your status?"

"I still cannot move my legs because the Dagger has me firmly pinned. I have tried lowering the landing struts, but they have nothing solid to support them."

"Roger that. We will see what we can do to get something under them."

I looked around at the collapsed mess surrounding us and saw a heavy door panel wrenched from its frame. I looked back at Klutch, who was rooting through the wreckage like an old boar hog. He had about half of one side of the Dagger cleared and called to me.

"Commander, I see Tria's legs. She is on the opposite side of the Dagger. There is a structural beam wedged under it, and it is pinning her legs. We need to raise the Dagger enough to remove the beam."

"Alright, Klutch, let's see if we can get something solid under the landing struts. Tria thinks if the Dagger can raise itself, she can get enough wiggle room to pull herself free."

Klutch stopped digging through the debris long enough to give me a thumbs up. I grabbed onto the door slab and started pulling it free from the frame. I was making good progress when something thumped down hard above us, causing debris to rain down. Klutch and I both stopped what we were doing. Two more thumps sent dust and trash falling into the cavity we had just cleared around the Dagger. Klutch came scurrying out of the mess, pulling his plasma projector from its clip. I commed Tria and told her what she probably already knew.

"Tria, we have movement above us. Sit tight until we know what is going on!"

"I do not have a choice. Nathan, please be careful."

Changing comm channels, I called to Sael. "Sael, get your ass back here now! I think we have at least three unidentified hostiles above us. If they crawl down after us, you will be trapped down there!"

"Moving!" she replied curtly.

132

Klutch grabbed my arm and pointed behind us. I turned and saw the metal spiked legs of a Prule Hunter that was attempting to crawl down the narrow passage. Sael was not going to make it back to our position. I cursed her for going it alone rather than staying with us. Adrenaline started flowing, and I could feel the beast commandeering my emotions. The Oolaran soldier manifested itself as a hate-filled sneer. The Prule crawled down until it filled the passage. Its capsule-shaped upper torso rotated in our direction, and a pale green corona materialized around it. I was going to give it a good reason to go elsewhere, but several blinding flashes exploded on the Prule's shield, making it flicker. The Operative decided to start the party without us.

Klutch shoved me aside and pointed the plasma projector at the metallic monster. A pinkish glow lit the passage, and in the blink of an eye, a blue glowing ball of energy hissed out from the weapon and splashed onto the Prule's faltering shield. Everything in the narrow passage that came into contact with the splattered plasma either melted or caught fire.

Klutch's eyes were as big as silver dollars. I heard him mumble loud enough over our comms to understand what he was saying.

"Tria was correct. This is not of Kashuga design!"

We looked on in disbelief as the Hunter's shield failed. It started flailing savagely as the hellfire engulfed it. Its lower appendages were starting to melt. Two more blinding flashes exploded on the Hunter, plowing large misshapen furrows completely through its armored torso. If it weren't for the rapidly spreading flames, it would seem things might be going our way.

That kind of defective thinking usually always got me in trouble, and this would be no exception. A powerful energy beam sliced downward through the debris-choked tunnel we had managed to excavate, collapsing our only exit. Another one blasted a hole not four feet in front of Klutch and me, knocking us sprawling. Klutch put his foot to my armored ass and shoved me toward the exposed end of the Dagger. I could hear Tria ordering her AI to arm the Dagger's defensive weapons, but Justice's subsystem replied it was unable to comply. Another shot from above collapsed the little hollow we had worked so hard to clear. We were now pinned against the side of the Dagger. I had my share of receiving and decided to start giving. Forcing my arm upward against the better wishes of my servos, I fired a beam shot that created a hurricane of destruction point-blank in our faces. The unsteady floor beneath was giving away. The Dagger along with the weapons turret rolled on top of Klutch and me.

We were now pinned with possibly tons of debris on top of us. The servos that assisted my movements gave me an assortment of warnings to stop what I was doing. Klutch's nonstop caustic dialogue let me know in no uncertain terms that he was firmly trapped as well. Thinking it could help, I tried moving with little burps of my gravity thrusters. That only made matters worse as more rubble settled in on us. Klutch got a little testy when he asked me to kindly refrain from trying to crush him to death.

There was one redeeming factor to my actions: Tria yelled over our comms that she was now free. Her exclamation was followed by a blast that felt like it was directly above us. I panicked and started yelling her name, adding to the confusing chatter of everyone talking at once. This was actually good because I could hear Tria and the Operative yelling over the top of Klutch's endless swearing. Unfortunately, an unfair percentage of my good experiences were always accompanied by bad ones. In this case, the bad was the loud creaking and crunching noises my external mic was picking up. The beast inside of me was attempting to dismiss the bad feeling I was getting when the entire floor went bye-bye.

Everything went crashing downward. The objects included on that list were the Daggers, turret, and a couple of Prule Hunters. Justice's subsystem chose a very opportune time to lend a helping hand and engaged our gravity thrusters. I was sent careening out of control upward through an assortment of trash. I quickly righted myself and came to a hover. My HUD showed two blue icons just behind me and to my left. Tria and Klutch formed up on me, but Sael was nowhere to be seen.

The dense dust cloud below us was settling, and I wondered if the Hunters were as fortunate as we were. The only thermal signatures I was picking up were the plasma fires burning in the rubble below us. We no longer had cover above us and would make good targets hovering in the open framework of the wrecked weapons tower.

"Tria, Klutch! Spread out and see if you can get a fix on Sael or the Hunters!"

We split up and dove to the corners of the gutted tower. Klutch sounded off.

"Commander, I have movement!"

"Hold your fire!" Sael shouted over our comms.

Klutch dropped to the rubble pile and yanked the Operative up and out of the debris. She jerked her hand free of Klutch's and got down on her hands and knees, rooting in the hole she once occupied. She pulled her rifle from the mess and slung it over her shoulder. I stomped through the wreckage with my fist raised at Sael. Before I could tear her a new one, we felt the junk under us heave and then settle. At least one of the machine monsters was trying to dig its way out. We boosted above the ruins and pointed our weapons at the quaking pile. Glancing around to make sure we didn't get any more unexpected guests; I spied the holes the Daggers had made through the tower. I got an idea that would upset the beast in me because it would not involve personally blowing the alien machines to pieces.

"Justice, activate the phase fields on all the Daggers!"

"Commander, you are within the minimum safe distance of the phase drive transition field," my suit AI warned. "I highly recommend vacating your current location."

That was all the warning needed, and we boosted to the top of the decapitated tower. Looking down into the debris, we saw it heave once more and then a metallic claw thrust upward. We took aim and were going to open fire when a tremendous roar made me shut down my external audio sensors. The massive pile below us was being sucked downward. Inside of the grinding suction typhoon were four blindingly bright pulsating globes of light. The Hunter that had managed to dig its way up through the rubble let out a warbling screech as it was pulled downward. I could see it flailing wildly trying to find something to grip onto. It disappeared into the brilliance, and the phase fields abruptly shut down. The Daggers now sat in perfectly round hollows of what remained of the rubble. Some unknown dimension of hyperspace just became our personal dump. I sure hope it was not inhabited.

We landed next the Daggers and armed their defensive weapons systems.

My anger once again flared at Sael for her disregard of my command. Tria, Klutch, and I all turned on her. Before I could say a word, she held up two of her arms.

"Nathan, there is no excuse for my actions. I have recklessly endangered the mission and my team because I resented your command authority. If this were a Chaalt mission and one of my subordinates were to do such a thing, I would have executed them. You would be well within your rights to pass that same judgment on me. I should have been focusing on the mission and not my petty vanity."

The old witch took all of the steam out of my rant and left me lost for words. She had already proven that she will say one thing and do another; it was just a matter of time. I was still pissed as hell, but it would do nobody any good to stand here and rip her a new ass. We needed to get moving because surprising the Prule was no longer an option. That thought was reinforced by two warning beeps in our helmet visors.

"Incoming aerial drones!" Tria called out.

We spread out and kneeled down in the debris. The defensive turrets popped out of the Daggers and their weapons rotated upward. The two aerial weapons platforms zoomed overhead, looking for targets. The Daggers turned them to clouds of fine metal dust. I was now wondering who was operating them: the Prule or someone else. I needed a no-shitter from the Operative.

"Sael, do you have any idea where the additional Prule forces are coming from?"

"I have already told you the remnants of Prule have been collected for a great many solar rotations. All were inert and were the objects of study. Many were only fragments. Other than the single active Hunter you turned over to my people, I cannot explain the presence of other Prule forces."

Klutch's helmet visor was transparent. I could tell he doubted the intel Sael was giving us. He grabbed her by the shoulder and pulled her down to his visor.

"The Hunters we destroyed did not appear to be fragments or inert objects!"

Sael pulled away from Klutch and turned to me. "I have given you all the information that I have. It is possible the Hivemind is using resources at this facility to repair and activate additional units. If this is the case, we could be facing several dozen."

When we started this mission, I felt our tactics and equipment gave us better-than-average odds of a successful outcome. Now those odds were favoring the opposition.

10

We had to push on, no matter the odds, but first things first. Sael was not going to get off that easily.

"You are now under Klutch's command. At his request, you are to give him the support and directions necessary for us to complete this mission. Is that clear?"

I was standing close enough to Sael I could see her reaction through her faceplate. She flinched as if I had struck her and gritted her teeth.

"Yes, I understand!" she spit out.

I glared at the Troop Master to wipe the large, toothy grin from his face. "We need to be able to control the shield dome. Give Klutch a heading to that location. I have no idea why the Hivemind has not sent additional forces to attack us. It is a historical fact from my world that you should never interrupt your enemy while they are making mistakes. If you have information you feel I need, give it to me now or let's move out!"

She cast her eyes downward then slowly looked up and locked them on mine. I could tell what she was going to say would not be a confidence builder.

"A lot has changed since I was last here. There has been a great deal of modernization. What was once a small collection of buildings is now the size of a settlement. I recognize a few of the older structures but nothing else."

That little tidbit set Tria off. She banged her armored fist into Sael's battle suit hard enough to make her back up a step. I grabbed her arm because she had balled up another fist and looked like she was ready to plant it upside Sael's helmet.

"Is there anything else you would care to share the truth about?"

"Tria, I never lied to any of you. I just omitted some of the facts in an attempt to manipulate Justice into thinking I was a necessary component of your team. I had hopes you would let me lead the mission."

I was more than a little skeptical as to whether or not Justice was so easily duped. I was leaning heavily on the theory she was needed more for her fighting skills than her brains. I had considered letting her lead, but not anymore.

"Sael, I want the facts without the omissions!"

"I do have rudimentary knowledge of the base's layout and defenses," she admitted. "We need to stay in cover and out of a direct line of fire from the weapons towers. They have a limited ability to fire on ground targets. As you already know, there is an unknown number of aerial drones with advanced antipersonnel weapons on board.

We need to avoid exposing ourselves to their detection sensors. There were originally several missile launchers seeded throughout the base in hidden locations. I speculate that due to the current size of this facility, there will be considerably more. You should also know that if we attempt to breach the shield control building by force, we will activate the internal defenses. The counter measures were very formidable. There are lockout contingencies that will render the systems inoperable by hostile forces. Once that happens, the only way to bring down the shield will be to destroy the power source built deep within the asteroid. I would also like to point out it would be madness for the Hivemind not to concentrate its forces at that location."

"I already had that figured out on my own," I said. "Let's get moving!"

Sael pointed to a structure in the distance that had high walls and a large orb protruding upward behind them. Our insertion point was in the shadow of a huge dish that pointed off into the void. We boosted through a large crack in the tower's wall and landed on a narrow-paved pathway. We pulled our shotguns, and Klutch took the lead with Sael at his side. Tria and I brought up the rear with both of us taking turns glancing over our shoulders. We worked our way around the building with the dish and came to a much wider thoroughfare. Klutch put his arm out to halt Sael and then called to me.

"Commander, I just saw a shadow retreat into an alley down this access road on our right. If we move out onto the road, we will be exposed to the weapons towers and possibly an ambush from that alley."

Tria and I took a knee with our weapons pointing down the alley. Sael kneeled next to Klutch, pointing her large rifle out into the access road.

"Let's hear some options, Klutch."

The Tibor leaned down and stuck his weapon around the corner using his HUD targeting system to study the problem from a different angle. He surveyed the street for about thirty seconds then pulled his weapon back.

"I recommend we backtrack to the building with the transmitter dish and make use of that skybridge that spans this access road. That will keep us in cover and give us a vantage point to look down on whatever was hiding in that alley."

I got up and tapped Tria on the shoulder. She stood up and slowly walked backward with her shotgun up and ready. When I got to Klutch, he kneeled down and leaned around the corner so I could peek over his shoulder. I followed his arm to where he was pointing, and it looked like a good overlook location.

"I have toured that installation, and there is no ground-level access to the building," protested Sael. "It is the central comms transmitter for this complex. It is only accessible through an underground tunnel at the main entrance of this facility. If you intend to blast your way in, the Prule will have no problem tracking our location."

It was frustrating to finally make a little progress, only to turn around and go back the way we came. What Sael did not know was that we didn't need to blast anything to gain access.

"We're following you, Troop Master. Lead the way!"

Sael just shook her head but kept her mouth shut. We turned around and ran back the way we came until we were at the side of the large communications building. Tria stopped several feet behind us and took a knee, pointing her weapon down the passage behind us. Sael went several more paces up the passage and did the same. Klutch and I were standing together at the wall. He looked at me and pointed to the portal device. I gave him a thumbs up, and he slapped his shotgun to its clip and placed his fingers on the activation buttons. I leaned down and readied my weapon, then gave him a nod. The flash of the device triggering momentarily dimmed my HUD. We got a good portal first try, and I ran through with Klutch right behind me.

The Operative ducked when the device flashed. She spun around with her weapon and was dumbstruck to see me and then Klutch run into a glowing spot on the wall and disappear. Tria waved her over but Sael stopped short with a look of shock on her face. Tria none too gently helped her step through and then did the same.

I stepped out of the portal and went prone just to the right of my entry point. Klutch came through taking note of my position and did the same on the left. We were in a brightly lit room that had four lift tubes against one wall and a ramp going downward on the opposite side. If it were not for the dead decomposing bodies scattered about the floor, the lack of resistance would have made this an appealing entry point. The Operative came stumbling through the portal and froze in place. She was apparently still shocked by our newly acquired tech. She should have kept moving because Tria came through and collided with her, knocking both of them to the floor. Klutch promptly hit the kill switch, and our only means of escape disappeared.

Tria rolled away from the Operative and took a defensive posture. Sael should have done the same but instead pushed herself across the floor until she was at my side. She seemed oblivious to her surroundings and only had a single subject on her mind.

"You could have told me you now have transporter technology!"

Not wanting to go into any details, I was going to blow her off but remembered something she had once said to me. I was sure she wouldn't miss the nuances of sarcasm interlaced in the retort.

"It is information that we wished to keep secret, so it was disseminated on a need-to-know basis. We decided you didn't need to know!"

Nothing was moving around us, so I pushed Sael away from my side and called to Klutch and Tria. "Make a quick sweep of the area and check for survivors. Sael, see if you can ID any of the bodies!"

Without comment, Sael got up and started checking corpses. She must not have found any council members because she made her way to the ramp that went down to another level and descended. Tria, Klutch, and I worked our way around the room until we converged on the lifts. We counted forty-one dead bodies. All were Chaalt, and all the corpses showed signs of mutilation. My guess was the Prule needed biological materials. For what, I had no idea. Judging by the decomposition of the bodies, they were all killed roughly a week ago.

Tria was shaking her head and stepped close to Klutch and me.

"They are research scholars and security personnel," she explained. "The Prule may have taken the precaution of sterilizing the complex. If this turns out to be the case, it does not bode well for the council members."

This was just another grim reminder that it was the intended goal of the bio machines to do this very same thing to the entire galaxy. I was going to call Sael and tell her to get her ass back here, but she called me first.

"Contact! I have at least one Prule Hunter and three more unidentified targets moving in the tunnel that leads to the entrance to the complex."

I pointed at Klutch and then the ramp. He nodded, then ran to the top of the landing, exchanging his shotgun for the plasma projector. I pulled a grenade from my leg storage and tossed it in the bottom of the down tube. Tria did the same to the other one. If something came down from above, we would have fair warning. We ran to where Klutch waited and quietly navigated the crisscross ramp till we reached the bottom. It was dark enough in the tunnel that my low-light sensors kicked on and I could see Sael laying prone near a low wall. She had her weapon pointing down the tunnel peering over the long barrel.

"They have not reacted to our presence and appear to be guarding the entrance to the tunnel."

We crouched low and kneeled behind the wall. I carefully eased the barrel of my shotgun around the corner. Using my HUD targeting system, I increased the magnification to maximum. I frowned because I could easily identify the Hunter, but the other targets were a mystery to me. They looked like the cobbled-together junk one might see at a steampunk convention. They did, however, have what looked like two Chaalt assault weapons mounted on short struts protruding from their sides.

"Sael, are those Chaalt weapons?"

"Yes."

"You told me the IFF on your weapons are tied to the DNA of your people and the military chips are implanted in the owners. I don't think the Prule would waste time mounting them unless they were operable."

"That is correct, but I fear the Prule have worked around those precautions," Sael said. "The mutilations on the bodies we discovered are consistent with the forceful removal of the hosts' military ID chips. The Prule were either adept at the procedure or Gredda's assault team medic showed them how!"

The disgust in Sael's voice indicated the hard-on she had for Gredda Porsha was now a permanent fixture. The traitor was going to die a horrendous death if Sael had anything to do with it.

"Can you still detonate the weapons?"

"Unknown. I have the capability, but the transmitter in my armor has a limited range. There is a security check point about halfway to the targets. We already know our cloaking capabilities will not conceal us from the Prule's sensors, so unless you want to bypass them altogether, we will be forced to do it the old-fashioned way and attempt to sneak up on them."

This was turning out to be a waste of time. I very much doubted we could sneak more than three hundred yards through the tunnel without being discovered. A shootout would only reveal our location to hostile forces. Justice had already foreseen the need to destroy the facility to prevent any possibility of spreading the machine infection. The traitors in the Chaalt government were planning to do it as well. I guess it was up to me to get that party started.

"Fall back to the lifts on the upper level, I will join you momentarily."

I could tell Klutch didn't like the idea and was going to protest. I jerked my thumb over my shoulder.

"All of you, now! That's an order!"

They grudgingly moved toward the ramp, but not before Sael saw the look of distress on Tria's face. She looked back at me with a frown. Klutch gave her a shove, and she turned her venomous looks on him. They started up the ramp, but Sael couldn't keep her piehole pinned.

"Nathan! What are you going to do?"

148

I decided I didn't want to have this discussion right now and didn't need to explain myself to her. The less she knew of my intentions, the better. According to Tria, my next course of action was at the very top of the Chaalt no-no list. I used my implants to call up my weapons menu. I selected weaponized nanites, and the high-pressure nozzle on my wrist extended from its port. If we got this joint to jumping and Sael's intel was correct, all latecomers to the party would have to pass through this tunnel or the skybridge that was our current waypoint. I gave the tunnel a twenty-second stream of the highly concentrated nanite gel. My team was waiting for me in a defensive perimeter at the top of the ramp. I pointed to the lifts.

"Lead the way, Troop Master!"

Of course, Sael could not stand it and had to run her mouth. After all the time we had spent together, you would think she could tell when I was not in a talkative mood.

"Nathan, what have you done?"

"Sael, shut up and move out!"

It took more than a few seconds for her look of rage to downgrade itself to anger. In that time, her weapon swung around almost one hundred and eighty degrees. If it were not for Tria swatting it aside, the arc of the barrel may have ended with the business end pointing at me. The old Kala Mor Dee was still in there somewhere. I guess my natural human charm had a way of bringing out the best in Sael. She gritted her teeth, turned around, and stalked over to the lift tubes. Justice was going to have to explain

149

in detail exactly why he wanted the Operative on board for this mission. So far, she has been nothing but a pain in my ass.

"Klutch, you and Sael take the left tube, and Tria and I will take the right. If we get separated, make your way to the skybridge, and we will meet you there. If scat hits the ventilator, sing out and we will try to flank any opposition."

Klutch gave me a thumbs up. Sael gave me the stink eye. The Troop Master must have liked Sael's stare as much as I did. He grabbed the back of her armor and pulled her into the tube. Tria and I jumped into the other side and were whisked upward. We stepped out of the lift into the control center of the comms array. We were not alone. There were more than a dozen of the bizarre junk collections standing around. Now that I was close enough to clearly see them, I winced in repulsion. The frameworks of junk supported a grotesque glob of mutilated flesh inside of them. They seemed just as surprised to see us as we were surprised to see them. They all started scurrying around on an assortment of different protrusions that passed for legs. Several were armed and opened fire. Tria went left and I went right but not before catching a glancing blast on my right leg that spun me to the floor. I rolled over and yanked a grenade out of my storage pouch. The beast was taking control. I wasn't sure where Tria ended up but could hear her giving them hell with her shotgun. Against the Oolaran soldier's better wishes, I yelled out a warning.

"Grenade out!"

I tossed the gift from the Chaalt people into the air, and it came to a hover near the large structural support beams above us. It immediately started passing out souvenirs that left no doubt this place was going to need some serious repairs. It was not one of my better choices because pieces of shrapnel were wrecking equipment and hostiles alike. More than a few stray ricochets pinged off my armor. The rapping impacts brought with them the haunting cackle of the crazed killer lurking inside of me. One of the mechanized surrogates came around the side of a console as I was raising my shotgun. Everything was moving in slow motion. The beast must have been on the trigger because I don't recall pulling it. The machine was on the receiving end of a penetrator slug at point-blank range. The abomination, sans gut sack, hobbled on its protrusions a few more paces before collapsing on the floor next to me. The Prule must have been throwing these things together willy-nilly. They didn't have shields to protect them, so they were vulnerable to all our weapons. The room was suddenly still, and Tria called to me. Her voice pushed the demon aside and cleared my thoughts.

"Nathan, are you hurt?"

"No, how about you?"

"I am well, but I don't think we got them all. I'll go high, you go low!"

I was going to acknowledge Tria's plan of action, but the words caught in my throat when a pulsating circle appeared on the overhead. The Troop Master fell through, croaking out his favorite Tibor oath on his way to the floor. He was quickly followed by the Operative, who came through with both her swords drawn and pistols out. She chose to slow the fall with her gravity boosters, making her a prime target. One of the machines hit her in the side with a volley from close range before she could open fire. She was blasted into a wall and disappeared to the floor somewhere behind the free-for-all Klutch started. Tria and I charged around the control consoles as Klutch unloaded a magazine of explosive buckshot. Parts of the machines flew in all directions. Several rebounded from the fronts of Tria's armor.

"Check your fire!" she warned.

Klutch dropped his shotgun and dove on a machine with his climbing hooks extended. Sparks flew along with various parts of his victim. The hostile that shot Sael was trying to turn its weapons on Klutch. I savagely kicked it into a console and jammed my needle gun against its torso. A one-second burst of hypersonic shards turned the biomass inside of the machine into a crimson cloud of gore. I was not aware that Sael had regained her footing and was attempting to join the melee. She popped up from cover with her pistols ready, only to catch a portion of the mess along with a few deflected needles right in the faceplate. She reeled over backward out of sight. Tria finally put an end to the chaos with well-placed slugs from her shotgun. I stepped around the wrecked consoles and found Sael. She was wiping the mess from her faceplate, apparently okay. I reached down to help her up, but she swatted my hand away.

"The equipment in this room was our only means of communicating outside the shield dome. Your careless misuse of the weapons I so foolishly supplied you was unwarranted," she reprimanded. "The murderous demon inside of you has stripped us of that option!"

The reality of her statement sucked. I would have liked to get a heads-up from Justice. The dome was blocking our outbound comms, and I had no way of knowing whether he had returned from his mission. Sael stood up glaring at me. If anything, I shortened the battle. Sael was delusional if she thought this place would still be operable after all the indiscriminate fire from the hostiles. It would be a waste of time giving her a fact check. I turned my back on her and waded through the wreckage to Tria and Klutch. My teammates were reloading their weapons and looked at me questioningly.

I shrugged and commed them on a discrete channel. "Sael is learning the hard way, but she is learning. It remains to be seen whether or not she will continue to resist or finally adapt to her position in our chain of command."

The Troop Master croaked out a laugh. "Her decision to join us has left her no choice. She will adapt or die trying!"

Tria stepped close and brushed pieces of gore from my armor.

"Sael did not receive the title of Kala Mor Dee because she is inept or stupid," Tria said. "She will overcome the

153

clumsiness of working with a new combat team. Her only remaining obstacle is her inability to accept your position as commander. She was trained from a very early age to be a leader among the warriors of my race. To accept an alien male from a primitive race as her leader is something that goes against everything she knows or believes."

I smiled because I knew Tria was right, but I was going to have to say it anyway. "You and Klutch did not have any issues elevating me to the position of commander. Both of you were more qualified, yet you chose to saddle me with that responsibility. I still question your decision on a daily basis."

"It is because we understand what Justice sees in you," Tria said. "We embrace what Sael refuses to accept. You are just the beginning. At some point in our future, the human race will arise and become the cure for what has sickened this galaxy."

I quickly hid my skepticism with the monstrous image of my war face. If they knew just how screwed up the power-hungry leaders on my world really were, they would probably vote to take us off protected planet status.

I slapped a fresh magazine of penetrator slugs into my shotgun and pointed to a corridor I hoped would take us to the skybridge. Klutch masked his features then moved out with his shotgun up and ready. I glanced over my shoulder to confirm Sael was covering our backs. Klutch gave us the all clear from the corridor, and we moved in that direction. We made it about a dozen paces before we felt the twin thumps of the grenades we had left in the lower level. Something must have passed very near the down tubes and triggered our booby traps. A warbling screech identified the recipient.

Klutch came barreling by us. "Commander, we should take cover and give that Throgg a warm welcome!"

There was no arguing with that logic. We ran back out into the control room and took up firing positions. The Oolaran soldier inside of me was fairly quiet in our last engagement, but now it was egging me on to make use of the most lethal tool in my arsenal. I lifted my arm and made ready with my beam weapon. When Sael realized what I was doing, she dropped behind the consoles and moved to the back of the control room. Tria eased up beside me and commed me on a private channel.

"You are in command, Nathan! Lead, and the beast will follow!"

I shook my head to clear my thoughts but did not lower my arm. What happened next brought a grim smile to my face and a look of horror to the Operatives.

Two large spiked appendages dug into the edge of the floor, and the Hunter pulled itself out of the tube. Its shield was flickering as it staggered forward. It looked like the lower portion of the metallic monster's capsule-shaped body was rotting away. It had made it this far on only two legs; the other four were missing. The shield failed, and one of the machine's remaining legs buckled under its weight. It collapsed, thrashing wildly with its last appendage. It suddenly broke away, flying across the room and crashing into the wall just above Sael's head. She didn't even flinch. She instead ran to the Prule Hunter and stared down at it.

"Nathan, you fool!" she cried, turning to me with a wild-eyed look. "All the crimes we have committed up till now were forgivable. Releasing weaponized nanites within my people's exclusion zone is not! There is no amnesty for such a crime! Now, no matter the outcome of this mission, we will be judged guilty of breaking one of my peoples most prohibitive laws!"

"If you want to wait around and tell them, go ahead. We are going to continue the mission whether you are with us or not."

"I will not have to tell them anything. Chaalt scientists will discover the evidence!"

"Oh really? Take another look at the evidence."

Sael turned back around and watched the last of the Prule melt away before her eyes. The floor where the machine dissolved bubbled and steamed until the corrosive completed its task. She opened her mouth to say something, but I cut her off.

"Tria and Justice have discussed this scenario at length. All our contingencies are based on the use of our entire arsenal. It would be the height of stupidity to purposely hobble ourselves by not using every weapon available to us. We came here to win! There is no other plan of action! This is the last time I will explain myself to you. If you are not ready to follow orders and continue this mission, you can stay here because we will have no use for you."

Turning to Klutch, I jerked a thumb over my shoulder. "Troop Master, we are done wasting time. Get us moving!"

Klutch took off with Tria and me right behind him. I did not bother to look back and see if the Operative would follow. I was beyond caring what she thought and wanted to get on with the reason we had come here.

11

We turned a corner and found ourselves at the skybridge entrance. Klutch was short enough he only had to lean over slightly to avoid being seen through the observation windows that lined the walkway. He went across first, momentarily stopping to take a quick peek down into the alley. He commed us the all clear. Tria and I bent low and crossed. Looking back, I saw the Operative was still with us. She hazarded a quick peek out of the windows, then bent and ran to our position.

"I saw an open doorway two buildings down on the left side of the alley," Klutch said. "When we exit the skybridge ramp, cross the alley quickly and take up defensive positions against the far wall. Cover me while I investigate the doorway. If all is clear, we will move on to shield control."

He made eye contact with the Operative to make sure she understood. She nodded, and he ran out into the alley to the opposite wall. He took a knee with his plasma weapon pointed up the alley at the open doorway. Tria had her shotgun poked around the edge of the skybridge entrance covering his rear. We waited for what seemed like an eternity, and then Klutch waved us over. Tria and I crossed and went prone against the wall with our weapons pointing in both directions. Sael waited until we were set then came running across. She crouched just down the wall from us and waved us toward Klutch. I slapped Tria on her munitions pack, and we took off to Klutch's position. He nodded to me and went low through the doorway. It was taking forever, and I was getting ready to call him. He came over our group comms with a surprising statement.

"Commander, I have a live civilian, and he thinks I am here to kill him!"

"Tria, Sael, find out what his story is!"

I waited until both the Chaalt warriors were inside and then followed. I could hear someone pleading for their life in the Chaalt dialect. I motioned to Klutch to give Tria and Sael some breathing room because he still had his war face on his face shield. I wanted to close the open doorway but had no luck with the controller.

"Troop Master, see if you can get this door closed."

Klutch started fiddling with it the same as I had done. My frustration must have been contagious because he pulled his shotgun and was going to butt-stroke the device into submission. Tria came up behind us and grabbed the barrel of his weapon before he could make any adjustments to the stubborn control switch.

Tria stepped close to me. "Do not bother. We are leaving."

159

"What did our friend have to say?"

"His name is Drillen, and he is a power source engineer. He and his work crew had just been relieved by another engineering team that monitors the asteroid's power generators. Two shifts consisting of six engineers' man the reactors around the clock. The other members of his team were going to eat before they retired, but Drillen decided to go to his quarters and sleep. When the containment breach alarms sounded, he attempted to make it back to the security station in the lift building. If he could have made it in time, the high-speed transport cars would have taken him seven thousand feet below the surface where the power plant control room is located. He reports once the building was locked down, the lifts were disabled from below, making it impossible to reach the reactors and safety. On his way to his barracks to find his coworkers, he witnessed them being confronted by Chaalt military forces. He said for unknown reasons they were all shot where they stood."

"It sounds like Gredda's strike team might still be here, and they don't want any witnesses."

"Possibly, but we will not know for sure unless we find them, or they find us first."

"I was concerned about engaging Chaalt forces if we encountered any. Now I am not."

Tria nodded in agreement. "Drillen recognized the Senior Operative, and she should be able to obtain a more complete debriefing. She says we need to move to a safer location."

"Where would that be?"

"Sael wants Drillen to lead us to the building that houses the lifts for the reactors. They are located in a storage warehouse that is on our route to the shield control compound."

"I assume she thinks our portal device will get us into the lift shafts?"

"Yes, if we can make it below and access the reactor room, we will have control of the shield. That will give us the option of bypassing the shield control room and any Prule forces that may be concentrated at that location."

"Did Drillen have any data on the location of the council members?"

"No, he seemed shocked that we would even inquire about their presence here."

Damn! I was hoping since we caught a small break, the gods of war might look down upon us with favor. That thought was just a fabrication of my simple mind; you would think that I would know better by now. Past experiences have shown that when things seemed to be getting easier and going your way, you were probably in for a world of hurt.

"Nathan, I have convinced Drillen to take us to the location of the reactor room lifts." Sael interrupted my misgivings. "We can make use of your transporter to gain access to the shafts. Once inside, we can make our way to the reactor and take control of the power supply for the entire complex."

Yep, this was sounding easier by the minute!

"Okay, Sael. Where to?"

"We go up the transport road to the fourth building on the left. We need to use caution because we will have to cross open ground that exposes us to direct fire from two of the defensive towers. We can limit our exposure by using your transporter to access the buildings on the way to our destination."

Now I was thinking piece of cake; things were finally going our way!

"Klutch, check out the alley between here and the next building."

The Troop Master went low out the door and against the building. I covered his back until he disappeared around the corner. Turning around I could see that all my ducks were indeed in a row. Tria was behind me with Drillen hunched over behind her. The Operative was bringing up the rear. She was kind enough to hold her tongue but impatiently waved me forward. She frowned when I gave her the finger. I was smiling behind the horror image that hid my face. She had no idea what the symbolization represented. Tria pulled my hand down and gave me a not-so-gentle shove toward the doorway. The Troop Master bailed me out.

"Commander, the alley is clear, and I have no movement on either transport lane."

"We are on our way, Troop Master!"

I hightailed it up to the corner of the next building and went prone. I quickly glanced down the alley and saw that Klutch was doing the same. Tria peeked out of the

162

doorway, and I waved her on. She, Drillen, and the Operative ran up the walkway and into the alley behind me. I backed away from the corner.

"Make a hole, Troop Master!" I called to Klutch.

The Tibor was really getting into being our portal operator. He jogged up the alley and stopped beside Sael and Drillen. He then gestured for Drillen to move away from the spot he had chosen. I rolled my eyes in exasperation because he could have picked any number of places other than that one. He called out a warning.

"Cover your eyes!"

I turned my head away from the bright flash of the device triggering and turned back to see he gotten a good portal on the first try. I bent low and was going to charge right in, but Klutch stepped in front of me, pulling his plasma projector from its clip. Before I could start bitching, he went through. I looked back in time to see Drillen plaster himself against the opposite wall of the alley in disbelief of what he just witnessed.

I commed Tria. "Wait until you see the portal start flashing before you bring Drillen and Sael through. That should give us enough time to make sure the building is reasonably secure."

Tria nodded, and as I turned to go, she slapped my armored ass with one of her hands. I ran through and found myself in a room full of supplies. There were items of every description ranging from mechanical devices to clothing. Klutch was peeking out of a doorway with a fist held up. He commed me.

"Commander, I think something or someone is on the level above us. It looks like there is a walkway up there that would be a good place to ambush someone if they entered the building."

"Have we been detected?"

"I don't believe so. The only way to know for sure will be to take a look."

"Right beside you, Troop Master."

We quietly stepped out of the room and turned around to get a look above and behind us. To our surprise, two Chaalt soldiers wearing heavy combat armor stood next to a large barreled weapon that was mounted on a tripod. They had their backs to us, looking out the windows that ringed the upper floor. Both had assault rifles in their hands. I was going to give Klutch a recommendation as to our next course of action, but he came up with one of his own. He loudly cleared his throat over his external mic.

"When you Throggs are done pleasuring each other, I want you to throw those weapons down here on the floor!" he called out to them.

It was a cringeworthy statement and almost funny had it not been for the fact they were both well-trained soldiers. They turned on us in the blink of an eye and opened fire. The bolts of energy from their weapons passed very close over the tops of our heads. Klutch never gave them a chance to correct their errant fire and sent a ball of plasma into them that made a burning six-foot hole through the wall behind where they had been standing. Their upright legs were the only evidence that they were ever there. The shelves loaded with supplies rapidly caught fire, turning the whole upper floor into a burning inferno. Tria, Drillen, and the Operative came running out of the backroom shocked at the blaze consuming the building. One of the legs from the Chaalt soldiers tumbled from the collapsing walkway and bounced to the floor at our feet. Drillen took one look and retched up the contents of his stomach. Klutch seemed frozen in place by the destruction he had just unleashed. I shoved him at a wall that had not caught fire yet.

"Klutch, get us out of here now!"

He shook off his daze and ran to the wall. We turned our backs to the flash of the portal forming. It was a good hole, and I waved Tria through. Klutch picked the engineer up by the back of his uniform and jumped through with the Operative right behind him. I took one last look and jumped. My team was weapons out in a small perimeter with the engineer lying prone in the center. I looked up at the hole Klutch had shot through the wall. Thick black smoke was pouring out announcing our exact location to the entire complex.

"Make another hole, Troop Master! We need to put some distance between us and the burning building before someone comes to find out what we are up to!"

Klutch quickly flashed another portal into existence, and I jumped through. I found myself inside a personal residence. It was small enough to see it was unoccupied. I ran across to a door and hit the controller. It slid aside, and I took a peek. This was an apartment complex: Doors lined the hall, and ramps took you to the upper levels. I decided we needed to keep moving rather than take the time to search all the quarters. My team was now holed up in the room behind me waiting for me to move. I ran across the hall and hit the door, leading with my knee. It caved inward, exposing another vacant apartment. I waved to Klutch and pointed to the outer wall.

"Let's keep moving!"

He ran inside and made another portal. I charged through with Tria behind me. We were once again in an alley between buildings. The warehouse was one building over, and I wanted to get there sooner than later. Klutch rushed by and started another portal. If we were not careful when we exited this structure, we would find ourselves in the firing line of the defensive towers. It turns out the towers were going to be the least of our worries.

My armor sensors detected multiple aerial targets

"Incoming drones!" Tria yelled out.

I was puzzled as to why it took so long for the hostile forces to react. The destruction and telltale smoke cloud left in our wake was pointing out our progress toward the shield projector compound. The shield would have been at the very top of any saboteur's target list. If, for some reason, the opposition overlooked that information, we surely brought it to their attention now.

Sael instructed Drillen to find someplace to hide and shoved him through the portal. Klutch closed the opening, and we cloaked, taking up positions in the alley and thoroughfare. I again felt the presence of the beast haunting my thoughts and actions. I took a knee at the corner of the alley and readied my beam weapon. Tria was across the transport road from my position and had a better view of the incoming targets. She threw her arm up and sent a beam shot at the oncoming drones. The lightning flash was accompanied by two of the seven targets disappearing from my HUD. The drones dispersed and opened fire on us with energy beams. Apparently, our cloaking systems were unable to keep us from being targeted.

Pieces of the building structures around us rained down from all directions, prompting us all to return fire. My HUD targeting was operated by Justice's subsystem. It gave me a target box that intersected with one of the drone's flight paths. I moved my arm up and left, turning the box green. I quickly sent a beam shot into the distant target marker and was rewarded with the disappearance of the drone from my HUD. Klutch took down another, and to my surprise, Sael downed one with a shot from her rifle.

I was again thinking things were going our way. Tria fired again, and now there was only one target moving wildly up and down trying to get a firing solution that would not result in its destruction. I got a piercing alarm warning in my helmet.

"Incoming troop transport!" Sael called out before I could turn around to identify the threat.

Damn! I was really hoping we could skip the world of hurt this time around! Rolling to the opposite side of the alley, I looked behind us. A large shuttle flying just above the buildings was heading in our direction. Tria was still hunkered down across the road, taking intense fire from the remaining drone. I could see Chaalt combat troops jumping out both sides of the shuttle. Klutch was covering Tria and attempting to shoot down the drone. I got to my feet so I could get a clear shot on the transport. I had a good target box and was going to engage when something detonated on the front of my armor, sending me flying out into the street. The pain in my chest and my double vision informed me I was still alive. I could faintly hear urgent shouts over the ringing in my ears. My eyes came back to focus, and I saw the Operative run to Klutch's side and pull his plasma projector from its clip. The shuttle was yawing its nose around so the troops inside could fire down on us while the rest advanced on our location. Sael sent a plasma ball into the side of the cockpit and another into the open hatch. The transport was engulfed in flames and rolled wildly over and dove in our direction. Burning bodies and molten metal rained down as it plowed nose-first into the warehouse building right next to us. My team was flattened by the explosion from the shuttle's impact. I held out little hope that Drillen had somehow survived in the conflagration triggered by the crash.

I felt myself being jerked along the ground. Tria was on her hands and knees pulling me from the flaming wreckage. I could finally hear her yelling my name over our comms telling me we had to move. To my relief, I heard Klutch calling to the Operative telling her to do the same. Reaching up, I grabbed Tria's arms and pulled myself up on

168

my knees. I started crawling as fast as my shaky body would let me. Every breath was a painful reminder that the beast and my armor did not make me invulnerable. Tria helped me stand, and I pushed her toward the alley across the street. I could hear Sael calling over our comms; she was taking fire from the street and buildings behind us. That statement was followed up by the Troop Master's colorful language and a loud exclamation over his external microphone.

"Eat scat, you traitorous Throggs!"

I saw a pink glow light up the far end of the alley, and the Operative immediately started cursing in a sentence that ended with, "Put that away before you manage to kill both of us!"

Flames were flaring more than one hundred feet into the air, and the building on the other side of the alley was fully engulfed. Sael and Klutch came running up out of the blaze, trying to make it back to our position. Sael took a shot to the back and went down hard on her faceplate in the fiery debris. Klutch slowed down enough to scoop her up and throw her over his shoulder. I thought he was stumbling under the weight of Sael's heavy armor. When his shotgun was blown from its clip, I realized his wobbly gait was from taking repeated hits. Our cloaking systems were proving to be worthless. Klutch dumped Sael and ran back into the firestorm. I was going to tell him there was no point in searching for Drillen's body, but he ran back out of the flames carrying both his and the Operative's weapons. The Tibor was a hardcore warrior through and

169

through. The thought of leaving perfectly good weapons in the hands of our enemies must have chafed him in all the wrong places.

The Operative was not seriously injured and was leaning against the wall of the building we had taken refuge behind. She had a pained expression on her face and slowly stood up. The gravity thruster pack she wore on the back of her armor and one of her prized swords were now scrap. I suspected we were on the receiving end of an anti-transport rifle like the one she carried. She manually released several clamps, and the remains of the wrecked equipment fell from her back. She had a prominent blackened indentation in the back of her armor, but it showed no sign of a hole. My armor had a visible dent from the weapons warhead but nothing more. If it were not for Sael's thruster pack soaking up the blast of the explosive round, it was hard to say what might have happened.

An amplified voice called out from somewhere behind the burning warehouse. We went prone weapons out, not knowing what to expect.

"It is the traitor Gredda Porsha!" Sael whispered to us. "I thought I knew the plans of the traitors, but it seems everyone in this conspiracy is working toward a goal of their own making!"

"Sael Nalen, are you still alive?" Gredda called out. "If you are, I know you are gravely wounded. I did not want to shoot the Principal Investigator of our people, but you left me no choice. You need to listen to me. The Prule have offered to make the Chaalt people the rulers of this galaxy. They only ask that we share the overabundance of resources that are available to us. If you surrender to me now, you will receive medical attention and the right to willingly serve your own kind. You can take your rightful place as head of our military forces and assume the title of Kala Mor Dee once again!"

"I suppose I don't have to guess who is going to be our supreme ruler?"

"Would that be so bad, Kala Mor Dee?" Gredda responded. "We are cut from the same cloth. The two of us will do what no others have dared. With the help of the Prule, we can make the Chaalt people the dominant race of this entire galaxy!"

"What of the council? Have you already disposed of them?"

"In exchange for their lives, they have agreed to go before the Chaalt people and nominate me as the new leader of all the Chaalt worlds. They will also have a place in our government and are only answerable to me."

"How are you going to explain your partnership with the Prule?"

"That will be the easiest part of all. I will be seen as the only leader to ever broker a permanent and lasting peace agreement with the Prule!"

Gredda and her crew were double-crossing the council, and there was nothing the council could do about it. I was lying next to Klutch and saw the vents in his armor lock into the open position. I was pretty sure the Troop Master was getting ready to do something really nasty. I grabbed his leg and shook it. He looked back at me with a look that confirmed my suspicions. I held a finger up to him and shook my head. I cleared my visor so he could plainly see the stern look on my face. I knew Sael Nalen could be a real pain in the ass, but she was no traitor. We needed to see how she was going to play this out. I was already having a major tug-of-war with the beast, and I was losing ground. If the Tibor started something, I knew the monster in me would push aside my attempts at control and happily join in. Tria must have been reading my mind and commed me and Klutch on a private channel.

"Sael will not stand for this! She is stalling to determine a plan of action. We should follow her lead!"

I hoped for all of us Tria was right. We were in a tight spot and outnumbered by well-trained experienced troops with powerful weaponry. The weapons we would have to use to extract ourselves from this scat would more than likely cause serious injury to us all. I called up antimatter in my launcher menu. I immediately got dire warnings from my HUD. The warnings were in my teammates' visors as well. Tria rolled to my side and gripped my arm, while Klutch just nodded and gave me a goofy smile. Even the lowest attenuation of the antimatter settings gave me targeting arcs well beyond my intended target area. Sael must have somehow sensed my deadly intentions and was waving me down with two of her hands. She cleared her visor and looked at me pleadingly. I drew my finger across the neck of my armor and pointed in the direction the voice was coming from. She again waved me down.

"The human and Tria Burlor died when the shuttle crashed down on them," Sael called back to Gredda. "What about the Tibor Troop Master?"

"The Prule Hivemind wants the spacecraft that you penetrated the shield with. If the Tibor turns them over to the Prule intact, he will be allowed to leave with his life!"

I was getting the feeling this bullshit session had more to do with Gredda stalling us instead of the other way around.

"Tria, see if you can get a look behind us without exposing yourself to a weapons tower."

Tria quickly crawled across the transport road behind us. She slowly eased up to the corner of the thoroughfare and pointed her shotgun around the corner against the ground, using the weapons sight in her HUD to get a safe look.

"Nathan! There are three Prule Hunters moving rapidly up the main transport road," Tria whispered. "We need to move now, or they will have us surrounded!"

Gredda was still trying to keep Sael distracted until the Hunters jumped us.

"I need an answer now, Sael, or you will die!"

The hellish fire burning the remains of the warehouse and the shuttle was disrupting Gredda's strike team enough they had quit sniping at us. There was a good chance their sensors were being overwhelmed by the blaze and intense heat signature. I called to my team and Sael.

"Everyone on me now! Klutch, we are going to get as close to the burning warehouse as we can, and I want you to start making portals until you hit the underground tunnel that leads to the power station!"

The news of the Hunters bearing down on us was all the encouragement Sael needed to give up whatever plan she was working on.

"It took you long enough. I did not think I could stall Gredda much longer!"

I shook my head, knowing she never had a plan to begin with. She was counting on me to pull our fat from the fire. I should have let her know it was desperation that drove me to this last resort. We ran to the edge of the scorching blaze, and Klutch made his first attempt and got nothing. His second attempt was the same thing. I was thinking that the world of hurt routine was coming around for seconds when Klutch yelled out he had a good hole. He didn't even wait to tell Sael to jump; he just pushed her in and grabbed Tria by an arm and went through, pulling her with him. He just saved me a massive amount of grief because I was going to shove her in before she could try to pull me with her. I momentarily stood there as the three Hunters came barreling around the corner. I dialed up a full-yield antimatter round and set it for a descending air burst at thirty feet. The Hunters came to a skidding halt and noticed me standing at the edge of the inferno. They turned in my direction and spun their weapons around. I launched the shell straight up into the air above me and dove through the portal.

12

I came crashing helmet-first to the floor of a huge tunnel. Before I could yell at Klutch to close the portal, he shut it down. I jumped to my feet.

"ANTIMATTER OUT!" I yelled.

Tria and I grabbed Sael by her arms and boosted down the tunnel hard enough she groaned out in pain. My HUD showed Klutch was wasting no time bringing up our rear. I was wondering why the scat was taking so long to foul the ventilator. As if on cue, the whole damned asteroid seemed to jump up in front of us. The tunnel that was straight just a second before somehow changed direction. We plowed into the tunnel wall, losing our grip on the Operative. The tumbling stop on the tunnel floor reminded me how much it hurt to be shot by Chaalt weapons. I sat up only to be freight-trained by Klutch. The collision had me wondering if the evil robot had installed a Tibor ass magnet in my helmet. A grinding crash and thick dust cloud let us know that going back to the shafts that could have given us access to the power generators would no longer be a viable option. The tunnel had collapsed behind us, leaving a solid wall of debris blocking our path.

Sael Nalen slowly rolled over and sat up. "You primate! Couldn't we have just slipped away without trying to kill us all!"

I almost cracked a smile. There was some of the old Sael still left after all. Sarcasm coming from her was a lot more tolerable than her endless bitching that seemed to be the norm lately.

"I was just thinning the herd, Senior Operative. Get ready to move out! We need to get back to the surface before any of the survivors can regroup. Klutch, find us a spot to go up and make a hole."

My retort muzzled any reply that Sael might have had. She unslung her rifle, quickly inspected it, and nodded. We moved down the tunnel about another hundred yards and found it dead ended into a large lift. There were three gravity sleds loaded with different pieces of equipment sitting on it. Looking at my HUD map, I could see we were underneath another warehouse at the base of a weapons tower. We were also to the rear of the Chaalt forces. Klutch climbed up on the equipment stacked on the sled. He leaned back and projected a portal but got a negative red band, and it closed. I heard him swear something about scat parked on the lift doors, and he adjusted his aim to the corner of the shaft and tried again. We got a good hole that was smaller than usual, but it was a clear passage. Klutch boosted up and through. Fifteen seconds later, we saw his arm poke through and wave to us. Tria and I grabbed Sael and sandwiched her between us so we could negotiate the smaller diameter opening. She was forced to embrace me; it had us helmet to helmet. The look on her face and the way she was gritting her teeth insinuated I should not comment on this unlikely position. Me being a primate and all meant I could not keep my primitive mouth shut.

"They call this a 'ménage à trois' back where I come from."

I was confident Sael knew nothing of the French or their language. It must have been the silly smile on my face that defined the comment. She headbutted me with considerable force. Tria leaned around Sael's shoulder, and I noted there was nothing silly about the look on her face. We boosted up through the hole, and Klutch shut it down. The first thing I noticed was the front of the warehouse was blown inward at a forty-five-degree angle. There was a huge rend to one side of the wall. I bent low and moved up to it so I could see the results of my handiwork. In the distance, plasma fires and pieces of buildings were splattered everywhere I looked. The epicenter of my detonation was barren of structures for several hundred yards surrounding the crater of the collapsed tunnel. I started getting sensor warnings on pop-up targets. Pop-up wasn't exactly the right phrase. There were Chaalt soldiers crawling around and, in some cases, dragging members of their strike team with them. They must have been trying to encircle our position when I left my party favor behind. Welcome to my world of hurt.

"I have twenty-two targets that appear to be combat capable," Tria said from my side. "There are eleven targets down showing small amounts of movement and thirty-seven fading heat signatures. I have no Prule machine emanations present in the area."

Klutch called out that there were no aerial targets and requested permission to disable the weapons tower. There was little chance the tower could depress its main battery at a steep enough angle to shoot down at us if we moved out of the building. If we decided to close the distance with the Chaalt strike team, that would change. It presented a clear and present danger that needed to be dealt with sooner than later.

"Take Sael with you for backup. Try to disable it without drawing attention to our position."

They ran to the back of the building, and Klutch made a hole. They both jumped through and it disappeared. I was going to concentrate on the targets in front of us when Tria leaned down next to my helmet.

"What is a ménage à trois?"

I almost bit my tongue trying to stifle my reply. It was not a good time to have that discussion. The hesitation in my answer was not overlooked.

"It means three's a crowd!"

"The truth will prove to be less painful than the bullshit you seem to have an endless supply of."

At least she said it with a small smile on her face. Not knowing when I would be forced to pay for my Earth boy sense of humor was bothering me more than the how. It would remain a mystery as to how Klutch may or may not have known that I had my tit in a wringer. His method for remediating the situation would not have made it on my list of approved actions. It started with a rather loud exclamation from Sael over our group comms.

"Nathan said not to draw attention!"

Tria and I both turned and looked up through a hole in the partially collapsed roof. Our view of the weapons tower suddenly brightened with a burst of plasma fire jetting from its upper reaches.

"I think we should leave now," Klutch calmly told Sael.

A hole appeared in the back of the building, and Sael ran through cursing the Tibor's indiscretion. Klutch quickly followed and then shut down the portal, declaring with no uncertainty that he had accomplished his mission. I was honestly lost for words. Tria and Sael ran to the front wall to observe the enemy's reaction to the fact we were probably still alive and causing additional havoc. This was accompanied by the weapons tower collapsing inward, sending a fountain of flames and smoke into the already congested atmosphere.

"Here they come!" Sael warned.

Klutch and I took up positions next to Tria and the Operative. The Chaalt troops were indeed charging what they must have perceived as an ambush. We hit the floor as they opened up with everything they had. The collapsed wall shuddered under the impact of the fusillade. The wall became so riddled with holes it fell inward affording us no protection or cover. I felt the beast pull free of its cage and assert itself over me. I pulled my beam weapon up and fired multiple times into the rallying combatants. The leaders were blown to pieces, and the shock waves flattened more than half of the oncoming troops. Klutch's follow-up shots broke the back of the charge and left no one standing. Tria ran to me and pulled my arm down.

"Nathan, they are finished. Cease fire!"

I shook my head to clear my thoughts. The beast skittered away into the back of my mind, leaving only its haunting laugh at the murderous mayhem. I could see the pain on Tria's face. She had not fired on the troops with her beam weapon. She had little stomach for slaughtering her own people, traitors or not. Sael Nalen stared wide-eyed at me. For a change, she had nothing to say.

"Commander, it is advisable to strip the survivors of their weapons," Klutch said, bringing us all back to the reality of our situation.

The comment seemed to snap the Operative out of it, and she moved out, weapon up and ready. I suspected she was wondering if anything remained of Gredda Porsha. Tria nodded to me, and we spread out on line to check for survivors. All the combatants that were out in front of the charge were reduced to unidentifiable body parts. Out of the corner of my eye, I saw the Operative kneel next to a body and then draw her pistol and fire point-blank into the soldier. We went on a little further, and I saw Tria do the same with her needle gun. While the beast in me thought of it as revenge, the human in me knew it was a mercy killing. Most of the bodies were blown apart or missing appendages. Klutch was going around collecting weapons and throwing them in a pile. I turned to Sael when I heard her talking to one of the downed soldiers. The warrior was groping at Sael and begging to be killed.

The Operative stood over the soldier. "Where is the traitor Gredda Porsha?"

The warrior's hand pointed to a group of bodies in the distance. I heard the soldier say that Gredda was severely wounded in the blast we unleashed upon them. Sael stood and then shot the soldier in the head. She stalked off to see if Gredda still lived. Klutch reported he had collected all the usable weapons. I waved him over as I walked to Tria. She turned and looked up at me. It was not hard to see the sadness on her face.

"There are no more survivors."

I helped her to her feet and pointed to where the Operative was going. She nodded and moved out without a word. I called to Klutch, "When we are a safe distance, burn it!"

We were most of the way to where the Operative stood when a pinkish glow lit the street behind us. I turned and saw Klutch send a plasma ball into the stacked weaponry. He looked a tad close to be burning live ordnance. What I thought might be a simple meltdown turned into a flaring pyrotechnical display that ended with an explosion that nearly knocked me over. I reflexively ducked and then looked up to see the Troop Master picking himself up off the ground. He came running by me with a stupid smile on his face and threw me a jaunty salute.

"Mission accomplished, Commander!"

There were times when I thought the beast in me was the only maniacal psychopath on the loose. I was now revisiting that thought. I hurried to catch up with Klutch. He ran to Tria's side and stopped because she would go no farther. The results of my antimatter shell were just as morbid as the damage from our beam weapons. There were dead Chaalt soldiers laid out in rows. Most were horribly mutilated and unidentifiable. I stopped by Tria and Klutch and watched as Sael worked her way around the bodies. She paused just long enough to try to identify whether the remains were those of Gredda Porsha. She suddenly stopped by a body propped up against the wall of the building they were sheltering behind. The body was missing two of its arms on the right side and had a large gory chunk torn out of the armor on an upper thigh. The helmet was peeled open and revealed a partially charred face. Sael kneeled next to the soldier and pulled the body closer to her helmet. Groans of agony escaped the soldier's incinerated lips. If it was indeed Gredda, she was still alive.

"In all the stories throughout our history that involved treason, not a single one was about the glorious rise to power of a traitor! None! Not a single one!" Sael yelled at the body. "What made you think you would somehow be an exception? The Prule only told you what you wanted to hear. They were never going to share power with any race. You would only have placed our people at the end of their extermination list. Once the Prule had a firm foothold in this galaxy and started reproducing in mass, all would die! There would be no exceptions!"

Gredda's head lolled to one side, and she gurgled out, "Kill me now, Kala Mor Dee. I would not have stood over you and gloated!"

"I am not gloating, you fool! Your treachery has endangered the entire galaxy. We must try to stop the Prule Hivemind before it is too late! Where are the council members being held?"

"What makes you think I would help you?"

"Because your actions are only suspicions at this point. If you want me to try to clear your name and restore the honor of your clan, you will help me undo the treasonous poison you have unleashed upon us all!"

Gredda's remaining eye grew large, and tears flowed from it.

"They are held in the crew quarters of the engineering labs. The four remaining members of my strike team guard them. A few resisted and were executed, but the rest still live. As for the Hivemind, it is hiding down in the weapons lab on sublevel three, where it is building an army of abominations."

The Operative stood and then pointed her pistol at Gredda's head. I saw the Chaalt warrior close her eye and nod. Sael shot her and turned away. She cast a disapproving eye at Klutch.

"The Troop Master is correct," Sael said. "We should eliminate the remaining defensive towers. We need to move quickly before the Hivemind decides the council members are no longer a bargaining chip. If I might suggest a plan of action, it would be for the three of you to make aerial strikes on the seven remaining towers while I investigate the shield dome complex."

It sounded like a reasonable plan, and I was definitely tired of skulking around the alleys and streets of the complex. Tria, Klutch, and I divvied up the towers among ourselves. Tria had twice the launchers, so she got the three towers to our south. Klutch got two to the north, and I got two to the west. We would make a single pop-up pass by each target and give it a high-yield antimatter shell. I was confident there would be no follow-up strikes. When we were done, we would rally at the shield dome building and find Sael.

Tria was ready to move out and stopped next to the Operative before departing. "Are you really going to try to clear Gredda of her treason?" she asked.

"No, I said what I thought would be necessary for her to reveal the information she wished to die with."

Apparently, Sael had nothing else to say about it, so I mentioned our plan to use antimatter shells to resolve the tower issue. She took off at a dead run in the direction of the shield building and never looked back.

My suit AI had a decent amount of information on the complex now that we had managed to crawl around more than half of it. It laid out a planned attack route for each of us. The plans included decoy maneuvers designed to attract the tower's targeting systems. When a tower attempted to engage one of us, another would attack it from a different vector. We boosted low level down the street and made a hard-right turn at the end and then split up. I made the first pop-up maneuver, which got the desired attention. The buildings I dropped behind took a hit that left nothing but a massive smoking crater. I made another hard turn, and my first target appeared highlighted in my HUD. The tower fired a burst at one of my crewmates, and I sent my response against the upper portion of the structure. My AI nosed me over and accelerated to maximum. The tactic was blindingly quick and dropped me so low to the ground, I involuntarily put a hand out in front of me that made contact with the pavement. A huge shower of sparks flashed from my gauntlet, and a warning tone sounded in my helmet.

To my surprise, Justice's subsystem gave me a warning laced with deadpan sarcasm. It brought back a memory or two of my childhood.

"Commander, it is advisable to keep your hands in the ride at all times."

It's hard to say where he picked up that shit from, but it was funny and I would have laughed if it were not for the multiple high-order detonations that rippled across the complex. My next pop-up maneuver filled my HUD with the return signals of flying debris coming down from all directions. I got a highlighted target and pumped out another shell. Once again, I nosed almost to the pavement but refrained from reaching out to touch it. My mind turned in another direction, and I started wondering what Justice was doing. The thought was interrupted by more massive explosions. The Chaalt warships that were once in close proximity to the base would have no problems detecting the blindingly bright flashes of the detonating antimatter. My suit made another course correction, and I was now rapidly moving in the direction of the shield dome building. My HUD beeped at me when a blue triangle with Klutch's name above it exited an alley to my right. An explosion in the distance let me know Tria had just finished off the last of the towers. Another blue triangle appeared in my helmet. Tria confirmed what I already suspected.

"All targets destroyed!"

I located the Operative against the wall of the shield compound. She was standing in the debris of several buildings and waved to me. I quickly landed next to her, as did Klutch and Tria.

"Nathan, if we breach the wall at this location, it should put us very close to the main access of the shield control room."

"I have been thinking hard about our next move and I don't think trying to take this building should be at the top of our priority list," I said. "We need to secure the council members sooner than later. Is there any way to bring down the shield temporarily without taking the control room?"

"Not that I am aware of."

"We need to get the Legacy inside of the dome. If we manage to secure your people, the only safe place to protect them would be aboard my ship. It might also be the only way for us all to get off of this rock."

The Operative looked at me with a strange look on her face. If I had to describe it, I would say it might have been newfound respect.

"I must admit that I had not considered that option. The shuttle that Gredda Porsha used to transport her troops was the council's personal shuttle. It should have been more than obvious to me that it was the only transport at this facility. I apologize for my failings. I am only focusing on the goals that I have formulated, and I am compromising the mission by doing so."

"It will not matter unless we can come up with a way to get the Legacy inside the dome. I still think we should secure the council's freedom before we worry about the shield controls. A pitched battle inside the control room may yield the same results as the comms building. If the shield comes down for keeps, your people are going to swarm this facility, and we are not going to know who to trust with the future of your people. Tria, Klutch, do you have anything you would like to add?"

My crewmates looked at each other.

"No, Commander, we are ready to move on your orders," Tria said.

"Sael, where is the engineering crew quarters located?"

When Sael did not answer right back, I turned on her ready to bite off a piece of her ass. I held my tongue because she was holding up a hand to me and looked deep in thought.

"Nathan, there might be a way to bring down the shield for a matter of seconds. I have no way of knowing for how long, but if the Legacy is close, Justice might be able to clear the shield before it comes back up!"

"If I know Justice, he is cloaked and very close to the dome. He doesn't like being out of comms with us any more than we do. If we can bring it down for a handful of seconds, Justice will get inside. What do you think it will take to shut it down?"

"The energy conduits that come from the power source have multiple standbys. They converge into the base of the control room in several locations," Sael explained. "If we can locate the active conduits and disrupt the power supply, we could possibly bring down the shield for a very short period of time while it transfers the power load."

Klutch piped in with the billion-credit question. "How are we going to know which one is carrying the load, and how are we going to find it?"

"There will be switching stations below the control building. We will use the portal device to find them and search each until we find the active conduits."

"If we are thinking this might work, there is a very good chance that the Hivemind has as well," Tria said, shaking her head. "The switching stations may be guarded. At the very least, the active one will most assuredly be. It would be foolish to think the Prule will let us wander around inside the walls of the compound while we perform a random search."

It really didn't matter to the beast in me if I battled Prule inside the compound or outside. What was bothering me was that we needed to continue our momentum and assault the Prule no matter where we were. If we went with Sael's plan, it might have the positive effect of drawing hostile forces to this location and away from our priority target, which was now the engineering building.

13

"Klutch, let's skirt the wall to another location and make a hole!"

The Troop Master threw me a thumbs up and took off through the wreckage heaped around the wall. We followed with Sael bringing up the rear. I was starting to think it would be a good idea to use the Daggers as air cover, but Sael had previously warned us about a large number of missile batteries that were still unaccounted for. I was not going to risk our only other means of transportation if everything went to hell in a handcart. We quickly made our way around the side of the wall, and Klutch stopped about halfway down. We dispersed into a defensive perimeter and took a knee.

"Proceed, Troop Master!"

We saw the flash of the device activating but heard Klutch grumble an oath under his breath. Apparently, he chose an unsuitable location.

"Moving!" he called out to us.

We got up and followed as he chose another spot about thirty feet farther down the wall. We took a knee and waited. The flash of the machine was not followed by any cursing, so I turned to look, and Klutch had his back to the portal waving me over with his usual goofy grin. I was going to tell Tria and the Operative to get moving, but it froze in my throat. A Prule Hunter's leg and the capsule-shaped upper body started to step through the portal.

"Klutch, kill the portal now!"

The Troop Master spun around and fell backward on his ass at the sight of the Hunter staring back at him. He hit the kill switch just as the Hunter was deciding it was going to pay us a visit. Two of the machine's legs and part of its upper torso sheared off cleanly and fell to the ground at his feet. If I had to guess, I would say the Troop Master's waste disposal systems were busily tidying up the lower half of his armor. We had used the machine an unknown number of times. This was a first for anything coming from the other side of the portal. We should have never assumed something would not get curious about a large round opening, and not want to take a look. We would not be making that mistake ever again.

Klutch got up and called out once again. "Moving!"

He ran all the way around the wall to another side and then stopped. We still had no movement outside the wall, so this time we chose to turn our defensive perimeter to look in and not out. Klutch got a good hole first try, and I ran up beside him. Waving to Tria and the Operative, I made a circle motion with my hand and pointed behind myself and Klutch, then held up a finger. Tria quickly nodded, and she and the Operative took a knee just behind me. I tapped Klutch on the shoulder, and he went through with his weapon ready. I was right on his heels and stepped out of the portal to Klutch raising his beam weapon at two Hunters. They were standing at the location of our first good hole and were carefully inspecting the sheared off parts of the Prule that stepped through our portal. I didn't need any encouragement from the beast and slapped Klutch hard on the shoulder. I fired a beam shot striking the unshielded Prule in the middle of the torso, and Klutch fired on the second one. Both were blown to scrap, and we searched for more targets. Tria and the Operative came through the portal, and Klutch quickly shut it down.

Before I could say anything, Tria opened fire with her beam weapon on a Hunter that came charging around the corner of the control building. The energy discharge was blinding and brought down the bio machine's shield. A fast follow-up shot from Klutch left the remains smoldering and scattered in all directions. We waited to see if we had any more takers, but nothing happened.

We ran to the side of the control building, and I went to one corner and Tria and the Operative to the other.

"Clear!" I called out.

"Clear!" called Tria a second later.

"I can see the entrance and have no movement!"

I could only hope we had taken out the Hunters that were guarding the grounds and that any inside might possibly be unaware of the racket we had just made. It was doubtful, considering the explosive force of our beam weapons, but I would remain hopeful.

"Klutch, turn that thing on and start searching the ground around the building!"

After seeing multiple flashes followed by an equal amount of swearing, Klutch called out.

"Commander, I am finding no voids underground at this location!"

"Move farther away from the building and keep trying!" Sael yelled out to him.

After another round of less than appropriate words, Klutch moved away from the building and started working a new search pattern. He got a good hole on the fourth try. It was a lot smaller than any we had previously encountered. It would be one person per jump. I grabbed Klutch before he could go first and let him know I would be the one jumping. He didn't like it, but it also wasn't a question with a multiple-choice answer, either. I pulled my shotgun from its clip and jumped before he could tag team with Tria. I was a little surprised at the sudden drop of about thirty feet. Before I could react, I glanced off of the riser tubes going upward into the building. Using my gravity boosters, I arrested my fall and righted myself before hitting what I assumed was the roof of the switching station. I set down as gently as possible and used my no-light sensors to find the service hatch that was snuggled up to the power conduits. I called to my team, gave them a sitrep, and told them to hold tight in a defensive perimeter. Tria came on and gave me just enough backwash to let me know she still cared. I swallowed my cheeky reply and let her know I needed some time to work the problem. Talking wasn't going to solve the issue. If I lived through this, I felt I would somehow pay for my remarks.

I carefully examined the hatch, and it was easy to see that there was nothing high-tech about it. There was no other way to access this tunnel unless you entered from the room below me. It was a simple tab of metal on a turn latch. All I had to do was turn the tab and let it fall into the opening. I reached down and grabbed the tab, turning it slowly until it was ready to open. I pointed my shotgun down and let the door fall free. It was faintly lit inside the room, and there was nothing moving. I dropped inside and quickly looked around. If this was the machinery operating the shield, it sure didn't look like it. There were two lights on a panel that were close enough to the color of red, that I went ahead and made the leap of faith it meant it was in the off position. Klutch called down and said the portal had just started flashing. I told him I was on my way. And as an afterthought, I pulled a grenade then tossed it inside. It would suck to be the first hostile through that door. I boosted hard up the narrow tunnel and saw the portal stepping up in the frequency of flash. I cleared the opening with enough velocity I would have flown to the bottom of the projector dome. Klutch foresaw this eventuality and stood over the opening. I hit him at a fair clip, but he held on. We were both dumped against the side of the building as the portal disappeared.

"Ha! You still had at least three seconds, Commander!"

The looks I was getting from Tria and the Operative did not seem as lighthearted as Klutch's. We got up off the ground and moved back to the rear of the building. Klutch had paced off the distance to the location of the shaft and got a good hole right off. I stepped forward, but Tria grabbed the back of my weapons pack. She came up on one of our discrete comms channels.

"I have heard you use certain statements in the past when you thought one of us might not be getting a job done in the proper amount of time. I am only going to repeat it because it is, after all, an Earth saying and not necessarily one that other races would consider using. I do wish to make sure it is stated properly. Stop dicking around!"

She gave me a shove and down I went. This time I used my boosters to stop about a foot above the hatch. I eased down and readied myself. When I let the door fall, it bounced off the head of a Prule Hunter. Where the hell were all these pieces of shit coming from? It was one of those times where you didn't know which of us was more surprised to see the other. Thinking I could quickly resolve the situation, I held down the trigger on my shotgun, deciding to give it the whole shebang. The triphammer explosions of a dozen penetrator slugs to the machine's head drove it violently to the floor. The slugs made some impressive dents in the Prule's armor but did not penetrate. The Hunter thrashed around on the floor and quickly let me know that a dollar's worth of nickel knots was not going to dissuade it from trying to kill me. I could hear the whine of its energy weapon getting warmed up as the machine's power whip smashed upward through the ceiling. I boosted backward from the opening and sent a beam shot in reply. I will never know what caused the massive explosion that followed my shot, because I was blown back up through the portal. Tria and Klutch were standing ready to arrest my ascent, but the attempt was in vain. I hit them with such velocity they were knocked to the ground. The huge blast that belched me from the opening canned the Operative as well.

I stopped my spin and righted myself. As I looked up, I could no longer see the opacity of the shield dome that had once dominated the star-filled horizon. Just about four heartbeats later, it flickered back into place.

"Justice?"

"I am here, Commander!"

I had to admit; the voice of the quirky AI was an overwhelming relief. As of that point forward, all of his past annoyances were officially forgiven!

"I have a lock on your position, Commander, and will upload your battle armor's recorded combat data for current intelligence assessments. I have also located the Daggers for retrieval and have identified a large number of hostile targets moving in mass toward your coordinates. All are emanating Prule machine communication signals. I recommend you shelter in place, and I will address the situation."

"Roger that, Justice! Setting up a defensive perimeter and will move on your recommendation."

I quickly landed, and we went weapons out with our backs to the building. I cleared the demonic image from my visor and made eye contact with my team. Even the old witch had a smile on her face for a change.

My audio pickups detected a rumbling in the otherwise quiet hum of the shield station. The noise gathered in volume until it was felt as vibrations in my boots. Justice was hammering the machine shit out of the Prule and their minions. I tried my best to keep from thinking things were going our way. It had proven to be a faulty philosophy on more occasions than I care to remember. Try as I might to suppress it, I was feeling more upbeat every second the ruckus in the distance grew louder.

"Commander, I request permission to initiate sterilization protocols."

"You are weapons free, Justice!"

The smile that was on the Operative's face turned to a cringe at Justice's call. She knew what was about to happen and surprised me by not saying a word. She may have finally realized that our success so far was pure dumb luck, and we had stretched it to the breaking point. I heard three hissing pops that were followed immediately by jarring booms that echoed across the complex. When there were no more reports, I knew the deed was done. The Prule were going to find that the environment in this place would no longer be to their liking. The beast stalking the peripheries of my mind was snickering because there would be no relocation plan the Prule could fall back on. They would never leave this place.

"Commander, I have suppressed the last of the anti-ship systems defending this complex. We now control the hostile airspace, and I am detecting no movement in your area."

"Roger that, Justice. We will move outside the shield control complex and await extraction."

"Affirmative, Commander. I am in route to recover the Daggers and will have a sitrep available for your dissemination once you are aboard. ETA five minutes."

I pointed at the exterior wall and slapped Klutch on the back of his armor. We moved quickly across the open ground, and Klutch made a hole. Tria ran through with me at her back. The Operative and Klutch stepped out last. We made our way out into the middle of the thoroughfare, weapons out. The five minutes pickup time Justice had alerted us to seemed much shorter. That would be a first, because it was usually just the opposite. Justice swept us up with the tow beam and set us down in the hangar. The combat stress that had gripped me earlier eased considerable.

"Commander, I have taken the liberty of activating Tria's third-generation Zaen battle armor. I have taken note of the Senior Operative's battle damage and have determined she will be a liability in combat without fully functional battle armor. If she is to continue the mission, I recommend she make use of the battle suit."

"Sael, report to the science lab, and Xul will assist you in getting suited up. Justice will make sure you know what you need to and will make the transition as seamless as possible."

Without comment, the Senior Operative headed out of the hangar. This was a side of Sael that I could come to enjoy. She was not known for shutting up, no matter the circumstances. Her quiet compliance might be a small indication she was finally willing to accept my command.

"Justice, bring us up to speed on everything going on outside of the dome."

"Commander, before I departed for the Chaalt home world of Athella, I commandeered a large number of IST communication frequencies. I broadcast messages to Chaalt assets that appeared to balk at orders to attack the Legacy. I sent misleading information that indicated the Senior Operative was in charge of a rescue operation supported by us with the intention of freeing the council and eliminating the Prule."

"Other than Sael being in charge, that doesn't sound like it was very misleading."

"I broadcast it from the Operative's IST and used her voice recordings to simulate her orders to stand down."

That raised my eyebrows because it was a new angle on getting things done. I had no idea the AI would take matters into its own hands and make the decision to go in that direction. Justice was wargaming at levels that were bordering on disturbing.

"I have to admit, I would like to discuss this with you in detail at some future date, but now is not that time. Out of curiosity, what effect did it have on Chaalt warship movements?"

"More than seventy percent broke off engagement maneuvers and have stationed themselves in a very high orbit above this base. The remaining warships attempted to engage with all available weapons. It necessitated my excursion to Athella and drew those forces away from this location to cover the traitors claiming power. They have declared military law and issued statements claiming we are rogue elements of a coup instigated by Sael Nalen. They are claiming it is our intention to install her as leader of the Chaalt people. The false council has proclaimed Gredda Porsha as the new supreme commander until our treasonous actions are crushed by the military."

Apparently Gredda's ambitious plan was the only one the traitors had left to fall back on. It was nice to know something good came out of us wrecking the comms array. The fools that were in charge didn't have a clue as to what was going on. They were blindly assuming their new partners could handle all comers. That mistake was going to be a big nail in their coffins. If nothing else, the real rebels just shot themselves in the foot as far as their leadership appointment went. When the dust finally settled on this shit stack, the real perpetrators would be easily identifiable. The trick now, would be to save as many of the legitimate rulers as possible, before things stopped going our way. It would be important to show we were only here on a rescue mission and nothing more.

"Is Sael privy to this intel?"

"No, Commander."

"For now, let's keep it that way. There is no point in relighting her fuse."

"I concur, Commander. I have nutritional supplements and hydration liquids for all crew members to consume that will alleviate combat fatigue and renew acuity. The Operative has already ingested the supplements and is undergoing armor acclamation training at an advanced pace."

"Are you equipping her with full armament?"

"Yes, Commander, she will have a first-generation beam weapon and limited antimatter bombardment capability. I will remain in control of all weapons of mass destruction to limit the possibility of fratricide."

I flinched a little. I knew the AI spent quite a bit of time in the early days of my combat missions doing exactly the same thing with me.

"I have replacement munitions and repair components for your armor staged in the ready room. When you are ready, we will move to the engineering building and initiate rescue operations."

We went to the ready room and stepped out of our armor so Justice could start the repair process. Sitting on the top of our lockers was a pitcher of water and what looked like breakfast bars. Klutch had his mouth stuffed full and asked for seconds. I sat with Tria and ate the slightly sweet nutrition bars and chased it down with the water. The pick-me-up was needed, and within ten minutes I felt like I had inhaled a bucket of coffee. I heard a thumping in the corridor and turned in time to see an armor-clad Sael Nalen run past the ready room hatch. Justice was not kidding when he said she was getting up to speed quickly. In the time it took Justice to repair our armor, the Operative went by the ready room two more times, running and using the gravity drives. I would leave it up to Tria whether or not she would let Sael keep the armor. After the amount of weaponry and equipment Sael has given to us in the past, the beam weapon technology would just about even us up.

I kissed Tria then slapped Klutch on the back.

"Let's settle this scat once and for all," I said. "We have better things to do than hang around the Chaalt home worlds."

We armored up and went to the hangar. Sael was standing at the open hangar door looking down on the research station. When she saw us coming, she stepped away from the opening and pulled her rifle from the clip Justice had engineered for it. Klutch took his place in front with Tria and I just behind him at his sides. Sael stepped up behind us, and Justice moved us rapidly across the complex. He stopped us just above the third largest structure on the asteroid. The Legacy was cloaked but could not hide the large opening of the hangar door. Our presence registered as a non-event with no reaction from below.

"This is the engineering building," Sael called to us. "The crew quarters are on the top floors."

I rapped Klutch on the back, and he jumped with the three of us close behind him. The drop was about a hundred feet, and we arrested our fall just above the roof deck. We eased down, and I pointed to a spot on the deck. Klutch wasted no time and gave us a good hole first try. Tria and I went in with the Operative backing us. We landed in a dark hallway with a light at the far end. We moved to the side as Klutch dropped in and closed the portal behind us. A quick sweep revealed nothing, and Klutch gave us another hole in the same location as the last one. This time, things got a little livelier when Tria and I landed on top of the junk piles the Prule were turning out for their army. I cut my gravity drive and landed full weight right on top of the five-foot bio machine. Grabbing onto the machine's weapon, I wrenched it off of its makeshift feet and body-slammed it into the wall. Jamming my needle gun into the crimson gore cradled inside of the metallic framework, I gave it a burp of hull shards. This did the trick, and it collapsed at my feet. Tria made quick work of her target with her climbing hooks. She pushed the mess away and stood ready to back up Klutch and the Operative as they made well-placed shots on the remaining three Prule soldiers. It was all over in less than two minutes. The hostiles never got a shot off before we overwhelmed them.

Sael sprinted to the end of the hallway and leaned into the drop tube.

"There is movement at the bottom of the lift! I think they are moving the prisoners!"

It would have been foolhardy to use the tube to pursue whoever was down there, so I had Klutch start making holes. The floor below us had two more Prule soldiers standing at the lifts. We sent their scattered remains into the tube, and Klutch moved away from the lifts.

"They know we are coming, Commander. We need an access point that can't be easily ambushed!"

We moved back to the end of the hallway, and Klutch blasted a door open with his shotgun. The room was a mess and showed evidence of recent occupation. He made a hole, and I jumped with Tria. We landed in a matching room, but it had two mutilated Chaalt bodies dead on the floor. It looked like they had made an attempt to barricade themselves in, but the futile move cost them their lives. The Operative was the last into the room and quickly peeked out the shattered doorway.

"There is a large number of Prule guarding the lift tubes!"

I was going to shake a grenade at her to show my intentions, but Sael had two out and looked at me for acknowledgment. I made eye contact with Klutch and Tria and pointed at Sael. They nodded, and I made a pitching motion at Sael. She threw the grenades down the corridor. The blasts came simultaneously, and I felt the concussion in the hallway on my armor. We charged out into the hallway, opening fire on anything that moved. We got an unexpected surprise as the entire end of the building blew up in our faces. The shockwave and flying debris scythed us down and sent us flying back in the direction we had come from. Some of the upper floor collapsed onto us. I called out to my team and got quick replies. Other than getting the shit knocked out of us, we were unharmed. Sael was pinned under heavy floor supports that we had to move to free her. Her scathing review of the incident was a wake-up call: things could have turned out much different.

"I saw the last members of Gredda's strike team just before the blast. The fools are scared and set off their trap too soon. They should have waited until we were in the transfer tunnel before detonating the explosives. Your portal device is still an unknown factor, and they cannot come to a consensus on how we are able to appear in such close proximity to their forces. They are starting to believe the stories."

"Sael, what the hell are you talking about? If they hadn't screwed up, we would be buried or worse right now!"

"Nathan, I have noted you are becoming adept at constraining the vile creature inside of you, but your aura broadcasts its presents for all to fear. You emanate the deadliest of intentions, and the blackness of your aura makes my skin crawl in repulsion. Tria and your followers seem immune to your horror. All else who feel its presence are smothered by fear and uncertainty."

There was no doubt my good guy Earth boy image just took a ding. I didn't know what to say, and decided I would let people think whatever the hell they wanted to.

"Klutch, get us outside of this mess and see if we can still access the tunnel to the labs!"

The Troop Master turned to the nearest door and pulled his shotgun. He gave it a blast of explosive buckshot, turning the door to scrap. We followed him in as he went to the exterior wall and ported us a hole. We jumped through and ran around the edges of the collapsed building until we came to another structure. This had to be the ground floor of the weapons labs. Klutch started working the ground, using his favorite expletives to keep us abreast of his progress. It didn't sound promising because the cursing was turning into compound words. Tria and I were weapons out and watching his back. Sael decided to work her way back into the debris field and see what she could find on her own. I would have discouraged her from doing that, but I didn't like sitting out here in the open any more than she did. This was one of the times it paid off to remain silent. The Operative came running from the wreckage.

"Nathan! I think I have found an access point!" she called to us.

We followed her back into the rubble, and she stopped at a spot that was depressed from a cave-in below the location. Just in front of the depression was about six feet of level ground.

Sael pointed at the spot. "Try here, Troop Master."

Klutch leaned forward and activated the machine. We had a good, usable hole. Klutch gave the Operative a nod, and we stacked to jump. If Sael was correct, I was hoping my deadly intentions preceded me and would possibly scare off anyone waiting to ambush us. I was taking no chances and had my beam weapon up and ready when Tria and I went through. The fall was long enough I had time to hit my boosters before I made contact with the floor. It was pitch black, and my no-light sensors kicked in to give me a look at our surroundings. Sael and Klutch touched down, and he killed the portal. We were on the other side of the cave-in. At our backs was about a hundred yards of tunnel that stopped in front of a large, heavily reinforced door. We moved cautiously toward it and stopped to get a closer look. The door was marked with a lot of warnings saying to stay the hell away. As with most things posted in this manner, it only made you want to be on the other side of the door that much more.

14

I pointed to the side of the door, and Klutch made an attempt that was a no-go. We tried the other side with the same result. It was solid to each side of the door, which probably meant that there was more tunnel to deal with once we gained access. We were left with no other choice but to go up the middle. My butt kinda puckered, because I was thinking that it was going to get messy when we did. They wouldn't have put this big ass door here without making sure they could secure it. The beast was goading me and wanted to take action. Waiting was not something I was known for anyway, so I made the decision to use a can opener instead of a corkscrew. I waved my team back down the tunnel. They didn't have to guess what was going to happen, and we all went prone just in front of the collapsed tunnel. Tria and I were to one side, and Klutch and the Operative the other.

"Single beam shot on three! One. Two. Three!"

The tunnel flared into brilliance as the door blew inward in an explosive blast. We boosted from the floor with our gravity drives and flew into the smoke-filled tunnel. My sensors showed wreckage and bodies scattered in all directions. There were three Prule Hunters attempting to right themselves. We cut them down with multiple beam shots that obliterated the check point they were guarding and started a huge fire. The remains of several Prule soldiers were thrashing about on the deeply gouged tunnel floor. Klutch and Sael put an end to their tribulations. I noticed Tria bent over, looking at what may have been a Chaalt soldier. I went to her side, and she cleared the image from her helmet. The hurt in her eyes was evident.

"These are the remains of Gredda's strike team. I will never understand why they have chosen this path. Their auras are so diminished, they have no spirit to renew. They are lost forever for the crimes they have committed against their own people."

I wanted to say they got what they deserved but held the comment in check. I had no idea what would make these soldiers turn their backs on everything they once cherished. I felt it had to be something the Hivemind had done to them; there could be no other reasonable explanation. The time they spent on the Prule salvage ship must have somehow affected them. It no longer mattered because they would never be able to tell us.

"Incoming hostiles!" Klutch shouted.

My helmet sensors pierced the smoke-filled tunnel and revealed a mass of bio machines boiling out of a side corridor. They quickly filled the tunnel from wall to wall.

Most of the targets defied description, and I realized that most were only partially able to move. They were being pushed along by the ranks behind them. The largest of the targets were two Hunters, and it was obvious they were an assembly of scraps. They were pulling themselves along on a single appendage and pushing the others along in front of them with their power whips. I could hear the Oolaran soldier inside of me, barking out orders of death and destruction. I gritted my teeth and took a knee, spinning up my minigun. I sent a nonstop stream of explosive shells into the wall of hostiles. Tria and Klutch joined in, and my sensors became overwhelmed by the flying machine parts and gore exploding inside of the tunnel. When the minigun ran dry, I sent all two hundred rounds of antipersonnel from my launcher tube into the mass of shattered machinery.

I felt several sharp raps on my shoulder and realized Klutch was calling to me. "Commander! Cease fire! There are no more targets!"

I slowly lowered my arm and looked up at the Troop Master, then at Tria. They pulled me to my feet, and I turned to find the Operative. She was standing with her back against the tunnel wall, staring back at me in silence. I couldn't think of anything useful to say that would make everyone believe I was in control, so I did what all soldiers do: carried on.

"Klutch, take point. Let's not give them any time to regroup!"

The debris was so thick on the tunnel floor that Klutch boosted above it and we made our way to the corridor that the enemy wave had come out of. We set down in the knee-deep carnage, and Klutch poked his shotgun low around the corner. Using his weapon sight in his HUD, he took a good look at what awaited us. It was not encouraging when he started cursing.

"Commander, there is a lift at the end of the corridor, and the Hivemind is herding several Chaalt into it!"

Damn! I leaned my head around the corner and saw the Hivemind push its way into the lift loaded with Chaalt. They had to be the council members we were here to rescue, and the machine was not going to let that happen. The bio machine saw me looking and raised some kind of weapon. I jerked back around the corner, pulling Klutch with me as a bright flash of energy impacted the corner above our heads. The energy blast knocked us sprawling on the gore-covered floor. We got back to our feet and charged around the corner in time to see the lift disappear up the tube. I had no idea what the Hivemind was planning to do, but we had it on the run. Taking the council members meant it was down to its last bargaining chips. They would be the Prule's only shield against our retribution.

"Nathan! As far as I know, there is only one exit to this building other than the tunnel behind us, and it opens to the exterior shuttle pad," Sael commed us.

Her heads-up gave me a feeling of dread. Things were about to come to a reckoning sooner than later.

If that was the case, I was hoping the Hivemind would make the mistake of going out onto the shuttle pad. I knew for a fact Justice would put an end to the bio machines' plans no matter what they were. We ran to the lift tube, and I gritted my teeth in frustration. The lift had stopped one floor below the shuttle pad. We would be forced into another confrontation that could spell doom for the Chaalt council.

I pointed back down the corridor. "Klutch, pick us a spot and make a hole. We need to get up to the fourth floor and find out what the bio machine is planning to do!"

Klutch took off running, and stopped after about a hundred yards. He leaned back and activated the portal device and got a good hole.

"Don't stop until we are on the fourth floor, Troop Master!"

We boosted up through the hole two at a time, and Klutch closed one side and activated another. We didn't bother to stop and were on the same level as the lift in less than three minutes. This floor was unlike the others because there was no open hallway leading to the lift. It looked like we were inside of a sizable storage area. I could only guess, but it may have been the supply depot for the lab areas. Klutch ran to a large doorway at the end of the room. We quickly followed and stacked to the side that had a large button that said "open" above it. I tapped Klutch on the shoulder, and he hit the button. The door opened with a slight hiss, and we could see the lift across from us. It was open and empty. A voice boomed down the corridor in the Chaalt language.

"The failure of one faction's ambitions of power only slightly diminishes my bargaining position. I know there are others who place great value in the biological vermin I hold here with me. They will be dissected a piece at a time if you do not yield to my demands!"

Well, there it was. The place I knew at some point I would be but thought I could come up with a plan to avoid it. The big problem was I had no idea how to get the council out of this alive. I would be damned if I let the Hivemind leave this place. I moved to the corner of the corridor and used my shotgun as Klutch did. I saw the Hivemind backed into the corner of a large common area with fourteen of the Chaalt council members, four being held by their appendages. I sent the video feed to my teammates.

"Klutch! Get outside of that wall and have Justice bring the Legacy in as close as possible. If I can distract the Hivemind, I want you to make a hole and pull as many out as you can. Wait for my call and do whatever it takes to try to save them. Sael, back him up as best you can. We may only have one chance at making this work!"

The Operative and Klutch ran to the exterior wall and ported out. Tria stepped in close to me. And I put my arm around her. The determination in her eyes wordlessly told me what I already knew. This would stop here and now.

"Nathan, we may be forced to sacrifice some to save the rest," she said. "I can think of no scenario where they will all see another star rise."

I was going to lie and tell her she was wrong but was interrupted by a blood-chilling scream.

"I have come to the conclusion that biological infestations are not capable of clear and precise thought," the voice boomed out again. "Past experience has shown me your respect for your superiors is only reinforced by displays of power. Since you obviously lack the thought processes necessary to communicate or bargain with me, I will demonstrate my resolve."

Another bloodcurdling scream forced my hand, and I stepped around the corner and into the open. I stood staring at the Hivemind. The bio machine had taken the parts from Prule Hunters and manufactured legs and arms for itself. What was once jokingly similar to an oversized light bulb was now a horrific abomination. Revealing myself did have the effect of stopping the Hivemind from doing whatever it was going to do to the elderly Chaalt female it was holding in its spiked hand.

"You! I should have foreseen it would be the minions of the ancient enemy!"

The beast in me stifled the indecision fogging my senses. I felt its rage building. My breath became heavy and deep as I reined in my murderous intentions. I had to try something, anything, before I unleashed an attack that would undoubtedly kill everyone in the room. My mind was working enough to remember my last encounter with the Prule Hivemind. I had disguised my voice to ensure nothing would point to humans or the planet of my birth.

"You wanted to bargain, so I will bargain with you," I said in the Scrun dialect. "Set the prisoners free, and I will allow you to leave this place."

"You insignificant piece of effluent, do you think I would err and make such a flawed decision? Here is an error you should have considered before spouting your mindless nonsense."

The bio machine lifted the Chaalt it was holding and held her out toward me. The end of its power whip extruded a glowing rod. It whipped it downward and, with a hiss of burning flesh, sheared two of the arms from the council member. The screams of agony had me raise my beam weapon and point it at the Prule. Tria ran to my side, pulling my arm down.

"No, Nathan! There has to be another way!" she yelled over my comms.

The whip came around again and sheared off the Chaalt's legs. The Hivemind tossed her aside and raised another.

"Here is a bargain even a parasite like you should understand. The two of you will shed your armor and stand before your god and master! Then, I will release the biological waste you have come here to save!"

Tria knew the Prule had just sealed the fate on itself and the remaining members of the council. She saw the blackness that surrounded me and felt the rage of the monster coming forward. There was only one option she could think of that would bring me back from the brink and save the council members. She did the incomprehensible. She called Klutch and Sael and told them to port in on the count of three. She then popped the seals on her armor and stepped out.

"Here is the only option that will spare your existence!" Tria called to the Hivemind. "I will stand in the place of my people!"

The world around me froze. The words from her mouth were like swords shearing away the darkness blinding me. The reality of what was going to happen swept the Oolaran soldier aside with a tidal wave of fear. Tria was going to sacrifice herself for the council.

"Tria! No!" I cried.

I tried to move in her direction, but the Prule Hivemind saw the truth in Tria's words. It dropped the council members and charged across the room. If I opened fire, she would die by my hand. A portal appeared on the back wall, and the Operative and Klutch ran through. They did not hesitate and started pushing and shoving the Chaalt council through the opening. In a handful of seconds, they were all out, and my team took up firing positions. The Hivemind snatched Tria up from the floor and held her as a shield. It turned to see that the Chaalt council was gone and it was now surrounded by the beings responsible for its capture. The piercing note of its rage and indignation could be felt as vibrations on our armor. The bio machine shook Tria like a rag doll, then pulled her across the front of its torso.

She called to me in anguish, "Nathan! Do what must be done!"

The beast was blinding me with hate. I raised my beam weapon, but something inside of me snapped and I let it fall to my side. All of these events were my fault because I failed to listen to the psychopathic killer imprinted into my brain. I should have never let the Hivemind leave the lifeboat alive. Nothing I could do now would change the past. The final choices that led me to this crossroads were mine to make, and I once again let compromise be the deciding factor.

The Hivemind wasted no time trying to capitalize on its new bargaining position. "Throw your weapons down, or I will disassemble this soldier a piece at a time."

Klutch and the Operative looked to me for guidance. The hesitation cost Tria a lower arm as the bio machine flicked its power whip's cutting tool down her side. She gasped out in pain. In a move that surprised me, Sael threw down her weapon and stepped back. Klutch grudgingly did the same. The blackness surrounding me blotted out all but the Hivemind, and I raised my beam weapon and pointed it at the loathsome machine. The machine pushed Tria out in front of itself.

"I sense you value this soldier more than the prisoners I once held! Abandon your armor and surrender yourself to me, and I will spare the female's life!"

The howling rage of the monster inside of me was deafening. My conflict with the beast, brought another scream of pain from Tria, as the machine sheared away her other lower arm. It held the cutting tool next to her legs.

"Step from your armor now! My patience is at an end!"

The reality of what just happened was like a sledgehammer blow, and I was suddenly free of the Oolaran soldier conflicting my mind. I popped the seals on my armor and stepped down to the floor. The Prule threw Tria at Klutch and the Operative's feet and quickly snatched me up from the floor by my neck.

I spit out what I thought would be my final order. "Get Tria out of here now!"

Klutch opened a portal and pulled Tria inside with Sael backing in behind them with both her pistols drawn. The portal disappeared, and I resigned my fate to the will of my maker. This was never how I envisioned my end to come. Now that it was at hand, I tried to find solace in the fact that I did make a small difference in the lives of others who had no future until I intervened. The bio machine whipped me around, tightening its grip, and my vision started whiting out.

"Order the intelligence of your ship to transport us aboard now, or I will prune your appendages a fragment at a time!"

For reasons unknown, I thought the bio machine's order was funny, and I laughed out loud. The only response that came to my mind was an epithet. "See you in hell, you piece of shit!"

The Prule obviously do not possess a sense of humor. It slammed me into a wall for my lack of capitulation. The explosion of pain was a tidal wave blotting out my world. As blackness enveloped me, I saw a shimmering circle appear behind the Hivemind, and then my world blanked out.

15

When I was young, I had a lot of things to be thankful for according to my grandparents, and they were right. Out of curiosity one day, I asked Granddad what he was the most thankful for. He smiled at me and said waking up another day knowing you are with the people you love. At the time, I accepted the response as any inquisitive child would have. I now realize what an understatement his answer was.

"Commander, I have stabilized your condition and need you to speak with Tria," Justice's voice said. "She is refusing surgery necessary to remove the sheared bone fragments from her wounds. We must assure her that you are well and in command. I have introduced nanites and stimulants into your system that should allow you temporary mobility. I recommend we convince Tria to undergo surgery immediately before she suffers further neurological and physical damage."

I could not see out of one eye and didn't know why. My other eye felt like someone had stepped on it, but it had enough vision I could see Klutch and Sael Nalen standing at the edge of my med pod.

My voice came out in a hoarse whisper. "Get me out of this thing!"

They tried their best to gently stand me up. Even with the work Justice had done to me, I could tell I was in piss poor condition. Whatever he was using for pain blockers must have been at a dose level to allow me to speak without slobbering, because I hurt everywhere. It was an effort not to groan out with each step I took. I could feel Klutch holding me up from behind. His grip felt like knives stabbing into me. Out of my good eye, I could see Tria in an open med pod. She was staring at me. I could see the sheared off bones protruding from her sides and tried my best to keep a neutral expression on my face. It would be one of the most difficult things I had ever done.

"I took a little damage, but Justice says I will be fine," I reassured her. "Unless you allow Justice to repair your wounds, I will also refuse further medical treatment until you come to your senses."

She tried to hold an arm up to me but did not have the strength. I did not know how much blood she had lost, but it had to be substantial. She was in shock, and I could see tears running down her cheeks. I put my hands on the edge of her pod; the effort was rewarded with pain. I felt Klutch grab the back of my uniform and keep me from falling face-first onto her. I kissed her as gently as possible.

"I will be here when you awake."

Her eyes clouded over and her head lolled to the side. Klutch pulled me away, and Justice's extruded arms urgently went to work. The med bay started making some unusual gyrations, and the next thing I knew, Sael Nalen was in my face. She turned her head and called to Klutch.

"He is back with us again!"

For lack of anything better to say, I told her she needed a mint. The frown my comment elicited turned to a small smile.

"Primate!"

"What happened to the Hivemind?"

"Justice took it upon himself to have Klutch activate a portal, and he sent a nanite missile through with the tow beam," Sael said. "It was an admirable shot and struck the Hivemind dead center. When the missile released its payload, the bio machine lost all interest in using you as a hammer. The Troop Master collected a sample of the Hivemind before it was completely consumed. He is holding the containment vessel in isolation and refuses to give me access. I have informed him that the biomass that sustains the Prule collective of entities must be hydrated with biological fluids or the sample will cease to function. On his orders, Xul has sealed the brig, so I am unable to determine the status of the sample."

"What about the council members?"

"Other than being scared for their lives and deprived of food for several days, they are as good as can be expected. They have been supplied with rations and water. Justice has them locked in the crew quarters. They believe the internment is for their own protection and they are compliant for now."

"Is there someone on the outside we can trust to tell your people what has really transpired?"

"My most trusted commanders already know, and the captain of the Fury should be covertly spreading the word to all the right people. Unfortunately, the traitors have more time to prepare for the coup than we have to stop it. All the major communication hubs are firmly in their control, but that will change with time."

I briefly closed my good eye and took a deep breath. While it hurt to do, it reminded me I was still here and the Hivemind was not. Or was it?

"Klutch! Why do we need any part of the Prule Hivemind?"

Sael stepped aside and the Tibor's face filled what little vision I had.

"Commander, it was a decision that Justice made. The only reason I complied was because I told him if I collected the sample it would be in my control, and I alone would decide its fate until you were back in command. He has agreed, and I have a small sample in a containment vessel designed by Justice and the Overseer."

"I would like a few minutes to speak with Justice. The two of you have done an amazing job. The mission would have failed without you. Take some time to rest, and I will be expecting recommendations on our next mission goals."

They both turned and left the med bay. When the hatch closed, my anger at Justice's decision to get a Prule sample burned like a live coal inside of me.

"Justice! I want that Prule shit off this ship now!"

The AI knew when to use tact and went to work on deflecting my anger as much as possible. He did choose the one subject that would stop my oath-laden tirade.

"Commander, Tria is now stabilized and will make a full recovery. While it is not possible to restore her severed limbs, I ensured that there would not be truncated appendages to inhibit her or the necessity to create prostheses she must adapt to."

I was angry, dizzy, and felt like a mudhole that had been stomped dry by Klutch. The path Justice chose to deflect my anger was becoming more perplexing than his decision to keep a Prule sample.

"What the hell are you talking about?"

"Commander, Tria is a veteran of many conflicts. She has witnessed a significant number of battlefield amputations. She is also well-aware of how advanced mechanized prosthesis can be. I assured her I could return full mobility to her severed limbs with military-grade prostheses. She has informed me of her wishes, and they will not include the use of robotics."

My head now felt like a drum that someone was playing a war beat on. I could not think of a reasonable explanation for the cryptic doublespeak I was getting from Justice. My anger was once again on the rise, and I was going to need some straightforward answers before I popped my cork! The AI was very perceptive and knew when to lay all the cards on the table.

"Tria told me to make her look more like a human!"

"What?" I shouted.

"Rather than rely on the use of artificial appendages, Tria has decided to adapt to using only two. She instructed me to remove the severed arms in their entirety. The procedure was without complications, and she will be back to limited duty within the week."

I was thinking the galaxy had gone mad. Yes, Earth had a very large percentage of truly wonderful people, but we also had our share of some who were bent in all the wrong ways and nothing would change them. The infatuation of other races to be more like humans had me dumbfounded. They chose to see only what they perceived as a way to change everyone for the better. While it was inspiring to think that contact with humans would give others hope, they really needed to take a tour of my planet so they could see the flip side of the coin. Humans as a people had come a long way from our savage roots, but we still had a long way to go.

"Commander, I am going to sedate you now and repair your battle damage."

I was so preoccupied with my thoughts I couldn't muster a comment to Justice's statement. The last thing I remembered thinking before I blacked out was, I did not have the right to question Tria's motives. She was the master of her future and destiny. I would never cross that line even if given the choice. She had made her decision, and I couldn't fathom why it should bother me. Perhaps something deep down inside of me liked the fact her extra arms gave her a marked advantage when she was physically dominating me.

I awoke to a less than palatable taste in my mouth and Justice talking to me.

"Commander, you will still have discomfort due to the large number of blunt force dislocations inflicted on your skeletal system. All corrective alignments were successful, as well as the repair to the cartilage damage associated with them. You will make a full recovery. The effects of the concussion you received are now minimal. The swelling to the right side of your cranium has receded, and your sight will return to normal shortly. The bruising and tissue discoloration will ebb in the coming days, and I see no reason you cannot return to noncombat duty."

I slowly processed everything Justice told me. The distinct notion I should be mad at the AI for some reason floated back and forth through my thoughts like a flashing billboard. Justice picked up on my contemplation and pushed on to a topic that would guarantee a change of subject.

"I have temporarily brought Tria out of her recuperative coma so she might speak with you."

My med pod popped open, and my thought processes all shifted to a single subject. I slid my feet to the floor and stood, trying to assemble coherent thoughts that might somehow belay my concerns for Tria. She was keenly attuned to my sensibilities, and I did not wish to add additional stress to her healing cycle. The stunt she pulled to keep me from annihilating the Hivemind along with the council brought a sudden flare of anger that quickly passed. She knew exactly what it would take to clear away the hate-blackened veil the beast had been blinding me with. It was stupidity to think Tria would not have sacrificed her life for her people's future. She did what she had to, and we paid a relatively small price for a victory that would ultimately benefit all races. I leaned over the side of her med pod, and she looked up at me with a small frown.

"You look like scat."

The comment got its intended response. I smiled.

"I have had better days."

"I was not trying to throw away my life needlessly. I did what I had to because I foresaw what it would take to give us all a better future," Tria said. "While it may have seemed like madness at the time, the outcome has proven my choices correct."

There was no arguing the truth of what she was telling me; she was right.

"I know. It just takes a backward-thinking human a little longer to process the facts."

It was her turn to smile. I could feel the warmth of it caressing my spirit.

"I wanted to tell you that it was my idea to make sure a small sample of the Hivemind would be preserved," she said. "I know there is a great deal of valuable information that can be extracted from the bio machine's remains.

Information that I am confident we can use in our war against the Prule. I wanted you to know this before you determined that Justice made the decision on his own. While Justice did agree with my assumptions, he also strongly stated that we would be doing so in conflict with your standing orders. I believe it is the reason Justice turned over responsibility of the sample to Klutch. We already know what the Troop Master thinks of the Prule. There is a good chance that the entities residing inside of the sample may have already perished."

There it was! The one thing I wanted to ream Justice a new ass over. Now my justification for doing it was baseless. Knowing Klutch, Tria was right; the Troop Master would never waste a second of his time trying to maintain an environment healthy enough to keep the sample habitable. I leaned down and gently kissed her.

"I am going to need you as a sounding board for our next plan of action. Sael may have some good input, but it will be your recommendations I will place most of my faith in. I want you to rest and get healed as fast as possible."

She gave me another golden smile as Justice closed her med pod. Her eyes blinked several times and then closed.

"Okay, Justice, you are off the hook. I was ready to have a meltdown, and now it is pointless. Even though you were overruled, you did make an attempt to enforce my orders. I will let the Troop Master know he doesn't have to pretend he is caring for the containment vessel anymore."

"Commander, Klutch is in fact maintaining the biomass to minimal inhabitability parameters. His methods have caused several hundred Prule entities to perish, but there are more than six hundred that still cling to their awareness."

I was genuinely shocked at that piece of information. I would have never guessed the Troop Master would knowingly help the Prule survive. Now I had to wonder what exactly the Troop Master was doing. Unless he had some input from Justice, the Prule were as good as dead.

"So, you are actively helping him?"

"No, Commander. Klutch has received no aid from me, nor has he made an inquiry on how to maintain the biomass."

"You're kidding me, right?"

"While I am familiar with the concept of 'kidding,' I can assure you, I am not."

"That only leaves Xul, and I know he would only help if Klutch asked him to. Klutch would never do that, so what is he doing to keep them alive?"

"The Troop Master is urinating on the Prule biomass daily."

It hurt to laugh, so I hurt for close to four minutes. Klutch didn't give a damn whether the Prule survived; he just liked pissing on them. The comedy in what the Tibor was doing was therapeutic. Yes, I was beaten, battered, and bruised, but now felt right as rain. I made my way to the command deck, where I found everyone but Tria. It was hard not to smile at Klutch as I walked by him. I slapped him on the shoulder and made it a point to tell him to carry on. He scratched his bullet head and looked puzzled, but it changed to his usual big toothy smile. Sael sat frowning and finally approached me as I sat in my command chair.

"I would like your permission to enter the brig___"

"No, there will be no scenario where anyone but the Troop Master or Justice will have access to the containment vessel," I said. "Do not waste your breath debating the matter. I have made my final decision, and nothing will change my determination. We have more pressing matters, so I suggest you pick another topic."

The frustration on the Operative's face was something I had grown used to seeing. She gathered her dignity and moved on.

"Is it still your intention to terminate this asteroid?"

"Yes, even with the level of weaponized nanites we released into the complex, the only way to be sure of complete sterilization is to reduce this place to atoms. Justice, do you have a briefing for us?"

"Yes, Commander. The antimatter device is now assembled. It will require an excursion to the asteroid's power supply so it can be placed against the generator's containment field. Klutch and Xul have already volunteered for the mission and have been instructed on proper placement. I will move the Legacy to the location of the lift shafts on your order. Before we can detonate the device, we must warn off the three Chaalt battle fleets that have encircled this station. I believe it will take a warning order from the Operative to gain the level of credibility that would ensure compliance."

231

Sael nodded.

"I will be the one to set the destruct charge," Sael said. "I want it to be known it was me and not another race responsible for destroying more than a trillion credits' worth of research station."

I could tell Xul was good with that, and I had no problem with it either. The trick now would be the timing of our escape. We had to shut down the shield dome in order for Sael to send any warnings of the base's destruction. Once the dome was down, we needed to get the hell out of Dodge. I was pretty sure when Justice was out joyriding around the Chaalt home worlds, he managed to ruffle a lot of feathers. Hanging around to figure out if we were still on a first-name basis might not be in our best interest at the moment. Apparently, the Operative was brainstorming the very same subjects.

"Nathan, I will put the warning order on a comms buoy and have Justice launch it before we drop the shield. It set to broadcast the message on a continuous loop with a countdown timer of eight minutes? If the fools cannot jump clear by then, they deserve whatever happens to them. I also have a recommendation as to what I think should happen next. I hope that you will consider it carefully before committing to another course of action."

As far as I was concerned, everything she was saying made sense and she was batting a thousand.

"Okay, Sael, I am with you so far. Let's hear it."

"I have coordinates that will give Justice the location of the Fury. I propose that we jump to that location, and I will take the council with me. We will then decide how best to repatriate the traitors and reestablish the rightful ruling party. Your presence is no longer needed for now, as many would see it as another unnecessary distraction to what many will decide is a power struggle of the ruling parties. It could also be misconstrued as proof the traitors were right about my ambitions of leadership and that you are backing me."

I nodded that I understood.

"Nathan, I want you to know the Chaalt people owe you a tremendous amount of gratitude. I would like to think that one day, they will know just how much they really owe you and your followers. I doubt what has taken place will ever be publicly disseminated. I can almost guarantee you it will be buried in a dark corner, and only those who were involved in this mess will ever know about it."

As far as we were concerned, the mission had a successful outcome and we were ready to move on. However, I felt there were still some unspoken issues that needed to be addressed.

"Tria put her life on the line to ensure the freedom of the council members. She was butchered for her efforts. I want you to personally tell the council that Tria's military status is retired. You can come to us and ask if she wishes to serve, but I better never hear you say she is being reinstated to active duty under anyone's command."

"The council members saw what the Prule did to Tria. None will deny your request."

"It was not a request."

Sael looked me in the eye and nodded. "I will make sure they understand."

"Justice, what is the status of your scans?"

"I have found no life forms or active Prule machine emissions in the complex. The only location that harbors the possibility for survivors is the power generator control room. That location is heavily shielded, and the reactor emanations further degrade my scan capabilities of that area."

"Move the Legacy to the power plant lift shafts and make the Operative and Klutch an entry point."

"Moving, Commander."

"Klutch, gear up and meet the Operative in the hangar bay. I want you to port in and bring out any survivors while Sael sets the antimatter charge. I am going to have Justice send the termination codes to the weaponized nanites. He has warned me the acid discharge will spark fires throughout the complex. A large number of the fire suppression systems in the complex were infected by the Prule and will no longer be active. You should expect heavy smoke and flame to fill the shield dome in a short period of time. We will be standing by with the tow beam to collect you and any survivors. Once you are aboard, we are going to destroy the shield control building and jump to the coordinates of the Fury. Any questions?"

Klutch looked sideways at the Operative. She shook her head. "We are good to go, Commander!" he answered.

Klutch and Sael headed to the hangar, and I decided I would visit Tria in the med bay to give her a briefing. Justice alerted me he was going to use the rail cannons to uncover the lifts shafts. He quickly reported he had a usable access point for Klutch and Sael. As I entered the med bay, Tria's pod opened and I waited until she became aware of my presence. The look of confusion on her face slowly turned to a small smile when she reached out to touch me. I realized she may have attempted to use the other arm she no longer possessed. When I was in high school, I had a friend who lost part of an arm working on a combine. He told me he still felt his lost hand and subconsciously tried to use it. Tria would have to make the same adjustment, and I suspected she would have to undergo training that would instill two-handed fighting techniques. She was crazy dangerous with all four arms, and now she could rely only on two.

I brought her up to speed on our current activities. She insisted on being moved to my quarters. Justice had no objections, so I helped her out of the med pod and wrapped a blanket around her. She was a little woozy but could walk on her own without difficulty. As we passed through the command deck, Xul promptly stood at attention. He could not hide the look of sadness on his face.

16

Once I had Tria squared away in my quarters, I headed back to the command deck. I wanted to know when Klutch and the Operative were on their way back to the Legacy. Normally, time seemed to whisk by, but now it seemed like an eternity had passed and still no word from my team members. Several minutes more went by, and I was going to start bellyaching.

"Commander, the Operative and Klutch are now using the lifts to bring out five Chaalt engineers," Justice said, alleviating my concerns. "The charge is set, and once the strike team is aboard, we will be ready to evacuate to the location of the Fury. Past data suggests it will take the Chaalt no more than eighteen minutes to determine our DEHD core destination and dispatch military units to that location. It will remain to be seen if it is their intention to pursue us. I have preprogramed maneuvers to disrupt continued tracking of our movements. If it becomes necessary, I also have contingencies to discourage further pursuit."

I was hoping it would not come to contingencies. The Chaalt should be able to figure out on their own that we bailed them out in a big way. Of course, thinking along those lines would put that subject under the heading of "things going our way."

"Commander, I have taken our crew members and the Chaalt engineers aboard. On your orders, I will destroy the shield control building and jump clear of the Chaalt exclusion zone."

"Get us out of here, Justice!"

The view of the shield control building filled the command center. One second it was there, and then the screen whited out from a brilliant flash. The brilliance continued filling the command deck, and everything around me faded from reality. The return to normal space-time was uneventful, and it felt like a huge weight was lifted from my shoulders. Justice put the image of the asteroid up on the view dome. The Legacy had lingered long enough before we jumped to record the destruction of the base. The screen flared as the base exploded. As the flash faded away, all that was left was a rapidly expanding cloud of rock and dust. I breathed a sigh of relief, but it was a temporary feeling. The weight I had felt I was free of suddenly doubled.

"Commander, I have no contacts to report, and that would include the Fury."

Klutch and the Operative walked into the command center with what could only be described as looks of satisfaction on their faces. That was about to change. I was going to tell Justice that it should be a piece of cake to locate one of his subsystems, but now that Sael was present, I would refrain from letting that particular cat out of the bag. Since Justice didn't enlighten them, it was up to me to cast some shade on their jovial moods.

"Sael, we are not picking up the Fury in this quadrant," I said, breaking the news. "Normally I would not question your coordinates or intel, but Justice ran thorough scans of the space around us. We are alone out here, and the timer is ticking on whether or not your people will follow our DEHD core signature to this location."

The Operative stopped in her tracks and frowned at me. "The Fury will be cloaked, but you have always been able to get a location on us in the past."

I couldn't tell if Sael was stating the facts or if she was hinting that she knew Justice was stowed away on the Fury. Either way, I chose to ignore it and move on with a larger search area.

"Justice, engage our stealth systems and move farther away from our entry point. We will wait and see if the Chaalt decide to come after us and at the same time start searching deeper into the void."

"Affirmative, Commander. I would like to note that our present location is at the very edge of the updated star chart information supplied to us by the Chaalt. I will update our records as we progress with our search for the Fury."

Klutch sat at his usual station. Sael decided she was going to hang out on the command deck, but I wanted her to give the council members a briefing. They needed to be current on everything that was taking place. I also wanted a heads-up if there was something they could do to dissuade their military from pursuing us. The Fury not being at the rendezvous point had her distracted enough that Sael had the council on the back burner. Justice was monitoring their conversations but said they had little to say since their rescue. They did, however, request permission to speak with Tria when she was able.

It took the Chaalt fifteen minutes and forty-two seconds. Justice reported the transitions and verified we had sixteen battleships and five light cruisers sniffing around in all directions trying to get a lock on us. Considering how many ships were in the area when we departed Chaalt space, this was a good sign. It would have to be determined at some point who the captains of these ships served. Were they looking to pick a fight, or were they in search of the rightful council? It was time I had a word with Sael and the Chaalt council members. I made my way to the crew quarters and stepped into a discussion I guess wasn't for my ears, because it promptly stopped. After several awkward seconds, Sael turned and grabbed me by the arm. She walked around to each member and introduced me. They all seemed grateful for what we had done to rescue them, and most spoke of rewards and remunerations. They all inquired about Tria's condition, and I was happy to report she would recover just fine without going into details.

The most senior member, Chandra Maring, identified herself as such and stated that Tria would be receiving the star of heroism. It was the Chaalt version of the Medal of Honor. I politely nodded, and when she continued to list the other awards due us, I held a hand up and interrupted. I explained what was going on outside of the hull and that we needed to figure out if it was a hostile pursuit. This put the room into chaos. I had about as much of that crap as I could handle. I pulled Sael aside and told her to get the council to make a message we could put on a buoy, and we would figure out things from there.

I left without further comment and went back to the bridge. Justice cued me in on the discussion they were having prior to me entering. The council members had been ordering Sael to tell me to take them back to the Chaalt home worlds. It was their belief the Fury must have been destroyed by hostile actions. Going back into that hornet's nest not knowing who would shoot and who wouldn't did not appeal to me. The urge to space them all, including Sael, crossed my mind more than once.

With Justice's help, Sael showed up on the command deck with a message that in no uncertain terms declared the council on the Legacy the rightful rulers of the Chaalt. The message also stated that anyone disputing that fact was a traitor and would be executed for treason. I shook my head and swore under my breath. Apparently, yours truly was going to be the executioner if they didn't back down. How nice of them to discuss it with me! My dark thoughts elicited a haunting heckle from the beast. Sael must have felt my reaction and stepped back.

"Nathan, I had nothing to do with the council's statement. I find it distasteful that they would continue to hide in your shadow. I must also admit they have no others to cower behind at the present."

"Justice, we need to deliver the council's message, and I don't care how you do it."

That got the Operative's attention. Justice made a snap jump that put us right in the middle of the Chaalt ship formation. The Legacy came into contact with at least three of the ships' shields. We were bounced about by our warp bubble pushing the much larger ships aside. Justice dropped the buoy and jumped deep into the uncharted void.

"Sael, I would like to hear your thoughts on why the Fury seems to be missing. Are there alternate coordinates that we should take a look at?"

My question seemed to snap Sael out of a trance. She stared at me with a frown. "I have a few theories, and none of them are good."

"Give me the best-case scenario."

"There is no best case. There is the possibility the captain I entrusted with my command may have betrayed me. I would like to think that Captain Cirral thought we were killed on the insertion to the research center and decided to fight the coup on her own terms. I no longer believe that is the case. All of my IST comms are going unanswered. She knows I live. My comms not being acknowledged could mean the Fury was destroyed, which I doubt, or the comms are being ignored."

That bit of news made me shake my head in derision. What the hell? Had one of the most technologically advanced races suddenly all gone mad? I stared at the Operative and wondered if this new twist was some kind of elaborate plan cooked up by her to expose the fact that Justice had indeed infected the systems of the Fury. The expression on her face gave nothing away. This entire mess had me looking in all directions for the next conspiracy. The best solution I could think of was to return the rightful council to Athella.

"Justice, jump us to Alpha Base."

"Roger that, Commander. DEHD core operations will be available in eleven minutes. I would like to report that the Chaalt warships that pursued us to our jump destination have all jumped out of the area with the exception of one. It is broadcasting on several IST channels attempting to contact the Operative. Shall I allow open IST comms traffic to receive on our systems? I must caution you: it will allow the Chaalt to locate the Legacy."

Sael scowled. "You have the ability to eavesdrop on my IST or block it?"

Why Justice would choose to reveal that information after I already told him to suppress other data pissed me off. The only thing I could come up with was it could make the Operative speak the truth about her communications with her military counterparts.

"Put it through to Sael."

Her scowl turned to a face I had seen only when she was executing Gredda's troops. She then verbalized out loud her orders to whoever was on the other end of the discussion.

"Release the crew from detention but confine them to quarters until I can speak with them. The rightful ruling council will determine our next course of action. I want all military commanders of the ships that followed the illegal orders of the traitors arrested. Let them know if they refuse, they will be executed. Those who comply will be given every chance to exonerate themselves of all charges. You will be updated directly from the ruling council from this point forward, so expect orders within the hour."

Sael's oration left little to my imagination. It sounded like the coup was put down when it became known we had rescued the legitimate rulers. I just needed the details to figure out where we fit in. The scowl disappeared from her face.

"Nathan, I need you to take me back to your base and load my shuttle. We will then need to return to Athella so I can return the rulers of my people to power. Captain Cirral has indeed betrayed me and the people she once served. She jumped the Fury to Athella and placed the crew in detention. She then took on a new crew of her choosing as well as the leaders of the coup and jumped to an unknown destination. I need to brief the council on what has taken place. We need to return as soon as possible. I will see to it you and your followers are compensated for your service to my people. For now, I can only thank you for what you have done."

The end to this mess was finally in sight. If it were not for the injuries Tria had sustained, I would have felt overjoyed at the outcome. We had jumped headlong into hell. While I could not say we escaped unscathed, I thanked my maker we made it out at all. I reached out and grabbed Sael's arm.

"Just so we have an understanding that Tria's service from this point on is voluntary."

"You have my word, Nathan," Sael said. "I will make it known that she is no longer an asset to be used to obtain your compliance."

The bridge started flaring a brilliant white as my reality faded away.

"Commander, I have four hundred and twenty-two Chaalt warships in the neighboring star systems," called Justice upon return to normal space-time. "All are cloaked and appear to be monitoring the space around our planetary system. I have uploaded an intelligence brief from Alpha Base. The data shows that most of the ships took up station when it became known we were making our rescue attempt at the research station. None have made an attempt to enter our system. It would be speculation on my part, but I believe their present locations represent a defensive posture."

That information put a smile on the Operative's face.

"There are many who have not forgotten your service to my people," she said. "I will return shortly with the orders of my council. It may no longer be necessary to jump back to my home worlds."

I hoped she was right. We could all use some rest.

"Justice, what is Tria's status?" I asked.

"She is sedated but doing well considering the trauma she sustained. Her prognosis is good, and once she adjusts to the use of only two appendages, she will make a full recovery."

"How about Coonts? Is he going to fully recover from the weaponization?"

"Yes, Commander. Coonts no longer requires coma recuperation and is now undergoing light physical therapy. He should be able to return to normal duty within the week. I have downloaded our mission to his implants, and he is hoping to meet with you and the rest of the crew."

We were back to things going our way, and for a change I did not feel like it was going to bite me in the ass. I headed to the galley for a quick meal. Justice had warned me the Troop Master was already there. He was packing away rations at a rate that would entail us making another supply stop in the near future.

"What about the Prule biomass sample?" I asked Justice.

"The Troop Master has cut back on his daily ministrations to every other day. The Prule are perishing daily. The data from the containment chamber confirms the live entity count is now one hundred and sixty-two. What remains of the Hivemind's existence is begging for

245

its life. The live count will drop below one hundred in two days. It would be a good time to ransom information."

The thought of getting usable intel from the enemies of all in exchange for Klutch pissing on the piece of pus they lived off of almost made me laugh out loud. The murderous bastards were finally getting what they deserved. As I rounded the corner into the galley, I was met by Xul.

"Commander, you might want to consider coming back after the Troop Master has finished his meal. It is questionable whether or not he has ever had table manners. As of right now, I can testify that he does not."

The little Grawl turned and walked away, shaking his bulbous head. I had seen the Tibor eating enough times that I had grown immune to his rather messy habits. I would make it a point to sit on the same side of the table and out of his spew zone if he tried to strike up a conversation. Normally when he eats, he eats and has little to say. I was hoping it would be one of those occasions. I got my tray and sat two spaces down from him. He gave me a nod and kept shoveling it in. I thanked my maker for the small favor.

I had about half my meal down when Sael and the council stepped into the galley. I stood and told them to make themselves at home, which most of them did. I made it a point to tell Sael to seat them behind the Troop Master. When she saw the food splattered around his table, she nodded and instructed the council accordingly. When they were seated, I picked up my tray and joined them. They were polite and quietly ate, but the noises coming from the Troop Master finally left them staring wide-eyed. Most pushed their trays away and decided to let me know what was on their minds. Senior member Maring asked for a word in private. I got up and walked into the corridor, and they all chose to follow.

"Nathan Myers, it is our wish to return to Athella, but not on one of our ships that have encircled this star system. While we would like to think our security could not be compromised aboard one of our own vessels, the uncertainty of what has taken place brings a certain amount of doubt as to the loyalty of our commanders. There is no such uncertainty about our security aboard the Legacy. We kindly ask that you transport us to Athella, and we will depart in the Principal Investigator's shuttle. Sael Nalen will ensure our safety from that point forward."

"Justice, what is our ETA to Alpha Base?"

"I have finished my scans and have no hostile ship movement in our star system. ETA twelve minutes. I will have the Chaalt shuttle loaded within fifteen minutes of our arrival. DEHD core operations will be available in thirty-eight minutes. I have the location of the military garrison near the capital of Athella plotted as our outgoing destination. If the council has another destination in mind, please have them alert me before we depart."

I guess Justice decided to let them know he did a little mapping while he was out joyriding around the Chaalt home worlds. Council member Maring cleared her throat and stated that was their intended destination. The council members all politely excused themselves and went back to the crew quarters. Once they were gone, I decided I needed a no-shitter from Justice.

"Justice, what are you doing? You seem to be giving away sensitive information for no other reason than to rub the council's and Sael's noses in it."

"I have been carefully studying the Chaalt council members and have determined that most of their interactions with us are from the standpoint of superiority. It is my intention to let them know that what they perceive as a marked technological advantage is, in fact, not the case. I can assure you that my observations now reveal they have changed their viewpoint. They now believe more than ever that a lasting alliance with us can only improve their chances of gaining tech that will bring them parity with our present technological levels. Those were lead council member Maring's words, not mine."

I should have known the scheming AI was working angles that I would have never thought about. Justice was taking out insurance policies that would pay future dividends. I just wish I was in the loop more often but could find no reason to chastise him for his methods. He was always working to our benefit, but I needed him to occasionally tell me in what way. He knew he had made his point and moved on.

"We are making our approach to Alpha Base and will touch down in one minute."

17

Our touchdown in the hangar gave me a feeling of closure. The worst of the mission had come and gone. Justice alerted me the Grawl were all present and waiting for us to disembark. I went down to the crew quarters and told the Chaalt that it would be a small delay before we left for their home worlds. I told them the base was at their disposal and the cafeteria was available for those who were hungry. All asked to speak with Tria if possible. I told them if Justice cleared it, she would be available before we took them home. This seemed to make them all happy, and as a group we headed down the boarding ramp.

The roar of applause that came from the Grawl surprised even me. They have been known to get a little rowdy, but I had never experienced anything like the greeting they were giving us now. The Chaalt quickly moved aside and stood staring at the celebration. Standing in the front of the gathered crowd was Coonts. He had his hand held high and wanted to be the first to touch mine. The once frail looking Grawl was now a v-shaped wedge of muscle. Several of the Chaalt were pointing in disbelief at his new physique. The crew and I waded into them and made hand contact with everyone. They all inquired as to when they could see Tria. I told them Justice would give them a heads-up when she was ready. Coonts let me know that he wasn't waiting for anyone's permission and went aboard the Legacy with Graf, Jaran, and young Felix in tow. They returned shortly grim faced and angry. All I could do was nod and shake my head. Young Felix stepped close and put his hand on my shoulder.

"Commander, I will begin working on a new battle armor configuration for Tria. I should have a design specification within a day and will proof it with Justice when it is complete."

The young Zaen made me smile. He was everything that we had ever hoped for in an engineer and then some.

"I take it you have already redesigned Coonts's battle suit?"

"Yes, Commander, it is queued into the replicator behind the missile replenishment order."

I told the young engineer to carry on. I turned back around and went to check on Tria's status. When I got to my cabin, she was awake and alert. She held an arm out to me, and I could see the effort caused her pain.

"You look tired. You should rest with me."

She hit that nail right on the head: I was beat.

"We will be leaving for your home worlds as soon as we load Sael's shuttle and bring our weapon magazines back to capacity," I said, then yawned. "You are right. I do need a small nap."

I peeled off my uniform and gently crawled into bed with her. That was the last thing I would remember until Justice called to me more than two hours later. I woke with a start and frowned because Tria was no longer in my cabin.

"Commander, we are in orbit above the Chaalt home world of Athella. Tria is aboard the Principal Investigator's shuttle and is about to conclude her meeting with the council. I want you to know it was by Tria's orders you were not alerted to our departure."

I wanted to be mad but felt one hundred percent better than I did a couple of hours ago. The headache I had been experiencing since to Hivemind used me as a flyswatter was gone. I got up and put on a fresh uniform then went to the hangar to see my guests off. Tria, Sael, and Chandra Maring were standing on the boarding ramp.

"You look much better, Commander Myers," Maring said, stepping forward. "We are ready to depart, and I want you to know that you and you followers are now honorary members of the Chaalt military. The Legacy has been issued special IST transponder codes allowing you unrestricted access to the Chaalt exclusion zone. After the briefing from Tria, we now know all you have done to help the Chaalt people. The Principal Investigator has also explained in detail why it was necessary to destroy the research facility and end the Prule infection before it could spread to our home worlds. You have the endless gratitude of the Chaalt people."

Apparently, a lot had taken place while I was napping. I turned and cast an inquiring eye to both Sael and Tria. The looks they gave me said shut up and go with the flow. I hoped my briefing was as idealistic as the one the Chaalt council must have gotten. I could think of no better course of action than to step up and give Chandra Maring a good old fashion Earth hug to seal the deal.

"Please call me Nathan. All my friends do," I said, hugging her.

The look of shock ebbed from her face as she finally returned the gesture. What was surprising was how long it took for Maring to release me. When she did, she smiled as she turned and walked up the shuttle ramp.

"You scat stacking primate!" the Principal Investigator hissed under her breath as she walked by me with an incredulous look on her face. "It is forbidden to touch a council member!"

I scratched my forehead with my middle finger, and Sael's frown grew darker. I hoped she wasn't wearing a sword when she finally figured out what that meant to Earthlings. Tria promptly turned me around and not so gently nudged me in the opposite direction.

"Just because Sael calls you a primate does not mean that you should act like one."

"I am glad you are healing quickly. I have some primal urges that need to be addressed."

My comment got the desired effect, and Tria finally laughed. We turned and watched as Justice picked the Chaalt shuttle up and pushed it out of the hangar.

"Justice, I want you to fly close cover until they set down!"

"Affirmative, Commander."

The Legacy flew alongside the shuttle as it landed on the military base. We sat stationary above it until a large contingent of troops encircled the shuttle. A transport rapidly approached and then waited until the council was aboard. It then made a hasty turnaround and disappeared into an underground revetment. Justice gave them a courtesy call alerting them that we were departing Chaalt space.

We jumped back to Alpha Base an hour later. Tria and I were both fast asleep and did not wake for more than nine hours. After my morning routine, I went with Tria to the med bay. Justice inspected his surgical work and replaced her medical wraps. The scarring was evident, but other than that, the wounds were healing at an advanced rate. Justice cleared her for more intensive physical therapy. She also started training on Oolaran two-handed fighting techniques. She absorbed the imprinting like a sponge because it was what she was born to do. Tria insisted on training at least five hours a day. As her training partner, I suffered more than a few bruises as she achieved higher levels of proficiency.

It had been a week since our return, and we had taken note that no one on the base has asked anything of us.

Everyone greeted us warmly but made it a point to give us a wide berth. I knew Justice and my crew could handle the day-to-day operations, but Tria and I were both ready to get back to kicking ass and taking names. Felix made it a point to let me know Tria's new armor was ready and waiting. We waited until the cafeteria was mostly full and called everyone to attention.

"Tria and I would like to thank you for the time you have given us to heal," I said. "We are officially declaring our rehabilitation over with. I know there is a great deal we need to do, so please submit a priority list to Justice so we can get on with the business of fighting the enemies of all."

This netted us both a rousing cheer. It quickly spread throughout the base that we were ready for offensive operations. Justice would be the metering valve for our plans and gave us our first briefing.

"Commander, the Prule biomass is now at critical levels of life support for the surviving entities. The containment vessel is now down to fifty-two life signals and diminishing. With your permission, I would like to open communications between the remaining Prule and the Overseer. We still have encoded information recovered from the Prule lifeboat that we have been unable to decipher. We also know the Prule entities that still survive are the oldest and most senior inhabitants of the Hivemind. The rest have sacrificed themselves so that the few that remain may live a little longer. Now would be a good time to ransom information necessary for us to counter any unknown Prule activity."

"Are you absolutely sure that our firewall can contain any active machine viruses?"

"Yes, Commander," Justice assured me. "The containment vessel is completely isolated and cannot be accessed without direct input from me. The Overseer is protected by multiple firewalls, and voice comms is the only allowed interaction."

"I take it the Overseer is ready to go?"

"Yes, Commander, he has taken this on as a personal crusade against the Prule. He is elated that he can be of service to his people once more."

"Okay, I give you my blessing but also want you to know that I have no reservations about letting them all die, whether we gain information or not."

"I believe that is the consensus of all, Commander. The Overseer has already determined that it will eventually be the outcome of our manipulations, regardless of the intel revealed by the bio machines."

"Proceed, Justice, and keep me updated to your findings."

Xul, Coonts, Jaran, and Graf were next to approach our table and sit down. I was still having a hard time adjusting to Coonts's new physique. It wasn't natural to see a muscle-bound Grawl. He quickly noticed Tria and I eyeballing his new build. The overcooked ham started flexing his muscles. The not-so-subtle moves made the other three Grawl turn their heads and grimace in annoyance.

"Coonts, is there something you would like to report?" Tria asked, annoyed.

The Grawl looked like he got caught with his hand in the cookie jar. He cleared his throat.

"Yes, Tria," Coonts replied. "Xul, Jaran, and Graf have made a detailed study of the data recorded on the high-energy beam weapon that the Quill have on their habitat ship. They have brought their findings to my attention. We have come to the consensus that the weapon is very similar to our own ship's mounted beam weapons. There is some speculation among the scientists, the crits may have reverse engineered the tech from Oolaran salvage. We already know they achieve the destructive power output by shunting all available power sources to the weapon and then directing the collected energy through a large focusing point. We have run simulations that show our new Oolaran power supply can surpass the demonstrated power levels of the combined generated capacity of the Quill habitat ship."

I found this tidbit of information a little hard to swallow. The sheer size of the Quill habitat ship was massive, and the amount of power sources aboard that ship had to be considerable. The looks on my scientists' and engineers' faces said they knew with absolute confidence they had their facts right.

"So, you are telling me a single Oolaran power generator can produce more energy output than an entire Quill habitat ship?"

"Yes, Commander," Coonts said. "The energy required to form the anomaly discharged by our main weapon is a magnitude greater than a discharge from the Quill weapon. It appears that the Quill systems are so inefficient that they are forced to make a collective transfer of energy to achieve such a high level of destructive force."

"Okay, I take it you have found a way for us to use that information to our advantage?"

All four of the Grawl bobbed their heads, smiling.

"Your assumption is correct, Commander. With the proper modifications to our beam accumulators and a newly designed focusing aperture, we can surpass the destructive capabilities of the Quill weapon," Coonts said. "The previous modifications that were made to our transfer switches will easily accommodate the necessary power requirements. We will need to have Justice go over our data, but it is believed we can develop a superior weapon based on our existing designs. Since our specifications will be based on the smaller diameter focus points of our current weapons, we will be able to produce a more concentrated energy beam. All of our simulations point to a forty-six percent faster recovery rate and twenty-one percent better range than the Quill weapon can achieve."

I held up my hands. "We would have to do some extensive testing before I would take a working weapon system off the Legacy."

I could tell Xul wanted to say something but was deferring to Coonts. I gave him the nod before Coonts could say anything else. "Is there something you would like to add Xul?"

"Commander, since Alpha Base makes use of the same weapon, we can use it for our testing. We have already calculated and formulated the design specifications. Felix has agreed to allot the replicator time required. The work will not begin until we have fabricated all of the necessary components. If we dedicate seventy percent of the scientific and engineering staff to the project, the base's defensive weapon will be down no more than sixteen hours for the retrofit."

I had to hand it to the Grawl: it sounded like they had all the bases covered. The Earth boy in me always did love guns with a bigger boom.

"Justice, what is the status of the Chaalt picket ships?" I asked.

"I have the scanned locations of one hundred and twenty Chaalt warships actively patrolling the systems surrounding Alpha Base. Their defensive posture has not changed."

"What is your recommendation on the weapons modifications?"

"I am still processing the information but can already conclude it is a noteworthy and viable modification. I

258

recommend we proceed. If testing yields the predicted results, I will dedicate additional processing time to altering the Legacy's weapons to conform to the new specifications."

I gave the Grawl the go-ahead on the new weapon design, and they quickly departed. Klutch was quietly sitting at the end of the table. I guess he was waiting for everyone else to clear the room before he approached.

"Klutch, is there a problem?"

"No, Commander, I guess not. Justice informed me he has made you aware that I was not knowingly caring for the Prule. I might have implied that I would take responsibility for their survival, but it was not my intention. It is my understanding that the majority died because of the manner in which I treated them. I wanted you to know that I was not honoring Tria's orders to the best of my abilities. I want to apologize."

Tria and I both stopped him before he could say another word. I looked at Tria and let her take the lead on clearing up the Tibor's indiscretion.

"Klutch, given the circumstances associated with my order to preserve the Prule sample, we will overlook what you have decided is dereliction of duty," Tria said. "While Justice may not have informed you of the outcome of your actions, you did in fact help prolong the lives of the entities."

The final part of Tria's statement netted us tears. The once pristine scent of the cafeteria's atmosphere took a turn for the worse. I needed to pacify the Troop Master before he contaminated any more of it.

"Klutch! A lot of people have to eat in here! Would you please calm yourself? The small number of Prule that managed to survive are going to die unless they give up information on their activities in our galaxy. The Overseer is interrogating them as we speak. If they do not give us what we want, I will happily join you, and we can piss on their biomass until they drown."

That seemed to mollify the Tibor. He slammed his fist down on the table. "Yes!"

With that said, he nodded to the two of us and got up to see if he could aid the engineers in any way. I was glad that his warrior's scent for the most part went with him. The next order of business was something that I thought Justice would have already given us a sitrep on. Since he was apparently avoiding the subject, I was going to have to ask.

"Justice, why have we not been able to track down the Fury?"

"They have disabled all IST and BS equipment in an attempt to elude capture by Chaalt forces. I have no means to reach out to my subsystems without an active data link. There is a small possibility we may obtain information on the Fury's whereabouts from the surviving Prule entities. I have directed the Overseer to start his inquiries about biologicals and not Prule assets. It appears this strategy may be the correct one. The Overseer has informed me he has an open dialogue with three of the

260

remaining entities. All are presently making unveiled attempts to coerce our negotiations to their advantage. Both the Overseer and I find their offers of ruling this galaxy comical."

I could find nothing comical about the Prule's continued stance of superiority. Even when confronted with the loss of reality, they still believed they had some sort of bargaining position. I hoped that their blind ambitions would one day be their ultimate demise. There were a lot of things on my plate that I could have occupied my time with, but one kept brushing the rest aside. I wanted to know exactly want intel Sael Nalen had on the whereabouts of that no-good piece of shit Eiger.

"Justice, I want a secure IST link to the Operative."

This got me a small frown from Tria. She got up and walked off without comment. I don't know if she was cued in on my thoughts or not, but this was one itch that I needed to scratch.

"Comm link is open, Commander."

"Nathan, I thought it would take a much longer time period before you would want to communicate with me again," Sael said, not mincing any words. "Have you uncovered any intel that will help us locate the Fury?"

"No, Sael, nothing yet. How are things on your end?"

"The rightful government of our people has been restored, and we are actively correcting the mistakes that have come to light. That is all I am at liberty to say. Is there another subject you would care to discuss that does not encroach on restricted security matters?"

"Yes, Sael, there is. I want all of the intel you have on Eiger. I want the location of his home world and the coordinates of his base of operations."

"That is a question I have been wondering when you would get around to asking. I will be honest with you. Back when we were pursuing Eiger, I was ordered to withhold the information from you so you could concentrate on goals that mirrored our own. I found it distasteful then and still do. I am no longer restricted by the constraints that I was previously subjected to. The success of my collaborations with you have freed me of the meaningless scat rained upon me by certain command personnel. I am finally able to make certain decisions I feel necessary to improve our alliance. This will be one of them. I will send you the data packet but caution you on the repercussions of a less than sterile operation.

"The Murlak have thirty-seven home worlds and a well-established military," she continued. "They have been to war on numerous occasions, and while their victories have been costly, they persevered in more than they have abandoned. An assassination on one of their home worlds by another race would be considered an act of war. Eiger is no doubt being shielded by the highest levels of his government. If you go into that scat hole, you need to make sure that there are no evidence or witnesses left behind that can point to you and your followers. You are currently an unknown, but your accomplishments are making waves throughout the galaxy. Don't make the mistake of thinking you will remain anonymous forever."

"Thank you, Sael. I will take everything you have told me under advisement. I give you my assurance we will call if we have information on the Fury."

"Good hunting, Nathan."

The IST channel closed, and Justice alerted me that he had received the intel transmission. A grim smile crossed my lips. I more or less knew where Tria would be and went to the makeshift training area that Justice set up for us in the back of the hangar. As was expected, she was there, working out with Klutch. They were both wearing their recon armor and using short batons as simulated weapons. The scent wafting around the back of the hangar implied Klutch was not on the winning end of their combat exercise. So much for the him helping out with the weapons retrofit. I suspected that none of the Grawl would want the Tibor within smelling distance, and all politely turned him away.

It was still too early for Tria to be on a combat mission, so I decided to withhold the Eiger intel for a later date. Another idea came to me, and it put a genuine smile on my face because it didn't involve combat. Once the weapons were upgraded and ready to be tested, I would take everyone to Haras to celebrate our successful mission at the research facility. We were in need of another supply drop, and the excursion would help me check that off my to-do list.

"Justice, call Broza and alert him to our needs. Give him your best estimate on our time frame. Let me know if we need to adjust our schedule to coordinate our departure times."

"Affirmative, Commander."

I made a quick left turn into the ready room and put on my recon armor. I picked up two batons, twirled them a couple of times, and headed out the door. A free-for-all was in the making, and it would be everyone for themselves.

More than an hour later, the three of us sat on the deck, sweating and leaning against the hull. It would be a toss-up as to who bested who. I thought at one-point Tria and I would gang up on Klutch, only to have her stab me in the butt on more than one occasion. When I tried to turn the tables on her and team up with Klutch, the ungrateful Tibor did the same.

"Commander, Broza has responded to my call and will be available for our resupply," Justice interrupted. "He will have our freighter at outpost 9765 in five days and will wait at that location until we have contacted him."

I stepped away from Tria and Klutch, who decided to go a few more rounds.

"That will be perfect. Are there any updates on the Prule?"

"No, Commander. The live entity count is now nineteen. They have yet to respond to the Overseer's inquiries on the location of any biologicals that were subjugated recently or in the past. They may very well perish without answering."

"So be it. What else have you got for me?"

"The Grawl scientists and engineers have started the retrofit process to the base's main weapon system. My observations predict they will have it ready for testing more than two hours earlier than their previous estimate. Engineer Coonts has finished the work on the power transfer cable. The Legacy is now capable of transferring the power load from the Oolaran power generator to the base's main distribution panels."

Tria looked like she could use a break. I raised my voice so she could easily hear me. "That's good news, Justice. Let me know when they are ready to test it. If you need me, I will be napping in my cabin."

That earned me a mischievous smile from Tria, and a large toothy one from Klutch.

18

A little over fourteen hours later, I awoke to Justice alerting me to the pretest countdown the Grawl had initiated. I was a little groggy and hungrier than a bear that just came out of hibernation. Tria rolled over and didn't act like she was interested in the weapons test.

In the shower, I turned up the temperature in hopes of soothing some of the aches I had somehow suffered in the past several hours. I thought I had most of the kinks worked out of my muscles when an overpowering wave of Sha'Leen left me in a heap on the shower floor. I rolled over and groaned, only to find Tria standing over me.

When we finally made it to the cafeteria, the population of the base was already present. Most just smiled and nodded, but Coonts sat at the lead table looking annoyed. I was going to issue an apology but the look Tria gave Coonts erased the sour expression from his face. Rank has its privileges. We took our seats next to Klutch, Xul, Jaran, and Graf. Coonts stood and went to the front wall.

"Justice, we are ready to proceed with the test."

Justice put a large view screen on the wall that showed the planet our moon orbited around. The thin, almost nonexistent atmosphere appeared as a light haze around the desolate planet. Coonts must have had plenty of time to think about his presentation. He waved an arm at the screen.

"Justice, please highlight the targets."

Twelve target boxes appeared on the screen above the planet at varying distances. Two looked like they were fairly close, and the rest were almost over the horizon of the planet. The rotation of the moon was taking us away from them at a decent clip.

"Commander, we have taken twelve of our comms buoys and fitted them with special telemetry arrays. The highly reflective shielding we installed over the transponders should give us a microsecond or two of data on our test shots before the targets are destroyed. We are ready to fire a calibration and focus shots at the first two targets. I will proceed on your order."

"Carry on, Coonts, you have our full attention."

"Justi—"

The screen blinked and the target box disappeared before Coonts could finish. He flinched and turned around with a scowl on his face. It earned him more than a few snickers from the crowd of scientists and engineers. He stalked to our table and sat down fuming. Justice decided he would take it from there. I rubbed my temples. Here we go again!

"Calibration shot successful. Focusing optimization shot in three, two, one."

The second box was gone with a blink of the screen.

"Beam focus successfully optimized. Ready to proceed with maximum beam output and regeneration testing."

The screen blinked in fourteen second intervals. All ten of the remaining buoys were disintegrated.

"Testing has revealed there is a slight lag in the power transfer cable. The beam recovery cycle was two percent under the simulation predictions. The Legacy will not be subjected to the same lag due to the direct feed of the generator. The range of the weapon was four percent greater than predicted and should reflect a slight increase with the direct feed. The only shortcoming, I foresee, is that it will be necessary to allow the anomaly weapon an additional twelve seconds of generation time after firing the beam weapons."

"So, is it your recommendation to install the upgrades on the Legacy as well?"

"Yes, Commander."

This got a cheer from the Grawl. Their engineering skills had produced another superior upgrade to our arsenal. Felix got up from the table and approached us.

"Commander, the manufacturing sequences are already queued into the replicator. I could have the parts necessary for the upgrades produced in under four hours."

"Okay, Felix, get started and let the Grawl know when they are ready. Before you leave, I have an announcement

I would like to make, and it concerns you as well as everyone else."

The young Zaen nodded, and I got up from my seat, raising my hands to get everyone's attention. The room quickly quieted.

"The first thing I would like to do is thank you for your hard work and dedication. You have once again proven that we can effectively challenge even the most technologically advanced adversaries. What not too long ago seemed like an impossible goal is now a reality. We are making a difference!"

This got me a rousing cheer from everyone. I held up my hands once more.

"When the weapons upgrade to the Legacy is complete, we are all going to outpost 9765 for a celebration feast. The owner of Haras has had enough time to acquire the ID chips necessary to give you all new identities. Those who wish to undergo the procedure can do so at my expense. We will stay a few days so you can actually have a chance to spend some of your wealth on items you may have been desiring. The sooner we get the Legacy updated, the sooner we will leave."

The roar of applause that got me was almost deafening. Everyone moved in mass to exit the cafeteria, leaving Tria and I sitting alone.

"We are going back to 9765 so you can visit with the Earth female?"

"I haven't got the faintest idea why a warrior of your stature would be jealous of any female," I said, raising my eyebrow. "It should be obvious to all that you have already captured the heart of the finest backward-thinking alien this galaxy has to offer."

She laughed out loud long enough to let me know that much of it was sarcasm. She put her arms around me and gave me a kiss, then slapped me on the ass.

"If we hurry, we can get the number two beam weapon pulled out of the weapons hatch and the focusing aperture disassembled."

"Lead the way, oh goddess of war. Your wish is my command."

She made an unflattering noise with her lips and shoved me toward the lift tubes. When we got up on the gravity lift to work on the number two weapon, it became obvious we would be in the way. A dozen scientists and engineers were already stripping away the cowlings from the weapon. There was no place for Tria and me that would not interfere or slow their progress. We gave up and went to the replicator building to see if we could at least ferry the parts for the retrofit. As was typical of the Grawl, once they started a project, they seldom ever rested until it was complete. From start to finish, it took twenty-nine hours to complete the upgrades for both weapons. Justice ran several systems checks and came up with only two minor fault readings that were quickly rectified. The Legacy was ready for weapons testing. I let everyone know we would do the testing sometime while traveling to 9765. No one could argue that logic, and every last scientist, engineer, and replicator operator took a bunk in the crew quarters.

"Justice, load the Eagles into the hangar and prepare to get underway."

"Roger that, Commander. Estimated time of departure is sixty-nine minutes."

I had Justice move the Prule containment vessel to the underground storage area below Alpha Base. The Overseer would continue his attempts to gain information from the remaining entities. Their numbers were down to fifteen. I held out little hope at this point of gaining anything useful from them. As we prepared to depart, I got an update alerting me that four of the fifteen Prule entities had become incomprehensible and would cease to exist within the hour. I felt no pity whatsoever and honestly hoped there was a hell so they could burn for eternity along with the rest of the scat I had sent there.

Justice's subsystems locked down the base, and we launched fifteen minutes later. We made a courtesy call to the Chaalt picket ships that the Legacy was departing. We let them know we would alert them upon our return. We DEHD core jumped to well outside of the 9765 system and used the Sig comms array to contact Tam Lin. She was happy to take my call and informed me she had useful intel to share with me. She also wanted to know if I had brought any guests. I let her know that I had brought them all. The subject quickly changed, and she said a Sig escort would meet us to take the Legacy into a secure docking area. Pasta would handle all the accommodations and see to it no one knew we were at the outpost.

Justice's subsystem aboard our freighter pinged my implants, letting me know Broza and Hylet were already at the outpost and visiting with other Zaens that did business there. I let Pasta know that he should extend a private invitation for them to join us once we were settled in. I gave him a detailed list of the supplies we needed. He relayed the reacquisition order on to the supply depot so they could start loading the freighter. Tam Lin was going to bank a considerable load of my credits on this little joyride. I hoped that some of the intel she had for me might somehow turn into an income stream to offset my expenses. I didn't have a shortage of credits; I just liked the thought of checks and balances.

Tam Lin had a private dining hall set aside for our use. She had food menus based on our races sent out to us in advance so everyone would have a good selection of food items to choose from. She was bending over backward to make sure we had everything we needed. I was now wondering what she wanted from me in return. If it was details on my latest adventures, she was probably going to be very disappointed. I had nothing to say about the Chaalt fiasco that I cared to share with anyone. It was too soon to tell, but I hoped there was no rumors floating around about what had taken place. We were notified that Tam Lin was on her way. Tria and I headed to the large cargo transfer doors that separated the dock from the depot. Tam Lin stepped out of a pressure hatch to our right and froze in place, staring at Tria. This was probably going to be awkward to say the least.

"Damn girl, I knew you had it bad for Nathan, but I don't know if I would have shed a couple of arms over him!" she exclaimed.

Yep, awkward! Tria's face darkened slightly as she processed what Tam Lin was insinuating. Rather than let this get any weirder, I stepped in front of the Earth girl and gave her a warning look.

"I will not go into details, but Tria lost her arms in combat," I said. "That is all we wish to say about it for the time being."

"Holy shit! Are you kidding me? She gets a couple of arms shot off, and you tell me you can't talk about it?"

Tria grabbed my shoulder and pushed me aside. She leaned down into Tam Lin's face. "My arms were not shot off. They were cut off! And, no, I do not wish to talk about it!"

When Pasta saw what he could only determine to be a confrontation, he hauled ass over to us, trying to figure out what the problem was. Tam Lin held up a hand, and he stopped short.

"Tria, I am sorry. I was not trying to make light of your battle injuries. It was a poor choice of words. I will not bring the matter up again."

Tam Lin's apology quickly changed Tria's expression. Looking around, I saw the looks of dread on everyone's faces change to relief. Tam Lin reached out and grabbed Tria and me by a hand.

"Come, let's go to my office and discuss business. Pasta will take good care of your people. He already has a

273

schedule set up for the new ID chips and will see to it your merchandise is delivered to your freighter."

She led us through several heavily guarded check points to the large ornate double doors that opened into her office. She sat us down in two oversized chairs facing her desk. Going over to a vault-like door, she whispered something under her breath and put her hand on the door. It opened into a huge storeroom. I could see over her shoulder as she rummaged around on one of the many shelves. She finally selected a shiny silver bottle and exited the chamber. The door closed behind her as she sat at her desk.

"I have been saving this for reasons I cannot begin to fathom. This is a fermented beverage from a race called the Erkla. They are not an advanced society. They would be somewhere around nineteen twenties Earth as far as development and tech levels go. What they are known for is their ability to make some of the best liquor this Earth girl has ever tasted. The name of this particular recipe was so hard to pronounce I decided to just call it the good stuff. You don't have to worry about it being toxic. I have had it tested to the point I am down to this last bottle. I know that Chaalt rarely drink, but if you and Nathan would oblige me, I think you will be pleasantly surprised at how good this is. It is slightly over forty percent alcohol but so smooth you will find it hard to believe."

She reached into her desk and came out with three beautifully decorated gold shot glasses. She then poured the dark bourbon-colored liquor into them. The three of us stood, and she once again apologized for her comments. She then made a toast.

"To my friends!"

We poured down the shots, and she was right. It was some pretty amazing stuff. It reminded me a little of tequila, and it would have been in the same category as some of the finest Mexico had to offer. The warmth it imparted to my belly made me consider a nap rather than shoptalk. We settled into our chairs, and she got down to business.

"The first thing I wanted to discuss with you I suspect might be a touchy subject. A large number of races have been on alert because they believe Tria's people were preparing for war. With who is only speculation, but the intel comes from a great many trustworthy sources. Those same sources say the Chaalt have terminated their agreement with the Galactic Union on patrolling the exclusion zone. They now have large fleets of warships actively patrolling, and everyone, including the Union, is forbidden to enter. If this is something you do not wish to discuss, we can move on to other topics."

Tria did the talking, and I decided to keep my mouth shut unless things started getting uncivilized.

"We should move on to other subjects."

At least Tria said it with half a smile. Tam Lin seemed to take it in stride, and after a few more seconds of uninterrupted silence by me, she moved on.

"The Sig have been developing intel on a large fleet of Scrun ships. The covert sources are reporting that more than sixty Scrun warships were seen escorting eight slave carriers in a distant quadrant. We have been trying to get a tail on the fleet but so far have been unsuccessful. When the Scrun detect any ship that could possibly get a track on them, they start jump-and-run tactics that have managed to lose any of the assets we have put on their tail."

Now that was the kind of intel I liked to hear about. The Scrun were definitely a positive income stream for us. It didn't hurt that I had grown fond of kicking the shit out of the slavers. The fact they were now escorting their slave ships meant that we had them running scared. I know we had put the hurt to their currency distribution system. Apparently, it was being felt at the top of their food chain.

"Give us all the locations on the sightings, and I will have my AI start crunching the data. We might be able to come up with something that could give us a lead on where they are coming from or going to."

"I thought you might be interested, so I had the information ready and waiting for you," Tam Lin said, sliding a data cube across her desk.

"I now have something for you to consider," I said. "How would you like to go into the mining business with me?"

Tam Lin sat back in her chair and steepled her fingers. She closed her eyes momentarily.

"It would depend on what you were mining," she answered. "It would have to be very lucrative in order for me to throw my hat back into that arena. It has been my past experience that what seemed like a sure profit ended up being the opposite."

"Containium."

That got her attention. She sat forward in her chair with just a hint of skepticism on her face.

"Are you sure? That is supposedly an extremely rare artifact not commonly found in the known galaxy. I do not know of any race that has records on mining it."

"There was a race that was actively mining it. We have no information on them and probably never will. There is a strong possibility they are now extinct."

She sat back and frowned at my statement but contemplated it without comment. She still looked skeptical.

"Do you have a sample I could test to verify your findings?"

"I didn't bring one with me, but it won't be a problem getting one."

"I need only a small fragment of ore to run the proper tests."

"I guess I could bring you some ore, but I have about six hundred tons of pure Containium that you could sample instead."

She pushed back from her desk and stood staring in open disbelief.

"Are you messing with me or what? If you have six hundred tons, you don't need a mining partner. You need a storefront to sell it and enough security to keep every pirate and crook in this galaxy from trying to steal it from you."

I sat back wondering how best to make this a profit-worthy venture that would ensure we got the better end of the stick. Tria stole the words from my mouth.

"You could sell it for us. I don't think there are many who would attempt to challenge your security forces. We do, of course, have one question that will have to be answered in advance: exactly what is the smallest percentage you would be willing to take for handling the transactions?"

We knew Tam Lin did not get to where she was in the business world by being a half-ass trader. She also knew that I had some very deep pockets. It would remain to be seen if she would get greedy on me.

"Okay, first things first," she said. "What I said about a storefront was an exaggeration. We cannot set up a storefront to sell Containium. It will have to be handled with the utmost discretion. We can only sell small quantities to a select few who can be trusted to keep their mouths shut. Letting word get out that there is a large amount of Containium going to suddenly flood the market will drive prices down. We don't want that. We do, however, want it to be known that those who have the credits may now be able to own a limited quantity of this rare commodity. Are you following me so far?"

Tria and I looked at each other and then back to Tam Lin. We gave her an affirmative nod.

"As far as a percentage goes, I can live with ten percent. I must also warn you; it will take a long time to sell that much Containium if we want the prices to stay at their current inflated levels."

The percentage Tam Lin had stated was half of what I thought it would be. It was good to know she wasn't as greedy as the rest of the galaxy was turning out to be. If I wanted to get things done on a larger scale, I would need to work this project from a different angle. Just because she didn't sound like she was interested in being a mining partner didn't mean I wasn't going to start mining. The income potential was staggering, and I wouldn't have to go out of my way to pick on the Scrun to make up for any perceived shortfalls. I thought about that for another ten seconds or so. Screw that! Unless the Scrun royal family quit running slaves, I was going to tear them a new ass every opportunity I could! I pinged Justice with my implants and told him to make a data cube with all the recorded information we had on the mining site.

"I need some very experienced structural engineers and decontamination crews," I said. "The zone of operation is off the chart radioactive, and there are no usable resources other than what is at the mining site. It is my intention to reopen the mine. In order to do that, I will need some very robust atmospheric locks and decontamination systems in place to ensure the safety of the mining crews."

"It just so happens that the Sig have the people you need to get those jobs done. They are based right here on

279

9765. We will need detailed information in order to prefab the necessary equipment, but I foresee no problems getting it done. I want you to know in advance what you are talking about will have a premium price tag attached to it."

"Will a half a ton of Containium cover it?"

That brought a smile to the Earth girl's face.

"Yes, that should more than cover our initial expenses," Tam Lin said. "I also know of a large number of ex-slaves who would love nothing better than to make a generous living working for someone who actually cared about their welfare."

Now the Earth girl had both Tria and I smiling.

"The crew quarters will need to be properly surveyed, but it looked like it was capable of housing at least sixty. When we have the numbers figured out, I want to run the mine around the clock," I said. "I propose you organize crews for a one week on, one week off work schedule. They will have to have secure transportation to and from the site. I think this will inevitably involve Sig fleet escorts as well. I want the site and the location of the system kept secret. It will take a lot of security and credits to make that happen, and it seems to me you are the person to get that done."

Tam Lin leaned back in her chair and threw her legs up on the big ornate desk.

"You actually need the Sig more than you need me," she confessed. "Your existing partnership has already endeared you to them in ways you cannot begin to understand. They worship that crazy monster inside of you. The rumors being bandied about have a significant number of Sig believing you could walk through a firefight in your underwear and come out with nothing more than a hangnail."

I rolled my eyes, thinking this was going to be more difficult than I thought. In the long run, I knew she was right. The Sig have shown me on more than one occasion they had me covered come hell or highwater. They have never attempted to stab me in the back. I couldn't say that about a certain other race claiming to be on my side. Making them a partner in the mine made perfect sense. I just needed to know what stake I should offer up to get this done. Tam Lin was already contemplating the ratios.

"I'll tell you what I think, Nathan. I will be your outlet at the ten percent I have already agreed to. I will get with Pasta, and we will present your ideas to the Sig leadership and see what their response will be. I can already tell you they will want to be partners with you, no matter the percentages. Most all of them would follow you into hell just so they could see you kick Satan's ass!"

Oh boy, was it ever getting deep, and I didn't bring my bullshit boots.

"When we see you at dinner tonight, I will bring you a data cube with all the recorded information we have on the mine. After you see the data, I hope you will reconsider my offer. I have a lot on my plate, and the mine may need dedicated management. That is something I have very little experience doing. You, on the other hand, have had years of practice."

Tam Lin threw her hands up, and I could tell she wanted to change the subject. She plopped her legs to the floor and brought up a holo screen in front of her. A Sig in a lab coat appeared on it.

"What is the status of our guests?"

"The procedures are complete and all have been successful. I will send out the registration data and get our asset to start processing it as soon as possible."

Tam Lin thanked him and closed down the screen. She turned to me.

"I will see you tonight, and bring your check book. My private transport is waiting out front, so please make use of it. You and your people should take some time and check out the outpost. There is an amazing number of products from around the galaxy."

19

The outpost was like Las Vegas. It was brightly lit and operated twenty-four hours a day. Tria and I didn't feel like wandering aimlessly around in the crowds that roamed the marketplaces, so we went back to the Legacy. The Legacy was nearly vacant, so I had Justice fill me in on the whereabouts of the crew and the Grawl.

"Commander, Coonts and Xul are in the market areas along with a number of the scientists and engineers. Klutch is at the Tibor Guild and no trouble has been reported from that location. Broza and Hylet completed loading the freighter and confirmed they will be present at dinner tonight. The data module you have requested was delivered to Tam Lin by Jaran."

"Thank you, Justice. Do you have anything else for me?"

"Yes, Commander. I believe you should remove all of the prepackaged Containium from the mine site before you send in the repair crews. The incapsulated packaging will make it a simple matter to decontaminate before removal."

"I was thinking the same thing. We should jump to the mine as soon as our business is finished here. Is there anything to report from Alpha Base?"

"No, Commander. Our new IST comms devices are functioning at optimal performance and without interference from the Chaalt systems. My tests indicate our comms are secure from Chaalt monitoring."

It seemed that all things were good and everyone was relatively safe. It was as good a time as any to start thinking about things I would like to do while I was here. Even though I could not remotely guess how far away from Earth we currently were, I felt the need to do something that could be associated with the normal behavior of a human. It quickly came to mind that it was customary to take your significant other out and buy them nice things. I was thinking some new dress attire was in order for our dinner party.

"Justice, ping Tam Lin's private comms channel and leave her a message to call me at her convenience."

"Message sent, Commander."

It didn't take but a few minutes for her to call me back, and Justice put her through.

"Is there a problem, Nathan?"

"No, not at all. I figured you could save me considerable time if you could recommend a clothing outlet where Tria and I could get some new attire for our dinner tonight?"

She laughed out loud, and I wondered if she thought I was nuts or something.

"That would be the last thing I thought I would hear coming from you. I was worried you would tell me some unknown doom was about to befall us all."

I almost thought it was funny myself, but not enough to laugh. It was my experience that there was always an overabundance of doom just waiting to be discovered.

"So, do you have a recommendation, or should we just wander the marketplace?"

"Of course, I have some recommendations," Tam Lin said. "Only two shops would be at the top of my list, but both are run by some pretty nefarious bastards. I also have a jeweler in mind, but he is worse than the first two combined!"

"What the hell is the deal with all the crooks? Are you telling me there isn't a reputable business run by honest individuals?"

"Nathan, running an enterprise on any outpost is a cutthroat business. If you are not up to the task of dealing with the huge amount of riffraff that comes through these places, you literally get your throat cut. All will smile as they attempt to separate you from your credits, but be aware they will have at least one hand on a trigger at all times."

"I will keep that in mind. Give me the names."

"The first place I would stop is Osa's wearables. He is a Gawanny trader and has cloth from all over the known galaxy. I am sure Tria is well-traveled enough she can fill you in on their background. The other is a trader called Droop. He is an Ilor, and if you haven't met one, they are easy to point out because they wear big puffy atmospheric suits."

"I am familiar with the Ilor and have no problems dealing with them. What about the jeweler?"

"Cralmo's rare minerals. He is a Kasulla and would steal the food from a baby's mouth if he couldn't pilfer it elsewhere. You cite my name when you deal with that son of a bitch. That should level the bargaining table. Tell him you want to see the Starfire he has been trying to sell me. They are iridescent stones that reflect light like a prism and weigh next to nothing. The beautifully inscribed metals they are mounted in are as impervious to wear and damage as the stones are. The word is they came from an artifact cache and are said to be a couple of thousand years old. He wants an ass load for them, but I somehow think you really don't care about the cost."

"If it is such beautiful jewelry, why haven't you bought it from him?"

"The biggest reason is that jewelry has never been my thing. The other is I don't like the way he looks at me whenever I see him. I get the distinct urge to bathe in a decontamination chamber every time our paths cross."

"That's a lovely thought!"

"On the contrary, it is anything but! I will send you the locations of the shops, and you can decide for yourself if you want to spend your credits there. I will see you tonight at dinner and would appreciate if you would do me a favor."

"Sure, no problem. What can I do for you?"

"Please don't kill anybody," she said, "unless you absolutely have too."

It was my turn to laugh, but the silence that followed pretty much said she was serious. I went to find Tria and ended up waylaid. It was obvious she was healed enough to roughhouse because it was all I could do to keep her from kicking my ass in her quest to get exactly what she wanted. It would have been a lot easier on both of us if she would have just asked nicely. When we finally left my cabin to go shopping, most of the scientists and engineers were back aboard. Apparently, word had somehow spread around the ship concerning our activities. The big smiles and looks from everyone were more than a little embarrassing. It didn't seem to bother Tria in the least, but my cheeks felt excessively warm for an extended period of time. I assumed Klutch would be the source of the gossip but was informed by Xul he was still at the Tibor Guild. It did not take much imagination to figure out what he was up to.

Tria and I made our way from the docking areas and found Tam Lin's transport. I spoke to the AI that operated the coach and gave it Osa's location. It took off at a moderate pace until it got to a trafficway. It rapidly picked up speed and blended neatly into the flow of vehicles traversing the outpost. We took a tunnel that spiraled down a couple of levels then slowed before pulling into a large parking area. The solid appearance of the transport's sidewalls turned lucent. A business with an oversized gaudy sign above the door was highlighted on the view screen. Turning to Tria, I squeezed her hand and smiled.

"Do you have any history on the Gawanny you would like to share with me? I don't want them thinking you are out walking your primate pet."

"As long as I have credits, they won't care where I walk my pet," she joked. "Just don't relieve yourself on the floor once we are inside."

Her sarcasm got me laughing, and I leaned over and kissed her.

"I will make sure no one is looking before I relieve myself," I promised. "Do you have any more nuggets of wisdom for this backward-thinking alien?"

"It has been a long time since I have had any contact with Gawanny traders. I will give you the high points from my memories, but it is not much. They are a midlevel tech race that are, for the most part, industrious and hardworking. They have three known home worlds and a military that has ambitions of power but not enough capital to achieve it. I would go through the trouble of describing their appearance, but it is just easier for you to see for yourself."

The side of the vehicle opened, and we stepped out into the moderate crowd moving up and down the walkways. Tria took my arm, and we went to the storefront door but could not find an obvious way to open it. This wasn't the welcome I expected and was going to turn away. Tria held tight and spoke to the door in Chaalt.

"We were going to Droop's for new attire but decided to take a chance and stop here first."

I smiled at Tria. I should have thought of that. With a small click, the doors parted, and we stepped inside. I was impressed. What the store lacked in storefront width, it made up for in depth. It was at least two hundred feet deep and had tall ceilings that glowed brightly. Thousands of bolts of cloth were stacked all the way to the ceiling. Down at the far end of the shop was an open area with a lone creature waving its six arms at us. It spoke to us in Chaalt.

"You do not want to waste your credits at a secondhand store! Peruse my wares and choose from the finest the galaxy has to offer," it told us. "When you have made a selection, I will tailor it to any specification you desire!"

Since I wasn't a connoisseur of clothing, I let Tria take point. I was confident she would have better taste that I did. I was a jean and T-shirt guy back on Earth. Smart cloth and battle armor were my go-to wardrobe out in the galaxy. I found a bench with several pushcarts next to it. I pulled a cart out and pushed it toward Tria, then sat on the bench for what I hoped would not be a long wait. She surprised me by coming back twenty minutes later with a bolt of a silver-gray material that was soft and silky to the touch and had a very fine pattern to it. I, of course, nodded my approval and went to finally meet the proprietor of the establishment. The alien was wearing a shiny blue cloth suit that fit his rather unique proportions perfectly. He had four eyes spread wide on his large head and a bushy beard that appeared to be made of coarse spines. He was about six feet tall with two thick legs that looked a lot like Klutch's. He had a rather large truncated rear end that he was sitting on. As we got closer, he leaned forward and rose up off it. This guy would never need to find a chair; he always had one with him.

He stopped short and stared at us for more than a minute. "You do not appear to be Chaalt?"

"Does it make any difference?" Tria shot right back in a voice that had an edge to it.

The creature quickly held up all six arms. "No! I did not mean any offense. Please step over to my scanner, and I will take the required measurements."

Tria stepped onto a grid pattern on the floor and was swept by a band of light. The Gawanny then pointed for me to do the same. When that was done, he went to a large monitor on a table and selected wardrobe designs that fitted the number of appendages we possessed. It was now time to figure out what we wanted our new duds to look like. I again let Tria take the lead. After more than an hour, she had designed some pretty snazzy getups. Hers was a pantsuit design, and both our jackets had storage for knives and handheld weapons. The overcoats were duster length so we could still conceal longer weapons if we chose to do so. Osa took Tria's selected bolt and scanned it with a small wand.

"The cost of the fabric you have chosen is forty-two thousand credits per outfit. Is this agreeable to you, or do you wish to select a less valuable material?"

This was the part I could handle without any input. "We are in agreement. Please continue."

"There is a custom manufacturing charge that will need to be added. It is twenty thousand credits. Are you agreeable to this as well?"

I nodded in agreement and told him to carry on. He loaded the bolt of material Tria had selected and fed it into a large fabricator. Twenty minutes later we had two new dress outfits. Osa insisted we try them on to make sure the fit was perfect. I looked around and didn't see a dressing room anywhere. When I turned back, Tria already had her uniform off and was looking at me like I was holding up the party. The Gawanny was staring with four large gawking eyes at the bandages wrapped around Tria where she should have had a set of arms. It didn't take him long to notice we had fighting knives in scabbards strapped to the inside of our arms and a pistol in concealed holsters at the small of our backs. He then looked over at me like I should have an explanation. He got one of my patented mind-your-own-business stink eyes. He suddenly found some setting on his replicator he needed to adjust. I ditched the uniform and slipped into the new suit. It was cool and slick to my skin, and the fit was perfect. We both stood in front of several mirrors, and I had to smile. Damn, we looked good!

I gave Osa my credit voucher. Before I let him pull it from my hand, I looked in into all four of his eyes.

"What you think you may have seen is a private matter and nobody else's affair. Your discretion is mandatory and comes with a bonus of ten thousand credits. If you agree to this, I will insist all of my associates patronize your place of business. If I find out you have done otherwise, I will tell them to spend their credits at Droop's and to spread the word that you cannot be trusted."

That did the trick, along with invoking Droop's name for a second time. The Gawanny swore on his clan and a number of other unknown things. We gathered up our uniforms and went to the transport. I told the AI to take us to Cralmo's. It took us down another level and drove for a considerable distance before stopping, this time in front of what looked like a fortress. The stuff this guy had inside was not leaving without a receipt attached to it. Looking around, I noticed there was not a lot of foot traffic in this section of the outpost. It may have had something to do with the two weapons turrets on the front wall of the establishment. It was a little off-putting but not enough to make me abandon the desire to give Tria the complete Earthman treatment.

I did not know if it had anything to do with our fancy new outfits, but the vault-like door opened as we approached. I took a good look around and noted no other pedestrians. Even the traffic on the roadway was nothing like the levels above us. While I did tell Tria about the new wardrobe, I didn't tell her I was going to buy her jewelry.

She had a small frown on her face while she scrutinized our location.

"Nathan, what is this place?"

"It is a jewelry outlet," I said. "I wanted to add a finishing touch to your new attire. It is traditional on my planet to give those we choose as our mates exotic adornments to show others how much we care."

My explanation made her laugh.

"You should know by now I really do not care what others think! I would personally rather have a new weapon."

I tried my best to hide it, but she obviously noted my disappointment, or somehow felt it.

"Perhaps some small embellishment would be appropriate."

I grabbed her by the hand and marched into the entrance. I stopped short just inside. We were boxed into a narrow hallway with a view screen on the wall and nothing more. A face appeared on the screen. I remembered Tam Lin making reference to the Kasulla as slugs, and now I knew why. The dark glistening head had two eyes on short antenna like stalks. Its four short arms were protruding from some sort of bodysuit.

"I am Cralmo, and this is my establishment," the face said. "I sell the finest ornamentations that credits can buy. May I see your credentials?"

Tria and I looked at each other, puzzled. Tam Lin didn't say anything about needing credentials to get in the place. I was on the verge of telling the slug that Tam Lin sent us, but Tria intervened before I could spit it out. She reached into her jacket and showed me one of her credit vouchers. I quickly did the same, and we held them up for Cralmo to see. A band of light flashed across them, and the slug's eyes both snapped forward. Without checking, we had no idea what the denominations totaled on the cards, but it must have impressed the Kasulla.

The walls around us rapidly rose up and disappeared into the ceiling. Around us were display cases loaded with jewelry of every description. Some of it was huge and other pieces were so tiny we had to squint to see what they were. Cralmo came forward on a gravity sled designed to hold his stubby wormlike body. The suit he was wearing covered all but his arms and head. There were several tubes attached to the suit that were connected to unknown devices on the cart. I quickly remembered the Troop Master's warning about staring and moved my eyes to the many displays surrounding us. Tria seemed more interested now that we could actually see some of wares this guy had. There were a lot of eye-catching pieces, but I wanted the best. It was a safe bet the really good stuff was not on display here. Rather than start throwing Tam Lin's name around and tying my reputation to hers, I tested the waters on my own.

"An associate of mine informed me you have a Starfire artifact for sale. I wish to see it."

I thought the slug's eyes were going to jump off their stalks.

"Who gave you that information?"

"Do you possess such an artifact or not?"

Tria was giving me the what-the-hell look and grabbed my arm. I was fairly confident she was going to turn me away and ask what I was up to. The Kasulla took it another way and though we might leave.

"Yes!" he cried. "Please come this way, and I will show you the very finest I have to offer."

Cralmo's conveyance turned around, and we went to the back of the room. Tria was giving me a small negative shake of her head, trying to stop me, but I would have none of it. Another wall lifted to the ceiling, and we were again facing another impressive vault door. The Kasulla turned back to us and two dangerous-looking security bots approached us from both sides. I felt the urge to go for my weapon but stifled it. The bots stopped on both sides of the door. I got the distinct impression it was just a display of power on the part of Cralmo, as well as a warning. Tria and I stood neutral-faced. After more uneasy moments of weird eye contact, he turned and messed around with the door for what seemed like several minutes before it opened. There were a few items in the vault, but only one that I could see was behind a power shield. It was a necklace or bracelet, depending on the size of the wearer. Tam Lin was right: the piece was stunning. It was a little large for Tria, but that would just make it hang a little lower on her chest. Looking at her new suit, I decided it would fit the low cut of her blouse perfectly. It would never hide her loss of two arms, but it should get people who knew she once had four to look at something else.

"How much?" I asked.

The way the Kasulla was acting indicated no one had asked him that in a while. My translator picked up a gurgling and sputtering noise but no translation. Tria was again shaking her head, and Cralmo did not miss that at all.

"It is the rarest of artifact antiquities and one of a kind. For you, today only, one billion credits!"

"Sold!"

I extended my hand with a couple of credits vouchers in it. I was getting a lot more gurgling and sputtering and still no translation. Tria looked at me like I was nuts, and she was probably right. It made no difference because I had already made up my mind. Cralmo stood staring at the vouchers in my hand like they were a live grenade.

"I said we have a deal."

He slowly reached out and took them. He put the first into the scanner he wore around his middle. It swallowed the card, and then he did the same to the next one. The device subtracted the additional four hundred and thirty million that was required and showed that I still had in excess of twenty million left on it. He handed back the card and was giving me the strangest look. I didn't like the vibe I was getting. Tria seemed oblivious to it because she couldn't believe what I had just done. The Kasulla's small hands were physically shaking when he turned off the shield and handed me the necklace. Turning to Tria, I held it up until she finally lost the incredulous look on her face. She leaned forward so I could place it around her neck. I could not think of a more fitting place for such a treasure.

"Thank you, Cralmo. I will be sure to tell all who inquire about the beauty of the artifact that I purchased it from you."

He stood there staring at me. For reasons unknown, I had the urge to run the hell out of there. I instead took Tria by the hand and walked out the door as if I didn't have a care in the world. When we got into the transport, she gripped my arm tightly.

"Nathan, I did not like the way the Kasulla looked at us. I have had my fill of squandering credits and think we should go back to the Legacy."

I nodded my agreement and told the transport AI to take us back to Tam Lin's private docking area. I made it a point to say we were in a hurry. It took off at a clip that verified acknowledgment of my wishes. A small amount of traffic quickly fell behind us. Our pace gave me a feeling of security, and I smiled at Tria. She was holding the necklace out from her chest, inspecting it.

"I must admit, I have never seen such a beautiful adornment. Thank you, Nathan."

"Does that mean we can fool around a little?"

She rolled her pretty green eyes and laughed.

"Possibly."

20

I leaned over to kiss Tria, and the world around us exploded. The transport flipped a couple of times, maybe more. I lost count because I hit my head hard enough that I blacked out. I came to with Tria yelling in my ear to wake the hell up! It was obvious the transport was now lying on its side. The seats we once occupied were not at the correct angle. Looking up, I could see the exit sign for the door was above us. Sparks and droplets of molten metal started shooting into the cabin from the edge of it. The inside of the transport was filling with smoke. I was having a hard time coming to grips with what just happened. Tria, however, was not.

"Nathan, we are being targeted by assassins!" she shouted.

That cut the fog from my head and got the beast stirring around in my brain. I could feel my demeanor change and my intentions turn deadly. With the beast egging me on, I went into combat mode. The sparks were from someone or something cutting its way inside.

Whoever or whatever they were, they had a fairly large circle almost completed in the side of our vehicle. Tria had her pistol out, and I was fumbling around, trying to get mine out from under me. The molten circle ripped up and out of the hole, and a head appeared in the opening. Tria shot it in the face at point-blank range. I rolled over in front of her, tearing at my holster, trying to get my weapon free of my new overcoat.

Something heavy and metallic bounced off the edge of the opening and landed in my lap. Instinctively, I flung it back over the side of the opening. The blast that followed turned the transport right side up. It also sent Tria and I spilling out of the ragged hole and onto the thoroughfare. Several bodies were scattered about, and they all possessed grasshopper-like legs and large upper torsos. These guys were Coram mercenaries, and I could think of more than a few reasons they might be here to kill us. I activated my IST.

"Justice, we have been ambushed and need some help!"

"I have already alerted Sig forces, and they are already on the way Commander," Justice calmly said. "Coonts and Klutch have been notified but have been ordered by Pasta to stand down. The outpost security forces might target them as hostiles if they intervene."

Coonts and Klutch both started calling on our IST, but I didn't need the distraction. I lied and told them we were fine and I would get back with them. I heard a loud explosion from somewhere down the road and wondered how many of these bastards were sent to kill us. Looking underneath the badly warped transport, I saw a set of oversized feet moving around to get an angle on us. I fired under the vehicle, shearing them off at the ankles. A Coram dropped face-first on the pavement, screaming for all he was worth. Tria put a shot into its head, silencing the assassin permanently. She took up a firing position at the rear of the wreck, and I took the front. Nothing was moving on my side.

"Do you have any targets?"

"No, only bodies!"

We heard a firefight going on to our front. The Sig or the outpost security were mixing it up with someone. Whoever was behind this had thought it out enough to have blocking forces box us in.

"Nathan, I have two transports moving to our rear!" Tria yelled from behind me.

I wanted to think it was innocent bystanders trying to flee the carnage. That thought was quashed when a couple of shots came from them and struck the wreck we were hiding behind. We both went prone and fired on the fleeing vehicles. We managed to hit the trailing transport enough times it slowed to a stop. We got up and took off running as fast as we could to close the distance. The door slid open, and several errant shots went over our heads as we hit the ground. We rolled away from each other and put fire into the car. Someone jumped from it and tried to run. Tria dropped him with a shot to the legs. I could no longer hear the firefight going on down the tunnel, and it became eerily silent. The silence was short-lived. I heard a booming voice that could only belong to Pasta calling our names. The sound of a large contingent of heavy combat boots running on the pavement filled the roadway around us. My IST was urgently beeping. I finally let the call go through and told Coonts the disagreement was over and we would be back to the Legacy shortly. It did not mollify him, but it did put an end to all of the IST comms traffic.

Pasta had his troops encircle our position.

"Do you or Tria require medical attention?" he asked.

We had small cuts and a lot of bruises, but other than that we were fine. Our new clothes were another matter. They were shredded and burnt in several places and blackened from the smoke and dirt. We looked like we had just crawled from a culvert.

"We are not injured, but I would like to know how the Coram mercenaries knew we were here?"

"We should get you to the Legacy before the outpost security bots arrive. They will want to detain you for questioning. I will leave some of my troops here, and they will explain what happened to them while shopping in this district."

I could only imagine what wild story Pasta's troopers would make up to cover our asses. I was gracious we wouldn't have to explain it ourselves. A large transport came barreling down the thoroughfare and came to an abrupt halt in front of us. The back door slid up and revealed several more Sig soldiers who were armed to the teeth. They stepped to the sides so Tam Lin could move from behind them. She was waving urgently to us.

"Nathan, Tria, get in! The outpost security is right behind us, so we need to get out of here now!"

Pasta all but picked us up and threw us in. He piled in behind us, and the door rapidly closed. Tam Lin went forward and sat down on a bench. She strapped herself in and pointed to the bench across from her, indicating we should do the same.

"I can't say much for your outfits, but that is a damn pretty necklace you have there, Tria."

Even though we almost got murdered by mercenaries, Tria and I looked at the sad condition of our garments and both broke out in laughter. Tam Lin just shook her head.

"You two are as crazy as they come. I should drop you both off at a thought reprocessing institute. What in the hell did you do to kick over that hornet's nest back there?"

I still had no idea. I carefully explained to her where we had gone and everything we had done. We were polite as far as I knew and could not explain the sudden attack. I did tell her it could have been an old score trying to be settled by a Coram warlord we once had an encounter with. The looks Tam Lin and Pasta were giving each other insinuated they thought otherwise.

"If you know something I don't, I would sure like to hear it."

"Nathan, there is a large number of Coram on the outpost. They have a guild a few decks below us, as do a number of other races. No one knew you were here except for my people and the two merchants that you visited. It doesn't take a genius to figure out who could be trusted with that information."

That narrowed the culprits down to just two. Of the two, only one gave me the creeps.

"Cralmo!" Tria and I blurted at the same time.

I looked at Tria's necklace, and the pieces started coming together. "That no-good son-of-bitch took my credits and then decided to kill us and take the necklace back!"

Tria told Tam Lin that another transport was at the ambush site and managed to escape. If I was a betting man, I would say Cralmo was aboard it waiting to take possession of the Starfire necklace.

"Turn this thing around and take me to Cralmo's!" I said.

Tam Lin quickly nixed that idea. "No, Nathan, that entire area is locked down and will be for some time. Let the dust settle and give it a day or two. Then we will go have a little face time with that slug piece of shit. Pasta has some of his crew gathering evidence. When he knows something, he will tell me."

Man, was my blood ever boiling. That slug had a billion credits of mine in his pocket, and he tried to kill me and Tria. He just got a permanent place on my to-do list, right next to Eiger. To take my mind off of skinning the slug alive, I managed to talk Tam Lin into stopping back at Osa's place. She personally got out and spoke at the door. When it opened, she hustled us inside. When Osa saw us and the condition of our outfits, I thought he was going to cry. He must have had it in his mind that Tam Lin wanted him to replace them for free. I produced the funds with another much larger tip for his silence, and he was all smiles after that. We had him box up them up, and Tam Lin impatiently hurried us back out the doors and into her transport. She made it a point to say she was not stopping again, even if it meant I would piss my pants.

When we got back to the Legacy, my crewmates were waiting. Trying to explain what we thought happened to Klutch left a bad odor in the hangar as well as our mouths. It took a lot of convincing to keep the Troop Master from paying the Kasulla an unpleasant visit. That honor would be left for Tria and me as far as I was concerned.

Dinner that evening was amazing as usual. I would like to say it was a light hearted and memorable event, but the tension in the air over the ambush left everybody feeling on edge. As we got up to go back to the Legacy, Tam Lin pulled me aside.

"Nathan, Pasta has some information. He alerted me he is on his way and would like to brief you personally."

I told Xul to take the scientists and engineers back to the Legacy and I would return shortly. Tria, Coonts, Klutch, and I stayed behind to wait for Pasta. I had Justice send a message to the Zaens. It had the jump coordinates to a location just outside of the devastated star system where the mining operation was hidden. It would take them longer to get there than it would the Legacy. By the time they arrived, we should have several blocks of Containium decontaminated and ready to transfer to the freighter.

Pasta showed up about fifteen minutes later, and he did not look happy. I had a bad feeling it was going to be contagious.

"Nathan Myers, my strike team picked up a wounded Coram mercenary from the ambush site before outpost security locked down the area. One of his legs was severed in the firefight, and he was unable to escape. We obtained information from him that points directly to Cralmo. Although Cralmo never identified himself, he told the Coram he was robbed of his most valuable asset. He showed them pictures of you and your transport, then promised a million credits if they could recover the asset before it left the outpost. The rest you already know."

We had the why and the how, but Pasta still looked very unhappy, and I knew there was more news that would leave me in the same condition.

"I take you have something else to tell us that we are not going to like?"

"Unfortunately, yes. I have surveillance teams watching most of the docking areas that belong to known mercenary groups. A Coram assault shuttle departed the outpost two hours ago in great haste. It did not request departure clearance and almost collided with an inbound freighter. After hearing about the departure of a Coram shuttle so soon after the mercenary attack, I decided to send in a covert team to detain Cralmo. His business and residence were both empty. All the merchandise was

305

removed and the business office chemically incinerated. I have teams out searching but already know we are too late. Cralmo is gone."

I cast a stinky eye at Tam Lin but could tell she didn't like it any better than I did.

"Nathan, I am sorry he slipped through our fingers," she said. "I didn't think he would up and leave. He has been doing business on this outpost for a long time. I thought sure he would deny all knowledge of the incident and pay everyone else for their silence."

I was pretty bent out of shape. To make matters worse, Klutch was putting the hurt to the once clean-smelling atmosphere.

"Take me to the Coram prisoner," I said. "Maybe he can tell us how to get a track on the shuttle."

Pasta shook his head. "That is no longer possible."

I had a feeling he was going to say that. There was nothing I could do but move on to other matters.

"We will be departing in the next few minutes," I said. "Let me know if you find out where the slug is hiding."

Pasta solemnly nodded. As I turned to leave, Tam Lin surprised me.

"Nathan, I changed my mind. I want to partner with you in the mining business. Sushi, Pasta, and I are assembling the necessary people to get the mine operational. When we are ready to start moving the engineering crews, I will alert you."

I stood staring at her for a moment wondering if she changed her mind because she felt she let me down. She must have been reading my mind.

"No, I am only doing it for the credits!" she protested.

That was bullshit. I knew for a fact she didn't need the credits.

"When we are ready to start operations, I will sit down with you, and we will iron out the fine print," I said.

"Deal!" she smiled.

I should have been feeling good about taking my first steps at being a galactic business owner. My thirst for revenge on the Kasulla for trying to kill Tria and me rained piss all over the prospect. Some of the animosity came from the Oolaran beast inside of me, but the rest came from my human side. You don't mess with my family and run, thinking you got away with it. There will be a reckoning. The guilty party will find out they are not the only ones with the deadliest of intentions.

Justice jumped us to the demolished star system and started a security sweep. I was brooding in my command chair when Tria decided she had her fill of it. She had no problem putting the assassination attempt behind her. In her mind, they had failed, and the culprits that made the attempt got what was coming to them. It was one of my Earth man failings to hold a grudge against the facilitator. Making matters worse was the fact that Eiger got away with it as well. It was now almost a year since he fled into the void. I was hoping the intel gathered by Sael would finally bring the piece-of-shit pirate's lucky streak to an end.

"Nathan, you should think of a name for this system," Tria said, trying to distract me. "Perhaps something that is not as bleak as your thoughts."

Coonts, Klutch, and Xul were monitoring their consoles and all turned to look at me when they heard Tria's comment. The looks, for the most part, were neutral, but deep down inside, they were like Tria and wanted me to get over it. They were right, of course, and I was setting a poor example of leadership by sitting around and letting it eat at me. Then a thought came to me. I scratched my head and sat up in my chair. I already knew Coram mercenaries had a base of operations on outpost 655. It was a long shot, but it was worth taking a look when we finished our business at the mine. Tria saw the sudden change in my mood and smiled. For now, I would let her take the credit for derailing my morose disposition. I smiled back and started thinking of a name. It came surprisingly fast.

"El Dorado comes to mind. It was a name given to a mythical lost city filled with treasures. There are some back on my planet who still hunt for it, hoping to become rich and famous."

I got nods all around, and Justice recorded the title. He then gave me a sitrep.

"Commander, the cargo bays on Eagle One and Two are now ready for decontamination operations. It will take three trips from each shuttle to remove all the encapsulated Containium. I have reconfigured Eagle Two's hangar in the Legacy's cargo hold so we can store the containers until they are transferred to our freighter. Once the transfer operations are complete, we can take Eagle Two back aboard."

"Coonts, Klutch, you will be on Eagle One, and Tria and I will take Eagle Two. We are going into the mine and removing all of the encapsulated Containium. One of you will run the tow beam while the other washes the blocks down with the decontamination boom. When you have as many blocks as you can carry, bring them out so Justice can put them in the Legacy's hold. I want you armored up for the additional radiation protection. If you don't have any questions, let's get on with it."

I got two thumbs up from Coonts and Klutch, and they headed for the lift tubes with Tria and I behind them. Tria took me by the arm and leaned in to me.

"I know you have other things on your mind," she said. "You can tell me now if you like, or I can wait until you decide to share it with us all."

Tria's perception was right on the money. It was getting progressively harder trying to conceal anything from her. I glanced at her. She may have said she would wait to hear what was on my mind, but the look she was giving me said otherwise.

"Outpost 655."

She stopped and turned me around. "The Coram black market outpost? You are not going to let the attack go, are you?"

I wanted to tell her it was a stupid question but didn't feel like getting my ass kicked. I had my fill of that lately. I knew a different tack was in order.

"Sael gave me all the intel she had on Eiger. Are you going to let that go?"

She frowned and pulled me along toward the hangar. Her silence said I made my point. We launched shortly afterward and followed Klutch into the tunnel entrance of the mine. Everything was the same as we left it. We took up positions on each side of the Containium blocks and went to work. We were able to take three blocks at a time out of the mine. We rendezvoused with the Legacy and dumped them into space. Justice pulled them aboard the Legacy with the tow beam and locked them down in the hold. It was on our second trip out that things started going south.

"Commander, Broza is on station at the rendezvous coordinates," Justice alerted me. "He is reporting that five unknown vessels have made an inner-system jump into close proximity of his location. He is being hailed to cut his drives and drop his shields. My subsystem is monitoring the Sig training crew. They are making evasive maneuvers and have fired warning shots trying to dissuade the combatants from attempting to board them. They are broadcasting their peaceful intentions but are receiving no reply other than to cut their drives and shields."

"Justice, have Xul armor up and tell him to pick a pilot for Eagle Two. He is to continue removing the Containium from the mine with Coonts and Klutch. Is the matrix charged?"

"Yes, Commander, the DEHD core is optimized for immediate operations. Xul has acknowledged your order and has chosen Jaran as his pilot. They will be standing by in the hangar awaiting your return."

Tria made a maximum velocity return to the Legacy. We retro braked hard to slow down enough for Justice to not so gently catch us with the tow beam. He pulled us aboard, and we exited the shuttle. I saluted my Grawl teammates as they ran up the cargo ramp of the shuttle. They closed the hatch, and Justice gave them a push into the void. I caught a little flak from Coonts and Klutch on our IST comms. They wanted to be where the action was, and hauling freight was not it. I reminded them that what they were hauling was worth hundreds of billions of credits. In a not-so-roundabout way, they both said they didn't give a scat. I finally ordered them to get the job done and quit bitching about it.

"Justice, jump us to the freighter. Do you have another report from Broza?"

"Yes, Commander, they are under fire. The Sig crew has taken command. They are making evasive maneuvers and returning fire. The hostiles were not expecting the freighter to have heavy weapons hidden on its hull, and they have disabled one of the attacking ships."

The DEHD core jump put an end to the report. When we returned to normal space-time, Justice cloaked the Legacy and put a sensor view in my helmet. I saw a single stationary blinking yellow box well off in the distance. Justice put us reasonably close to the engagement based on data from his subsystem aboard our freighter. The four hostiles were red triangles on the view screen, and they were closing with the blue one representing our freighter. The freighter was taking a lot of fire, but the Sig were pros. They were limiting the damage they were taking by spreading the concentrations of hostile fire over large portions of the freighter's shields. The largest ship in the enemy formation made a snap jump that put it well ahead of the freighter, and it rapidly turned to attack from another vector. Whoever they were, they weren't completely incompetent. They had divided the defensive weapons fire from the freighter and limited some of the evasive maneuvers available to the Sig pilot.

"Justice, designate the largest hostile ship as target one and fire when you have a solution," I ordered.

The jump the hostile ship had made put it at a considerable distance from our current position. Justice made a turn that aligned us with the target. I thought he was going to close with the target but was proven wrong when he opened fire. My HUD blinked, and the target turned into a debris cloud that spread like dust in the wind. Holy crap! The Grawl were not kidding when they said our beam weapons would be more destructive. It was like the hostile had no shields at all. Justice did not have to say it, but he did anyway.

"Target destroyed, Commander. On your order, I will target the remaining hostiles with only one weapon in an attempt to disable the ships."

I was still a little shocked by how efficiently our weapons killed the enemy. The other ships must have been getting sensor lag because they were not breaking off their attack.

"Target the closest aggressor."

"Firing!"

The entire rear of the hostile ship disappeared in a bright flash. The two ships following it didn't need sensors to determine what had happened. They abruptly broke off their attack and were going to make a run for it.

"Justice, hail them in the languages they used to call our freighter. Tell them to shut down their drives and shields or they will be destroyed."

"Message sent, Commander."

No dice. Why they thought they could still get away was beyond me. They attacked a Sig-flagged freighter without provocation. According to Tam Lin, nobody in their right mind would do such a thing. One explanation was the pirates that operate this far out on the fringe may just be the biggest dimwits in the galaxy. There was always the slim possibility they didn't know anything about the Sig, or perhaps they thought superior numbers would get them a quick surrender. It didn't make any difference at this point because they were not stopping.

"Justice, call our freighter and have them hold their position. Launch a comms buoy and alert the closest Sig fleet that we have stumbled upon a pirate operation that needs to be cleaned up."

"The freighter has acknowledged the order, Commander. They are reporting no injuries and only minor damage to three shield emitters and two defensive weapons. The comms buoy has been launched and will transition in thirty seconds."

"Take out the lead ship."

In a blink, the smaller ship was gone. Their shields were no hindrance to even a single shot from one of our beam weapons. You would have thought that the trailing ship would have thrown in the towel, but it surprised us when it transitioned. Justice alerted us that it was an intersystem jump. The hostile emerged from hyperspace and was now moving toward a small planetoid on the edge of an asteroid field. The weak central star was so far away, it cast very little light on the target's destination.

"Justice, let's follow them and see where they are going."

"Affirmative, Commander."

Justice jumped to within spitting distance of the vessel. It started launching missiles in response to our transition distortion waves. The pilot knew we were pursuing but could not detect our location. The missiles passed harmlessly to port, and we snuggled up to the fleeing ship.

"Commander, I am intercepting encrypted comms traffic to and from the planetoid. It appears the target's destination is a small base on the surface near the polar cap. I am detecting weapon tracking systems coming online. The count is twenty-seven fixed position missile and energy beam batteries. We have been swept multiple times, and the weapons are still in search mode."

We had more important things to do than chase pirates around the fringe of the galaxy. The pirate ship we were pursuing was not stopping. The captain must have thought the base's defenses could shoot us down if we got close enough. I had Justice send them a final warning, which, to their peril, they chose to ignore. Our range to the target was so close that a single shot turned the ship into a cloud of shrapnel. As we passed through the debris, they created glowing sparks cascading across our forward shields. I considered doing the same thing to the base, but Tria suggested we disarm the base and let the Sig deal with it. At some point they would give us a detailed intelligence report on who or what they found.

I was in agreement and told Justice to destroy the defenses. To make sure we were not missing any secondary defenses, Justice uncloaked and gave the pirates a stationary target to concentrate their fire on. It took the Legacy forty-two seconds to shoot down all the incoming missiles and destroy the base's last line of defense. As far as I was concerned, the engagement was a fitting test for our upgraded weapons. I considered boarding the disabled pirate ship that was slowly spiraling its way into the void but decided I had wasted enough time. We needed to get the Containium to a secure location and move on to the next mission I was trying to piece together in my mind.

We joined up with our freighter and jumped to a location that was closer to the mine but would not divulge its location. I wanted to make sure that El Dorado's location would remain secret for the immediate future. Justice notified me that a Sig comms buoy transitioned into the system where the pirate base was located. It was broadcasting using our encrypted codes. The Sig would have a fleet of twenty-six warships in the star system in seven hours. There was a good chance the life expectancy of the pirates at the base would only be another hour or so after that.

21

We left the freighter in what I hoped was a more secure position. It was drifting in the void and well away from any star system. I ordered Broza to power down the ship's drives to minimize their scan signature. Justice did a thorough scan of the surrounding space and verified we were indeed alone. We made a few random jumps to throw off anyone who may have been trying to track us. When we finally showed up at El Dorado, we found Coonts and Klutch impatiently waiting. They had all the Containium blocks floating in the void between the two shuttles. Justice started loading them into the cargo hold while he pulled Eagle One into the hangar.

When Coonts and Klutch debarked the shuttle, they cornered me in the hangar. Both were pretty wound up about not being in on the action. Even after I related the story of what took place and how well the new weapon upgrades performed, they were still a little pissy. They somehow felt that having to haul freight was a waste of their talents. Admittedly, they were probably correct, but I was not going to let scientists and engineers with no combat experience under their belts take on that responsibility. Their incessant grumbling was getting on my nerves. It must have bothered Tria that the two of them were bitching about such easy duty. She pulled me aside and whispered that it might be a good idea to let the pair stay behind with Eagle Two while we did the transfer to the freighter. That put a smile on my face. I liked the idea. I had Justice hail Eagle Two. I told Jaran to bring the shuttle in close to the hangar so Justice could lock onto it with the tow beam. He pulled the rear of the shuttle into the hangar, and I called the Grawl and told them they were being relieved. When they came down the shuttle's ramp, I congratulated them for a job well done. As I turned around, I saw Coonts and Klutch making a beeline for the ready room. They already determined what I had in mind for them.

"Coonts! Klutch!" I called.

They stopped in their tracks like they had run into a brick wall.

"You will be relieving Xul and Jaran from duty. The two of you are going to take Eagle Two and patrol El Dorado until we return and can take you aboard."

The pair slowly turned and were not hiding their dissatisfaction well. It looked like Coonts might have something to say about it, but Klutch elbowed him hard enough, it almost knocked him to the deck. The two walked by, slapping at each other but without further comment. They boarded the shuttle, and Justice wasted no time pushing them out into the void. Justice secured the last of the Containium blocks, and we jumped back to the freighter. Tria and I went aboard to let the Zaens and Sig know what a great job they had done.

Broza and Hylet were both physically shaken, but the Sig crew acted like it was no big deal. They were more interested in finding out if they could get weapons like the Legacy's mounted on the freighter. I could only imagine how blown out of proportion our pirate encounter would eventually turn out to be. We gave the Zaens coordinates that would take them to a point in the void that was halfway to Alpha Base. It would be more than fifty hours in hyperspace to reach that destination. Once at that location, the Legacy would rendezvous with them, sans shuttles, and take the cargo from there.

I watched from my command chair as the freighter disappeared into hyperspace. We made a standard transition back to El Dorado that lasted more than thirty minutes. It took Justice less than twelve seconds to locate Eagle Two, and we quickly ran them down and loaded the shuttle into the vacant cargo hold. Coonts and Klutch avoided eye contact with me as I thanked them for doing such a great job. They stalked off to the ready room, and I returned to the command deck.

"Justice, take us home."

"Acknowledged, Commander. DEHD core activation in ten seconds."

As everything around me glowed a bright white, I thought about what I should do next.

As my world faded back to reality, I was still trying to make up my mind. I would discuss it with Tria, and if we came to a consensus, I would gather the crew and see what they thought. We had more than forty hours until the freighter would reach the rendezvous point, which was more than enough time to make a decision on what to do next. When we landed at Alpha Base, everyone pitched in to get our supplies squared away. The Grawl and Felix were genuinely happy to be back to the place they called home. A great many of them went back to working on projects they had abandoned to work on the Legacy. I had a meal with Tria and quietly told her we had enough intel to go after Eiger, but I wanted her input first. Her answer gave me a lot to think about.

"Nathan, if we go after Eiger on his home world, even the smallest misstep could mean disaster," she said. "I don't deny Eiger needs to be dealt with, but at what risk to the other members of our crew? We should ask Coonts and Klutch what they think and make a decision based on everyone's input."

There was no arguing with Tria's logic. I would have got around to asking for other opinions sooner or later but usually after I had already made up my mind. We would go over the intel and then decide if the risks were acceptable. Before I could open my mouth and call a group meeting, Justice intervened.

"Commander, the Overseer is reporting a breakthrough. The last remaining Prule entity has provided the location of a base it claims was where Gredda's strike team was to evacuate the Hivemind. It also states that Gredda passed the information to the rogue council members. That opens the possibility the base may now harbor the Fury."

"Do you think the information is accurate?"

"Yes, but I must caution you the Hivemind might also have ulterior motives for giving us this specific information. I would also like to add that if we do not provide aid to the entity, it will perish within the hour."

I was thinking about calling Klutch and having him provide the aid, but there was a good chance it would end up killing the Prule anyway.

"Okay, Justice, minimal life support. Make it known that information will be the bio machine's only lifeline."

"Affirmative, Commander. I am processing the information, and it appears the base's location is in uncharted space."

I now had to make a decision on what to do about the freighter. It was still more than twenty hours from the drop-off point. Should we act on the information immediately or wait until we collect our cargo from the freighter? I decided to have a talk with Graf and Jaran. I found them in the base cafeteria and told them what was going on. They came to the consensus that our priority should be to investigate the Prule base. Jaran said they could use Eagle Two and our Coram shuttle to collect the Containium. It would take at least ten trips, but they smiled and said they had nothing better to do. I could not help but love those guys. They were nothing like the rest of their race and proved to me every day that change was possible. It gave me hope for my own kind. If the Grawl could do it, so could the human race. I thanked them.

"Alert the crew and tell them we are preparing for a combat deployment," I called to Justice. "I want Eagle One in the hangar and the Daggers in the hold. I want a full mix of nanite and antimatter aboard; I don't want to leave anything to chance."

"Message sent, and I am queuing the ordnance for loading."

The alert started a flurry of activity. Everyone from the Grawl to Felix made sure we had a complete loadout. I had Justice put the Prule containment vessel back in the brig. If the mission turned into some sort of trap or a wild goose chase, the Prule entity would not be on the return trip. The Legacy was loaded and ready for war in just over an hour. Everyone was anxious, but that was normal for one of our deployments. Our encounters with the Prule have never been without injury. I was hoping this would be an exception but knew it was wishful thinking. The beast inside of me stirred with anticipation.

We launched, and Justice made a DEHD core jump to the edge of known space. It would be suicide to jump directly to the coordinates not knowing what would be awaiting us there. We opted for a scan and jump routine that would get us there eventually. We wanted to make a stealthy approach, and this method would give us the best chance at doing it. We had already made two jumps equaling eighty light-years each. We still had two hundred and ninety to go. It was on our third scan in preparation for a jump that Justice called out.

"Commander! I have two separate transponder threads emanating from both Guardian Transponders. The threads are so close together they appear as one. I speculate this phenomenon is caused by the thread's termination points being in close proximity to each other. Both threads have terminated at one hundred and forty-two light-years. I have recorded the data for future reference."

We had made so many DEHD core jumps that it was easy to forget we had Guardian transponders. Now that we were making a number of standard transitions, the magical alien tech would have a chance to make detections. My curiosity was piqued, but the threads would have to wait until we investigated the Prule base.

"Go ahead and jump to the next waypoint when you are ready, Justice."

Our jumps had been uneventful; this time, however, our prejump scan detected distant ship traffic. Justice engaged our stealth systems, and we closed with the contacts.

"Commander, I have identified the contacts as Scrun motherships. They have detected our transition, and power emanations suggest they are preparing to jump to hyperspace."

"Can we stop them from jumping?"

"No, Commander. We will be unable to close the range before they transition."

That fact was verified when the two red triangles on the view dome disappeared. The chances were high the ships had slaves aboard.

"What do you get when you backtrack their course?"

"If the Scrun ships did not alter their trajectory, the course intersects a star system less than one light-year from our location."

"Jump to the edge of it and let's take a look."

An eye blink later, the jump revealed a red giant central star and two planetary bodies. The larger of the two was being cooked by the star, but the second smaller planet was distant enough it could support life. The noted white hue hinted it was perpetually winter on the surface. Since Xul was now on the crew, we would give him a designation to associate with our planetary discoveries. The planet would now be recorded as X-Ray One unless we found data that said otherwise.

"Commander! I detect a Scrun mothership in low orbit of the smaller planetary body. I am also detecting emanations from six shuttles climbing out of the planet's atmosphere."

"Disable the mothership's drives in case it tries to run!"

The Legacy accelerated to maximum and fired a glancing shot to the Scrun ship's shields with the beam weapons. As we passed the mothership, Justice poured a stream of rail cannon fire into the depleted shield. A shimmering hole appeared where the shield was flaring the brightest. The rear of the ship started going to pieces and jetted clouds of pressurized atmosphere. The defensive systems on the Scrun ship locked onto our weapons discharge. Return fire blazed against the Legacy's shields, revealing our location. A salvo of missiles leaped from the ship in search of a target to lock onto. Justice made a short jump to lose the missiles and let the shields regenerate. Justice alerted us that the Scrun shuttles were now diving for the surface of the planet.

"Justice, hail the mothership," I ordered. "Tell it to cease fire and shut down its shields."

We turned back to the target and jumped in close. Justice sent the message, and the Scrun mothership replied with more blind weapons fire. Justice pounded its shields until they failed then shredded the upper decks before jumping away. The damage left the ship defenseless against incoming fire. The Scrun broadcast a surrender message. Knowing they were born liars, I had Justice jump back in and blast the weapons turrets from their hull. Our recorded blueprints of the mothership allowed Justice to make precision shots on known chokepoints and main corridors. Heavy smoke and debris were jetting like fountains from the back of the wrecked starship. Those unfortune enough to be in the rear of the ship would find it difficult to make their way to the forward spaces. The Scrun commander was now pleading for us to cease fire. Justice had purposely avoided shooting up the hold and the hangar bay.

I was going to give the Scrun a chance to return any beings they might have taken for slaves back to their home planet. I had Justice send a message to them. It stated that if they harmed any of the beings they took as slaves or tried to use them as hostages, I would show no mercy and kill them all. It really didn't matter if they believed I would show them mercy or not. I had already proven I was capable of delivering on the final part of the message. It did not take but a few seconds for the commander of the ship to reply with a message that almost made me laugh. Almost. The message stated they had no slaves aboard and were here to aid the primitive lifeforms that lived in tunnels below the ice on the surface. I suspected the next thing the prick would try to do was sell me oceanfront property in Arizona. The frowns on my crew's faces turned to sinister smiles when I told Justice to park the Legacy right over the bridge of the slave hauler.

"Armor up. We are going to go over and see if that Throgg is telling the truth."

Tria cocked an eyebrow at me but was right on my heels when I jogged down the corridor to the lift tubes. I thought she might comment on how reckless of an idea it was to go aboard the slave ship with only a four-member strike team. She never uttered a peep. It's not like we had not done this before. We had intimate knowledge of the ship's layout and what weapons we would face. This time around, our portal device would give us an extra edge. They would never in a million years expect us to walk right onto the bridge. We were going to bring the boom before these guys could figure out what was happening.

When we got to the ready room, Coonts and Klutch were already geared up. Klutch stunk the place up because

I made him leave his prized plasma caster behind. We had mission goals that I wanted to accomplish, and they would be infinitely easier if the ship was not burning down around us. One of those goals would be to gather intel from the ship's navigation computers. I wanted to know where the ship had been and possibly where it was going. Tria and I slipped out of our uniforms and put on the specialized suit liners. I asked her if we could access the Scrun NAV computers without input from them. The answer was no, we would need command-level access. As usual, I would have to wing it and hope for the best once we were on the bridge.

Tria smiled at me. It was like she was doing the mind reading thing again.

"I am sure you will think of some way to get the information we seek."

It was almost strange seeing Tria's armor with only two appendages. I hoped like hell we would not miss the extra launchers she used to have at her disposal. I pulled my shotgun from its rack and inserted the twin magazines. Charging the barrels, I pulled the mags and put two more rounds from my ammo pouch into them. I looked around at my team and gave them a thumbs up. They returned the gesture. We were topped off and ready to roll.

"Justice, what are the Scrun assault shuttles doing?"

"They landed in a crevasse and shut down their drives. The location appears to be a makeshift staging area. They have abandoned the shuttles, and I believe they are attempting to hide in a bunker deep under the ice."

We would take care of those fools when we were done with the mothership. We went to the hangar, and Justice had the hatch open and waiting. Looking down on the massive mothership below us, I pointed to the protruding bridge structure. There was a large open area in between the sensor arrays on the antenna farm. Directly below was the bridge.

"Klutch, when we touch down, I want you to port a hole right between those antennas. Tria, Coonts, and I will drop in first, and then you follow. I want you to use your own judgment, but I want the commander alive. Everyone else is expendable."

I got three more thumbs up and then I jumped. I engaged my gravity drives and dove to the hull of the ship, righting myself before touching down. We stepped back to let Klutch do his thing. He got a good hole first try, and we jumped into it with the deadliest of intentions. The first thing that greeted us was the low urgent tone of alarms. The ship was crying out its distress to its masters. We hovered above the deck and opened fire on the stunned crew standing at control consoles. Klutch came dropping through but went right by us. He landed in the lap of some hapless fool. The Scrun squalled out in pain as his legs were crushed by Klutch's mass. The Troop Master silenced him with a blast from his shotgun and dove on another who was trying to draw a pistol. Another blast from Klutch's shotgun ended all resistance in the control room. In less than thirty seconds, we had control of the bridge. There were seven Scrun officers permanently down and out. The commander and two of his staff sat in their chairs with arms extended and fingers splayed upward. They seemed to be in shock at our entrance.

Coonts and Klutch took up positions at the two entrances to the bridge. Tria stood by me with her weapon pointed at the two officers sitting in front of their commander's chair. There are a handful of things I could think of that truly disgusted me. Right at the moment, I could only think of twenty-two such things, and they adorned the head slaver's atmospheric suit. I stepped up on the commander's raised pedestal and rapped my shotgun against his face plate. Each strike threatened to dislodge the offending award trinkets. My translator grunted out the Scrun language.

"I am going to give you another chance to tell me what you are doing here. For your sake, you better get it right the first time."

I stood, expecting a quick reply, but the Scrun sat there staring at me with his crazy big eyeball and his grotesque hairy-lipped mouth hanging open. I was going to need a little more cooperation than that. I gripped my shotgun like a bat and brought it down just above his faceplate. It was not a killing blow by any means. It was more of a wake-up call. The blow laid the big bastard out on top of his two underlings and set him to screeching out unintelligible nonsense. I expected sentences that were more coherent than that. I jerked him back into his chair for another Q&A session but got interrupted. The hatch next to Coonts swished open, and a Scrun soldier ran through hollering something that sounded like the Scrun word for fire, which is exactly what Coonts gave him. I wished he would have used something besides an explosive penetrator slug. Tria and I, along with our three captives, were now wearing various pieces of the deceased.

Coonts probably already knew the looks he was getting from behind our war faces. Rather than wait and see if I would comment on his decorating skills, he called to Klutch and then jerked a thumb over his shoulder to the corridor. They both stepped out and closed the hatches behind them. My sensors picked up the faint sound of gunfire, and then I felt the thump of an explosion. When I got no report from my teammates, Tria ran to the hatch and opened it, taking a quick look. She turned back and shrugged. I guess that meant they were fine and just taking care of business.

I turned my attention back to the commander. "Do you have slaves aboard?"

"No, they were on the shuttles that returned to the surface."

"Call the shuttles and tell your people to release the slaves and return to the ship."

"They witnessed what you did to my ship," the commander said. "They are not likely to follow my orders."

It wasn't the answer I was looking for. My sensors again picked up gunfire from the corridor and a couple more thumps from explosions. We had been dicking around for more than fifteen minutes, and my patience was wearing

330

thin. Coonts called and stated that he and Klutch had cleared the cargo hold control room. They now controlled the lifts to the bridge.

"Can you see any occupied slave crates on the monitors?"

"Negative, Commander. All I see is a lot of Scrun down there. It may be an evacuation point for those escaping from the aft part of the ship. Judging by the open crate count, I believe they were getting ready to receive at least a hundred slaves, maybe more."

"Decompress the hold and use the security turrets on anyone that doesn't get blown out."

"Roger that."

I felt a slight rumble under my feet when the hold violently flushed into the void. The Scrun commander's face looked a little paler. He knew his future was in doubt.

"Recall the shuttles now!" I demanded.

He jumped up and went to a console and started grunting out orders. He stood there waiting for a reply. When it never came, he started yelling and repeating himself. It was obvious the shuttle crews had no intention of answering. He again held his hands out, fingers splayed upward in the Scrun sign of surrender.

"They refuse to answer and will not comply. We know of you and what you do to our people!"

It was nice that the word was getting around that someone was taking a stand against the slavers. The indignant tone of the Scrun's voice seemed to insinuate I was doing it for no reason.

I looked the commander in his big cyclops eyeball. "So, you think it is a crime for me to defend those who cannot defend themselves against the technologically superior races?"

The fool realized his comment might not have been in his best interest. His eyeball grew a little larger, and his tongue started flicking in and out of his mouth, trying to wet his hairy lips. One of his officers suddenly stood. I guess he was trying to impress me with Scrun logic in hopes it would deflect my anger from his commander.

"It is an honor for the lesser races to serve their masters! We bring order and duty to their primitive irrelevance," the Scrun officer said. "We save them from the perpetual ignorance of their primal ways and raise their awareness to what the future may hold for them."

The clown must have been the commander's political officer or possibly the guy in charge of inducting new recruits. The way he spewed his bullshit had me thinking the moron believed every word of it. He did succeed in turning my anger from his commanding officer. Unfortunately for him, he was now the target of my derision. Tria must have decided her scat filter was at capacity and saved me the trouble of expending any additional munitions. She raised the Scrun officer's awareness to the overhead and several consoles with a blast of explosive buckshot.

"We have wasted enough time on this filth," she said. "We need to get back to our primary mission."

She was right. We needed to wrap this up and move on. Her unexpected response to the Scrun's oration had their leader on the verge of a mental breakdown. I would throw him a lifeline. I wouldn't let on that it was going to be a temporary one at best.

"I want the data files from your navigation computers," I told him. "The information is the only bargaining chip you have left that will convince me to spare your life. You have ten seconds to comply."

I pointed the twin barrels of my shotgun at him. He jumped from his chair and went to a console. He worked it like he was playing a piano. In less than a minute, he extended a hand to me with a data cube in it. Tria stepped forward and snatched it from him and stowed it in her ammo pouch. She swung her shotgun around and put a couple of slugs into the comms station. The Scrun dove to the deck, avoiding the flying debris. We went to the exit hatch and stepped into the corridor. Tria made it a point to extract a grenade from her kit and show it to the Scrun commander. She then tossed it to the overhead in the corridor and closed the hatch. We called to Coonts and Klutch, alerting them we were on our way to the hold control room. When we arrived, they were sitting with their feet up on the consoles like they had nothing better to do. I waved the wise guys over and pointed at the large cargo hold view screen.

"We are not taking the lifts."

I blew the screen out with a blast of buckshot, decompressing the corridor to the bridge. We were sucked

333

out of the opening and into the vacuum of the hold. I heard Klutch laughing at Coonts, saying he knew I wouldn't use the lifts. I assumed the conversation involved a wager Coonts had just lost.

"Justice, we are ready for extraction and will be exiting the cargo hold."

"Affirmative, Commander. Tow beam is on standby."

"Is the motherships orbit decaying?"

"Yes, Commander, it will enter the planet's atmosphere in five hours and three minutes."

"Any chance the Scrun can correct that problem?"

"Negative. The damage to their drives was critical. They ejected the antimatter power cells to prevent catastrophic detonation. The odds of a maintenance tug arriving before the ship burns up in the planet's atmosphere is currently less than two percent."

We boosted from the hold and were snatched up by Justice. He pulled us into the Legacy's hangar and moved away from the Scrun mothership. My teammates retracted their helmets and stood waiting for additional orders. I could tell they were wondering what I was going to do about the shuttles. I answered the inquiring looks by ordering Justice to take us down to the crevasse where the Scrun shuttles were sheltering. It made Klutch's day when I told him to bring his plasma caster.

22

The scene that greeted us when we arrived over the crevasse brought my blood back to a boil. The beast in me that for the most part had remained silent was now rattling the bars of its cage. The slaughtered remains of more than forty of the centaur-like creatures that inhabited the planet were scattered about the site. They were the size of a pony and had the heavy fur coat of a yak. The two short arms on the upper bodies were scaly and had large cord-like muscles. The four-fingered hands had thick, sharp claws, as did the four feet of the creatures. It wasn't hard to guess how the many caves that lined the crevasse's icy walls were excavated.

Justice highlighted the entrance to the bunker the Scrun had taken refuge in. I thought about using the Legacy's weapons to annihilate the Scrun, bunker and all. Cooler heads prevailed, and Tria suggested I choose a method that would not harm the surrounding tunnels or stress the inhabitants any more. We jumped from the hangar and touched down next to the shuttles. The hold doors were open and the cargo areas empty. The tracks in the snow and ice went from the shuttles to several of the caves lining the walls of the crevasse. The inhabitants of the planet wasted no time leaving the area. I thought about trying to get information from the flight computers on the shuttles but nixed the idea. If I had to abandon my only ride off the planet, I would set booby traps in hopes of getting a little revenge for being stranded. I went to the tunnel that led to the Scrun bunker. It was a fairly recent excavation, and I assumed it was built to protect the teams of slavers from the frigid conditions. They probably had all the comforts of home down there. It was an indication that this was an ongoing operation that wasn't intended to end any time soon. That was about to change.

"Klutch! The slaver pieces of scat might be getting cold sitting down there in that bunker," I said. "You have my permission to rectify the problem any way you see fit!"

Coonts and Tria started backing away from the Troop Master. It looked like the smart thing to do, and I joined them as they boosted up out of the trench and took shelter in the hangar of the Legacy. A pink glow lit the crevasse as Klutch poured shot after shot of plasma down the bunker shaft. Huge jets of steam screamed up from the frozen ice-covered ground, obscuring our view. I was wondering what was taking so long. I stepped to the edge of the hangar door and looked down at the glowing steam cloud. I was relieved when the Troop Master finally popped up out of the cloud bank and landed in the hangar.

"Mission accomplished, Commander."

"What about the shuttles?"

"I thought they might explode and collapse the crevasse if I set them on fire. I decided to put a couple of grenades in the drive nozzles. I put a tamper delay on them. If someone engages the drives or climbs into the nozzles to inspect them, they are in for a big surprise."

I knew the Tibor was an expert when it came to mayhem. If it was good enough for him, it was good enough for me. I doubted if the creatures that lived on the planet would get anywhere near the shuttles. The experiences they associated with the Scrun spacecraft had to be horrific.

"Justice, get us back on course for the Prule base."

"Initiating prejump scans, Commander. We will jump to the next programed waypoint in four minutes thirty seconds."

We went to the ready room to get out of our armor, but it turned out to be premature.

"Commander, I have detected a transition into this system, and the drive emanation is of Scrun origin. The target is making a course change that will align it with the planet we have designated as X-Ray One."

"Please tell me it is not a service tug."

"Negative, Commander. The drive signature matches that of a Scrun mothership."

"Engage our stealth systems, and let's go meet them."

"Affirmative, Commander. Reversing course now."

Justice swung us around and headed back toward the Scrun ship we had disabled. Justice alerted us that the new target was hailing the doomed ship.

"Commander, I have decoded their transmissions. The new target is here to take on slaves."

Unless the Scrun crew members were asleep at the wheel, their scanners would be painting them a bleak picture anytime now.

"Commander, the target's shields have come online, and it is slowing."

"Engage them when you are ready, Justice. Make it messy. I want the Scrun to easily figure out what happened."

Justice launched a four-missile salvo that jumped to hyperspace. He then opened fire with our beam weapons. The Scrun ship's forward shields flared brilliant white and then failed under the multiple shot barrage Justice hammered them with. The Scrun defensive systems attempted to lock onto our weapons discharges. They only managed a couple of shots that passed well aft of the Legacy. Our antimatter missiles transitioned back to normal space-time and made contact with the mothership's hull. The front half of the ship disintegrated into a large glittering cloud of debris. The back half of the ship was spinning like a top and headed toward the planet. I was convinced it would end up sharing the same fate as the first Scrun ship and burn up in the atmosphere. I was proven wrong when a high-order detonation turned the remains into flying scrap. Justice confirmed the first target would receive a fatal peppering of debris just before making its final reentry. I had hopes that any Scrun ships coming to collect slaves would not stay after determining the nature of the space junk orbiting the planet. Justice recorded the discovery data so we could turn it over to the Principal Investigator. The Chaalt would see to it the planet got on the list for protected status.

I had Justice hang around the system for an additional four hours while the crew and I slept. When we awoke, Xul reported no additional Scrun activity. We jumped from the system to our next waypoints and all were vacant of any ship activity. The Legacy was now a single jump from the location of the Prule base. As a precaution, Justice was going to jump three-quarters of the way to the target area. We would cloak and use our stealth systems to make the rest of the journey. Our transition to the insertion point could be detected. We were gambling that the distance to the target would leave doubt as to our actual destination. We would be relying on the capabilities of our Oolaran systems to keep us hidden from any hostiles that might be in the area. As we closed with the system Justice gave us an ominous sitrep.

"Commander, my sensors are picking up a massive debris field. It appears to be the remains of several types of vessels. I can only speculate on the number but would put it at more than a hundred. None have power source or life readings that I can detect. The greatest concentration of wreckage is orbiting the small planetary body that is our destination coordinates."

Justice put a magnified view up on the bridge dome. The sight was awe-inspiring and horrendous at the same time. The pieces large enough to identify as being from a starship had holes shot through them at every possible angle. The battle that took place here was incredible. I shook my head wondering what the original ship count must have been when the shooting started. Judging by the appearance of the wreckage, any ship disabled in the battle was shot to smithereens. It didn't look like anyone involved in the conflict had the intention of taking prisoners. You were victorious or you died. It was the only explanation for what I was seeing. Justice had to start weaving the Legacy through the wreckage. It was thick enough we could not avoid colliding with the small stuff. Our forward shields were sparking from the impacts. The greater the number of impacts, the more likely we could be tracked. The disturbance created by our passage was setting things in motion that were once stationary. If someone or something was paying attention, it would not be hard to track our progress.

"Are you getting any readings that might indicate the Fury is on the surface somewhere?"

"Negative, I have been broadcast—Commander! I am detecting an energy spike on the surface!"

It was one of those times when I hated being right. An energy beam lanced up from the planet's surface and plowed through the debris. It struck the Legacy's shields amidships. It did not penetrate but did manage to weaken the shield to forty percent of capacity. Justice dove for the surface of the planet. Our forward shields were flaring from the constant collisions. We were now a target with a visible reference point. Another shot hit our aft shields. It was not degraded as much as the first and pulled our shields down to a dangerously low twenty-two percent. I no longer wondered if we would find Prule. Justice didn't hesitate to use the biggest stick we had at our disposal. He fired our anomaly weapon down the vector of the hostile fire and followed it with a barrage of six full-yield antimatter missiles. We were now below the debris field and hugging the mountainous terrain on the surface. Our shields were regenerating and would be at full capacity in a couple of minutes. A bright corona came from the area we took the fire from. It flickered and then faded away.

"Commander, the hostile fire came from a derelict ship that appears to have crashed on the planet's surface. The remains fit the description of a Prule resource gathering platform. It had no shield emanations, and our weapons made direct hits on that location. The chances that the weapon survived our attack are zero."

"Did you detect other ships on the surface?"

"It will require me to make a more detailed scan of the planet. The surface is littered with debris. While the concentration is less than what is orbiting the planet, it is still considerable. The planet has no atmosphere but does have a gravity reading of point five G. Our passage through the debris field has sent wreckage falling from orbit and raining down on the surface. If the attack on the Legacy was an automated response, the falling debris should have triggered additional weapons fire. I have not detected any retaliatory fire. The chances of other weapons being hidden on the surface is high. Now that we are out of the debris field, our movements can no longer be predicted. Doing a thorough scan of the planet will expose any additional weapons sites if they exist. The probability is low that there is technology present that can actively track the Legacy while cloaked. Since I cannot completely rule out the possibility, I will take the precaution of staying close to the planet's surface."

"Do you think the Hivemind purposely sent us into a trap?" I asked the AI.

"A trap would not be an entirely accurate description. It did give us what it thought was information on an active Prule base. That would make any species other than Prule a target. The debris in orbit appear to be centuries old. The information from the Hivemind may be just as dated. I surmise on some level the Hivemind assumed we would be captured and subjugated, then it would subsequently be set free to have its revenge upon us."

"Just before we were attacked, you started to tell me something related to finding the Fury."

"Yes, I was telling you I am actively broadcasting a minimum power IST signal," Justice explained. "The signal is well below the power threshold for hyperspace transmission. It should only be detectable inside of this system. If the Fury energizes its IST receivers, my subsystem will pick up the signal and respond. So far, I have nothing incoming on the system."

"Okay. What is your take on the attack, and do you have a theory on who targeted us?"

"Our retaliatory strike most assuredly destroyed any evidence or remains of our attackers. I do, however, suspect it was active Prule forces. The energy beam used in the attack exactly matches the power profile of the weapons used against us by the Hivemind's lifeboat."

I was getting bent out of shape. The Hivemind sent us on a fool's errand in hopes of us getting killed or captured. Justice had more or less warned me it was a possibility that was the bio machine's intent from the beginning. I had let the thought of recovering the Fury cloud my judgment.

Tria must have felt my anger mounting and came over and put her arm around me.

"Nathan, the discovery of this planet is not a total waste," Tria said. "We now have proof that the Prule are still active in this galaxy. My people can take the evidence we have uncovered and present it to the Galactic Union. They will now be forced to take the threat seriously."

"I don't know if I am ready to get the Union involved just yet," I said. "The level of Prule activity on this world is still questionable. For all we know, Justice wiped out any proof we might have had."

"If that turns out to be the case, Nathan, we can still sell the salvage rights for all the scrap in this system to my people," Tria said. "I would be guessing, but I would estimate the value at several hundred million credits."

I had to admit that was an angle I had not thought of. The sheer volume of materials that could be harvested was staggering. If Justice was right and the wreckage was a couple of hundred years old, that would make us the owners of the discovery. A grim thought crossed my mind. We may not have been the first to make this discovery. We may be the only survivors able to capitalize on it. I pushed that thought from my mind. There still may be active Prule somewhere on the planet. They would have to be eradicated before we could let anyone near it.

"You have a point, Tria, but don't you think it makes more sense to put it up for bids?"

A frown flashed across her face. She was probably thinking I wanted Tam Lin to get in on the action. I knew she would never admit it, but deep down, she was jealous of the Earth girl. I knew I was skating on thin ice and closed my mouth rather than justify my comment. She jumped on my hesitation and justified hers.

"Nathan, by revealing this discovery to my people, we will be showing any who have had doubts about our motives when we destroyed the research facility that we are staunch allies and supporters of the Chaalt."

"The council should already know that."

"I agree, but there was still a large number of forces that stood against us. The amount of salvage to be collected would create jobs that could last for years. Many of those same detractors could end up working on a project of this magnitude. What better way to show them they were misguided in their distrust?"

I threw my hands up in surrender. It would be hard to argue with someone who was right about things a hell of a lot more than I was. The smile that replaced her frown said this was a win-win situation for me.

"Okay, Tria, you are now officially in charge of the salvage negotiations once we are sure we have eliminated any remaining Prule."

I felt like I had an abundance of brownie points that I would redeem on some future date. For now, I had bigger fish to fry. I had made up my mind the Hivemind intentionally lied to us. Even though we had no idea how many Prule were on the planet, I wasn't going to let the remaining entity know that. It was not the only one who could stretch the truth. It would be the last thing the Prule entity would ever hear.

"Justice, have the Overseer tell the Hivemind we have reached the target coordinates. Inform it the Prule forces that once occupied this planet have all been destroyed. Make it known that it will perish here as well."

I headed to the brig to take care of some long overdue business. Coonts and Klutch decided they would join me. Tria acted like she had better things to do and waved me on. On the way to the lifts, I heard Klutch make a wager with Coonts. It involved the amount of urine it would take to kill the Hivemind. Their discussion turned into an argument that I wanted no part of. That freaking Tibor! There would be no pissing involved in the Prule's demise. The Overseer's awareness would be evacuated from the containment vessel, and it would go out the hangar door.

Our defensive beam weapons would turn it to dust. I would wait until we were almost to the brig before I burst Klutch's bubble. There was a good chance Coonts would claim to be the winner by default. The close quarters of the brig would be no place I wanted to be right after that happened. In the time it took us to get to the down tube, the Hivemind's survival instincts must have kicked into overdrive.

"Commander, the Hivemind has offered to give us the exact coordinates of a subterranean facility," Justice said. "It states that if the biologicals who attempted to manipulate it survived to make it to this location, they had the access codes to give them safe entry into the site."

I stopped in my tracks so suddenly that Klutch and Coonts, who were still arguing, bowled me over. I went headfirst into the down tube. I righted myself and stepped on to the hangar deck, frowning. My two crewmates stepped out a moment later, apologizing for the collision. My stare silenced them.

"I take it the Hivemind will give us the access codes if we continue its existence?" I asked Justice.

"Yes."

"I want specifics or no deal. What kind of facility is it?"

"The facility was designed to repair battle damaged assets. Hunters, to be exact. It is also a biological materials storage area."

"Are there active Hunters?"

"The Hivemind claims its queries to this facility are more than two hundred years old. At that time, the active unit count was ninety-seven."

I gritted my teeth and slowly shook my head. I wondered when it would finally dangle a carrot in front of our faces. The blatant hint that there were other secret facilities was now out on the table as a bargaining chip. I didn't doubt for a minute that this one was just the tip of the iceberg. My instincts were telling me to doubt the Prule's reason for leading us here. This was feeling more and more like it was the Hivemind's last-ditch effort for revenge.

"Justice, what are the odds of this being another trap of some kind?"

"Fifty-fifty."

Well shit! I didn't need a super intelligence to tell me that. My simple mind had already come to that conclusion. The Hivemind admitting there was at least ninety-seven Hunters roaming the planet reinforced Justice's theory that they were behind the attack on the Legacy. It was also leading me to believe the Hivemind was playing us for suckers. If the attack on the Legacy would have been successful, it would have died along with the rest of us. It really didn't care if it lived or died. This was all about getting back at the first biologicals able to capture it. Coonts and Klutch were both waiting for me to come to a decision.

"Change of plans," I said. "I am headed back to the bridge."

As I suspected, Coonts claimed to be the winner of the wager. Another heated argument broke out. Coonts's new physique must have come complete with a reinforced spine and an even bigger set of nads. He was in the Troop Master's face and poking at his chest. I was at the lifts, and the smell was already eyewatering. How Coonts could stand it was beyond me. I had not heard any threats yet, but it was time to shut them both down.

"Hey!" I yelled at them. "Knock that scat off and make sure your battle kit is ready. We are going to investigate the Prule facility!"

That did the trick, and they both ran to the ready room. When I returned to the bridge, I was surprised to find Tria on the IST talking to the Principal Investigator. She must have taken my words to heart and got right on the deal. Even though I had said nothing about contacting Sael, she took it upon herself to do it. I caught the last of their conversation and heard Sael say that her best containment teams would be on their way within five hours and the salvage fleets would follow once the planet was cleared. I sat in my command chair and hoped I would hear a good explanation.

"Nathan, it is time that we started sharing the risks we have been taking," Tria said when her call with Sael finished. "Sael has stated the Chaalt people owe us a huge debt of gratitude, so I am giving them a chance to prove it. I want this to be one less possible threat that we have to face alone. They are now aware this was a Prule stronghold and will come prepared to deal with whatever they may find. Sael will also be bringing several of our best salvage experts to assess the extent of our find and establish a reasonable value."

I had a lot of reasons to be mad but could find no fault in Tria's decisions. Everything she had done was in the best interest of us all. It didn't change the fact I still had plans that I intended to move on a lot sooner than five hours from now. I was also questioning why she would call Sael so quickly.

"I was planning on taking a look inside the Prule base, and it didn't include waiting for Sael," I said.

"I know. I will see you in the ready room."

She gave me a dazzling smile and went to the down tubes. That was interesting to say the least. It had always been my experience to hear some less than friendly exchanges between Tria and the Operative. Apparently, that was not the case this time around. That in itself was a strange occurrence. Then, not a word about the dangers of going into the Prule base alone, just "I know, let's go."

"It's probably a trap!" I yelled after her.

She stood waiting at the lifts until I caught up with her.

"It's never mattered before. Why should it now?"

She was correct. I was never known for stepping over a steaming pile when I could land both feet right in it.

"You seem rather jubilant after talking to Sael," I said. "That doesn't happen very often."

"The council wants me back under their command. They have offered me the rank of Senior Operative and a free hand in decisions that would normally require their stamp of approval."

I stopped dead in my tracks and slowly turned to her. "What did you say?"

"I would think about it."

I grimaced and started rubbing my temples. It sounded like one of those routines where we took a step forward, only to find we had to take three back. Tria interpreted my reaction for what it was. She put her hand on my shoulder and pulled me close.

"I have generated considerable enthusiasm among the leadership of my people to again obtain Prule artifacts. We did, after all, destroy their entire collection," she reminded me. "I am laying the foundation for future concessions from the council. There will come a time when they will offer us whatever we want in exchange for continued access to discoveries."

Once upon a time, I heard those very same words from the Operative. They didn't bear fruit then, and I doubted if they would now. I wasn't happy about some of the decisions Tria was making. It may have had something to do with me not being in on the discussion. We had to go through a lot of bullshit to get her away from being manipulated by the council. Now it seemed like she was intentionally putting herself back in that position. The look I was giving her gave away the consternation I felt. She embraced me and kissed me lightly on the lips. Her smile never wavered.

"Nathan, in the time that you have known me, how many times have I made decisions that we have not benefited from?"

"Well, I could probably name ..."

"For the sake of this conversation, let's leave our combat engagements out of the equation!"

It was my turn to smile. I was pretty sure she was done playing games. Whatever she was up to had to be good, or she wouldn't be this exultant.

"I would be interested in hearing everything that was said."

"I told Sael we found an ancient debris field around a planetoid in uncharted space. We were considering the sale of the salvage rights, and they would go to the highest bidder. I told her to let us know if she wanted to submit an offer. She stated she would pass the information on to the appropriate people. With that said, it seemed reasonable to tell her while surveying the wreckage we were attacked from the surface of the planet. When she asked who was behind the attack, I told her evidence suggested there were active Prule units on the planet's surface. I might have also thrown out the theory that the planet was once a Prule base of operations in this galaxy and the salvage was the wreckage from the attack on the base. Sael being Sael demanded I turn over the coordinates. I, of course, refused without consulting you first but did go on to say the salvage would take years to remove once we sanitized the planet. I ended the transmission and was going to consult with you on my actions. Sael commed me back on my IST minutes later and started making offers, the results of which I have already stated."

"Are you really considering being a pawn of the council again?"

Tria frowned. It indicated to me I might have hurt her feelings. I guess I could have worded it differently but was still a little pissed for being left out of a command-level decision. Relationships were full of give and take. Commanders to subordinates, not so much. Her frown eased, and she shook her head.

"Not in a million solar rotations, but Sael does not need to know that. She is not the only one capable of subterfuge."

"You didn't leave us much time to take a look around before Sael shows up and starts stepping on my toes."

"I am going to use an Earth phrase that you have used on more than one occasion. I think this is the appropriate time to repeat it: We have more than enough time to find out if we are biting off more than we can chew."

23

When we got to the ready room, Coonts and Klutch were already wearing their suit liners and inspecting their weapons. Xul was wearing his Zaen armor and met Tria and me at the door.

"Commander, all battle suits are at full munitions capacity, and Justice has filled the reservoirs with weaponized nanites," Xul reported. "They are preprogramed to the same parameters as our last mission. Justice has briefed me on the target area, and it will be necessary to use the shuttle for the insertion. He has selected an equal loadout of nanite and antimatter missiles for the launcher magazines and topped off the expendable ordnance. I will be in Eagle One prepping for departure. If you need me, I will be going over my checklists."

The little Grawl was another fine example of what his people were capable of being. He was now fulfilling several different duties. What started out as the Legacy's science officer turned into a combat pilot position out of necessity. He willingly filled the spot and had already proven he could handle whatever was thrown at him.

"Carry on, Xul," I said, giving him a smile and a thumbs up. "We will be boarding shortly."

We suited up and checked one another's kit for anything that might possibly indicate a problem. The front of Klutch's armor had a hardened bell around the portal device's projector. Justice had made it a permanent fixture on his armor. I rapped on the bell and gave it a couple of hard tugs. It wasn't going anywhere unless the Troop Master had his suit systems release it. Up in the top of my HUD, I had three green bars indicating the status of my teammates. We were good to go.

Justice put the target area video on my helmet HUD. He highlighted the insertion area. It was on the opposite side of a massive crater that was more than two miles across and easily that deep. The crater wall was the reason we would be using the shuttle for the insertion. It rose up to a height of twelve-hundred feet and obscured what Justice had determined was the tunnel entrance to the facility. The scan returns showed nothing usable aside from unusual density readings spread out over a large area. If the weapon that had made the crater would have hit two thousand yards to the south, we would not have a reason to look around.

"Commander, I have included some extra equipment in your battle suit's inventory," Justice informed me. "The strike team will be carrying the extra equipment as well. You now have six communication drones that should allow continuous comms with the Legacy, as long as there is unobstructed signal continuity. I can track your progress through the facility. It is advisable to place them in strategic locations along your route. I have also created a data capture device designed to penetrate Prule processing units like those found imbedded in the Hivemind's biomass. You and Tria will each have one. It is still an experimental device, but if the opportunity should present itself, place it on anything you determine to be a Prule computer system. The longer it is in contact with the processor, the greater the chance to collect valuable information. If for some reason you fail to collect it, the internal clock will release weaponized nanites to neutralize the device along with the processor it is in contact with.

"The final addition to your loadout is two antimatter charges. Their destructive power is equal to four of your launcher tube's full-yield munitions. They have tamperproof ignition systems that interphase with your HUD. I have included a menu that should cover most any deployment scenario, and they can stick to any surface once activated. You should use extreme caution if you decide to deploy them."

It was nice to know that we now had the option of doing some major damage to the facility without bombarding it from space. The more I thought about it, the more I liked the idea. If there was something we did not want to fall into anyone else's hands, we could now blow it up without expending launcher munitions. It gave us the option of proclaiming our innocence to any interested parties. Justice was still wargaming a hundred steps ahead of me.

"Thanks, Justice," I said. "You know how much I like new toys to play with."

That comment got me the stink eye from my crewmates. There had been a few times when my propensity for mayhem had proven to be just as dangerous to them as it was to the enemy. I shrugged and smiled back at them. Justice put the latest scans of the insertion point up on the hangar wall so we could all take a final look before we departed. There was just enough room for the shuttle to fly in between the crater wall and the mountainside the tunnel entrance was located on. It may have been easier to jump in, but Justice nixed the idea. If we were subjected to another surprise attack, the shuttle's shields might be our only salvation. Xul had Justice's subsystem preset all the Eagle's heavy weapons for a retaliatory snapshot in case the worst came to pass. At the very least, it would slow any follow-up shots long enough for us to get clear of the area. If need be, Justice was on the other side of the crater wall and would turn the site into another pothole. I felt we had our asses covered and couldn't think of anything else we needed to do. We boarded the shuttle, and Justice pushed us out into the void.

Xul had the shuttle cloaked and flew low over the tortured landscape. We had to make a couple pop-up maneuvers to clear the ridges between us and the ravine that would take us to the cave entrance. Each time we gained altitude, we got better scan returns of the ground below. It was desolate and without life or visible power sources. It was disheartening to see this much destruction and know the planet was still occupied by hostile forces. It painted a grim picture for those who came here to defeat the Prule.

"We will be over the target in thirty seconds, Commander!" Xul called out to us.

We stood up and made our way to the shuttle's hatch. Klutch took the front position. He had his plasma caster up and ready with Tria and me behind him. Coonts rapped on the back of my armor, letting me know he was in position and ready. It was a rough ride at the speed Xul was flying, so we locked our boots to the deck, waiting for him to pop the hatch. When he finally did, it was to a dark, featureless rip in the ground. Our no-light sensors showed us the remains of a huge landslide caused by the crater wall heaving up from the surrounding terrain. There was evidence of large machinery and possibly weapons buried all along its leading edge. The entrance was nothing more than a three-foot by four-foot hole that had not been completely buried by the onrushing ground. There was no evidence of activity around it. The soil was pulverized and loose, showing no signs of being disturbed.

Klutch used his armored boots to push the soil into the hole until he had an opening big enough to accept his large dimensions. The rest of us had formed a semicircle around him with our weapons pointing outward. He disappeared into the hole. What sounded something like a whoop came over our group comms.

"Klutch! What the hell was that?"

"Nothing, Commander," Klutch replied. "That first step is what you would describe as a doozy. I have no movement, and the tunnel looks clear. It drops off in the distance, so I am unable to tell what is farther down."

Tria went down next with me right after her. Klutch was right. It wasn't so much of a step as it was a fall. The tunnel was over one hundred feet tall, and the landslide had filled the entrance all the way to the top. I slid almost straight down the rocky slope, looking for Tria below me. I hit the bottom and rolled. I heard a clipped laugh on my private comms and looked up to see Tria. She had made the decision to use her suit's gravity drive to suspend her above the floor and avoid the haphazard slide altogether. I was going to give her some stupid reason for not doing the same, but Coonts came rolling into me. He started swearing at Klutch for not being more specific on the nature of the fall.

I got to my feet as Tria landed next to us. I pulled Coonts up and extracted a comms drone from my fanny pack. I tossed it up the slope, and it took off to the ceiling of the cavern. It hovered at the hole we used to make our entrance. I called to Xul for a comms check. He came right back loud and clear. I told him to go back to the Legacy and wait for us there. I had no idea how long we would be and did not want him sitting up there as a stationary target. He commed back an affirmative, but I could tell he did not like it.

Tria, Coonts, and I got our bearings and located Klutch well down the passage. He was kneeling where the tunnel dropped down a slope. We boosted to his location. He was studying the floor of the tunnel.

"What have you got, Klutch?"

"Commander, unless it was destroyed, there is a very large tracked vehicle around here somewhere. Look at the size of the track marks."

The tunnel was eighty feet wide, and a set of track marks went down the middle, leaving little room on either side. I could only speculate, but my mind conjured up a huge tank with a gazillion weapons sticking out in all directions. The chill that ran up my spine vanquished the image, and I turned to look down the slope. It leveled off sixty feet below us and continued out of sight. Coonts made an ominous observation.

"Commander, the way the dust and debris were disturbed by the passage of the vehicle indicates the direction it last took. If the vehicle was going out of the passage and to the planet's surface, the mounds of soil pressed from beneath the tracks would be at the tunnel side of the track. It is plain to see that is not the case. The soil is pushed out on the entrance side, indicating the vehicle went down the passage and not out of it."

I tried to paint a good picture of the situation. Maybe it was just a big tow truck of some kind that hauled other crap back for repairs. This was, after all, supposed to be a

359

repair facility. Then I started thinking about how many times the Hivemind had misled us. Nope! It was going to be a big ass tank loaded with every weapon the Prule had ever built.

"Coonts, Klutch, you take the right side, and Tria and I will take the left. Use your gravity drives to stay close to the ceiling of the passage. I know cloaking hasn't helped in the past, but do it anyway. If we see a big tracked weapons platform, we will retreat back up here and make another plan of action."

My crewmate's cloaked avatars appeared in my HUD. We boosted to the ceiling and eased our way down. The tunnel went three hundred yards and dropped again. We followed it down another step, and this time it terminated at a huge blast door. If the vehicle was down here, it was somewhere on the other side. I had the access codes and the carrier wave necessary to gain entry. I stood in front of the door and again thought about the Hivemind. It was a backstabbing pile of bio-shit that no doubt wanted us dead. I would love nothing more than to loot this place and go back to the Legacy to rub it in the bio machine's awareness.

"Klutch, choose a spot on the door and make a hole."

Tria pulled a comms relay from her kit and tossed it to the top of the tunnel ceiling. It probably was a good idea, but I doubted if we would have comms on the other side of the door.

The Tibor pulled his plasma caster from its clip and checked the charge on the energy pack. The business end glowed a pinkish blue, and we all took a step back.

"Anytime, Troop Master!"

He turned and gave me a toothy grin and hit the button on the portal device. We had a good hole. Tria and I raised our beam weapons and ran through with Coonts right behind us. We spread out and took a knee. Low light was no longer necessary. There was plenty of light on this side of the door, and our audio pickups were assaulted by the din of machinery. It was loud enough we would not have to worry about the small amount of noise we made while moving. Klutch came through behind us and shut down the portal. My HUD notified me we were in an atmosphere. It was high in nitrogen, carbon dioxide, and ozone. It had only a minute amount of oxygen. Breathing it if one of our suits got breached was not a healthy option. The G load went up from point five to a constant two.

Klutch crouched down behind us with his plasma caster up and ready. I wasn't sure if I was comfortable with it that close to my back but had other things to occupy my mind. The tracked vehicle was indeed a tank, and we were crouched in its shadow. It did not have the number of weapons my imagination had conjured, but the large twin barreled turret mounted on its top was all it probably needed to do the job it was designed for. I waved us forward, and we scurried underneath its belly. Tria and I had to bend over, but Coonts and Klutch had no problem standing under the mammoth weapon. We could see

361

another tank behind the one we were sheltering under. I wondered if this was the only exit. If it was, they were trapped by the crater wall at the end of the tunnel. More unpleasant thoughts passed through my mind. There was always the possibility they could blast an opening big enough to make it to the surface. I shook my head to clear the crap screwing my concentration. My view from underneath the tank was limited. I could see an open area in the distance. We weren't going to see what was going on in here if we didn't get moving.

"Klutch, take point," I ordered. "Move us to the next vehicle."

He came forward, and we formed up behind him. The distance to the next tank was about twenty yards. We had no way to tell if someone or something was up on the rear deck of the tank. We would move fast and hope our cloaked battle armor hid us from detection. Klutch went first and looked up at the rear of the tank.

"Commander, it looks clear, but I think I see what could be an open hatch."

"Tria, you go across to Klutch and cover me and Coonts. We are going to take a look up above."

Tria gave me a quick nod.

"Be careful, it is still too early in the game to let the enemy know we are here," she said.

She was stating the obvious, but I didn't mind. I thought sure she would insist on coming with me. As second in command, she made the right decision. If I screwed up and got fragged, she could carry on the mission. Coonts huddled close to me.

"You take the right side, and I'll take the left," I told him. "Come up slow and easy. If you make contact, don't start shooting unless you have to."

He gave me a thumbs up and went to the right track. He waited until I gave the signal, and we used our gravity drives to slowly climb the fifteen feet to the back deck of the machine. Klutch was right: a large hatch was open on the rear deck. Coonts and I came from two different directions until we could look down into it. It was a missile magazine and was partially filled with thirty-foot-long blunt-ended black tubes. Now that we could see the back side of the turret, we could also see the four holes of the launcher. We didn't see any hostiles, and the tank behind us covered a direct view of our location. I pulled a couple of grenades from my storage pouch and pointed into the far end of the magazine.

"Proximity, with remote detonation activated."

Coonts nodded and climbed down into the well. I did the same and wedged one of my gifts under the business end of the weapons. Turning around, I put the other grenade in the launcher feed tube. Coonts crawled back out of the magazine, and we both dropped back down to the floor of the tunnel. We formed up with Tria and Klutch.

"We rigged the missile magazine to blow in case we need a good diversion," I said. "Did you get a look out into the complex?"

Tria leaned in close. Our comms broadcasted on frequencies so low they would not carry beyond our position. If someone was actively searching for the communications, they would find us. But the chances were low that sensors of that nature were deployed inside the base.

"Not much to see from here," she said. "A large crane is blocking our view of what lays beyond. We could use the crane to get a better look. The platform on the top would be a good hide."

Klutch commed right back and pointed upward at the tank. "We should make sure this one cannot be used to block our exit."

"Make it quick, Troop Master. We will be waiting for you. Coonts, cover him!"

They went back toward the front of the tank and boosted out of sight. We heard Klutch comment over our comms. He told Coonts to take the left one while he did the right. It did not take a genius to figure out they were spiking the projector tubes on the turret. Coonts called out he was done, but Klutch sent him a curt reply, stating more is always better. Coonts grumbled something under his breath, but I was sure he complied. They both dropped down from the front of the tank and rejoined us.

"Take point, Klutch. We want to get to the top of the crane carriage," I said.

We watched Klutch's avatar run out of the tunnel entrance and stop at the base of the crane's support leg. He boosted up and over the edge of the carriage. We heard him let out a croak and something that sounded like "scat."

"Commander, you better come and take a look," Klutch said.

We hustled out to the support leg and glanced around. Machinery and stacks of parts surrounded us on all sides. We were in a machine assembly area. I boosted upward with Tria and Coonts right behind me. I landed on the edge of the carriage and saw the Troop Master laying prone and peering downward over the front of the platform. I got down on all four and crawled up next to him. If scat was indeed what he said, it was an understatement.

On the floor two hundred feet below us, were thousands of aliens of every description. The bluish-white electrical current we had witnessed on the Hivemind's lifeboat danced among the metal protrusions sticking out of their bodies. The floors and walls around them were alive with the current, and it jumped to them from every direction. It was like watching an ant hive. The aliens were picking through a massive pile of debris. They selected pieces and parts, placed them on a conveyor, and went back for more. The conveyor moved the debris rapidly into a large separator that had chutes coming out of it in all directions. The chutes fed machines that produced the loud buzzing hum and grinding noises that permeated the complex.

It was no longer a myth cooked up to scare the lesser races. The Prule were active in our galaxy. If this evidence was not convincing, I didn't know what could be more damning. The survivors of the battle to free our galaxy were not sitting idle. They were making preparations, and it didn't look like it was for innocuous purposes.

"Commander, there is an atmospheric lock by the debris pile, and it is cycling," Coonts called to me. I moved to his side.

He pointed to a spot on the far wall to the right of our position. About four hundred yards away, a red strobe light was flashing. It stopped, and a large hatch parted in the middle. Eight Hunters came through, followed by gravity sleds loaded with more debris. They dumped the sleds down a chute that carried the gathered booty to the massive pile being picked over by the reanimated beings. Although we had no idea where it went, we now had another exit to choose from if scat hit the fan. Tria was at my side and pointed out the Prule were actively salvaging the surface of the planet. Where they were doing it was a mystery. Justice did not detect any movement in the area, and the location of the air lock was not that far from where we made our insertion. That bit of intelligence meant there had to be tunnel networks that were shielded from detection. I guess the Prule had nothing better to do for more than a couple hundred years. It seemed logical to make their rebuilding efforts as covert as possible. The chances of being able to contact Justice would be slim to none. We needed to get our collected intelligence uploaded to the Legacy. If things went south on us, we would at least have some proof to show for it.

"Klutch, we are moving back to the tunnel entrance," I said. "I want to send our data to the Legacy, and I don't think I should try it from here."

The Troop Master eased back from the edge, and dropped over the rear of the platform.

"All clear, Commander."

We quickly joined him and ran underneath the parked tanks and back to the pressure door. I pointed at it and gave Klutch a nod. He put a portal in the same spot we entered through, and Tria, Coonts, and I exited the complex. Klutch stepped through seconds later and shut it down.

"Justice, do you have a copy?"

"Yes, Commander. Are you ready for extraction?"

"Not yet, Justice. Have you detected any movement top side?"

"Negative," Justice replied. "I have made several excursions around the immediate area. My scans show no power sources or life forms. I have found nothing other than debris from starships and other vehicles strewn about the surface. Just east of your position is another large crater with a crashed spacecraft of unknown origin. The front half of the ship is buried, but the rear of the vessel is relatively intact. It would be worthy of investigation when your current mission is complete."

That had to be where the Prule were gathering salvage. The ship's hull was shielding them from detection. The only way to know for sure would be to go investigate, but at the moment, we had other plans.

"I want you to upload the data from our battle suits and give me an assessment as quickly as possible. We will hold our position until we hear from you."

"Affirmative. Uploading now."

We huddled against the pressure door to await Justice's synopsis. He didn't make us wait long.

"Commander, I will continue to examine the data but have found several interesting items worth noting. I have identified a new Prule asset working among the reanimated slaves. They are larger than Hunters and only have four legs instead of the six normally seen on the Prule we have encountered. They also have twelve upper appendages with multiple tools on each. I have singled them out on the frames of your video. They are maintaining the vast amount of machinery in this part of the complex. The next item of interest is the video of them picking up slaves that no longer appear to be moving and inserting additional conductors into them. Once they determine the proper number of conductors, they put the beings back on the work floor and the current reenergizes them. The final item in this briefing, is that everything processed in the lower machine complex is being piped through the wall into another part of the facility. If it does not expose you to additional hazard, it would be very desirable to see what they are doing with the refined materials."

"Roger that. We are going back inside."

I didn't think it could be possible to expose ourselves to any more hazards than we already had. My grandparents had always said I was a curious child, and I lived up to that reputation all my life. It made sense to go back in and find out what the Prule were doing on the other side of the wall. Klutch made another portal, and a few seconds later, we were all sneaking back under the tanks. When we got to the crane, Klutch pointed to the myriad pipes and ductwork on the ceiling of the complex.

"Commander, we should work our way to the far wall by using the overhead piping as background cover," Klutch suggested. "If a Hunter detects our cloaking systems, we can always attempt to hide in one of the ducts."

It was as good a plan as any and should get us to the other side without interference from the activity below.

"We will follow your lead, Troop Master."

We formed our combat diamond and boosted to the ceiling. We would be able to stay behind the piping in a few places but most of it was too small to give us cover. I was happy that Klutch didn't like dicking around up here anymore than I did, so we moved along at a rapid pace. Our cloaking systems were doing the job, and the opposite side of the complex loomed in front of us. As much as I hated to admit it, I was feeling like things were going our way.

"Commander, two of the Prule maintenance machines are climbing the ramp leading to where the tanks are parked," Coonts said.

I stopped and looked back across the complex. I magnified my view so I could determine what the Prule were up to. My HUD gave me a distance reading at just over a thousand yards. We had about two hundred to go to reach our destination. Coonts was right. The Prule were up in the assembly area and climbing aboard the tank that had the open missile hatch. I had a feeling, and it wasn't pleasant. It was something akin to needing to use the bathroom really bad only to find somebody beat you to it. The crane boom swung around and moved over the tank. The feelings of dread were now being reinforced by the unsportsmanlike conduct of my bowels.

"Klutch, get to the wall and make a hole now!" I shouted.

The Troop Master had already surmised what was about to happen. He knew we needed to be someplace other than where we were. If the Prule removed those missiles, everybody on this side of the complex was about to have a bad day. The four of us braked hard with our gravity drives to keep from colliding with the wall. Klutch fumbled with the portal device's buttons and projected a hole that immediately closed. Tria pushed him lower on the wall.

"Try again!" she shouted.

The second one was a good hole. That's when a massive explosion detonated at the other end of the complex. Tria, Coonts, and I boosted hard through the portal. Klutch came barreling into us a second later. We crashed into the side of a structure and landed in a pile on a catwalk. Klutch managed to hit the right button as he fell, and the portal closed behind us. The shockwave from the blast bowed the wall we had passed through and fractured it like a jigsaw puzzle. The material chutes were blown off, sending their contents out like giant shotgun blasts. The facility shook hard enough to bring down the overhead pipework on top of us. The catwalk ripped loose from the structure we had landed on and sent us falling with the rest of the wreckage to the floor below.

24

Of all the scenarios I had thought of while booby trapping the tanks, what just happened had not been one of them. Doom on me! We were pinned up against a building structure with tons of busted crap on top of us. I could move my legs a little but not much. The commentary coming from my strike team made it clear they were not injured but were stuck under the debris as well. My helmet's HUD showed their locations, and Klutch's icon was beside mine. I could feel movement under me and assumed it was the Troop Master. I pushed my suit servos to their limits and managed to bend forward about a foot, which freed my arms. The movement under me increased, as did the swearing coming from Klutch. I started digging between my legs and uncovered the Troop Master's faceplate. In the past when disaster struck, it was usually the Tibor's ass sitting on me and not the other way around. The horrific look on his face implied I should in no way make light of the situation. Tria and Coonts were against the building when the catwalk collapsed. Their icons were above and left of Klutch's and mine, with Coonts being the farthest up.

Coonts was the first to report he was making progress and managed to get his arms extricated and was working to free his torso. Tria's icon was about two feet or so below him. The unladylike grunting coming from her comms channel let us know she was still in the same predicament as Klutch and I but was working on it.

"Commander, I need silence on the comms channel!" Coonts suddenly called out.

I was wondering what kind of calamity could possibly make our self-inflicted woes any worse than they already were. I cringed because I knew the sky was the limit when it came to pain and suffering. Considering where we were and what we would be held accountable for, things were unlikely to improve. We stopped struggling against the debris and stayed off the comms channel for what seemed like a long time.

"Commander, we are not the only ones trying to extricate themselves from the wreckage," Coonts finally said. "I have movement from three different directions. One of the sound sources is coming from the building we are pinned against. If I had to speculate, I would say that something is trying to smash its way out!"

I sat still and increased the volume on my audio sensors. I picked up the telltale thumps coming from behind me. The last time I heard similar noises, it was a Prule Hunter wanting a piece of my ass for the mayhem I had caused. The odds were in favor of it being the same situation.

"Coonts! Get Tria dug out as fast as you can!"

"I am working on it, Commander!" Coonts shouted.

I started thrashing around until my servos were giving me stress warnings in my HUD. I must not have been doing Klutch any favors because his vocabulary digressed to unfiltered profanity. He called to me in a voice I could tell was straining for control.

"Commander, I would really appreciate it if you would stop what you are doing! I have managed to roll on my side and am going to trigger the portal device. If you continue to push more debris down on me, I might inadvertently miss my intended target and send you lower torso to another dimension."

I had to give him credit: it was succinct and to the point without a lot of overtones suggesting disrespect. Not wanting to lose any of the body parts I actually enjoyed using, I quickly answered.

"Roger that, Troop Master. Please carry on!"

I heard some more strained grunting and felt the debris under me shift a little more.

"I am ready, Commander," Klutch said. "Triggering in three, two, one!"

I suddenly found myself falling down and sideway in a rush of wreckage. The next thing I knew, I was sprawled out in a pile of debris with the Troop Master across the room from me. He got a good portal on the side of the building we were pinned against, and we fell through the opening. We were now inside a room filled with machinery. My maker must have decided that my freedom from the trash pile would be my only acorn for the day. My sudden stop was accompanied by something pushing me aside. We were not alone. I tried to get my feet under me but was jerked off the floor by one of the four-legged Prule maintenance machines. It started smashing electrodes into my armor. The sharply spiked tips were breaking off or bending with each blow. That didn't deter it from trying to get another one into me and only convinced it to strike harder. I got a grip on two of the arms and was trying my best to rip them from the bio machine. It had ten more, and they were all pummeling me with spikes or tools.

"Commander, I have freed Tria's arms and should have her extricated shortly," Coonts called.

My vision was blurring from the heavy shots I was taking to my helmet. I wanted to answer Coonts but didn't think any response I might have made would be coherent. I was, however, going to make an effort to call Klutch and ask why he was not doing something about the ass kicking I was getting. Before I could grunt out a rational request for help, rapid fire blasts from the Troop Master's shotgun disabled two of the machine's legs. It pitched forward onto the floor, but not before it unceremoniously threw me into a wall. I fell to the floor with the beast in me screaming out to use my beam weapon. I sat up and was seriously giving the idea some thought but saw the Troop Master was standing over the flailing bio machine, putting shot after shot into it. When it finally went still, Klutch gave it another half of a magazine of penetrator slugs. More was always better, and he took that motto seriously. He ruptured a fluid reservoir on the bottom of the bio machine's torso, splattering us with a brackish substance that had the consistency of jelly. If it was the biomass the machine sustained its inner being with, then Klutch had revealed a weakness we could use to our advantage. Tria called over the group comms and the urgency in her voice said things outside were not going well.

"Incoming Hunters!"

Her exclamation was followed by a jarring blast that caved part of the wall in, giving me a view outside of the building. I was going to boost up and out of the opening, but a Hunter stepped into my line of sight. I threw my arm up and shot it with my beam weapon. The back blast blew the rest of the wall out, knocking both Klutch and me to the floor. Klutch never saw the Hunter and was yelling at me to check my fire. Tria and Coonts appeared at the opening, yelling the same thing. They jumped inside and pulled me to my feet. Klutch looked like he still had more to bitch about, but Tria cut him off.

"You destroyed the second Hunter before it could identify us as a threat," Tria said. "The Hunter Coonts engaged never got a lock on us. They were both buried under debris and had just freed themselves. Heavy smoke is pouring out of the material chutes and degrading visibility on this side of the complex. We should clear the area before they can determine the nature of the threat."

"Coonts, have you tried to make a connection with the comms relay?

"Yes, Commander, several times. We still have no comms to the surface."

"Klutch, take point," I ordered. "We want to stay in the buildings as long as possible. Get us to the other side of the complex and try to find an exit."

The Troop Master slapped fresh magazines into his shotgun and led us to the wall in the back of the building. He made three attempts to get a portal, all failing. Coonts pointed to a ramp that went up a level, and Klutch quickly nodded. He made another attempt with the device and got a good hole. We found ourselves in another room filled with machinery that had an open corridor on the opposite wall. Klutch ran to the opening and took a knee. He took a good look and waved us forward. He pulled a grenade from his storage pouch and wedged it between the wall and a machine console. Anything coming through the corridor behind us was going to get a rude awakening. We ran down the corridor on line and hit a junction that went right and left. The passage was a lot larger than the one we had been in. As far as I could tell, the building we were in was against the complex wall. The left-hand turn obviously went to another section of the underground base. Not wanting to go deeper into the maze of passages, I waved Klutch to the right. Tria and I took one side and Klutch and Coonts the other. We could see the end of the passage ahead. It was well-lit with large floor-to-ceiling windows. Klutch held up a fist, and we took a knee. He eased forward until he was at the end of the passage. He took his shotgun and used the HUD targeting mode to get a glimpse of what was around the corner. He hastily jerked it back and scurried to our position.

"Commander, there are six Prule in a large control room," Klutch reported. "They look a lot like small versions of the Hivemind we captured."

The Troop Master used his HUD to transfer the video. The effort was not necessary because one of the machines came around the corner and stopped. Its reaction told me our cloaking was not enough to keep us hidden. Tria shot it twice with penetrator slugs, bursting its bulbous upper torso like a balloon. We had no choice but to charge the control room in an attempt to kill them all before they could sound an alarm. Klutch jumped up and led the way as we ran around the corner. The five bio machines turned to us and froze. Nope! Cloaking was still detectable by their sensors. The time it took them to start reacting told me they must not have comprehended the danger they were in. It was as if they thought we would beg forgiveness or maybe self-terminate. They got explosive buckshot and slugs instead. It took us less than fifteen seconds to remedy their faulty thinking. The machines were not armored, indicating the brighter minds running this outfit must have felt no threat could ever reach them here. You would have thought that blowing up the raw materials side of the complex would have set off major alarms. I couldn't begin to understand why it had not. It was a gross miscalculation on the part of the supposedly brilliant machines.

"Nathan! You need to look at this!" Tria called. The edge to her voice made a chill run up my spine.

I turned and saw Tria and Coonts were looking out the large windows. I pointed at a pressure door on the other side of the room, and Klutch gave me a thumbs up and headed in that direction. I ran to Tria and Coonts to take a look. My eyes opened wide and everything I had eaten before we started the mission felt like it turned to water and was heading for the out door. A couple of hundred feet below us was an assembly line. It was turning out Prule Hunters. Hanging on racks that went from floor to ceiling and spanned the length of the complex were thousands of the Prule machines. They hung like jackets on hangers. The machines were salvaging the raw materials from the wreckage on the surface to build more troops. If this was going on in secret facilities throughout the galaxy, things could take a turn for the worse if another invasion fleet came from Andromeda. I guessed the Prule had no problem losing a portion of their operation as long as this part remained intact. As we watched, we saw hundreds of the Prule maintenance machines moving in the direction we had just come from. A grim smile crossed my lips. Good luck trying to fix the amount of shit we just broke. Coonts went to the consoles the Prule were operating.

"Commander, this would be a good place to deploy the data collection modules Justice gave us," he said, snapping me out of my thoughts.

I had forgotten all about the devices. Tria and I ran to a console and placed the compact collection device on top of it. Klutch could see through the window on the pressure door and didn't think it would be healthy to hang around.

"Commander, this door leads to the ramp that goes to the assembly area," Klutch reported. "We need to find another exit sooner than later. If they send even a fraction of those Hunters up here, we will be visiting our makers shortly afterward."

As if I needed any more convincing, the console I was standing next to lit up with flashing lights. I looked at some of the other consoles, and one by one they started doing the same thing. The Prule must have been performing damage control from this location. We had put a major hiccup in the operation of the complex, and now, no one was controlling what was left. If things were going to turn to shit, they were going to do it in a big way, and fast. Klutch called out a warning.

"Commander! Several of the Prule maintenance machines are turning back and climbing the access ramp. I count fourteen coming this way, and they are moving quickly!"

"Tria! You and Coonts backtrack down the corridor and see where it leads. Klutch and I will handle the machines."

Tria and Coonts ran down the corridor, and Klutch started messing with the controls on the pressure door. I could tell by his ongoing commentary we were not likely to get the door open. I pointed my shotgun at the large view window and blew a hole through it. Klutch frowned at me and swung his big armored fist into the remains, knocking a hole we could walk through. The loud hammering racket of machinery assaulted our audio pickups. Klutch started to unclip his plasma thrower, and I grabbed his arm.

"Unless you want every machine in here to know where we are, you should hold off on using that thing until we have to," I warned.

I could tell he didn't give a crap if they knew our exact position or not. I was glad when he went ahead and humored me. Drawing our shotguns, we stepped out onto the ramp and started putting well-placed shots into the legs and lower abdomens of the oncoming machines. The muzzle blasts from our weapons barely noticeable above the din. We knocked the lead machines down, and the others slowed to a stop. It looked like they were attempting to perform repairs on their fallen comrades. Before I could throw shade on the idea, Klutch took this as his cue to toss a grenade. It bounced once off the ramp and landed at their feet. The explosion was spectacular and blew most of them off the ramp and down to the floor below. It crossed my mind he was looking for an excuse to use his damn plasma caster, and now he had one. The machines were now focused on the explosion and heading directly for the ramp. Tria called to us and said the corridor ended at another large pressure door and Coonts was having no luck at getting it open. I told her we would be along shortly.

What seemed like unorganized chaos down below abruptly stopped with the detonation of the grenade.

Either the victims of the attack blew the whistle on us or smarter machines finally determined that we were the source of their current woes. An eight-foot section of the railing below us disintegrated in a flashing release of energy that knocked us both on our asses. My HUD could not pinpoint where the shot had come from. What it did show in great detail was the river of hostile icons had reversed direction and were all moving our way.

"Klutch, it's time to go!"

I thought he would hose the ramp down with his plasma caster. It surprised me when I saw him raise his launcher. I assumed he was going to rain high explosives on the hostiles as a parting gift. My HUD started flashing red as my antimatter proximity warning gave off a piercing beep. He emptied his magazine of all twenty rounds, and they were set to maximum yield. He rolled over and gave me a horrific smile as he pulled me to my knees. I stared at him in disbelief.

"Are you out of your mind?" I cried. "We don't even know if we can get out of here!

"Not to worry, Commander. I put a two-minute delay on the detonation timer."

I hastily threw a grenade down the ramp and scurried back through the hole in the control room view screen. Another blast showered us with high-speed fragments of the observation window and the landing we just vacated. My grenade detonated somewhere below, and I heard the warbling shriek of an enraged Hunter. I grabbed the data devices and shoved them in my storage pack. I looked over my shoulder to ensure the Troop Master was bringing up the rear. He was right on my heels and gave me a healthy push down the corridor.

"Commander, you should pick up the pace!"

I bit down on my retort and boosted down the passage. We covered the remaining distance to where Coonts and Tria waited in silence. I could have said a lot of things but knew this little adventure was just the tables being turned on me. The looks my fellow crewmates were giving Klutch, were reminiscent of the ones I used to get when the beast in me made decisions that proved detrimental to the team. He shrugged them off and pointed the portal device at the wall next to the pressure door. There was a loud crash from the passage behind us. Tria and Coonts tossed grenades down the corridor, then crowded in close to me with their weapons ready. The timer in my HUD said twenty-two seconds until detonation.

"Klutch, when we go through, get us as far from here as possible!"

He waved me off and hit the button. His indifference to our current plight had me at the tipping point, and I was considering giving the portal device to another team member. The alien device was evidently capable of further enlarging an already inordinately large set of nads to Oolaran beast-like proportions. One such set was bad enough, but two could be downright hazardous to our health. We had a good hole, so we cloaked and jumped through. We found ourselves in a construction bay that was so huge we could not see the far end. In the middle of the bay, sitting on an antigravity cradle, was a massive starship that stretched into the darkness of the gigantic cavern. Its blunt hull design was reminiscent of a Murlak Warbringer. The large vessel was festooned with weapons. It was easy to see where the battle damage it had once sustained had been repaired. The ship was crawling with thousands of Prule repair machines. Klutch guided us to the upper superstructure of the ship. It was one of the few areas that did not appear to have Prule activity. A low rumble could be heard over the strident construction noises, and the cavern shook. Dirt, rock, and small amounts of debris came down from the overhead, creating a haze that was rapidly spreading throughout the cavern. I was more than a little disappointed it was not as spectacular as our first feat of destruction, but it was sure to have put the hurt on the Hunter production lines. Klutch guided us into the shadows of a large antenna array. We landed and went prone on the hull with our weapons pointing out in all directions.

"I am going to reconnoiter the area and make sure we are secure," the Troop Master called to me.

"Roger that, just don't start any trouble until we can find a way out of here."

I thought I heard the big lummox chuckle at my statement. He got up and went toward the rear of the superstructure. So far, our cloaked battle suits had not been detected. As long as we were not in close proximity to the machines, I think our luck would hold.

"Commander, the area is clear," Klutch said. "You should move the team to my location."

We made our way to where Klutch was crouched at the rear of the ship. He held up a fist and then got down on his knees. Tria and I did the same, then we crawled to the edge of the deck. Coonts stayed behind and covered our rear while the rest of us took a look. We had a good view of pressure door where we had made our entrance. What seemed like a nonevent the first time we caused stuff to go boom was no longer the case. The Prule were abandoning their work and moving in mass toward the Hunter production area. This was an unexpected turn of events. I knew I could not count on them all leaving, but it sure looked like the vast majority were going to do just that. Security in this facility was almost nonexistent. I guess after the battle for the planet was won, the Prule had more than two hundred years of undisturbed peace to rebuild the base. The weapons that attacked us on the surface probably doomed any interlopers who may have stumbled upon the planet. The Prule's complacency with the status quo was going to cost them.

I frowned as I revisited the circumstances that led us here. If it were not for the Hivemind giving us this exact location, it was hard to say how long this operation would have continued unabated. I had pretty much decided to kill the Hivemind once we returned to the Legacy. I wondered if the Overseer could get it to divulge more information on other bases. As much as I hated to think about it, the Hivemind may have anticipated my

385

intentions. There was a good possibility the conniving piece of scat was insuring itself a stay of execution by throwing us this bone. I still had reservations concerning the access codes it gave us. My intuition said it was another trap of some kind, and that was the reason we did not use them. Tria nudged me with an elbow, purging my mind of the past and focusing me on the present.

"I have no intention of returning to the Legacy with the antimatter charge Justice gave me. This would be a good place to leave it," she said.

I had to agree with her. There was no way we could leave without at least trying to make the Prule ship a permanent fixture of the base.

"Coonts, where can we do the most harm with our munitions?"

"The ship's star drives. A chain reaction detonation on the antimatter containment vessels could do irreparable damage."

I looked at the other strike team members, and they nodded in agreement.

"Okay, Coonts, you take the lead and pick the spot, and Klutch will make a hole. Let's rig this thing to blow and get out of here so the Legacy can evac us off this rock."

We were all in agreement. It was time to get the hell out of there, but not before doing the Prule one more nasty. The Tibor gave me a big toothy smile. He loved to blow things up. I pointed to Coonts, and he gave me a thumbs up. We eased over the back of the ship and slowly descended toward the engine room. The mass exodus of

Prule was now just a trickle. Several bio machines were in and around the ship, but most went to the Hunter production area. The access hatch they were using had clouds of noxious-looking smoke flowing out of it. The haze around us was getting thicker by the minute. The less visibility the better. Coonts slowed us to a stop. He found a repaired hull plate that he reasoned would have breached the internal spaces or it would not have been repaired. It was also within a couple of hundred yards of the discharge nozzles of the star drives. He slapped Klutch on the shoulder and pointed to his selected spot. We got our weapons ready, and Klutch gave us a good portal. We charged through and found ourselves in a dark cavity between the hulls. It was filled with giant cables, power conduits, and piping that stretched as far as the eye could see. The engine room had to be close. Klutch took the lead and headed off in the direction of the star drive discharge nozzles. We had gone about fifty yards and found an access hatch that for sure would take us into the interior spaces. We did not mess with trying to open it. Klutch made a portal right in the middle of it. We stepped out of the portal into an occupied corridor. Two Prule maintenance machines were moving down the passage away from us and did not turn around. We crowded against the wall and, as quietly as possible, started working our way in the opposite direction.

Our progress came to a complete stop another thirty yards up the corridor. It had only one exit and was out into a large access passage that ran directly into the engine spaces. There was a huge blast door that protected the engine spaces. It was locked open about twenty feet up, and we could see a large number of Prule working on various pieces of equipment. Out in the passage, there were hundreds of Prule, and the chances of us not being detected were pretty damn slim. To make matters worse, Coonts called out a warning.

"Commander, we have Prule coming down the corridor to our rear!"

This may not have been such a good idea after all. We were between a rock and a hard place.

"Klutch! Make a hole!" I yelled.

Before he could active the device, a Prule maintainer stepped into the hallway and froze. Klutch threw his arm up and put a stream of armor-piercing rounds into its belly. It pitched forward onto the deck and started slinging the contents of its biomass reservoir all over the place. Coonts opened up to our rear, and two high-explosive blasts shook the corridor. Our asses were officially in the fire after that. Klutch jerked his plasma caster out in front of him and sent two big squirts of hellfire out into the group of Prule that were moving in our direction. We had every machine in the place zeroing in on our location. Tria called over the group comms.

"We have to move now or we will be trapped in here!"

Coonts's minigun firing to our rear left us little choice as to where we could go.

"Klutch, get us to the engine spaces!"

The Troop Master sent another stream of plasma out into the gathering Prule and then boosted for the engine room. As soon as I cleared the edge of the hallway, the first thing I saw was a large gravity lift loaded with equipment. Just beyond it was a large group of Hunters rapidly moving across the passage to intercept us. I sent a beam shot into the lift, blowing some of the equipment to pieces and sending it nosediving for the deck. Tria saw what I was doing and put a follow-up shot into the control cab. The aft section blew off, dumping the whole flaming mess down on to the Hunters. Coonts must have decided we were going to be sucking shit shortly. The antimatter proximity warning went off in my HUD. It went from red to yellow, which still meant we were in for a rough ride. I could not see the threat that was encouraging him to blow us all up. Visibility was crap because Klutch had everything between us and the engine room blast door blazing with plasma fire. If that wasn't enough to get my juices churning, the blast door started coming down. We dove for the deck at the base of the rapidly descending door. The only thing I could think of at that moment, was whether or not we would be welcome in the presence of our maker.

25

A lot of people do not believe in divine intervention. I would tell any who asked that there was indeed such a thing, or our maker wasn't quite ready for us to soil the carpet of his heavenly abode. The shockwave from the detonation of Coonts's antimatter shell blew us to the deck and under the engine room door. I have always known we were lucky, but not that lucky. If that was not the hand of our maker giving us his nudge of approval, then we died in the blast and this would be our hell for the rest of eternity.

My HUD was blacked out from the detonation. Justice's subsystem that made the operation of our armor possible put the stick frame outlines of our surroundings on the HUD view screen so we would not blunder about blindly. This feature enabled me to see the clawed appendage of the Prule maintainer just before it smashed into my torso. The blow did not do any real harm to me but did give me a damage warning indicator for my ammo pack. I rolled to the side before the next blow could land. My wits were now working on all cylinders, and I fired a burst of armor-piercing rounds up into the bottom of the machine. It collapsed on top of me but was blown off by a blast that sent me flying into the pressure door. The warbling screech of a Hunter let me know I had bigger problems lurking in my immediate future. I boosted hard for the ceiling just as another blast hit the door. My HUD highlighted my target and also showed me the whereabouts of my strike team. We were scattered about the huge engine room and were all fully engaged with hostile targets. The entire engine room radiated from explosive blasts and weapons fire. The beast in me was tearing its way out of it cage, and I could feel its rage taking over. It had been a while since I felt the monster's hate-filled anger and, in some ways, it was reassuring. If I was going to die, it was going to make sure I had plenty of company going with me.

I rolled hard to my right, and my beam weapon came up with what seemed like no effort on my part. I hit the Hunter dead center, knocking it down and dropping its shield. My next shot explosively scattered its remains in all directions. While I got the beast's approval, I did not win any from my team.

"Nathan! Cease fire!" Tria yelled out over our group comms. "If you breach the star drive's antimatter containment fields, we will all die!"

The reality of the warning my significant other doused me with was enough for me to wrest control back from the beast. The blast from my beam weapon had caused collateral damage to two Prule that were in close proximity to my target. The maintenance machines were attempting to drag themselves back into the fray. Coonts hosed them down with his minigun, blowing their remaining appendages to shrapnel.

"Commander, you must not let them open the blast door!" Coonts warned. "I do not have a clear shot!"

My HUD flashed a warning and highlighted two Prule up on the level above us. Coonts was engaging more targets, and Tria and Klutch were back to back sending streams of armor-piercing rounds into the Prule surrounding them. I boosted for the Prule on the landing above me, but my target fixation earned me a penalty shot from somewhere below. I was blown cartwheeling into the machinery above my targets and dumped on the floor at their feet. My vision was blurry, but I could still see enough to make out the clawed feet that started hammering me nonstop. I was fortunate because my attackers were the small versions of the Hivemind and were unarmed and unshielded. That made them relatively soft targets, but the blows they were raining down on me were anything but.

"Commander! The door is opening," Klutch shouted. "Do not make me come up there and close it myself!" The Troop Master must have thought I was napping, and the deadly edge to his voice meant he had all the trouble he could handle.

It's a shame the smell of a Tibor had no effect on Prule. It crossed my mind that the odor Klutch was giving off at the present would probably kill a great many lesser races.

392

Between the testy insubordinate tone of my Troop Master and the ass stomping I was once again on the receiving end of, I again let the beast in me off its leash. My launcher came up and pointed at the control panel the Prule were standing at. The beast must have triggered a round of high explosive, because a lucid person would not have done such a thing. The distance was maybe four feet to the recipients of my hate. The explosion blasted the Prule into numerous pieces and sent me flying more than thirty feet over the upper level rail to the deck below. While my armor did soak up the punishment it had received, that didn't mean there wasn't pain involved. My brain was rattled like a peanut in a beer can. My vision was wonky as hell, and I had major fault warnings on my minigun and needle weapon. It was hard to get any clarity as to our current state of affairs because my audio pickups were zoning in and out.

I felt myself being pulled across the deck and I was not in the mood to play patty cake with another machine piece of crap. I was going to give the high-explosive route another go, but felt my arm being pushed down. My vision was coming back, and I was greeted by Coonts's upside-down helmet filling my faceplate. My hearing was on the mend as well. He was yelling over my comms channel to hold my fire. I pushed his helmet away from my faceplate and rolled over with a groan. The blast door had stopped moving. It had risen about a foot before I put a spanner in the works. The other thing I noticed was there were still several hostiles in the area, but they were all thrashing around on the deck like brainless idiots. Even the Prule I could see through the gap under the door were having wild seizures. My brain finally put together more coherent thoughts, and I realized the symptoms were nanite-related.

Tria and Klutch pulled me to my feet. Tria cleared her war mask and put her faceplate to mine.

"Commander, Klutch and I have expended our nanite reservoirs," she said. "It will not hold back the Prule for long. Their numbers are too great. We need to get out of here before they attack in mass."

My brain was back to understanding complete sentences. We did not possess enough weaponized nanites to protect us indefinitely. The large area and number of hostiles would effectively dilute our attack to the point it would no longer incapacitate the bio machines. We were screwed unless we could get out of here.

"Coonts, you take our charges and put them where they will do the most damage," I commanded. "Set them so they cannot be tampered with. Program them for remote disarm and detonation. Set the fail-safe for twenty minutes. Klutch, find us a way out of here. I don't care how you do it."

We gave Coonts our scuttling charges, and he boosted up onto one of the gigantic drives. He momentarily looked around and then disappeared into the maze of machinery. Klutch started putting portals on every spot that he thought would have a void large enough for us to make our escape. We would be able to tell if he was successful if

394

the nonstop cursing that was being mumbled over our comms ceased. Tria and I got down on our knees and peeked under the blast door. The amount of carnage we had inflicted on the Prule obscured our view. The machine carcasses stretched into the distance. We both knew it would be foolish to think the Prule had given up. Somewhere out there, they were massing for an attack. Our options were quickly going to run out if we didn't get out of here soon.

Just to keep the scat eaters honest, I put my arm under the door and raised it to what my HUD suggested would give maximum distance. I cranked the yield on an antimatter round until I got an orange release warning. As soon as Tria got the warning, she boosted away from the door. She called out a warning even though the rest of the team got the same messages. I let the round fly and boosted for the upper level, where Tria and Klutch took cover. The detonation shook the ship and blasted pieces of Prule and other debris through the gap under the door. In response to the high-order detonation, the door finally decided it should do what it was originally designed for and slammed down to the deck, sealing us inside. The upside was we didn't have to worry about the Prule sniping at us through the gap. The downside was unless Klutch could portal us out, we were trapped like rats in a dumpster.

Coonts dropped down from the drives and joined us. In the top right-hand corner of my HUD, a small green remote detonator box appeared. It had the word armed in the middle of it. Coonts had transferred control to me. In the event I was not capable of doing the deed when the time came, the control would pass to Tria and then back to him and finally Klutch. He was putting contingencies in place if things went really bad for the chain of command. I was hoping like hell it would not come to that.

But Klutch's mood and demeanor were making me think we were in a steamy one up to our eyeballs. He was still probing for a good portal location only to have the hole promptly close on every try. Between curse words, he alerted us the device was starting to lag between attempts. I had to give it to the Prule: they knew how to protect the engines and antimatter containers on their starships. Klutch jumped down from the upper deck and slowly shook his head. It was now confirmed. There was only one way in, and one way out. He had a look that I had rarely seen on his face: gloom. This place would prove to be our tomb unless we took drastic measures. Not wanting it to come to that, I decided to go to plan B, even though I had yet to come up with one. My team gathered around me, and I wasn't about to let them think I didn't actually have a backup plan.

"Klutch, make a portal on the blast door," I said. "I am going to send a full-yield antimatter round through. After the round detonates, you make another portal, and we get out of here. My plan is for us to get to the utility access where we boarded."

Tria commed me on my private channel. "I know you just made that scat up. I just wanted to tell you it would have been my plan as well."

Tria boosted with Coonts to the bulkhead on the side of the door and went prone on the deck. Klutch looked at me, and his gloomy expression changed to a goofy smile. He was game no matter how nutty the idea was. I took a knee so I had a good upward angle and gave Klutch a nod. He gave me a hole about ten feet up the door. I let the round fly; dire warnings be damned. He closed the hole, and we both boosted to where Tria and Coonts were waiting. We landed on our bellies and slid to a stop next to them. Tria reached out and grabbed my armored glove. She squeezed hard enough I could feel the pressure. There was a tremendous metallic clang, and the deck jumped hard enough to make me think the ship had slapped me in the face for the damage I had inflicted on it. I rolled over and glanced to the upper deck. All the control consoles were flashing with warning lights, and alarms were now blaring. The ship was telling us what we already knew: we had worn out our welcome, and it was time to get the hell off.

We got up and ran to the door, which had a very pronounced bow to it. Klutch activated the device but something huge must have been blocking the backside of the door. The portal closed. Klutch didn't hesitate and pointed the projector to the top of the door. To my relief, he got a good hole. He jerked his plasma caster from its clip and boosted up and through. Tria, Coonts, and I were tight to his back. Klutch wasn't going to need his plasma caster because we flew into a blazing inferno. The walls of the passage leading to the engine spaces were folded outward, exposing other decks and corridors. I was shocked at the amount of Prule that had gathered to attack us. As far as we could see, their mangled bodies were in smoldering heaps. The blast had pushed their remains up the walls, all the way to the overhead. There was a large rend in the ceiling, and smoke and flames were being sucked upward into it. Klutch never even slowed, and we flew right for it. He wasn't going to hear any bitching from me about stopping and trying for a portal. It was the only sure way of getting away from where we were. We popped up through the flaming hole and found ourselves in a giant cargo hold. The freight that occupied the deck where the blast penetrated was on fire as well. Fire suppression systems were blowing out geysers of a thick gray foam that stuck to everything it touched, including us. What little our cloak suits did to hide our location was rendered useless.

Klutch started blasting balls of plasma in all directions, setting stacks of cargo ablaze, intensifying the spreading inferno.

"Klutch, save the plasma. We may need it!" I called.

"I have a plan, Commander!"

I didn't think boiling us in our battle suits was a noteworthy plan. When he didn't elaborate further, I knew he was making it up on the fly, just like I was. I had to give him credit though: the rapidly growing pyre was covering our retreat. The Prule weapons fire coming from the hold fell off drastically. Coonts had been firing nonstop to our rear, but he ceased. At the far end of the hold was a large open loading hatch. It was hard to say if Klutch knew it was there or not, but we needed a little bit of salvation and a way to get out of there would fit the bill perfectly. Klutch cranked up the speed, and we flew at maximum velocity for the opening. I could only think of one thing, and that was not to be trapped inside of the ship. Tria on the other hand, was thinking a little further ahead.

"Klutch, stay low to the deck so we are not exposed to the ship's weapons!"

I should have been the one to think of that and alert the Troop Master. In a way, I was kind of glad I didn't when I heard his curt reply.

"This is not my first boarding, Captain Burlor!"

After the cluster grope we had gone through, I could see where everyone might be a little testy. Tria could have chosen to verbally gig the Troop Master for his comment, but she let it slide. She knew how much stress Klutch was under to lead us the hell out of there in one piece. With the foam covering our suits, we were visible targets, so we started taking fire from the Prule Hunters on the upper deck. We were flying low and fast. Most of the fire was well to our rear but was progressively getting more accurate. I saw a flash just in front of Klutch that made him turn us toward the side of the ship. We ducked over the edge and stayed right against the hull. The ship was more than a mile long and we still had a way to go. Out of the corner of my eye, I saw a turret swivel toward us. I wouldn't have thought my sphincter could pucker any tighter. When the turret opened fire sending beams of energy a couple of feet above our heads, I though it somehow dragged my throat into my ass and was strangling me. Klutch had us flying so tight to the hull, it was less than a foot away. We got lucky because the weapons turrets could not depress their fire any further without hitting the ship. The star-like heat given off by the weapons fire had temperature warnings flashing in my HUD. I normally wouldn't claim being shot at could possibly have a redeeming factor, but in this case, it striped the sticky fire-retardant foam from our armor in bursts of fluffy ashes.

The business end of the ship was coming up fast. Beyond it was about five-hundred yards of open space and a gigantic pressure door that allowed the ship access to the facility. It was, of course, closed and sealed. I had yet to see a Prule warship that didn't have an inordinate number of heavy weapons mounted on the bow. It would be ludicrous to think this ship would be an exception to that rule.

I had never heard a story where someone kicked a hornet's nest like we had and only had one hornet wanting a piece of your ass for it. When we cleared the front of the ship, the Prule were going to stick it to us. Klutch must have been reading my mind because he slowed us down and went prone against the deck behind a shield emitter.

"Klutch, there are several thousand Hunters pursuing us," Coonts warned. "We should keep moving!"

Tria and Coonts sent streams of high explosives into the charging ranks of Prule. Their response was to fill the atmosphere around us with energy weapons fire. Our cover was being blown to pieces. It obviously no longer mattered how much damage they inflicted on their prized warship. They were determined to take us out, and I was thinking they just might succeed. I popped out my spray nozzles and purged my entire reservoir of weaponized nanites. It would slow the Prule down, but not stop them; there were too many.

"I would like to hear your plan. I am fresh out of ideas," I called to Klutch in a voice as calm as I could muster.

He pointed at the flames leaping from the ship's hold. "They will come to their senses anytime now! We need to be ready to go when they do!"

I was floored by his response. The Prule were already blasting the crap out of their own ship. It was highly unlikely at this point they would do something sensible. This turned out to be one of those times when I was genuinely happy, I was wrong. With a giant wrenching metallic groan, the giant access door split in the middle and started opening. The explosive decompression sucked us off the deck and out toward the void. We hit our boosters and bounced among the flying debris like pinballs. Over the top of the horrendous howl of rushing atmosphere and flying junk, Klutch yelled out over our comms to detonate the charges.

With a thought, the charges ignited, blasting downward into the antimatter containment fields of the star drives. Everything flashed a brilliant white, and the last thing I saw was the huge bow of the ship being propelled right at us as we were sent flying out into the void. My battle suit was working overtime to keep control of my uncoordinated flight. The AI started using opposing spurts from my gravity drive to arrest my considerable velocity. As I regained my senses and looked back at the planet, I saw an incredible sight. There was a massive volcanic-like upheaval, sending chunks of rock and who knows what else thousands of feet upward into the planet's light gravity. Looking down, I saw a beautiful sight. The front of the wrecked Prule ship was protruding out of the cavern's mangled access doors. It had corked the opening and allowed the blast to be directed back into the complex. The resulting geyser had me convinced we just dealt the entire complex a death blow. A smile parted my lips as a childhood jingle danced through my head: "All the king's horses and all the king's men."

"Commander, I have locked on to the strike team's locations and will collect you with the tow beam. ETA thirty-one seconds," Justice commed us, interrupting my revelry. "I want to alert you that Sael Nalen has arrived with a taskforce of twelve warships. I gave her our location and warned her to stay clear of the area. When the taskforce entered the planet's orbit, previously unidentified Prule defensive batteries attacked and lightly damaged two warships. The Chaalt are currently bombarding the surface from orbit and have one hundred and forty assault shuttles flying combat sorties near the poles of the planet. I also have interesting data collected from the Sig. I downloaded the intelligence report from our comms chain and will have it ready for your review."

I felt myself being tugged backward. I rolled around and saw the fast-approaching hangar of the Legacy as I was pulled inward. Xul was standing with Tria and Coonts with a look of anxiety on his face. Justice killed the tow beam, and I was set down on the deck. The Legacy made a hard turn and nosed back for the planet. My HUD highlighted Klutch's position, and we were on him in a blink of an eye. The tow beam locked on and pulled him aboard. We retracted our helmets and went to the Troop Master. When he retracted his helmet, he had his usual goofy smile on his face. Coonts took exception to his mood.

"How can you act like that after nearly letting us be overrun and destroyed?" Coonts asked, disgruntled.

"I told you I had a plan," Klutch said. "Even though the timing was tight, it worked out perfectly!"

Coonts's face went from mad to worse. "What are you talking about? If the Prule had not made the mistake of opening the access doors, we would be dead right now!"

Emotions were running high, and Klutch's reply didn't help matters.

"Hah! Apparently not all Grawl are as smart as they want everyone to believe," Klutch retorted. "Even the Commander and Tria were able to figure it out!"

Coonts turned to us with a questioning look of anger on his face. I didn't want any part of where this conversation was going and was not going to be caught in the middle of another argument between the two. Xul saw what was coming as well. He made up an excuse to be somewhere else and headed for the bridge. I was admittedly a little miffed at the part where Klutch said that even I had it figured out. I wasn't quite sure if it was a swipe at my intelligence or not. Rather than admit Tria and I were both a little puzzled by his comment, I quickly made a lame attempt to quell the silly bickering.

"Klutch, quit messing with him and spit it out!"

You could almost see steam rising from Coonts's head when Klutch started nonchalantly flicking debris from his battle suit. The looks Tria and I gave the Troop Master made him stop dicking with the Grawl.

"The Throggs had to open the access door. It was the only way they could attempt to quickly extinguish the fire I started in the cargo hold," Klutch explained. "I knew at some point they would decide to decompress the cavern to keep their prized ship from burning up. It took a little longer than I thought it would, but it worked out as planned."

Tria, Coonts, and I promptly turned and headed for the ready room. I was done with that conversation and had other things on my mind, namely what the Sig uncovered in the star system close to El Dorado. We stepped out of our abused armor and put on uniforms. Klutch hung back, muttering unkind things about the Grawl under his breath.

I knew he was a little pissy because he was not getting the attention, he thought he was due.

"It was a brilliant plan, don't you think?" Klutch called after us as we walked out of the ready room.

Tria looked at me out of the corner of her eye. I made sure Coonts wasn't looking at me and gave her a shrug. Klutch wouldn't leave it alone.

"It was the only course of action that made tactical sense, don't you agree?" he called again.

I didn't turn around but held a thumb up, hoping to end any more discussion on the supposed plan. When I looked down at Coonts, he decided a thumb was not the appropriate digit and gave him the middle one instead. For some reason, Tria gave me a frown and an elbow. There were a few Earth gestures she did not care for because she took most everything literally. She also knew that it could be learned from only one source. You would think by now that I would remember I was under constant observation. A great many things my crew have observed me doing rubbed off on them. Some were good, but a lot of it could be considered questionable. It made me wonder how much longer it was going to take Justice to figure out a way to manifest the taboo gesticulation. When you think of the devil, he tends to speak to you.

"Commander, I have several IST messages on hold for you from the Principal Investigator," Justice said. "I informed her you were on a mission and you would contact her when you returned. The catastrophic explosion of the Prule base was observed by Chaalt forces. You now have additional message traffic."

I wasn't in the mood to have a conversation with Sael. She most assuredly would want a full rundown on my activities. There was no doubt in my mind she would find fault in the way we handled the discovery of the Prule base.

"Are they still honoring our exclusion zone?"

"Yes, they appear to be fully involved with sanitizing the planet of Prule defensive weapons."

"Okay, I want you to take an azimuth from our insertion point to where we exited the Prule base. I want you to strike the halfway point between those locations with our primary weapon. Then I want you to do the same to the alien ship you discovered in the crater. The Prule were salvaging it from below the surface to avoid detection. I want to make sure that is no longer possible."

"Affirmative, Commander. Those locations are already on my targeting list. I will move the Legacy in preparation to make the strikes."

"What is the condition of the Hivemind?"

"It has not received additional nutrients or liquids since you departed for your mission. I do not believe it will perish in the next twelve hours, but its condition is precarious. To ensure its biomass has minimal sustainability, it will require assistance from us within that time period."

"Collate our mission data and download it to the Overseer. At the proper time, I want him to present it to the Hivemind," I said. "I have a gut feeling it did not believe we would survive and return from the base. We would like it to know with no uncertainty that we are back and in good health. While running around and causing havoc, we managed to get about twenty minutes of run time on the data collection devices you gave us. I would like a detailed briefing on what they recorded, if anything."

"I am already working on the decryption, Commander. If known Prule algorithms produce the expected results, I should have workable keys to unlock the data within the next few hours. The targets you chose for elimination are now void of Prule activity. It was necessary to make follow-up strikes on the underground base to ensure no Prule assets survived in the area."

"Okay, Justice, stay cloaked and move us out from the planet so we can keep an eye on the Chaalt. Let me know if it looks like they discovered anything we might have overlooked."

Tria and I stopped at the galley for a quick meal but Coonts kept going. He was still fuming about our uncomfortably close call with oblivion. It seemed like it was common practice for him and Klutch to play this game. I wrote it off as their stress relief routine. I had witnessed it enough, I really didn't care, as long as it no longer involved me. I figured we had maybe thirty minutes tops before Klutch cooled off and forgot all about being mad. As soon as that happened, he would decide he was hungry. I didn't want to be anywhere near the galley when that happened. We ate lightly in case my predicted time line was faulty. When we got up to leave, I suggested a hot shower and a nap before we started going over the data. The look of mischief in Tria's eyes, suggested she was good with the shower but not with the nap.

26

As it turns out, I got to enjoy another one of those rare times I was wrong about something and it didn't nearly cost me my life. Tria and I actually did get a small nap in before Justice woke us. That didn't mean I wasn't a little crabby from lack of sleep, and it showed when I responded to the AI's wake-up call.

"Yes, Justice, what is it now?" I snapped.

Biting off the AI's virtual head for waking us would probably net me an undesirable response at some point in the future. The machine knew how to use the human emotions it had learned from me to make payback a bitch in some cases. I didn't have a legitimate reason to be irritable. Tria had made certain of that. I guess deep down it had something to do with the AI carefully documenting my sexual proclivities. I felt that such things should be on a need-to-know basis, and Justice didn't need to know. The time it took for him to reply meant I would indeed be subject to an equivalent amount of future crabbiness. It was too late to apologize, and I would suffer whatever was coming to me, regardless of my effort. So, I didn't even try.

"Commander, the Operative is insisting to speak with you directly," Justice finally said. "She has ordered a Chaalt battle fleet to transition to our location. She is not so politely asking for permission to proceed."

"Open a comms channel to her highness."

Justice put Sael right through, and she didn't waste any time taking select bites out of my ass.

"Commander Myers, I find your habit of delaying, or possibly blocking, our communications during a major combat operation, irresponsible and disrespectful to me and the personnel under my command."

Crap! She was going to get all official on me. That meant she must have a number of her senior officers listening in on our discussion. I wondered why she would do that. In the past, she didn't want anybody to know that I usually talked to her any way I wanted and didn't give a damn if it pissed her off or not. Tria rolled over and mouthed, "Show her a little respect." I bugged my eyes at her in a show that stated it wasn't likely. She started doing other things to make me rethink my bullheadedness. I suddenly found it difficult to be irritable at the Operative. I changed gears and came up with noteworthy excuses instead.

"Principal Investigator, my strike team and I spent close to four hours in direct combat with thousands of Prule combatants," I said. "We escaped by the narrowest of margins and are lucky to have survived. While I know that

410

you and your troops would not need to recuperate after such a campaign, my crew and I do. I will be sending a copy of our mission data over to you shortly."

I was going to say more, but Tria was relentless. I promptly ended the IST transmission.

"Justice, send a copy of the combat video you were preparing for the Hivemind over to Sael. Please do it quickly!" I pleadingly called out.

I couldn't imagine what the Operative and her underlings were thinking right about now. Sael knew me fairly well. If she even remotely surmised the nature of my abrupt termination of our comms, she was going to have an epic meltdown. My interactions with Tria did manage to assuage Justice's feelings. He no longer seemed interested in displaying any spite for my earlier tactlessness.

"Data files sent, Commander. I will instruct Xul to take the Operative's calls if she has questions concerning your combat mission. I have already prepared a list of predetermined answers based on my observations of the engagement."

I was struggling to stay focused but did manage to say, "You can do that?"

"Of course, Commander. There are only so many logical questions the Operative could ask. I believe I have sufficiently covered the most important ones. The less cogent can wait until you are ready to answer them personally."

I was wondering if he would let me get away clean. That last little stab indicated he would not. A little tit for tat might be in order. Perhaps I would do my fornicating somewhere other than the Legacy and see what the AI thought of those apples. I cringed, thinking I just might have let the cat out of the bag. Justice could get a pretty good read on my intentions by interacting with my implants. Maybe I could absolve myself by giving Tria my undivided attention. It could turn out to be a win-win situation.

Sleep ended up being just a fleeting thought, at least for me anyway. Tria was out cold, and I had no plans of waking her anytime soon. The thought of laying around until the Operative called to annoy me made me shower again and go to the bridge. I wanted my briefings over with before deciding our next move.

"Justice, what info did you download from the Sig?"

"Commander, the Sig report they have captured eighty-seven pirates and have uncovered a huge cache of stolen artifacts and cargo. Interrogation of the pirates reveals the ships that were attacked and looted were intentionally sent to the star system for that purpose. The pirates assumed our freighter was one of the targets."

"Did the Sig find out who was sending the ships into harm's way?"

"Negative, Commander. The Sig did report they found the crews of the captured ships in a crater near the base. The mass grave contained tens of thousands of bodies, indicating the pirate operation has been ongoing for a considerable period of time."

I knew the Sig were very much an eye-for-an-eye society and probably didn't need to ask, but I did anyway.

"What is the current status of the base?"

"All but a select few of the prisoners joined their victims in the crater and the base is now a Sig military outpost. This will be advantageous to our mining operation because we will now have a secure storage and distribution hub well separated from El Dorado."

"Is that all of the report?"

"No, Commander. The Sig request a personal visit from you at your earliest convenience. They have additional subject matter that they will only discuss directly with you."

That last part had me scratching my head a little. Our comms array was widely dispersed across the void, and the chances of someone finding one of the buoys and figuring out how to decrypt the transmissions were slim to none. The Sig must have stumbled onto to something big or they wouldn't be asking for a face to face. Tria had already taken the steps to ensure our stake in this star system. Maybe it was time to turn it over to the Operative and her people so we could move on to other matters, the meeting with the Sig being the first.

Thinking of the Operative had me wondering why that particular burr under my saddle wasn't burning up my IST with her usual lighthearted banter. It was strange that now that our lines of communication were open, she had yet to call back.

"Justice, give me a secure IST to Sael."

"Secure channel open, Commander."

"Principal Investigator, I am ready to discuss the mission if you have the time."

"You can stop trying to grease my orifices, you primate! You know my staff is not privy to my secure comms."

"It's just that I was a little irritable during our last conversation," I said. "I feel that I owe you a little more respect than that and a proper explanation."

"You can stow that scat! I have no desire to hear you try to explain your primitive antics. They may have been lost on my subordinates, but not on me!"

Whew! The old battle-ax seriously needed to get laid.

"Sael, I . . ."

"Nathan! Do us both a favor and just stop for a moment and listen to what I have to say."

I guess I should have been happy that she was saving me the trouble of having to do any additional brownnosing. I was going to let her know what the Hivemind had told us but decided to hold off for the time being. I would let her have her way until I could no longer stand it. As it turned out, I was moderately surprised by her next comments.

"Nathan, the mission data you sent me contains some stunning information," Sael began. "I am not sure if it makes sense or not, but it is obvious in some of the data, the Prule machines fear you and your team. That runs contrary to the information we have been collecting for the last two hundred years. Some of my scholars are speculating the Hivemind somehow sent out a warning. We have no data to back up that assumption, but why else would the Prule fear an unknown without some prior warning of your capabilities."

I was more than a little dumbfounded by the Chaalt's conclusions. I would need Justice's input to verify their findings. The Operative and her people were competent investigators, so what she was telling me had a lot of credibility. At the time, I was only worried about getting our asses shot off and not what the Prule were doing while we were running for our lives. I was concerned only about surviving and didn't give a crap what they were up to. Tria walked onto the bridge with a frown. She heard part of the conversation, and just like me, wondered what the hell. I threw my hands up and shook my head. Tria had seen those human gestures enough that she sat at her console to listen in on the rest of my conversation with the Senior Operative.

"I can tell you firsthand, the Prule we encountered didn't act like they were frightened," I said. "I have to admit, they seemed shocked when they encountered us, but I never saw any indications they were afraid. All were trying their best to kill us. As for a warning, I guess there is a possibility they may have had prior notice."

"We are working on a theory the Fury made a stop at the base and revealed the outcome of the siege at our research facility. Unless you have intel, your mission video doesn't reveal, it will remain a theory."

I made a crude motion with my hand and winked at Tria. She just rolled her eyes.

"I was going to give you a briefing on what we had, but you insisted I shut up."

The silence that followed my statement implied I should carry on and Sael was going to keep a clamp on her piehole until I filled her in. I let the silence hang until Tria gave me the stink eye and waved me on. I kind of thought it was funny, but the scowl on Tria's face said to quit screwing with Sael.

"The location of this outpost came from information we extracted from the Hivemind," I told Sael. "The Hivemind also stated the coordinates were passed on to the mutineers who stole the Fury. I would say that makes your theory valid. We are still developing information we collected during our mission. As soon as we have it decrypted, I will give you another briefing."

It must have been enough for the Operative to digest at one time, or she didn't like the way I was yanking her chain any more than Tria did. She moved on to another subject.

"Tria has already taken the necessary steps to certify your discoveries and salvage rights," Sael said. "You will have exclusive rights to any future findings discovered on the planet. That being said, I am requesting your permission to move additional assets into the star system. Once it is secured, surveyors and salvage teams will begin documenting and cataloging your find."

"Sael, even though you have a habit of making me wonder at times, I trust you. I will leave you in charge, and you do whatever you feel is necessary. We have other information we are prosecuting and will leave this in your hands. I promise you if we come up with intel on the Fury, you will be the first to know."

"Thank you, Nathan. My people and I appreciate all you have done for us."

Even though I thought she was a little prompt in her thanks, I let it go. There was always the possibility the Chaalt might uncover another Prule base and choose to keep it a secret. Since we still had the Hivemind as a source of information, we had the possibility of discovering a lot more Prule assets. That all by itself would keep the Chaalt honest if they wanted continued access to our discoveries.

"Justice, jump us to the Sig's new base of operations."

"Affirmative, Commander. DEHD core activation in thirty seconds."

When the Legacy returned to normal space-time, I sat in my command chair, looking at the view dome. Justice highlighted seventy-two Sig warships with blue triangles. They were spread throughout the system and were patrolling in task forces comprised of nine warships each. There would be no doubt to any interlopers whose turf they were passing through. We were hailed by the Sig, and I was surprised that it was Sushi who made the call. If he made the trip from Haras just to brief me, it must be hot intel.

"Commander Myers, you are cleared to make an inner-system jump to the planet's orbit. I will meet you in the shuttle landing bay. I request that you wear your combat armor to keep your identity secure."

I was starting to get antsy. Whatever they found must be crazy good, or why the cloak-and-dagger routine. We would give the place a proper shaking when we jumped into orbit. They either didn't give a crap, or it was for the benefit of someone else. Justice alerted the crew we were changing our mission profile. Coonts, Klutch, and Xul joined Tria and me on the bridge. They were wondering as much as I was what the Sig discovered. We went down tube and armored up while Justice jumped us into a stationary position in orbit above the former pirate base. We boarded Eagle One, and Klutch piloted us into the void. He nosed us into a steep descent and took us down fast. I was standing behind the Troop Master as he skillfully lined us up with the base's shuttle hangar and made a picture-perfect landing. Sushi had an honor guard awaiting us. They stood with weapons extended and lined the walkway all the way to the pressure doors securing the base. I was kind of wishing that the Operative was here to witness how the Sig treated us. She might be less inclined to be a pain if she knew we were better appreciated elsewhere. When we exited the air lock, we were met by Sushi. We retracted our helmets and gave the Sig a customary bow.

"Commander Myers, it is good to see you again. After the failures of our last meeting, I hope this one will restore your faith in me and my people."

That explained part of the drama surrounding our meeting. Sushi was holding himself responsible for Cralmo getting away after his attempted assassination of Tria and me. It would be a waste of words to convince him otherwise. I was getting to know the Sig pretty well. Sushi wasn't about to let that smudge on our relationship go without terminal closure.

"Sushi, I in no way hold you responsible for Cralmo's escape," I assured him. "He obviously had a well-thought-out getaway plan. His luck will not hold out forever. One day we will meet again, and he will pay for his misdeed."

"Perhaps it will be as you say, Commander, but until that day comes, the Sig will not rest until we have rectified our miscalculation."

"I have had the same misfortune. Eiger, who is said to be the king of the Murlak pirates, has eluded me on more than one occasion. It is admittedly hard to put behind me, but sometimes there is no other choice."

The smile spreading across the Sig's face gave me a rush of adrenaline.

"There is a very good chance you will no longer have to put it behind you. We have uncovered information that may give you advance notice as to where Eiger will be."

Hot damn! I sure hoped the big Sig wasn't getting his crank yanked by some lowly piece-of-crap pirate. We had

419

heard stories like this before, only to have them proven false. Sushi must have seen the doubt on my face.

"Please follow me and you can verify the information by any method you see fit," he said. "We have two undamaged freighters in the loading docks and prisoners that have yet to prove their worth."

Sushi led us deep into the complex, and we took a lift to the lower levels. Our final destination was a room lined with chairs and a large monitor on one wall. Sushi approached the monitor and touched it. We instantly got a view of twenty holding cells made of a clear composite. The first seven were occupied. I recognized six of the aliens, but the one in the first cell was an unknown. There was three Murlak, two Grawl, and one Ilor. The prisoner in the first cell wore an atmospheric suit that was similar to the Ilor's. His ample girth alluded to the fact he, like Klutch, came from a world with higher than one gravity living conditions.

"Commander, the prisoner in the first holding cell is a Rugerian," Coonts told me on a private channel. "They are an advanced race that are closely associated with the Galactic Union. Why he would be at this location would require a noteworthy explanation."

"Commander Myers, you are free to interrogate the prisoners. With the exception of the Rugerian, the rest will be joining their victims in the mass grave we discovered not far from here. Once you hear the Rugerian's story, you will know why I recommended disguising your identities."

I looked at each of my teammates. They were feeling the same as I was. This might be the break we were looking for. If we knew where Eiger was going to be in advance, we could take steps to ensure he would not slip through our hands and escape. Sushi showed us to the holding room door. The exterior entrance was a heavy-duty armored piece of work. The interior door not so much. We saw a quickly gathering crowd of Sig file into the observation room. They were wanting to see how the demon warrior took care of business. If the information was as good as the Sig stated, we would corroborate it by any means necessary. Klutch pushed in front of me before I could take the lead. It was his usual spot in our combat formation, so I didn't bitch about his light use of elbows to get out front. We closed our helmets and blacked out our visors.

Klutch's entrance surprised me. It probably got rousing cheers from the Sig who gathered to watch. The Troop Master was eyeballing the lighter interior door and then took a couple of running steps and smashed it into the cell block. The reaction of the prisoners was priceless. They pushed back into the corners of their cells and slid down the wall. I guess they thought if they could somehow make themselves smaller, we might overlook them. Sushi added to their terror by opening all of the cell doors. I guess he wanted to see if they would find the courage to attempt an escape. If that was the case, he was going to be sorely disappointed. They all stayed put with the exception of the Ilor. He immediately stood at the opening to his cell and started offering up credits, artifacts, and information he claimed would bring us riches beyond belief. Klutch marched right up to him, and the vents in his armor locked into the open position. I knew for a fact the Tibor was going to shut the pirate up, which might leave the alien unable to speak for an extended period of time. I was actually kind of interested in hearing what he had to offer. I commed the Troop Master before he did anything nasty to the portly alien.

"Klutch, we can save him for last," I said. "He might actually have information we could make use of."

Klutch grumbled something ugly about pirate scum and pushed the Ilor back into the cell.

"If you speak again before we ask you a question, it will be the last mistake you ever make," he threatened.

It's hard to say whether the Ilor heard Klutch or not. He was acting bizarrely and it looked like he might have been fondling himself. Klutch gave me an incredulous look and tapped his helmet with his finger and then pointed at the Ilor. When I turned away, I saw Tria staring at one of the Murlak and giving off a deadly vibe. She was a Chaalt with a keen memory. If this was one of Eiger's enforcers that had brutalized her, he was about to have a bad day. She stalked into his cell and jerked him off the floor. She shook him like a ragdoll and pulled him up to her helmet. She cleared her faceplate so he could see her face. He started screaming out all kinds of nonsense. A lot of it had to do with how important he was and how wealthy he could make us.

"I bet you thought this day would never come," Tria said, cutting him off. "You broke one of my arms with the butt of your weapon and then kicked me in the face twice. You were laughing when you did it. I don't hear you laughing now!"

The Murlak's eyes were bugging out and his mouth hanging open. He must have recognized her. Tria extended a climbing hook and cut the pirate's arm off at the elbow. She threw the pirate to the floor, where he lay screeching. She reared back with her armored boot and kicked the Murlak in the head with such ferocity, it partially decapitated him. It was deathly quiet in the cell block.

"Isolate the cells so we can compare notes," I called out to Sushi.

All the cell doors closed except for the one I was standing in front of. The Grawl that was sitting in the corner of it peered up at me.

"Do you know who I am?" I asked him.

"Yes, you are the alien many call the demon warrior. It is said that you killed Drayen and destroyed his outpost."

"Now that we have established who I am, I want to know who you are and why the Sig found you useful enough to spare your life."

"I am the captain of the ship that was disabled and left to drift in the void."

"I still don't see why the Sig wasted their time saving you. You attacked and illegally boarded vessels doing legitimate commerce. You killed the crews and stole their cargo. It is my understanding you are now subject to galactic law. If I am not mistaken, the penalty for your crimes is death. I am going to ask you one more time. Why did the Sig spare your life?"

"I have knowledge of those who are responsible for sending freighters to this location."

"You have one choice, and that is to tell me who would knowingly send thousands of innocents to their deaths," I threatened. "I will decide if the information is worth turning you back over to the Sig. They may have other uses for you."

"Give me my freedom, and I will reveal the names and their locations."

The Grawl was in no position to bargain. There were way too many bodies in that mass grave for the little asshole to dictate terms to me. My anger at his arrogance quickly made up my mind. A three-second burst from my needle gun scattered his upper torso back into his cell. The macabre abstract painting on the cell walls would either loosen the lips of the next pirate, or their bowels, before they met their maker.

"Coonts, bring the other Grawl!"

Coonts carried the Grawl into the cell by his neck. He threw him beside the splayed remains of his captain.

"Your captain had a chance to bargain with the Sig for his life in exchange for information. You now have the same choice. Who was responsible for sending freighters to this location?"

"Genda Binar. He is the freight manager for Carsoon Galactic Shipping. He is also the captain's clan sibling."

"I want to know how to find Genda Binar, so that I can personally give him my condolences for his brother's passing."

The Grawl stood wringing his hands and staring at what remained of his captain. He hastily shook his head in acknowledgment.

"He can be found at Carsoon Shipping," he said. "It is one of the top ten shipping corporations in the galaxy. It has twelve shipping hubs. Genda resides at hub eight. The Sig will know the coordinates. You should also know he was handpicked for his job by the owner of the corporation, Bren Carsoon. Bren is clan sibling to Warla Carsoon, who is a level six Galactic Council member. You can verify what I say is true by asking the Rugerian. He is a level nine Galactic Council member and the covert intermediary between certain members of the council and the leader of the Murlak pirates."

Now we were getting somewhere. If what this Grawl was telling me was correct, he might get to leave this place upright and breathing. My crew had gathered around listening. Now that we had someone who seemed to be giving us the straight dope, Klutch had a good question for the Grawl first officer.

"Why would the Rugerian risk coming to this location?"

"When we had possession of the last freighter sent to us, we were to gather all the cargo and artifacts from this location and take them to a destination only known to Illam Pove. The Rugerian is present to validate the accountability of shares."

Tria weighed in with the next obvious question. "Who is Illam Pove?"

"He is one of the Murlak the Sig spared. I did not see whom you chose to kill. If it was Illam, the coordinates of the place the Murlak call Shurmosk died with him."

The Murlak word "Shurmosk" roughly translated to fortress. It had to be where the Murlak and other nefarious members of the illicit artifact trade stored their ill-gotten gains. We gave Tria a questioning look, and she shrugged her shoulders. She had not asked the pirate his name before she sent him to hell.

27

We marched the Grawl out of the cell. There was a one-in-three chance we inadvertently shot ourselves in the foot. I would not say it, but it may have been a good idea for Tria to question the Murlak before she killed him. Sushi was evidently listening to everything said because the cells of the remaining Murlak opened. The Grawl pirate took a look in the first cell and gave us a negative shake of his head. He approached the second cell and pointed into it.

"This is Illam Pove, and he knows the location of Shurmosk."

The Murlak howled in anger and attempted to dive on the traitor who had identified him. Coonts was standing next to the Grawl pirate and shouldered the Murlak aside. The Murlak tried to get to his feet but Coonts kneed him in the face, laying him out cold. If the Murlak knew where the fortress was located, then he had to be one of Eiger's most trusted confidants. It was just a matter of extracting the information without killing him in the process.

"Klutch, take this piece of scat to Eagle One and return to the Legacy. Put him in the brig and give him the isolation treatment. We will finish up here and be along shortly. Oh, and Klutch, before you leave the brig, I would like you to service the Hivemind's biomass. It needs to know we made it back from our mission in better shape than it is in."

The Tibor gave me a croaking laugh. "It will be my pleasure, Commander!"

Klutch grabbed the Murlak by the fur on his head and dragged him from the cell block. Tria, Coonts, and I stepped back to the first Murlak's cell. He was still pushed back in the corner and had a wild-eyed look on his furry face. His stock value had taken a huge hit, and he knew it.

"I had nothing to do with the deaths of the freighter crews. I was ordered to come here and to haul cargo under the command of Illam Pove."

"That does not change the fact that you are a pirate," I said. "The blood of the victims is on your hands, no matter what you claim."

It was obvious to me we would not get any groundbreaking information from the Murlak. Sushi probably tossed him in as a sacrificial lamb to gain us leverage on the others. We turned our backs on the cell, and the door closed on the pleading Murlak. Moving on to the Rugerian's cell, we crowded in around him. He stood face to face with my war mask. His pressure suit helmet hid his face but not his eyes. They suggested he was soiling his suit.

"I have been searching a long time to find the link between the illegal artifact trade and the Galactic Council, and here you are," I said menacingly. "You are the proof I need to show the other races on the council that corruption is prevalent everywhere. They need to look inward as well as out, and no one is beyond scrutiny."

"You would do well to free me. I was a prisoner here. The council will reward you handsomely for my safe return."

"You have an interesting take on reality. It seems to conflict with how the Sig discovered you here. I think finding you hiding in the hold of a pirate freighter gives the Sig's story a great deal more credibility than yours."

"The Sig are known to be merciless killers. I feared for my life after I escaped my captors," he pleaded. "When the Sig found me, I told them whatever they wanted to hear to ensure my safety."

I laughed at the Rugerian. He was so full of scat it was ridiculous. The fool thought we would somehow see things from his point of view. It was time to burst his bubble and yank him back to reality.

"There is no scenario where we will take you from this place and free you. I find it insulting you think we will believe the lies you are spewing at us," I said. "You are somewhat fortunate the Sig have some unknown use for you. If it were left up to me, I would kill you for your breach of trust. You obviously deceived a number of races into elevating you to your current rank as a council member. I find great satisfaction in knowing you will never return to the council to practice your treachery ever again."

The sniveling crook reached out and started pawing at my armor. He was blubbering and pleading to let him go. Coonts grabbed him by his pressure suit and threw him to the back of the cell. He slid down the wall, begging us to change our minds. We walked out of the cell, and the door closed behind us. I looked down the cell block to where the Ilor was held. The lunatic was down on all four, peeking out the doorway of his cell. To make the picture even more surreal, he began waving at us. I had thought I would be interested in what he could offer us. But it was clear to me the Ilor was raving mad. We would leave him for the Sig, and they could determine what to do with the crazy alien.

We left the cell block and met Sushi outside the observation room. I let him know that he should let the Cralmo fiasco go. The information Illam Pove would give us was a lot more important. I told him what I thought about the Grawl leveling with us. I suggested pumping him dry of any useful information and then dumping him of some remote world to fend for himself. Sushi seemed to agree with my assessment.

Before we headed back to the Legacy, I had to ask him about the Ilor and why he was even in the cell block instead of a thought reprocessing institute. Sushi gave me a frightening smile and explained that his years of contact with Tam Lin taught him that humans needed a certain amount of humor in their lives. He went on to explain that he doubted if the Ilor would knowingly hurt anybody. He also assured me he would have warned us off if it looked like we might want to hurt him. The strange antics of the alien brought laughter to his otherwise emotionless crewmates, and he thought we could use a little of the same. He said Tam Lin called such things a joke and that humans enjoyed the pastime. While I had to agree with a certain amount of his explanation, I would not have chosen the cell block as a place to pull the stunt. There was not a lot to joke about in there. Oh well, aliens do alien things, and humans are no different. It has a lot to do with whose eyes you are looking through. I put a fake smile on my face and waved at the Sig in the same manner the Ilor waved to us. He and several of his troopers laughed out loud. We said our farewells and made our way to the outer pressure lock. We stepped out onto the planet's surface and then boosted straight up with our gravity drives. Justice swooped down out of orbit and snatched us up with the tow beam.

"Justice, if the matrix is charged, jump us within scanner range of the transponder thread termination points." I said.

"Yes, Commander, I have the coordinates of a location that will give us coverage of both sites. I am ready to jump on your order."

"I have to know before we jump: did the Hivemind survive Klutch's goodwill gesture?"

"I can assure you goodwill had nothing to do with the Troop Master's contribution to the Hivemind's survival.

431

The unusually large quantity of his so-called goodwill gesture indicates he was purposely holding his normal waste relieving routine. I suspect his intentions were to inflict fatal damage to the Hivemind."

"I take it he failed."

"Yes, I am unsure how the Hivemind survived, but it hung on to its remaining self by the thinnest of margins. The biomass has since overcome the extreme dilution and the intake of questionable nutrients. It appears to be back to normal functions. The entity will endure for at least the next forty-eight hours before it will become necessary to assist it further."

"Now that it seems to be on the mend, have the Overseer transfer the data from our mission. If it should suffer a relapse, I will see if the Troop Master has it in him to aid it once more."

I guess Justice thought my sarcasm was uncalled for because he jumped the Legacy ahead of my order to do so.

"Commander! I am detecting a large number of Scrun warships in the orbit of one of our destination targets," Justice warned as we returned to normal space-time. "I now have a count of one hundred and thirty-three known Scrun spacecraft and three very large unidentified vessels. The Legacy is cloaked, and all stealth systems are engaged. Depending on the capabilities of the unknown spacecraft, there is a twenty-five percent possibility that our DEHD core jump was detected."

"Are you picking up any comms traffic from the unidentified bogeys?"

"I am detecting a data stream but cannot determine if it is communications or sensor feeds."

"Get us clear of our transition point and move us toward the other target planet."

"Already moving, Commander."

I went to the ready room and shed my armor for smart cloth. The crew and I headed for the bridge to get a god's-eye view of what was happening around the second target planet. We were almost to the up tube when Justice called out again.

"Commander, the three largest targets have brought their shields online, and I am detecting large energy spikes within their hulls."

The usual tone of Justice's voice changed slightly. It had an edge to it that indicated he might be experiencing the human emotion of anxiety. His next words sounded almost like dread.

"The unknown targets have transitioned!"

We were stepping out of the lift tube when it felt like something grabbed the Legacy and gave it a toss. Neither the artificial gravity nor the inertial dampeners could nullify the effects of the sudden forces exerted on the Legacy. We were thrown into the overhead and then two of the bulkheads; for all I knew, it could have been the deck. I rolled over groaning and wondering what the hell just happened. The feeling of pain throughout most of my body was a good indication I was still among the living. My vision finally made the necessary corrections, and I saw Coonts facedown next to me and Klutch crawling toward

433

us. Tria was attempting to regain her footing; blood was running down her face. The ringing in my ears subsided enough that I could hear her yelling.

"Justice, give me a damage report!" Tria yelled to Justice.

"We have minor damage to the portside shield emitters. I was able to bring our shields up before the unknown vessel collided with us. I made an inner-system jump to clear our datum. We were swept by sensors that may have given the unknown vessel targeting information on the Legacy. I am attempting to defeat their tracking systems by hiding among the large number of Scrun warships in orbit above the second planet."

That tidbit of information was the antidote for my punch-drunk state. I got to my feet and pulled Coonts up with me. Tria and Klutch gathered their wits, and we ran to the bridge. I took Tria's hand and pulled her close to me. I wiped the blood from the small cut on her scalp.

"Are you okay?"

"I am fine. It is just a scratch. We have bigger problems to worry about. I think it would be advisable to strap ourselves in."

I knew for a fact Tria was lying. We both had the nano weave lamination treatment when we underwent the Oolaran weaponization process. It took a hell of an impact to penetrate our skin. I looked at the bulkhead she collided with and saw the assortment of sharp protrusions sticking out on the ship's plumbing. She was hurt, but there was little I could do about it. She would refuse medical attention no matter what I said, so I had to let it go. I gave her a nod then turned to Coonts and Klutch. They both flashed a thumbs up, so I went to my chair and strapped in.

Our stealth systems worked well against the Scrun, but we knew nothing about the unidentified ships. They detected our transition and jumped near that location to investigate. Justice was making several course changes to avoid further detection when we were plowed into by one of the two-mile-long spacecraft. I had my doubts it was an intentional collision. The three ships were huge, and they were spread out to avoid each other when they reemerged from hyperspace. The chance meeting was dumb luck on their part and bad luck on ours. It didn't matter now because they knew we were here. Both the Scrun and the unknowns would have detected our escape jump and brief use of our shields. They also knew we exited hyperspace somewhere close to the planet they were orbiting. The Scrun's response was immediate. They launched thousands of missiles making the chances for a probable strike greater by the minute. Justice put the Legacy as close to the planet's atmosphere as he could without giving us a reentry plume. The Scrun were making wild maneuvers and continued to launch missiles. Things were tight and got even tighter when the big starships jumped almost into orbit above the Scrun. The unknowns had yet to take us under fire, so I would not start anything by ordering Justice to give them a dose of what we had to offer. My crew was looking at me, wondering if I was going to light them up. I chose diplomacy, or possibly, survival.

"Justice! Get us out of here!" I ordered.

"I am working on an exit vector, Commander!"

Justice was weaving the Legacy in and out of countless missile salvos. The view dome was a blur from the constant maneuvering. My eyes widened as we made several very close passes near Scrun warships. Justice must have finally found the out he was looking for, because we snap jumped to a location just outside of the star system. He again turned away from our transition point and put some distance between it and us. I personally would have liked him to jump the hell back to a safer piece of the space, but I think he was trying to collect data on the unidentified spacecraft. The view dome had red triangles highlighted all around the planet. But I didn't see the three big ones. I was starting to deliberate on their whereabouts when they exited hyperspace at our transition point. They were as determined as bloodhounds to track us down. Justice made another hard turn that had us going back toward the Scrun-infested planet. I didn't want to bust the AI's virtual balls, but I really wanted to be somewhere other than back in that hornet's nest.

"Justice, is there a reason we are still playing cat and mouse with these guys? If you were trying to piss them off, it is more than obvious you succeeded."

"I have concluded the sensors on the unidentified vessels are unable to track our Guardian-designed stealth systems. They are able to detect our transition distortion waves but quickly lose tracking data when we exit the area. The highly aggressive nature of the AIs that are operating the ships suggest the vessels belong to an advanced predatory race. I am gathering valuable information on their capabilities. They have already revealed the measurable power levels of their defensive shields. They are beyond those of the Scrun warships. It would take concentrated fire from all our weapons to bring them down to a point the Legacy could inflict significant damage to their hulls. It would be extremely useful if we could measure the destructive output and nature of their offensive weapons."

I would have found it extremely un-useful if the measurements he was referring to were being made on the Legacy's hull. We watched as the three ships split up and moved away from each other. They bracketed our transition exit point and started searching in patterns that gradually moved them outward from our last known coordinates. It was going to suck if we end up finding out their weapons were better than ours. Justice made another hard turn, and to my relief, we were moving away from both the unidentified bogeys and the planet the Scrun had so much interest in.

"Justice, did you get any useful intel on the planet's surface?"

"Yes, the areas I was able to map were abundant with primitive animal life, but no advanced life forms were detected. I did, however, identify a large construction site on the coast of the single continent I was able to scan. I

437

recorded thousands of Scrun communications. They reveal the new complex will be a permanent Scrun outpost. None of the comms traffic disclosed information pertaining to the unknown vessels."

"What about the other planet the Guardian transponder was pointing us to?"

"The second planet in the system is within the life zone of the star, but my scans detected a massive seven-hundred-mile-wide crater on its surface. That information, coupled with the huge amount of planetary debris in its atmosphere, indicates the planet suffered an extinction-level collision with an asteroid or other very large object in its recent past. I surmise it may take hundreds if not thousands of years for the planet to restore life-supporting conditions."

"Were you able to get a fix on the termination point of the transponder thread?"

"Yes, it is fortunately on the opposite hemisphere of the impact crater. I am currently moving away from our pursuers and will make course corrections that will take us closer to that location. With your permission, I would like to perform one last test of the unknown starships' detection thresholds."

"What kind of test?"

"I would like to launch one of our Chaalt-designed stealth missiles on a course that would take it toward the unknown ships. I will then have it jump into hyperspace and reemerge just beyond the vessel's location. At no time will the missile target any of the ships. It is my plan to degrade the stealth field of the missile to determine at what point the unknowns detect its presence."

That got me looks from my crew. They knew as well as I did that this could easily be interpreted as an escalation to an already tense situation. I had mixed feeling on the subject and was sure my crew did as well. We were probably all unanimous in thinking it would be wise to just slip away. It was a tactic that we had seldom ever used, but it seemed like the proper time to revisit that thinking. Before I could put words to my thoughts, Justice interrupted my doubtful inclinations.

"Commander, I am detecting another spike in the power levels emanating from the vessels searching for us."

I looked up at the three large red triangles Justice had highlighted on the view dome. They were spread out a considerable distance from each other. They were gradually receding targets because we were moving away from them as well. They suddenly flared as if on fire, and the whole view dome screen seemed to jerk sideways.

"Justice! What the hell just happened?"

"The alien ships fired all of their point defense weapons simultaneously in a predetermined pattern. It appears they were attempting to make a random weapons strike that would have revealed our location if they were successful. I performed a jinxing maneuver that prevented one of the beams from striking our hull. I would like to also add it was a brilliant but futile last-ditch effort on the part of the hostile AIs to locate the Legacy."

439

That got my juices working. It also made up my mind on gathering data to use against the vessels if it came down to duking it out.

"Justice, what is the status of the DEHD core?"

"The matrix will be fully charged in eight minutes, and DEHD core operations will be available at that time."

"Preprogram a DEHD core jump back to the Sig's new base of operations and proceed with your test."

"Coordinates locked, Commander. Launching missile now."

I watched the view dome as a pale blue circle appeared at our feet and moved away from us. It disappeared for about twenty seconds and reappeared behind the hostile ships. They immediately made a turn that hinted they got a detection. Their tracks indicated they didn't have a lock. This information could prove useful in the future. Their sensors could detect the minute transition waves created by our missiles, but they had to be close. The vectors they were taking put them several degrees off of a direct intercept course. The pale blue circle around our missile was slowly growing a deeper shade of azure. In the blink of an eye, the three ships pulsed with a golden halo and three white lines lanced out and disintegrated the missile. Even though it was on an outbound course away from the ships, they still chose to strike it. There was little doubt in my mind about their intentions. If they had detected the Legacy, they would have opened fire.

"Commander, the weapons used against our missile share parity with our own systems," Justice reported. "The destructive force is comparable to that of our beam weapons. The one advantage I am noting is their weapons have an extended range over ours due to a longer-duration energy pulse. This information reflects a direct correlation to the size of their power generators. The alien ships are formidable weapons platforms and should be considered dangerous adversaries. The one weakness I perceive in the data is the overaggressive nature of the controlling AIs. In that particular realm, the Legacy has a marked advantage."

I wasn't quite sure if Justice was just pointing out that Guardian-designed systems were superior to those of the unknown aliens. To me, it sounded an awful lot like the human peculiarity of honking one's own horn. The idea of hanging around and investigating the transponder thread was souring quickly. It made better sense to leave before we stirred up enough trouble to start exchanging fire with the unknowns.

"Justice, I have changed my mind about investigating the thread. Before we jump out of here, I want to let the aliens know they didn't scare us off. I want you to empty our magazines of stealth missiles. Target every Scrun picket ship that is not a slave hauler. Have the missiles transition to their targets after we jump."

That got me some smiles and nods from my crew. Inflicting damage on the Scrun was a whole lot better than just leaving them alone and sneaking out with our tails tucked between our legs.

"Launching now. DEHD core activation in thirty seconds."

We had never encountered a hostile with the same level of technology as the Legacy. This was the first time that we knowingly backed away from a fight. The hostiles had the numbers, and the odds were definitely stacked against us. Justice didn't even bother speculating on our percentages of a successful attack. That was a bad omen all by itself. There was one redeeming factor to our judicious retreat. When the missiles started hitting their targets, the unknown aliens driving those ships were going to look like suckers in the eyes of the Scrun. We would come back, and when we did, we would not be alone. As my reality faded away, I pondered the relationship between this place and the Scrun fleet sightings that Tam Lin reported to us.

Our return to normal space-time got us an immediate hail from the Sig's new base. Justice put it on the Legacy's open comms channel.

"Commander Myers, it is good that you are paying us another visit," Sushi said. "We had some company since you were last here. Another freighter jumped into the system. We alerted them we had an ongoing operation against pirates and they should be cautious of any ship approaching them without proper clearance. They departed within minutes of our communication. We suspect it was the freighter the pirates were supposed to capture. This was good for the crew of the freighter, but ultimately may prove bad for you. If you were planning a mission based on the information obtained from the pirates, you may want to advance your timetable accordingly. It is just a matter of time before those behind the criminal activity in this sector, find out the freighter did not go missing and made it to its original destination."

Crap! I was counting on having a little more time to question Illam Pove. This put a serious crimp in my timeline. We needed to put together a plan to pay Shurmosk a visit sooner than later. We did not want the Murlak to get a warning before we could take care of business. A place like Shurmosk would only have the people necessary to keep it secure. If the Murlak received advance warning the location has been compromised, they could call in reinforcements or evacuate their treasure and abandon it entirely. The latter scenario seemed much more likely. I thanked Sushi for the data dump and ordered Justice to jump us to hyperspace. It would take more than forty hours of normal transition time to reach Alpha Base. When the matrix was charged in the next hour, we would make the rest of the journey in seconds.

28

We returned to Alpha Base and immediately set to work on rearming the Legacy. As was now a common practice, all the scientists and engineers pitched in to help. Tria, Coonts, Klutch, and Xul joined me in the briefing room to put together a plan. We knew we had to get the information on the whereabouts of Shurmosk from Illam Pove. Our usual method for gaining info was to beat the hell out of the murderous pirates until they talked. Illam Pove had to be on really firm ground with Eiger to be entrusted with the location of his treasure stash. I was not above committing what many on my home planet would consider to be atrocities. If that was what it took to gain important info from an alien that committed such crimes on a daily basis, then so be it. It was our experience that the aliens who committed the most heinous of crimes rolled fairly quickly when they received the same treatment. We had to be careful how hard we pressed the Murlak. There was always the chance he might decide to die rather than cough up information.

It was decided we would make it a tag team effort. We drew a name out of a helmet to see who would pick the teams and go in first. Coonts won and chose Klutch as his partner. I personally didn't think it was the best combination. Why Coonts did not select Tria or me was a mystery. We occasionally disagreed with him, but we never got into the heated bickering contests he and Klutch were known for. Tria hooked her arm in mine and gave me a doubtful look. I shrugged, and we followed them into the Legacy's hangar. They started arguing right off about who should go in first. My patience was wearing thin. I was about to send them both on some meaningless errand. I had my fill of hearing them make wagers on the outcome and then nitpicking each other on how to go about it. When they saw the looks Tria and I were giving them, it ended the argument. Coonts got his way, and we entered the brig. Justice had Illam's cell blacked out. He configured the walls for a one-way view. We could see in, but the Murlak could not see out. Tria, Klutch, and I sat on the benches outside to observe whether or not the Grawl had any luck with the pirate. Since Coonts's recon armor no longer fit his new physique, he chose to wear a smart cloth uniform instead. The door on the cell opened, and he stepped inside.

"I will make this simple for you," Coonts started. "You give me the coordinates of Shurmosk, and I will save you a lot of pain and suffering. There is also the small possibility of freedom, as long as you don't attempt to waste my time."

The Murlak stood up and stared down at Coonts.

"You are the strangest looking Grawl I have ever seen," he spat. "Did the demon warrior feed you his scat to fortify your scrawny frame?"

Klutch acted like that was the funniest thing he had ever heard. He started braying and slapping his knees. I thought Tria was going to choke him out to shut him up. Even though the cells were soundproof, Coonts already knew what the Troop Master's reaction was going to be. He found no humor in the Murlak's statement. He squinted his eyes and took a step back. The Murlak must have mistaken the Grawl's posture for fear and leaned forward with a venomous look on his face. Coonts leaped up off the deck, leading with his knee. He caught the Murlak right in the mouth, knocking him backward and bouncing his head off the cell wall. The Murlak rebounded and went face down on the floor. Coonts casually leaned down and flicked the four teeth sticking to the knee of his uniform against the side of the Murlak's head.

"You will find it difficult to eat your scat rations without those," he taunted.

The Murlak rolled over, spitting blood and more teeth. It looked like he might have lost the end of his tongue as well. Coonts didn't cut him an inch of slack. He grabbed Illam by the fur of his head and drove his fist into his muzzle, knocking him out. Coonts kicked the Murlak over onto his face so he wouldn't drown on his own blood. The Grawl was yearning to test his new strength and Oolaran fighting skills. But if he was not careful, he might accidently kill the Murlak. Klutch stood up and gave the Grawl a clapping ovation. I don't know what he was celebrating. We got zip for info.

"Klutch, what are you doing?" I asked. "Don't cheer him on. He didn't get any useful information."

"I am cheering because Coonts now owes me five thousand credits!"

That earned the Tibor a sharp elbow from Tria and a stink eye from me. I should have known the two wankers would turn this into some kind of game. My temper was starting to rise, and the toothy smile on the Tibor's face faded.

"I want the two of you to quit screwing around and get us something we can use," I shouted. "We are running out of time!"

The Tibor jumped up from the bench and stood in front of the cell door. When it opened, he told Coonts to take a break and watch how a professional gets the job done. I thought I heard the Grawl say something about double or nothing. I gritted my teeth. They were starting to get on my nerves, and that was not a good thing. Tria squeezed my hand.

"They are doing what you call letting off steam," she said to me. "Coonts is exhibiting restraint. Klutch will do the same, if for no other reason than to win their wager. They know if they kill the Murlak, we will have nothing."

I was hoping one of them would get the Murlak talking. I felt that if I went in, Illam Pove would die for sure. Coonts sat next to me and shrugged.

447

"The Murlak will meet his maker before he will tell Klutch what we want to know."

Screaming from the cell suddenly got our attention. Klutch was sitting on the Murlak and holding up the alien's hand. Ours mouths fell open when he spit out a thumb. Illam was screaming and babbling nonsense, so the Tibor bit off a finger as well. He spewed it into the Murlak's face. I knew the Troop Master was a hard ass, but this was a step above that.

"If you do not tell me the coordinates of Shurmosk, I will give you eight more reasons why you should!"

It took two more fingers to get what we needed. Coonts stormed off a sore loser and ten thousand credits lighter in the pockets. Klutch stood with Murlak blood dripping from his mouth, laughing at Coonts. When he saw the incredulous looks from Tria and me, he told us Coonts was mad because he didn't think of it first. My crew used to think I was the crazy one. The Tibor now owned that distinction. I had Justice treat the Murlak's wounds. I had a feeling he had a lot of information that could prove useful in the future. On my way out of the brig, I saw Klutch go into the holding cell where the Hivemind's containment chamber was stored.

"Klutch! You have been more than helpful today," I called. "It won't be necessary to aid the Hivemind at this time."

The Tibor discharged a mouthful of crimson spittle onto the container and turned to me.

448

"I was just checking to make sure the chamber was still secure, Commander!"

We needed to get the Troop Master back into combat. He had a lot of pent-up energy that was going to waste. He could better serve us by expending his energy on hostiles who were expendable. The sooner we left for Shurmosk, the better.

"Your time might be better spent going over your combat kit. We will be leaving for Shurmosk by the end of the day."

As expected, that put a gory smile back on the Tibor's face. He threw me something that resembled a salute and ran out of the brig.

"I will be squared away and ready in half that time, Commander!" he called as he ran.

I was betting it would be less. Tria tugged me toward the lift tubes.

"Let's get something to eat before he decides he is hungry."

It was really questionable if I had the stomach to eat after witnessing the Tibor's interrogation. The warm, inviting smile on Tria's face changed my mind. I might end up needing the extra energy at some point before our departure. We found Coonts and Xul in the galley sharing a meal. They waved us over, and we joined them.

"Commander, Xul and I agree that you should ask the Operative to join us on the Shurmosk mission. We are confident that if you ask, she will join us. She may resent your leadership, but she respects your combat abilities.

We will need all the help we can get. Her skills as a warrior are unquestionable. She tries to give the appearance of indifference, but I know her spirit craves battle," Coonts said. "Xul has volunteered to go with us, but his combat skills are untested and his equipment not up to the task. The Operative, on the other hand, can make use of Tria's old combat armor, and her prowess as a killer will be welcome when the shooting starts. Her help may prove to be the difference between a serious injury to someone on the strike team and pulling off a swift and decisive victory."

Swift or decisive were not words that I would have openly used before kicking off our next mission. Even though the beast in me cheered on Coonts's rhetoric and instilled a sense of preordained victory, we would not know how big the steaming pile was going to be until we buried our boots in it. I looked at Tria, and she stopped eating long enough to nod in agreement. It was an easy decision for my teammates. Sael spent most of her time bitching at me and not them. In the long run, I knew they were right, and I would make the call. In the back of my mind, I could hear the haunting call of the beast confirming Coonts's insight. Sael enjoyed a good blood bath as much as it did.

I managed to get down six more bites before the Troop Master walked into the galley. He picked up two trays in preparation for his precombat feast. The four of us picked up ours and dumped them into the recycler. Three of us gave Klutch a polite nod on the way out. Coonts choose instead to give him an Earth gesture that earned me a sharp poke from Tria. The Tibor gave him a boisterous croaking laugh and mouthed the words "ten thousand" to him. A few short years ago, the two aliens would have never acted like this. I was still finding it difficult to determine what part of my behavior rubbed off enough to turn them into the stooges they were now.

I changed gears and started composing the message I was going to send to Sael. Tria had other ideas. More than an hour later and a hot shower to soothe a few bruises, I opened a secure IST channel to Sael. She answered without hesitation.

"Nathan, are you calling with information on the Fury?"

"No, unfortunately not. I do, however, have something you might be interested in."

"Let me guess. The Hivemind has enlightened you on the whereabouts of another Prule deathtrap."

I was starting to get a little agitated at the Operative's demeanor and considered doing the mission on our own. Why she thought that we should have information on the Fury hinted that she still thought Justice had a subsystem stowed aboard. Try as she might, she was not going to get me to admit it anytime soon.

"Perhaps I should call you later so you can find some fool to remove that stick from your ass."

"You primate! You are the stick in my ass," Sael snapped back. "What do you want?"

"We have developed some solid information on Eiger. I was calling because I thought you might be interested in participating in his apprehension. I suspect it will involve sending a large number of pirates to an unexpected meeting with their maker."

"Nathan, as much as I would like to participate, I have been informed by my superiors that no Chaalt will take part in any more missions that violate the territorial boundaries of the Murlak home worlds. I have been specifically told not to commit another act of war if I value my position as the Principal Investigator of my people. To be honest with you, we have a hold on all military excursions. The only exceptions to those orders will have to be Prule related."

"Sael, we will not be going to the Murlak home worlds. We have information on a Murlak base called Shurmosk. It is where the pirates and corrupt members of the Galactic Council store their stolen treasures."

The silence lingered long enough I started to ask if she was still on the IST channel.

"I have heard intel reports on such a place," Sael said slowly. "The stories vary enough that I wrote them off as a myth. How can you be sure you have accurate data?"

"The Sig captured a Murlak pirate by the name of Illam Pove. He is now in our custody. One of our sources has positively identified him as one of Eiger's highest ranking enforcers. The Troop Master convinced him to reveal the location."

"Pove is known to me, and yes, he is high in the ranks of the pirate leadership. You say you also have evidence that implicates members of the Galactic Council collaborating with the pirates?"

"Yes, as well as the involvement of their clan siblings."

"Why are you not asking the Sig to back you on this operation?"

"They would if I asked, but they have no fleets anywhere close to the base coordinates. The travel time involved to move a task force would be well outside of the time frame we have to execute the mission. Their equipment is inferior to ours, and I fear they will take unnecessary losses. You know as well as I do that a small, highly capable strike team can move faster and be more effective. Our weapons and equipment are a huge force multiplier. The longer we wait, the more chance there is of the pirates getting a warning that the base has been compromised."

"I will be at Alpha Base within two hours."

"We will be waiting for your arrival."

We transferred Pove and the Hivemind's containment chamber to the security cells under Alpha Base. Klutch and Coonts made themselves busy with swapping out the assault shuttles. They loaded a fully-armed Eagle Two in the hangar and were going to put all five of the Daggers in the cargo hold. We hadn't come up with a scenario where we would need them, so I nixed the idea in favor of an empty cargo hold. The Troop Master bitched about it until I told him we would be shooting and looting. I made contact with the Zaens and told them we might have need of the freighter. It was my plan to have it take up a covert

453

position within a short jump of Shurmosk. If our engagement was successful, we would take as much of the pirate's assets as we could and destroy the rest if we had to. It was my intention to decapitate the pirate leadership and deprive them of the wealth they used to continue their illegal operations.

Justice reported the sighting of a lone Chaalt warship entering our star system. The Operative had arrived. The ship rapidly moved above Alpha Base, and a few minutes later we heard the loud report of Sael transporting down. Tria and I were just leaving the munitions storage building and went to meet her. She was wearing Chaalt heavy combat armor with her sword and anti-transport rifle clipped behind her shoulders.

"I wonder if she did that just to rub in the fact, we don't have a transporter. At least it looks like the old witch is raring to go," I whispered to Tria.

Tria's response to my comments was a crushing squeeze of my hand that made me flinch. She chose to be a lot more cordial than I was.

"Principal Investigator, you will be wearing my backup armor on this deployment," Tria said. "Justice informed us how well you adapted to it on our last joint mission. If that is agreeable to you, please go to the ready room on the Legacy. Justice has the suit prepped and will give you a quick refresher course on the weapons systems."

We followed her to the Legacy and had to wade through the gathered scientists and engineers. Sael stood on the boarding ramp and watched as Tria and I made

454

hand contact with each of them. Jaran, Graf, and Felix waved to us.

"I will begin production on the torpedoes for the Legacy," Felix called to us as we boarded. You have a prototype loaded in the Legacy's launcher. By the time you return, I will have a complete loadout awaiting you."

I smiled and waved back. The young Zaen had proven his worth time and time again. He had risen to every technical challenge thrown at him and surpassed all of our expectations. There was no doubt in my mind that I had some of the finest minds in the galaxy working for me. Together they gave us a better-than-average chance of successfully completing all our mission goals.

"Justice, what is the status of our freighter?"

"Broza is transitioning to the jump off point. He estimates their transit ETA to be four hours and forty minutes."

"I was not aware Felix had finished his schematic and production program for the torpedo," I said. "I knew we recovered the parts for one at our artifact depot but didn't think it would be ready to deploy any time soon."

"The parts the Grawl collected were of a complete weapon. It only required proper assembly and integrating the onboard AI with my weapons core. The Guardian architecture rapidly assimilated my Oolaran targeting systems, and it is now ready in all aspects. Felix was part of the assembly team and carefully cataloged all of the weapon's internal specifications."

"Okay, Justice, take us to the freighter jump off point. I want to meet with the Zaens and their Sig crew. They need to know what we are going to do and what they will be jumping into."

"Roger that, Commander. DEHD core transition in twelve minutes."

Tria joined me, and we went to the ready room. We ran into the Operative, and she was suited up in Tria's armor. In the background I could hear the usual arguments and expletive-laden banter coming from Klutch and Coonts.

"Your influence on the Grawl and Tibor have rotted their brains!" Sael said to me.

I didn't even frown at the slight; she was probably right. I winked at her.

"I'm still working on yours."

She hit her gravity boosters and disappeared into the hangar. I was going to let her know about our encounter with the Scrun and their unknown allies. There was always the possibility the Operative had intelligence on the aliens. I decided my inquiry could wait. It had no bearing on our current mission goals. As we approached Coonts and Klutch, the Grawl was poking home his point on some unknown subject. He was doing it on the front of Klutch's armor with his index finger. When they noticed us coming, they promptly stopped whatever they were discussing. Both tried their best to look as if they were having a polite conversation. I wasn't buying it. The two of them were up to something, and I was pretty sure it had to do with another wager of some sort. My expression must have given away my displeasure because they both quickly exited the ready room. Tria smiled at me, erasing the frown from my face.

"Let it go. They could be doing a lot worse," she said. "Their behavior is no different than some of the others I have served with. It is how they deal with the stress of constant combat."

"I know, but Coonts has never been a good loser, and the weaponization procedure only made it worse. He should have it figured out by now that the Troop Master rarely makes a wager unless the odds are in his favor."

I was going to say more and ask Tria if she knew where a Grawl Guild was located. I knew there were much more pleasant ways to deal with stress. That thought was the last thing going through my mind as our reality faded away. Our return from interdimensional space was uneventful, and Justice alerted us the freighter's projected ETA was three hours and seventeen minutes. My mind was wandering back to the subject of stress elimination, but the Senior Operative flew out of the hangar and set down in front of us.

"Justice has cleared me for combat operations," Sael said. "I would like a briefing on our battle plan."

"Justice will use our stealth systems to get us as close to Shurmosk as possible. We will then use the portal device to covertly make an insertion into the Murlak stronghold. Once inside, we will eliminate any and all pirates we come into contact with. Our first priority is to locate Eiger and either eliminate or capture him. If our intelligence proves to be faulty and he is not present, we will attempt to gain control of the base. If we are successful, we will bring in our freighter to remove the pirate's financial resources or destroy them in place."

Sael surprised me by not asking a single question or bitching about anything. I looked her in the eyes, trying to get a read on her mindset. The grim determination staring back at me told me she would like nothing better than to drink pirate blood from her boot. She had more than enough problems of her own, yet here she was, ready to go. It had me speculating whether the council knew about this little adventure or not. I brushed the thought aside. Xul and Coonts were correct. The Operative was an asset to the team. When the scat came raining down, she only got meaner.

"Sael, we will be gathering in the galley," I said. "Justice has combat stimulants and nutrients selected for our prebattle meal. Please meet us there in an hour."

She nodded and went to the ready room. I was again unsettled by her lack of questions or bitching about any little something that didn't conform with her regimental command style. Sael was a lot of things, but quiet and cooperative was not one of them. Tria picked up on it as well and pushed me toward the ready room. I cocked an eyebrow and threw my hands up, giving her my what-the-hell look.

"I sense something is troubling Sael, and you should try to find out what it is before we depart," she said. "We need her help, but she needs to be focused on the mission and nothing else."

"I don't think she needs any of my human idiosyncrasies right at the moment," I replied. "You should go ask what is eating at her, and I will wait for you in the galley."

"She still treats me as a subordinate and will not speak her mind. Though she may not act like it, she considers you her equal in command authority," Tria argued. "You must find out if we are going to have a problem with her now, and not while we are on our deployment."

"You have got to be kidding me! She considers me something alright, but lately, I believe it has more to do with unpleasant things she may have stepped in."

"She does that for the benefit of others who may be watching your interactions. I know for a fact that she hides her true feelings for you. She respects you for the things you have accomplished. No one has ever been successful at what you are doing. You are winning a war few will even acknowledge. It is why she has finally chosen to follow you."

Tria wasn't going to budge on the subject. She pointed at the ready room and gave me her I-mean-it look. I frowned and stalked off. I was the ranking officer, and I was the one doing the marching. I went to the ready room and walked up to Sael as she stepped out of Tria's armor. She had a puzzled look on her face.

"Commander Myers, is there a problem?"

"You can save the commander routine for someone who cares. I came here to find out what is bothering you. I have grown used to your normal behavior, and you are not acting normal. If we have a problem, I want to about it now and not find out we have issues during combat."

I thought she was going to answer me. She instead decided to remove her suit liner. She was now buck naked, and we were about two feet apart. Her once chiseled muscle and bone physique, had a little more meat on it. She was filling in nicely, and I was having a little difficulty not taking an overly long look. She took a step closer. That was the last thing I expected her to do. My eyes were suddenly dollar-sized and my mouth a desert. She reached an arm out to me, and I almost fell backward over the bench behind me. She shook her head.

"My uniform, please."

I didn't realize I was standing in front of the locker it was hanging in. I quickly handed it to her. Try as I might, my composure was nowhere to be found. She seemed to be enjoying my bumbling behavior.

"You primate. Sit down before you fall and hurt yourself."

At least I got a response I was used to hearing. I sat down, and she sat right beside me. She didn't act like she was in any hurry to finish putting on her uniform. I don't think I could have been any more uncomfortable unless someone lit my ass on fire.

"Your observations are correct," she began. "I do have a number of issues troubling me lately. When my people called me Kala Mor Dee, my orders and decisions were never questioned. I felt I had the unwavering trust and respect of all my subordinates and demanded nothing less. After my many visits and interactions with you, I had come to the conclusion I was wrong. They all feared me, and I tried to change that. Unfortunately, when they lost that fear, the ones I counted on the most to carry out my orders turned on me. I believe it is why I have lost the Fury."

She was quiet for a moment, then continued, "I will be honest with you. When I saw the way your people respected you, I was at a loss as to why. You rarely ordered or demanded anything from them, yet they would follow you to their deaths if that is where you led them. They only feared what the Oolaran imprinting did to you, but all of them respect and trust you on a level I cannot begin to fathom. I wanted the same for those who served under me, and I got treachery in return. My superiors will not come right out and say it, but the loss of the Fury is a blot on my record that will forever haunt me. I have heard the rumors that there are some who believe my participation in the rescue mission was unnecessary. It is also said by many I should have stayed at my command and rallied the loyal troops to put down the rebellion."

"Maybe they need a reminder that it was you saving them from the Hivemind," I said. "Klutch could not have got them all out as swiftly as we did without you help. If it were not for your guidance, we could not have caught up with the Hivemind as rapidly as we did. I am sure that saved some of the lives of the council members."

"I still have the backing of most, but to some of the others, those are memories of convenience. They will not take action against me for fear of losing their connection with you."

"Maybe I should remind them that you are the only reason they have a connection with me."

"Nathan, please do not do that. It will be taken by those who oppose me as something I put you up to doing. I am trying to put it behind me. You asked, and now you know. I just want to move forward from here."

"With all that going on, why did you agree to come with us?"

The Operative sat silent for several minutes, staring at the floor. She took a deep breath and gave me a small smile.

"I keep asking myself the same thing. There is only one reasonable answer I can come up with: I guess I am hoping whatever makes you the popular Throgg that you are will rub off on me."

29

My laugh was contagious. To hear Sael do it with so much conflict going on in her life was a relief. She must have been serious because when we walked out of the ready room, she hooked two of her arms in mine. Tria had waited patiently by the lifts. I didn't realize my little heart to heart with Sael took almost an hour. When Tria saw the smiles on our faces, hers lit up as well. She grabbed my other arm, and as we walked to the lifts, she leaned over and whispered to me, "I hope you aren't getting any big ideas about a ménage a trois."

Freaking evil robot! He ratted me out! I closed my eyes and gritted my teeth, almost walking into the side of the lift tube. Tria pulled me inside at the last moment. Sael let go of my arm and gave us the strangest look. We stepped out of the tube and saw Klutch make the turn into the galley. Tria and I slowed down, but Sael kept right on going. I hissed at her to slow down, but she frowned and waved me off. She must have thought we were having a little jealous spat because she turned the corner into the

463

galley. Tria didn't seem to be upset about my less than truthful disclosure on my use of French axioms. She was, however, interested in knowing what was up with Sael. I gave her the summarized version. She shook her head in derision, then swatted me on the ass and pointed to the galley.

When we got inside, we saw that Xul and Coonts were already seated together. The Troop Master was leaving the chow line and moving in their direction. Sael was finishing making her nutrient selections. Klutch sat next to Coonts and they traded a few insincerities. Xul knew where that was going and left before it could blossom into the usual disparaging discourses. Tria and I again tried to get Sael's attention, but she was heads down, inspecting the rations Justice had selected for her. She headed for Coonts's and the Troop Master's table. I thought she would surely remember the Tibor's unique eating habits. When Coonts saw that she might sit on the opposite side of the table, he attempted a tactful rescue. He patted the bench beside him.

"Senior Operative, would you care to join us?"

Coonts got a polite nod, but Sael still sat on the opposite side of the table. She didn't make the foolhardy mistake of sitting directly across from the Troop Master and chose instead to sit across from Coonts. It was still close enough; she was inside what the rest of us considered the no-sit zone. Tria and I sat next to Coonts and waited for the fireworks to start. To our shock and surprise, Sael sat straight-faced when Klutch tore into his

464

nutrient bars. She never even looked up when he started making noises like a racoon ravaging a trash can. When the crumbs started flying, she brushed them away and carried on with her meal. We decided to do the same. When we finished, we went over our plans one more time. We would use stealth until it was no longer possible. There were no friendlies in the area of operation, so everyone was a target. Justice had a picture of Eiger that would allow our battle suits to use AI recognition programs to identify him out of a crowd if necessary. We would attempt to apprehend him if the opportunity arose. If not, he was going to be a dead man like everyone else. If we could take control of the base, we would call in the freighter and take as much as we could carry while Justice flew cover. The Sig were already sending a fleet, but it would not show up for another twenty-seven hours. We should be long gone by then. Justice alerted us our freighter had arrived.

I spoke to Broza and then to the Sig crew. They assured me the freighter's weapons and shields were performing to spec. We went over everything they needed to know. My confidence in the Zaens was given a boost when they seemed almost enthusiastic about going into combat. I think it had a lot to do with the way the Sig crew performed during the attack the pirates made on our freighter. Their actions obviously put some starch into the Zaens' spines. If our mining plans worked out, I would upgrade to a freighter based on a battleship platform. If anyone got wind we were moving large quantities of

Containium, we would need the extra firepower to protect our business interests. We went to the ready room and started our ritual of strapping on the tools of our trade. We checked each other's kit and made sure everything was secure. I made eye contact with Tria, Coonts, and Klutch, and they each gave me a thumbs up. As I stepped in front of the Operative, I could see her eyes wandering around her HUD menus before fixing on me. She gave me a Chaalt salute, and I returned it. Then she gave me a thumbs up. Every weapon was at capacity, and our suits were all in the green.

"Justice, take us to the surveillance jump point."

"Roger that, Commander. The matrix is charged, and we will be out of direct observation from our freighter in three minutes. DEHD core jump to waypoint one in three minutes and thirty seconds."

We marched single file to the hangar. Xul was sitting in the cockpit of Eagle Two and gave me a thumbs up. I thought it was pretty cool when the aliens under my command acknowledged they were good to go with an Earth man gesture. Xul would be flying in the event we needed an emergency dust off or some extra firepower. I was hoping we wouldn't have any need for it. My grandad taught me a long time ago to hope for the best and prep for the worst.

Our reality faded away and then back again. We now occupied a piece of the void two hundred and sixty light-years from our freighter and point five from our target. As far as we knew, the Chaalt were the only ones with deep space sensors that could detect DEHD core transitions. If we were wrong, we had knocked hard on the Murlak's door. Our stealth systems were online, and Justice was scanning. Five minutes later, he gave us a less than favorable report. We were close to the coordinates, but it was on the edge of a massive multi-light-year asteroid field. There were millions of asteroids spread out in every direction, and the majority were huge. You could hide an entire fleet of Warbringer's in that mess. Justice started throwing numbers at me based on his scan observations.

"Commander, of the one million eleven thousand thirty-three asteroids detected in my scans, one hundred and sixty-two thousand are large enough to harbor a base capable of docking a Murlak Warbringer-class battleship. I narrowed my search pattern and have eliminated all but two hundred and seventy-one that are concentrated around the coordinates given to us by Illam Pove. I am not detecting spacecraft or other telltale emissions in or around those targets."

I should have known just getting the coordinates would have made finding Shurmosk too easy. We would be forced to search. There was always the chance that Illam Pove was a tougher nut to crack than we thought and gave us erroneous intel. After thinking back on my observations of Klutch's interrogation, I dismissed any speculation on the Murlak's fortitude. Pove's shrill screams as Klutch slowly bit down on the last finger of his left hand gave little doubt as to his sincerity. I cleared the morbid scene from my mind and brought our present situation back in focus. It would be stupidity on the part of the Murlak to not have sensors and weapons on any usable route to their base. If Justice could get a whiff of those systems, they might lead us to where the base was located. We would again be relying heavily on our Guardian-designed equipment to shield us from detection. The complete lack of activity as we penetrated deeper into the asteroid field was a confidence builder. Our technological edge was holding.

"Commander, we are coming up on the coordinates of Shurmosk," Justice said. "I have no active detections to report at this time. There is a possibility the location revealed to us may have been a contact waypoint. It would be a way to identify friend from foe. Once a vessel is verified as an ally, the final route to the base would be transmitted."

It wasn't something I had considered. Now that Justice put the theory out for us to chew on, it was more or less the same thing we were doing with El Dorado. We were actively shielding its whereabouts from all but a few select allies. It made sense to limit the information so it could not be coerced or extracted by more diabolical methods. I was getting antsy. I thought we would be on the base by now doing our thing. I didn't like standing around with a thumb inserted in my out door. We were all dressed up with no place to go. If we had to turn around and go back to Alpha Base, I knew a Murlak who was going to go for a walk in the void without a suit.

"Commander, I am detecting transition distortion waves close to our area of operations. I am going to shelter the Legacy in close proximity to one of the nearby asteroids so we can observe and identify the vessel."

"Roger that. If it is the Murlak, maybe they will be kind enough to show us the way to Shurmosk."

"I have identified the vessel as a Murlak Warbringer-class battleship. It is moving closer to the asteroid field but is not on a course that will intersect with the coordinates you were given by Illam Pove."

Justice put a digital representation of the surrounding asteroid field and a red triangle indicating the Murlak ship in our HUDs. He extended a course cursor from the hostile ship that indicated its flight path. Justice was right. It would pass near the asteroid field, but unless it made a hard-ninety-degree turn, it would miss it completely. I was again thinking Pove had lied to us.

"Commander, I am detecting three shuttles launching from the Murlak ship," Justice said. "The hulls of the shuttles are exhibiting stealth characteristics. They are moving into the asteroid field on a course that will pass close to our position."

"What about the battleship?"

"Its course has not changed. It appears to be on a heading that will take it into the dust nebula that surrounds the outer perimeter of the asteroid field."

"How good is their stealth?"

"It is of fair quality. Their systems are redirecting over half of my passive scan return information. What it does

469

not do adequately is mask the drive emissions. I foresee no problems tracking them."

We watched as Justice tracked the shuttles in our HUDs. At one point, they were on a vector that would take them directly at the Legacy but veered off sharply and made a sweeping arc well behind us. Justice confirmed what was on our minds. The Murlak were making a methodical search of the surrounding area. We thought it was a matter of time before they would lead us to Shurmosk. I had Xul drop the ramp on Eagle Two, and we made ourselves comfortable in the cargo hold jump seats. I hoped we would get moving soon. After another hour of sitting, Coonts and Klutch were elbowing and swatting at each other. I was glad they closed their helmets; I could only imagine the conversation that was taking place on their private comms channels. The Operative sat quietly with her arms crossed, trying her best to ignore my other strike team members who were acting like ten-year-old children. The Operative of old would have had a meltdown by now. She would have been reaming me a new one over my crew's lack of discipline. After more than three hours of course changes and backtracking, the shuttles regrouped. It looked like they were moving toward the fringe of the asteroid field.

"Commander, the Murlak Warbringer is retracing its outbound course and moving back to the asteroid field," Justice reported.

"Is there a possibility they detected our position?"

"We were never targeted by any of the shuttles' scans. It is highly unlikely they are aware of our presence."

"Have you picked up any comms traffic?"

"Negative, Commander. They have maintained communication silence."

I was thinking the Murlak decided to load up and leave. We would be forced to search for the base once they left the area. I was on the verge of telling my strike team to stand down and stow their armor.

"Commander!" Justice said urgently. "Two additional shuttles have launched from the Warbringer. They are joining with the three-shuttle formation and moving back into the asteroid field."

My pulse quickened. We may have witnessed the ritual security sweep that preceded landing at the Murlak base. I was wondering who might be on the second set of shuttles. Was this Eiger's security team escorting him to Shurmosk?

"Commander, the shuttles are on a course that intersects with an asteroid with a diameter of less than five miles," Justice said. "If this is indeed their destination, a Warbringer battleship would have great difficulty accommodating its large size in such a restricted area. I am moving the Legacy a safe distance behind the shuttle formation, and we will follow until they reach their final destination."

We watched as the shuttles headed for the asteroid Justice had indicated. They slowed, and as they did, a rock formation on the surface parted and they disappeared inside. My crew was back to business as normal. We marched off of Eagle Two and made ready for a combat jump. Justice tucked the Legacy against the back side of a large asteroid that faced our target, then partially opened the hangar door. We jumped out. He quickly closed the hatch and slowly moved the Legacy away. We used our gravity boosters to take us around the asteroid to a point where we could observe the pirate base. We were about a thousand yards from our target, and there was no outward reaction to our insertion. We formed up and boosted toward the pirate fortress. We were vulnerable and exposed while crossing to the surface of Shurmosk. We should find out fairly quickly if the stealth features of our suits failed us.

To my relief, our touchdown on the surface was uneventful. We were close enough to the hidden opening the shuttles had used for access that we could make out the parting line in the rock. We stayed low to the surface and used small burps of our gravity drives to push us along. Klutch suddenly held up a fist and pointed at a row of rocklike protrusions sticking up from the surface. We were keeping our comms locked down to further avoid detection. He pointed left and right. I followed his arm and saw that the protrusions were an equal distance from each other and went in both directions. Klutch made a circle motion with his hand and again pointed at the rocklike pillars. I wasn't sure what they were for, but Klutch was right: it looked like they encircled the hidden access doors. He turned us away and I assumed we were going to try to find another way in. We slowly worked our way along the surface.

We came to a crater that was about thirty feet across. As we started to go over the edge, Klutch stopped us again. The crater was only about ten feet deep. At its bottom were rows of pencil thin antennas about two feet tall. They created a grid that was roughly six feet by six feet. While this was an interesting find, it was what Klutch pointed at to the side of the array that got my blood pressure up a couple of notches. The rocklike wall had the outline of a hatch on it. We skirted the sensor grid and stacked near the hatch. I pointed to Klutch's portal device and then at the door. He nodded and was going to pull his plasma weapon from its clip. I quickly grabbed the barrel of the weapon and pulled his shotgun for him instead. I wagged my finger in front of his facemask. We would try to use stealth before I would let him burn the place down around us.

He activated the device, and we got a small, single-person hole. He leaned forward into it and then stuck a hand back out behind him. He waved for us to follow. I was next with Tria, Coonts, and the Operative bringing up the rear. We were in a narrow, dark service tunnel. My no-light sensors gave me a great view of the Troop Master's ass but nothing else beyond him. His armor filled the tunnel, blocking our line of sight. We had no choice but to blindly follow. If he started a party, we would have a hard time joining the celebration until we could exit the passage. We crawled along for more than two hundred yards. It was a testimony as to the thickness of the outer shell of the asteroid. The Troop Master slowed and then finally stopped. I could barely peek over his shoulder and could see the passage dead ended at another hatch. Klutch was messing around with the backside of the access, and to my surprise, it opened. We dropped down into a large machine space that had an active generator.

Now that we were inside, I took a leap of faith that our comms would no longer be an issue with detection.

"Coonts, take a look around and give me an idea of what this equipment might be used for," I said. "Klutch, you and Sael look for an exit."

Turning to Tria, I pointed at a service panel. "See if it is something we can cause a little trouble with."

Tria went to survey the control panel, and I got a heads-up from Klutch and the Operative. They found two hatches and split up to guard each of them. Coonts returned and reported the generator supplied power to several surface arrays, but its size implied it powered other unknown equipment as well.

"This display is a monitoring station for several pumps," Tria said, pointing at the control panel. "It does not identify what they are pumping. The switches on the lower panel are the actuators. I think if we shut them down, someone would be here shortly to find out what the problem was. It would be a good way to get some information on the facility."

Coonts was standing next to me studying the board. Tria had a good point. If we could not get someone's attention with the pumps, maybe screwing with the power supply would get us a maintenance tech.

"Is there anything like this on the generator?"

"No, Commander, the generator is being monitored at another location. There are, however, a number of transfer switches that alternate the flow of energy. If we were to damage enough of them, we could trigger an automated shutdown of the generator."

There was no time like the present to start adding complexities to the lives of the pirates. I decided we would start with the pumps. If that didn't net us the results we were looking for, the generator would be next.

"Tria, shut down the pumps. Sael, Klutch, we will be expecting some guest shortly. I have no idea how many, but I need at least one to be alive."

When Tria shut the pumps off, an alarm sounded. I knew it would be doing the same elsewhere. Tria, Coonts, and I climbed up on a maintenance scaffold on the side of the generator. We had a good view of the hatches. We cloaked and settled in for what I hoped would be a short wait. About forty seconds passed, and the hatch on Sael's side of the room opened. Two Murlak wearing bright green jumpsuits hustled through the door. Sael was a little overenthusiastic. She clotheslined the first one, flipping him up and then prone on his back. He was gagging and clawing at his throat. She whipped the other around by his arm and smashed him face-first into the rock wall. The wet-sounding crunch had a definite note of finality to it. A short string of Chaalt oaths was heard over our group comms. It did not bode well for the health of either Murlak.

"Commander Myers, we will need another source of information," Sael reported. "I have two Murlak fatalities."

Klutch thought it was funny. I did not. I cut his croaking laugh off like a light switch.

"Klutch! Can that crap!" I yelled.

There was no point in jumping Sael's ass for killing the Murlak. It was why we were here and what we had planned on doing. She was not as finely tuned to the armor as we were. The suit-assisted reflexes and strength multipliers made it extremely easy to kill an unarmored combatant. Before I could tell her to take it easy next time, the hatch opened and a tall Murlak wearing body armor stepped in.

"Cancel that alar—"

His eyes swelled and his words locked in his throat as he stared at the two dead bodies. Sael didn't hesitate. She kicked one of the bodies with such force it flew into the hatch, slamming it shut before the Murlak could turn and run back through it. He fumbled with the door control, but Sael jerked him backward onto the floor. He attempted to draw a sidearm, and she wrenched it from his grip, snapping the bones in his wrist. He screeched out in pain as she picked him off the floor and threw him at the Troop Master.

"Here, Troop Master! Do something with this Throgg before I to kill it, too!"

Klutch turned his shoulder, and the Murlak slammed into it and fell to the floor. The air was forced from his lungs, putting a damper on his screams of agony. He lay groaning on the floor. We had a source of information.

"Tria, turn the pumps back on," I ordered. "Coonts, cover the hatch while Klutch searches the Murlak."

The alarms stopped their incessant wailing as soon as Tria activated the pumps. Sael busied herself by pulling the dead bodies up onto the maintenance scaffold and out of sight. Klutch stripped the gear off the Murlak and searched him. He stomped the Murlak's helmet and communicator into scrap.

"That is what will happen to you if you do not answer our questions," he threatened the Murlak.

I shut down my cloaking systems so the Murlak could see who he was dealing with. Kneeling down next to the Murlak, I pulled his face up to my war mask. Coonts was peeking out the hatch and interrupted before I could start my interrogation.

"I have three Murlak coming this way and they are wearing body armor!"

If I would have known the pump alarms were going to generate this much excitement, I would have come up with a different plan.

"Klutch, get the Murlak on his feet and keep him quiet."

Klutch pulled the Murlak off the floor and behind the generator. His method for keeping the Murlak from yelling out was simple: he punched him in the gut. The Murlak bent double trying his best to get air into his empty lungs. I cloaked while Coonts waited on the back side of the hatch. A moment later, it swung open and the three unsuspecting soldiers marched in. They were oblivious to Coonts standing behind the door. He pushed the hatch shut and decapitated the last one through with his climbing hook. The first two whirled around completely shocked as their fellow trooper collapsed headless onto them. The Operative took this as her cue to jump off the scaffold. She landed boots-first on the helmet of the leader. He was driven into the floor with a broken neck. Reaching out, she grabbed the remaining Murlak by the front of his vest and drove her armored fist into his faceplate three times in rapid succession. The first blow probably would have been sufficient and given us a second prisoner to interrogate. The other two might have been Sael's pent-up anxiety over losing the Fury or might possibly have something to do with Klutch laughing at her. Either way you wanted to look at it, there would be no use in trying to talk to him now. I hoped we would get what we need from our remaining prisoner.

I pulled the prisoner away from Klutch and lifted him off the floor. We heard there was a lot of cringeworthy scuttlebutt being spread by the Murlak about the demon warrior. I wanted the prisoner to get a close-up of my macabre war face so he had no doubt who was asking the questions. His acknowledgment of my identity led to a lot of wasted thrashing and screaming. I extruded a climbing hook and held it to his throat, and he quieted immediately.

"Where are the shuttle docks?"

The Murlak pointed at the hatch Coonts was guarding. "At the end of the passage."

"Where can I find Eiger?"

"I would not have that information. I am in charge of maintenance. His shuttle landed, and his security team escorted him away. I do not know where he could be."

"How many troops are stationed on this base?

"Base security has eighty. My maintenance crew has twelve. I do not know how many accompanied Eiger."

"Where is the artifact storage chamber?"

He pointed over his shoulder at the hatch he had come through. "At the end of this passage is the main corridor. Go in the direction of the shuttle docks, and it is the second hatch from the pressure locks. You will know when you get there. The entrance is like no others."

I dropped the Murlak on the floor at Klutch's feet. We had all the important information needed to get this party started. Eiger was here; it was just a matter of finding him. The first thing we needed to do was make sure he didn't have a ride off this rock. Tria commed me on a private channel.

"If Eiger is indeed here, we should make sure the Warbringer cannot send additional forces."

"We are going to the docks to disable Eiger's shuttles," I told her. "I will have Klutch port out and send a message to Justice before we initiate hostilities."

"Klutch, get the pirate on his feet. He is going to lead us to the docking area."

Coonts was holding the Murlak's helmet and waved it at me to get my attention.

"Commander, there is a lot of comms traffic on the Murlak's communicator."

We had spent way too much time in one place. It was a matter of time before someone came to investigate the lack of maintenance reports from the crew we had killed.

"Rig a remote detonated charge on the generator. Make sure it cannot be tampered with, and then we are out of here!" I told Coonts.

Coonts tossed the helmet and pulled an antimatter charge from his storage. He boosted up onto the maintenance scaffold. I commed the Operative.

"Sael, put a grenade outside the hatch and set it for antipersonnel. Give it a ten-second delay, and do the same to our exit hatch."

She turned and went to work without comment. Coonts jumped down from the top of the generator and gave me a thumbs up. Sael ran over with another grenade in hand and signaled she was ready to set the second one.

"Klutch, let's get moving!" I called.

The Troop Master opened the hatch enough to peek out. He had no hostiles in sight, so he pushed the Murlak out into the passage ahead of us. I cloaked, and we followed in our combat formation. We slowed enough to give the Operative time to set her next booby trap. She joined up with Coonts, and we started moving. There were four hatches on the left side of the passage, and the Murlak slowed as he came to the first one. Klutch gave him a healthy push for his tardy behavior, and we continued on. The passage was about two hundred feet long, and we could see a pressure door at the end. We had passed the third door when it suddenly opened. A Murlak stepped out and collided with Tria's cloaked armor. Tria grabbed him in a headlock and slapped a hand over his mouth. She jerked him hard up off the floor and shoved his head backward over her forearm. There was an audible snap as his neck let go. The Murlak's head lolled over at an impossible angle. Coonts and the Operative charged into the open hatch. We heard a brief scuffle, and then the Operative gave Coonts a "well done" over our comms. Tria threw the dead Murlak inside as Coonts and Sael stepped out. Coonts tossed in a motion-triggered grenade and closed the hatch after them.

Klutch and I were distracted by the commotion and turned to see what was going on. The Murlak could not see our response since we were cloaked but made the hasty assumption, we were looking the other way. He guessed right and took off running down the passage screaming for help. Klutch spun around and threw his arm up, giving the Murlak an overabundance of hypersonic needles. His calls of alarm were abruptly cut off as his head and upper torso seemed to melt away. The mutilated corpse flopped forward, sliding several feet down the gore-splattered passage. There was no way to hide the mess Klutch had made, so we ran to the pressure door. Looking through the observation window, I could not see anyone inside. The door had a touch pad locking system, and Klutch shook his head negative. He turned and pointed at the Murlak's corpse. Coonts ran back and dragged it back up the passage. He put the Murlak's hand to the pad, and the door swished open. Sael was the last through the door and put a grenade under the dead body as a parting gift.

We found ourselves in a control room overlooking the shuttle docks. We expected to see the five shuttles, but not the small armed freighter that was snuggled up to a loading area. There was a lot of activity going on, and it all appeared to be connected with moving cargo into the freighter. Our intel source stated this was the storage site for the pirate's ill-gotten gains. It didn't take a genius to guess what the cargo might be. Tria gave me a heads-up that we were in the dock's atmospheric control room. She pointed out that the pumps were we screwing with controlled the flow of the atmosphere in the dock. It was probably where the three Murlak we killed were stationed. At some point they would be missed, and things would start to get exciting. If the Murlak were loading the freighter in preparation of moving their wealth, there was a good chance they got tipped off this location was compromised. All this new data translated to the fact we were behind and needed to step up instead of playing catch-up.

I would have liked the time to come up with a new plan of action, but Sael upended the bucket of piss that perpetually hung over my head.

"Nathan! They are retracting the loading ramp!" Sael said.

I magnified my HUD and saw they were closing the cargo doors on the freighter as well.

30

We were running out of time, and like so many times in the past, we were going to wing it. I hated to be rushed, but things were happening at a pace that just wouldn't slow down. The pressure lock doors that went down to the dock started cycling. Somebody was coming to check on the missing crew. We spread out to both sides of the door and waited to see what kind of crappy hand we were going to be dealt next. The doors parted, and four Murlak wearing atmospheric suits were standing next to a gravity sled with a piece of equipment on it. They were talking among themselves. My assumption that they were checking on the missing crew was wrong because it didn't seem like they had a care in the world. I gave Klutch a push and went in after him. In quick succession, we gave each a one-second blast from our needle guns at point-blank range. It made a mess out of the air lock, but we were in a hurry. It was pointless to worry over spilled milk. The rest of my team piled in behind us, and I tossed a grenade out into the control room.

"We need to get aboard that freighter and make sure it doesn't leave with that cargo!" I said.

"Nathan, I am familiar with the freighter's design," Sael said. "I know where the bridge is located. If we use the portal device to gain access to the command center, we will have control of the ship's weapons and shields."

It was a better plan than mine because I didn't have one at the moment. There was only one logical thing I could say.

"Sael, take the lead, and we will follow. Klutch, be ready to make a hole! Let's move out!"

Tria cycled the air lock. When it opened, Sael led, and we boosted hard for the upper deck of the freighter. Klutch and I had Murlak blood splattered on our armor, and it degraded our cloaking systems. I hoped everyone on the loading area had better things to do than look over the top of the freighter. Sael set us down on the hull and ran forward to a position between the weapons turrets and the shield emitters. Clearing her faceplate, she got down on a knee and pointed to a spot that had a rescue hatch on it.

"The bridge command center is two decks below this hatch. We will have to pass through the inner hull maintenance tunnels. There is a chance we may encounter inspection crews since the ship is preparing to get underway," Sael said. "Troop Master, this vessel is a dated design and is not known for the quality of its fire suppression systems. Please do not use your plasma caster while we are aboard!"

When Sael was sure Klutch understood, she gave the order to activate the portal device. Klutch leaned forward to make a hole, and we heard a muffled thump. We looked up in time to be showered by the observation windows of the control room above us. A piercing alarm started wailing. The ventilator was officially fouled. I decided we might as well stir the pot a little harder.

"Coonts! Detonate the charge!" I called.

The explosion reverberated throughout the docking area. A large section of the rock wall bowed outward and broke away. It fell on the congested walkways that lined the dock, crushing an unknown number of Murlak who were working there.

"They are retreating to the shuttles!" Tria called out.

Several pirates were running for the shuttles. That was the last thing I wanted.

"Weapons free!" I shouted.

Three of the shuttles were docked below the stern of the freighter, but two were in our line of sight. I fired a beam shot that struck the first shuttle nose-on. The distance diffused the weapon's effectiveness but still blew out the front view screens. Coonts's and Tria's follow-up shots left huge gaping holes in its hull. We shifted our fire to the second shuttle, ripping the hold open and setting it on fire. Our attack did little to dissuade the surviving pirates from trying to board the remaining shuttles. It also drew a line directly back to us. The hostiles now had a location to focus their ire. Light weapons fire lanced up at us from every angle, but the curvature of the freighter's hull shielded us from most of it. We rained high-explosive and antipersonnel rounds down onto the scattered troops. A lot of it was ineffective, but it let them know their efforts were more of an inconvenience than a hindrance to our wanton destruction. I set an antimatter round for its lowest yield and targeted the long wide ramp that connected the shuttle dock to the asteroid. It went up in a tremendous flash, raining debris all across the hull of the freighter. The Operative ignored the distraction and let the Troop Master know we needed to keep moving.

"Any time, Troop Master!" Sael yelled.

The exhaust vents locked open on the rear of the Tibor's armor. I was glad when he didn't voice his opinion of Sael's leadership. He instead triggered the device, giving us an access hole. Sael jumped with the rest of us right behind her. The drop was only about twenty feet, and we landed in a well-lit corridor lined with pipes, wires, and conduit. The maintenance tunnel was not the only thing the Operative had correct. We came down a few feet behind an inspection team. The noise of our landings made them whirl around to face us. We were so close together that they could make out the blood-splattered outlines of Klutch and me. The shock on their faces was permanently erased by exploding buckshot from Klutch's shotgun. He gave the three-man team a whole magazine, blowing their remains well down the walkway. Sael yelled at Klutch and pointed to the deck. He jammed a new magazine into his shotgun and mumbled something disparaging under his breath. I cleared my helmet so he could plainly see my look of disapproval. He quickly made another portal. Sael took note of my reaction and incorrectly interpreted it as an endorsement of her leadership skills. She grabbed Klutch by his weapons pack before he could jump.

"We need the control room intact!" she called to us on our group comms.

Her stating the obvious did not endear her to the rest of my team. She was pushing her luck with the Troop Master and, for that matter, me as well. I was on the verge of reeling her in when she redeemed herself. Her choice of an insertion point was spot on. We landed just inside the bridge access hatch. There was no hiding the sound of our sudden touch downs. The two security guards outside of the hatch spun around to investigate. Klutch and Coonts jammed their shotguns against the Murlak's armored breast plates and gave each a penetrator slug. They were blown out into the corridor and against a bulkhead. Neither was moving. The twin blasts spurred the bridge crew to action. Those who had sidearms drew them and fired blindly at the hatch opening and at my partially visible outline. I was struck twice, but the low-energy pistol beams had no effect on my heavy armor. I extruded my climbing hooks and used my gravity drive to boost into the Murlak firing on me. I drove my shoulder into the skull of my first assailant and slashed the arms from the other. The command center erupted into chaos. Tria disregarded the free-for-all and kept a cool head. She jerked the Murlak captain out of his chair and open-hand slapped him to the deck, then put a boot on his back to hold him there. Sael, Coonts, and Klutch went medieval on the four remaining command staff. The body parts that littered the deck around the captain and the blood pooling against his face had him retching his guts out. Tria uncloaked and pulled the captain up off the deck.

"Lock down the ship's access hatches and activate the shields, or I will cut you up a piece at a time," she demanded.

It wasn't a stretch to guess the freighter's captain was no longer the master of his bowels. He was blubbering nonsense our translators could not comprehend, but he pointed to a console. Tria set him down, letting him gingerly step over the eviscerated members of his crew. He started working the controls with hands that were shaking so badly I was surprised he was able to use them at all. He finished and turned to Tria.

"It is done!"

Coonts was working his way around the bridge consoles, examining each of them. He stopped at one in particular.

"Commander, I have located the weapons console and can target the remaining shuttles with the aft batteries."

I had mixed feelings about destroying the shuttles. We had no way of knowing if Eiger had made it aboard one of them or not. I had it in my mind that proper closure of my Eiger vendetta would involve close scrutiny and accurate identification of his corpse. The shuttles were an imminent danger to the freighter, and as far as I knew, the only way for Eiger to escape. Like it or not, they were a clear and present danger that had to be dealt with.

"One of the shuttles is getting underway!" Tria said, expediting my decision.

"Coonts, destroy the shuttles!" I ordered.

An alarm sounded when we started taking fire from the shuttle. Its shields were up, and it peeled away from the dock. The Murlak pilot was concentrating his fire on the freighter's aft shield. It was flaring a bright white, triggering another alarm on the bridge. Coonts returned the favor, and the shuttle tried to veer away. There was little room for it to maneuver, and the larger weapons of the freighter finally penetrated its weakened shields. It blew apart, sending a large piece of its hull onto one of the docked shuttles. The impact ripped the ship from its mooring and sent it tumbling to the bottom of the docking bay. It exploded in a crash that triggered an impressive fire on several pieces of equipment. The machinery and pumps that maintained the atmosphere were no longer functioning, thanks to the tune-up Coonts gave the generator with an antimatter charge. The smoke from the fires was rapidly filling the entire docking bay.

The pirates who had taken refuge in the remaining shuttle finally decided the wisdom of doing so was faulty on a variety of levels. They unassed the shuttle only to find that the boarding ramp was no longer attached to the mooring pads. The twenty or so fools gathered at the end of the shattered walkway. I guess they were trying to figure out if they could leap the two-hundred-foot chasm my antimatter shell had created. Coonts wasn't taking any chances they might somehow sprout wings. He raked them with cannon fire and then shredded the shuttle, adding to the growing conflagration in the bottom of the docking bay. Coonts used the targeting screen to scan the loading area for more hostile targets. The surviving pirates retreated into the base, conceding the docking bay to us. The familiar sound of a Chaalt grenade detonating somewhere down the passage from the bridge pulled Coonts and I away from the weapons console. Klutch and Sael went in that direction to secure the approaches to the command center. I looked over at Tria, and she waved us on. We ran out into the passage and saw smoke rising up from the lift tube. It wouldn't be hard to track Klutch and the Operative. The trail of carnage left in their wake was easy to follow. We stepped out of the lift tube and found the mutilated recipients of the grenade. We were in a large corridor that led to the hold; the hallway had several bodies scattered down its length. Sael and Klutch were nowhere in sight.

"Klutch, give me a sitrep." I called.

"I am in the cargo bay, Commander, and it is now secure. The Operative went aft to the engineering spaces. You may want to take a look at what is in the hold."

"Roger that, Troop Master, I am on my way. Sael, what is your status?"

"I have secured the engine room and have the full cooperation of the engineering crew," Sael said. "Send the Troop Master to stand guard over them."

Sael's leadership was officially over. She had stomped all over my patience. Yes, she led us to a quick and decisive takeover of the freighter, but the turmoil of her command style had hit the tipping point.

"Negative! Hold your position," I ordered.

"I would be better—"

"Senior Operative! That was not a request!"

I took her silence as an acknowledgment of my order. I saw Klutch wave to Coonts and me. He was standing in front of the large pressure doors that sealed the hold. My exchange with Sael was over our group comms. I couldn't think of any other reason for the smile on the Tibor's face. Just inside the doors were seven or more dead bodies and several weapons scattered on the deck. It was hard to tell because most were shot to pieces. I was willing to bet the Tibor's minigun ran dry before he decided the pirates were no longer a threat. Several shipping crates full of credit vouchers also suffered from his attack. There were hundreds of vouchers scattered about the hold. Coonts disappeared among the crates and returned several minutes later.

"Commander, I can only speculate, but the value of the artifacts that I could identify are worth hundreds of millions of credits," Coonts said. "That is only what I could see on this side of the hold. Along with the unknown amount of credits, we are talking about hundreds of billions in wealth, possibly more. I would like to make a suggestion."

"Okay, let's hear it."

"I think we should take the freighter and link up with the Zaens and transfer the cargo. It will be less exposure to hostile retaliation if the Murlak call for additional reinforcements. It would be an error on our part to think that they have not already done so."

"Can you do it with just the captain and the engineering crew?"

"Yes, if the Operative stands watch over the engine spaces, we can do it. We still need to get out of the asteroid. If you can get the access doors open, I can get the freighter to the jump off point."

"I still want antimatter charges set in the cargo hold," I said. "If we fail to get to the jump off point, I want you and Sael to abandon ship and destroy the freighter."

"Roger that, Commander. Klutch and I will set the charges now."

Coonts was right. It made sense to steal the freighter since the Murlak were kind enough to load it for us. The transfer at a secure location would also keep our freighter from being identified by hostile forces. I didn't want it to be a target for retribution, especially if it was carrying Containium from El Dorado. Sael was going to crap a Throgg when she heard what the new plan was. She didn't have to like it; she just needed to do it. I might as well break the news to her and get it over with.

"Sael, I have made a change of plans," I said to her over our comms. "You are to stay in place and make sure the engineers have the star drives ready for departure on a moment's notice. We are going to take the freighter to the jump off point."

"The engineer Coonts would be the appropriate candidate for that duty," Sael protested. "You would be better served if I was on the assault team that attempts to get the access doors open."

"Coonts will be on the bridge with the Murlak captain piloting the freighter. You have your orders, and I expect you to carry them out. Are we clear?"

Sael must have been busy crapping more than one Throgg, because she failed to answer. I took that as a yes.

Coonts and Klutch finished planting the charges and joined back up with me. My heated exchange with Sael had big grins on both their faces.

"Let's get moving!" I said.

We went back to the bridge, and Coonts took over the captain's chair from Tria. My armor was a bloody, gut-covered mess. Without a thorough cleaning, my cloaking systems were useless. I approached the captain of the pirate ship. He tried to back away, but Tria stopped his retreat by stepping behind him. My appearance was probably doing additional damage to the already poor condition of his undergarments.

"Open a comms channel to the base," I told him. "Tell Eiger the demon that destroyed his outpost and his battleship wants to speak with him."

The captain hastily complied. His shrill, almost pleading voice added a nice touch to the transmission. Unfortunately, it did not inspire anyone to answer. I summoned the most sinister voice I could muster and called out over the open channel, "I am coming for you, Eiger!"

We were going to have to do it the hard way. I waved to Tria and Klutch. Before we could exit the bridge, Coonts grabbed Klutch and turned him around.

"You should take my minigun munitions. You may need them if the pirates decide to fight."

Klutch clapped the engineer on the shoulder and nodded. He ejected his empty ammo pack, and Coonts clipped his into place.

"All kills made with my munitions will be credited as mine. You are currently only six ahead of me," Coonts called to the Tibor as we turned to leave.

I knew the two meatheads had a wager of some kind going. Now I knew it was on how many pirates they could each kill. Klutch spun and faced Coonts, raising his finger.

"Move out, Troop Master!" I yelled.

He quickly complied without further comment. We didn't waste time messing with the boarding hatch in case it was being targeted by the pirates. We crawled up the rescue hatch into the hull maintenance tunnel. Klutch made a hole, and we were once again on the outer hull. The chamber was now filled with thick, dark smoke, which obscured the loading area. The fires down below were somewhat diminished due to the low oxygen levels. It was getting lower by the minute, and the inconvenience of not having breathable air would force the pirates to use suits or masks. I didn't know if they had another scrubber they could bring online. The probability of repairing the damage we caused on our insertion was low. The Chaalt grenades we left behind would discourage all but the most well-endowed in the nads department to make an attempt.

Coonts was monitoring our progress and dropped the freighter's shield long enough for us to clear the hull. We engaged our gravity drives and made a fast drop to the wrecked loading area. We set down behind a large gravity sled that got upended by my antimatter shell. We came under fire by automated turrets that dropped from the overhead in front of the atmospheric lock. They were blasting the gravity sled to smithereens. Klutch's answer to the problem was to burn them down. He unclipped his plasma caster and pumped four big glowing globs of plasma over the top of the sled and onto the overhead structure. Oxygen was a great accelerant, but plasma didn't need it to burn. The inferno Klutch started rapidly spread to all the equipment near the entrance to the base. First one turret went silent, and the other quit seconds later. The bad thing about Klutch's plasma toy was it burned at such high temperatures it wasn't healthy for us to go wading through it. We were going to have to make a hole somewhere other than here. I did not want to risk damaging our armor.

I pointed up at the rock bulging out into the docking chamber by the detonation of our antimatter charge. There was a chance the rock that fractured off of its surface made the remainder thin enough to use the portal device. We boosted up to the damaged wall, and Klutch chose the spot he decided would give us the best chance for a usable portal. Before he could trigger the device, a rumble resonated through the docking chamber that rapidly turned to a roar. The thick smoke that was helping to hide our activities was disappearing at an alarming rate. The pirates were opening the asteroid's access doors. Everything not securely locked down went flying out into the void. As the big doors slowly parted and the smoke and debris cleared, I could see an unpleasant sight: The Murlak Warbringer's huge weapons-covered nose filled the expanding opening. I should have known the pirates were up to something. I doubted if they were going to destroy their freighter, but they effectively blocked its exit. Eiger was forcing a standoff he thought he could win. The odds had shifted into the pirate's favor but rebounded back in ours as a very welcome voice came over our comms.

"Commander, are you in need of assistance?" Justice asked.

It was hard to say if the AI's casual inquiry was to instill calm to our rattled composures, but my reply was anything but.

"Justice! Strike the Warbringer now!" I shouted.

Two blindingly bright beams struck the battleship's shield amidships, causing it to flare a bright milky white. A pulsating ball of energy quickly followed. The brightness of the anomaly rivaled a star and blacked out our HUDs. Its velocity slowed slightly as it passed through the ship's shields. Its impact was dramatic and devasting. The massive battleship seemed to wrap itself around the wound inflicted on it and started melting away into the blinding pyre. I was awed and shocked at the same time. The power of the Oolaran weapon was frightening to witness. I hoped it had the same effect on the pirates as it was having on me. The momentum imparted by the massive energy release shoved the huge battleship aside. Coonts did not hesitate and accelerated the freighter out of the opening. It veered sharply away from the collapsing warship and disappeared into the asteroid field. I thought the Grawl was cutting the clearances a little too close, but his decision to flee proved to be the correct one. The Murlak ship parted in the middle, and the fat blunt nose careened into the asteroid, crashing into the edge of the access doors. One of the giant doors came loose and floated across the bay in our direction. We boosted hard to get out of its way as it struck the wall several yards from where we were going to make our insertion. The corner of the door saved us the troubled of porting through. It punched a large hole through the rock, decompressing the base's interior. As it rebounded off and headed for the bottom of the dock, it was being trailed by three flailing Murlak pirates and a considerable amount of unidentified junk.

We reversed our course and flew back to the rend created by the door. When the outflow of debris slowed to a trickle, we boosted inside. The interior lighting was flickering but still operational. We could see that safety pressure doors had slammed shut on both ends of the corridor we were in. The pirates still had a small quantity of usable atmosphere. That wasn't going to work for me. If we had to operate in the void, then the pirates would as well. I raised my launcher and gave the door farthest from our position a five-shot burst of high explosive. One or two would have probably gotten the job done, but the Tibor had rubbed off on me enough to imprint his philosophy of more is always better. The hatch blew inward, crushing an unknown number of hostiles. The void quickly claimed the bodily remains and sucked them from the opening with other assorted pieces of trash. Klutch charged forward and held up a grenade. When the gruesome discharge slowed, he threw it into the opening. We were disappointed when it did not detonate. I had my doubts that we had accounted for all the pirates.

"Justice, can you get an interior scan through the dock access?" I asked.

"Negative, Commander, the interior spaces are well-shielded."

Tria got my attention and raised her launcher. Klutch saw what she was doing and did the same.

"High explosive, five-second delay, five-round bursts," she called to Klutch.

He gave her a thumbs up and stepped up to the opening so he had a good angle to bounce them down the passage. They opened fire, sending the explosive shells ricocheting in both directions down the passage. The rippling detonations sent small vibrations through my boots. I pushed off the floor and floated to the junction.

The corridor was filled with clouds of debris, but there was no sign of the pirates anywhere. There was not a lot of base to hide in. Klutch went left, and Tria and I went right. We could see the front entrance because it still had plasma fires marking its location. We slowed up when we came to a large vault door. It was the former treasure chamber for the pirates. It was closed, and depending what Klutch could come up with, it had to be one of the few places left to hide. Klutch hailed us a few minutes later.

"Commander, I have no live combatants to report, and none matched Eiger's description."

It was an interesting way to word his report and did not include any additional information. I surmised he may have found live pirates, but they were no longer alive. I was not going to second-guess him, but it would have been nice to question someone as to the whereabouts of the remaining pirates. I looked back at the vault door, wondering if the pirates had indeed trapped themselves in the chamber. I could only think of a couple of reasons they would do that. The one that made the most sense was they were taking refuge until help could arrive.

"Justice, did the Warbringer launch any comms buoys?"

"Affirmative, Commander. They launched a total of eleven since their arrival in this system. The most recent were the three they launched just before they moved into the asteroid field."

"Don't you think that would be information I should know?"

500

"Unless the pirates are able to summon a fleet or they have developed new shields and weaponry, it will make little difference on the outcome of your mission."

The AI had a point. The Murlak's technology was no match for ours. If they sent other ships, they would share the same fate as Eiger's flagship. Klutch joined back up with us. He was examining the vault door with Tria.

"Did Coonts jump out of the system?" I asked Justice.

"Yes, Commander, he has sent an IST report back to me. He has rendezvoused with our freighter, and they are transferring the cargo. He estimates it will take them approximately three hours to complete the loading operation."

"Roger that. As soon as they get the cargo transferred, I want him to cut the Murlak freighter loose and let them go their own way. Tell him and Sael they are to stay with the Zaens and jump to the Sig base near El Dorado. We will join up with them there."

"Sending message now, Commander."

Tria and Klutch had disappeared down the corridor and into one of the side passages.

"Nathan, we have a wall that may be shared by the vault enclosure," Tria called to me. "Klutch wants to use the portal device to determine if we are correct. We will hold until you join us."

"I am on my way."

Unless we killed Eiger in the shuttles, he had to be hiding in the vault with the last of the pirates. It would have been a simple matter to port a hole in the vault door and give the scum hiding there an antimatter gift before we abandoned the base. But in order to get the closure on Eiger I was seeking, I would have to positively identify him. It made no difference if he was dead or alive as long as I could get a good look at his face. An antimatter shell in the confines of the vault would no doubt leave little in the way of remains to identify. I chose instead to leave a grenade against the door and set it to remote detonate. Boosting down the passage, I found the storage area where Tria and Klutch waited for me. Tria met me at the entrance and pointed to the rear wall.

31

The storage chamber once held the loading equipment that we destroyed in our assault of the loading dock. There were a few older gravity sleds that occupied the back wall. Their appearance alluded to the fact they were non-working junk that hadn't moved in a long time. Klutch was standing between two of the them, motioning at us to join him.

"Commander, if we can activate a good portal at this location, we should be to the rear of the pirate forces," Klutch said. "I doubt if they have figured out how we got into the base. It will be a complete surprise when we show up inside the vault with them."

"I left a grenade against the door," I said. "It should be just enough of a distraction to make them think we are trying to come through from that direction. When I detonate it, you try to get us a hole."

The Troop Master gave me a big, goofy smile and activated his war face. He checked his shotgun and gave me a thumbs up. Tria was standing next to me and changed out her mags for fresh ones. She made eye contact and blew me a kiss. I couldn't help but smile. Her faceplate changed to its evil-looking caricature, and she turned to face the wall. I put my war face back on and detonated the grenade. Reaching out, I rapped the Troop Master on his shoulder with my armored fist. He ported us a good hole, and we jumped through. We found ourselves standing next to a large, empty storage crate. Out to our front were twenty-four Murlak pirates. They were behind makeshift barricades consisting of overturned gravity sleds. The backside of the vault door had several blackened places around its perimeter. The fools had welded the door shut in an attempt to keep us out. The dust cloud shook loose by my grenade was still floating out from the door. We had a captive audience; all eyes were forward in anticipation of us coming from that direction. My attention was drawn to a tall pirate wearing bright silver armor. He was standing to the rear of the defensive formation. He had six pirates forward of his position wearing Zaen battle armor. They had their launchers trained on the vault door.

"Is that Eiger?" I asked my team.

Tria commed me right back and said, "If it is, the arrogant piece of scat is wearing the ceremonial armor of Murlak royalty!"

Klutch drew a bead on the pirate's back. "What does that have to do with anything. Dead is dead!"

Tria pushed the barrel of Klutch's weapon aside. "I will show you what that means!"

Before I could react, Tria boosted right at the pirate in shiny armor. Klutch and I had no choice but to follow. As we closed with the target, Tria flipped her shotgun around and caught it by the barrel. Klutch and I raised our beam weapons in case the hostiles wearing Zaen armor turned on us. When it seemed like Tria would collide with the pirate, she swung her shotgun like a baseball bat. It was a hell of a swing. The weapon made solid contact with the side of the pirate's helmet, driving him from his feet. The limp body rebounded off the ground, and she grabbed him in a headlock. The Murlak's helmet had a dent in the side and hairline cracks in the face plate. Tria pointed back the way we came and boosted for the portal. The lack of atmosphere left no sound to alert the pirates what was transpiring to their rear. Klutch looked like he was going to open fire into the backs of the pirates. I waved him off and pulled an antimatter charge from my storage pouch. He saw what was in my hand and boosted for the portal. I set the charge and gave it a fifteen-minute delay. As I approached the portal, I gave the charge a toss, sending it bouncing around in the empty storage crate. As I exited the portal, I almost ran into Tria and Klutch. They were stripping the Murlak's armor of weapons.

"Is it Eiger?"

Tria looked up at me with a grim smile. "Yes," she said triumphantly.

"Is he still alive?"

"For now."

I alerted them to the time on the charge. Klutch jerked the pirate off the ground by an arm, and Tria grabbed the other. We boosted out into the corridor. The entrance to the base was one hundred yards to our left. I wasn't about to mess with the door.

"Beam shot out!" I called out over our comms.

Klutch and Tria stopped and reversed course back into the storage chamber. I hit the doors dead center with a beam shot, blowing them out into the dock. The burning plasma splattered in all directions. We had a clear path to the docking bay. I turned back to Tria and Klutch. Eiger must have recovered from having his gong rang because they were beating the hell out of him. Their armored fists were making some impressive dents in the flashy Murlak armor. The pirate went limp, and Tria had to stop the Troop Master before he killed him. Eiger's armor had little in the way of protection. It was more for show than it was for combat. He was fortunate that Tria did not hit him with her weapon in the faceplate, or he would have decompressed. There was a good chance the showy armor was for his meeting with his corrupt business partners. I would pay a billion credits to see their faces when Eiger doesn't arrive.

We boosted out into the docking bay. Justice had the Legacy snuggled up to the dock access with the hangar bay open. We felt the pull of the tow beam and cut our gravity drives. He pulled us into the hangar, and I turned to look at Shurmosk for the last time. We had dealt the pirates a blow they may never recover from, but I knew it would not end their presence in the galaxy. The Scrun were proof of that. There would always be another waiting for the chance to take over the leadership position. I felt a small sense of accomplishment in that whoever would take over would have to come up with the funds to stay on top. I smiled when I saw a large plume of debris jet violently from the entrance of the base.

"Justice, it is my understanding, we have an experimental weapon aboard that is still untested."

"Affirmative, Commander. Would you like to commence testing?"

"Yes, Justice. Launch at your discretion."

"I will move the Legacy to the edge of the asteroid field and inform you when the weapon is ready to launch."

I followed Tria and the Troop Master as they dragged Eiger to the brig. The pirate's head jerked upright, and he started yelling something about paying to release him unharmed. Tria drove a pile driver of a punch to his midsection. He gagged and puked into his face mask. They threw him into a cell. Justice closed the door and blacked it out. He was going to experience the treatment he has doled out for an unknown length of time. His chances of living much longer were tenuous at best. We knew he had information on the corrupt members of the Galactic Union. That and the intel on other pirate operations would be the extent of his lifeline. He would tell us what we wanted to know, or the Troop Master would use his fingers as toothpicks. We would be able to corroborate some of the information he would eventually give us with

Illam Pove. Justice alerted me he was ready to launch the Oolaran torpedo.

"Commander, I have instructed the weapon's onboard AI to transition to Shurmosk and enter the docking bay. Once inside, it will power down and wait forty hours before it will self-destruct. If the Murlak should investigate the base before that time period expires. It will choose the optimal time to self-destruct, with the intent of doing the maximum amount of damage to hostile forces as possible."

The Legacy was unarmed when I discovered it in the Alaskan wilderness. The torpedo was the final weapon missing from its arsenal. I would now have the ship's complete weapons systems at my disposal.

"Okay Justice, launch the missile and jump us back to the Sigs new base."

"Affirmative, Commander. Launching torpedo now, and DEHD core transition in thirty seconds."

My reality flared a bright white and faded away. My return to normal space-time came with the usual report from Justice.

"Commander, I am tracking two hundred and forty Sig military vessels in and around this system. I have a lock on our freighter, and it is holding above the Sig base of operations. Coonts is requesting to speak with you on a private IST channel."

"Thank you, Justice, put him through."

"Commander, was your mission successful?"

"Yes, Tria captured Eiger alive. We are going to take him back to Alpha Base for interrogation."

"That is a surprising turn of events," Coonts said. "I would have thought the pirate would die before surrendering to us."

"Tria did not give him a chance to do either. Have you spoken with Sushi?"

"Yes, and we are both in agreement that it would not be wise to store the contents of our freighter's hold at a location known to the pirates."

"It is my intention to take it back to Alpha Base. I want you to politely explain to the Zaens that they will be staying with the Sig for now. I am sure they won't like it, but I am not ready to reveal the location of Alpha Base to them. I trust them, but it is better for us all if they are not able to divulge what they don't know."

"They will be very disappointed. They have been quite vocal about getting back to their usual trade route."

I really didn't want the two Zaens to be unhappy with me. They had been an invaluable source of tech and the sole reason we now have one of the finest replicator operators in the galaxy. The answer to the problem would require a little finesse, but the Zaens would ultimately come away pleased with my orders.

"Tell Broza and Hylet that we need to make sure the pirates never find the freighter," I said. "They will want revenge on the crew, and I will not allow that. Tell them I bought a new freighter and it will take a short period of time to properly arm and outfit it."

"I was not aware we had another freighter," Coonts said, confused.

"I haven't bought it yet, but they don't need to know that. I want you to get them off the freighter as soon as possible and jump back to Alpha Base. We will unload the hold and sanitize it. We will then trade it back to Tam Lin for a newer model."

"What about the Sig crew?"

"They will stay aboard. I am confident the Sig would rather die than betray our alliance. They can ferry the freighter back to 9765 when we are done with it."

"Roger that, Commander. I have another request before I brief the Zaens."

"Is there something I have not covered?"

"Yes, I would like to offload the Operative as well," Coonts said. "She has made the trip from Shurmosk quite unpleasant. I would appreciate if you could arrange for her to be somewhere else, preferably on her home worlds with her own kind."

I was wondering when Sael would wear out her welcome. It was going to be irritating, but I felt I owed Coonts some relief.

"We will come alongside, and you can tell her to report to me."

As usual, Justice was listening and brought us alongside the freighter's boarding hatch. He opened the hangar door in anticipation of Sael debarking. If she started in on me, I would grant Coonts his wish and send her packing sooner than later. It took her only a few minutes to show up at the freighter hatch and jump across. Tria and I stood waiting to see if she would ruin what had turned out to be a good day. Sael surprised both of us by not carrying on in her usual irritating manner. The look on her face betrayed her true feelings, but she kept them in check.

"May I inquire as to how your mission turned out?" she asked me.

"Tria captured Eiger alive, and he is currently in the brig."

Sael looked shocked at this revelation. She was temporarily lost for words, which was a good thing. It gave me a chance to move on to other things, namely getting out of my armor and into a hot shower.

"Can I see for myself?"

"Sure, Sael, knock yourself out. Tria and I are going to the ready room to stow our armor."

Sael gave me a questioning look. My Earth phrase had her stymied as to its true meaning. I decided to clarify my statement before she could take up any more of my time.

"Yes, Sael, you can see him."

Since the brig was on the way to the ready room, we walked with her, and I was glad she did so silently. Justice cleared our side of the cell wall so we could see in but Eiger could not see out.

Sael stared in at the pirate and then turned to us with a strange look on her face.

"Why is he wearing the ceremonial armor of the Murlak royal clan?"

I didn't have an answer, and how the hell would I know anyway. It was a statement Tria had made as well, but I really didn't care what the pirate prick adorned himself with. It was an interesting subject, but not enough to change the ruminations going on in my mind. I pulled Tria toward the hatch. Things were going my way, and I was going to make the best of it while it lasted.

"Sael, why don't you ask him yourself? Because I don't care!"

With that, Tria and I went to the ready room. We stepped out of our armor, and when we got down to removing our suit liners, Tria's help removing mine made the trip to my quarters a quick one. The stars in my little piece of the galaxy were all aligned. I didn't have a care in the world until Justice commed me.

"Commander, I realize I am interrupting you at a most inopportune time, but Sael Nalen has an urgent need to speak with you."

I couldn't believe it. Sael had a knack for bothering me at the worst possible times, and this was no exception. I was going to have a real hard time controlling the frustration in my voice.

"Put her through, Justice!"

"Nathan! I have found out why Eiger wears the armor of the Murlak royal clan!" Sael said excitedly.

I gritted my teeth in anger. Sael needed to know in no uncertain terms that I really didn't give a shit and she could brief me later. Tria put a halt to my rant and answered for me.

512

"Please continue, Senior Operative."

"I have questioned Eiger at length about the armor. He was more than willing to answer my questions."

I didn't know where this was going, but I had regained my composure enough and wanted to know what kind of crap Eiger was spoon-feeding her.

"Okay, Sael, tell me what he had to say."

"I know you will find this hard to believe, but Eiger claims he was giving up his position as the leader of the pirates. He has made an agreement with the royal clan's patriarch. He was going to turn over his share of the wealth you captured as a penalty for his past transgressions. He would then take a life mate from within the royal clan, and his past was to be erased. He claims that he was going to give his business partners their share of the wealth and was going to cut all ties with them," Sael said. "Nathan, if he became part of the royal clan, it would make little difference to the Murlak people what Eiger's past once was. The only things that will matter to them is what he does going forward."

"Sael, I don't care what he has to say. He is never going to make it to his royal appointment. He will answer for the countless murders and crimes he has committed."

"Nathan, the royal clan is the wealthiest in all the Murlak home worlds. The bloodlines date back thousands of years," Sael said. "Even though they no longer rule, they have the ears of the most powerful government and military officials. What they want, they get, and their opinion is generally the government's official view on all matters. By capturing Eiger, you have made yourselves the enemy of the whole Murlak race."

"I have yet to meet a Murlak who wasn't a pirate, so I don't care what they think. They can be pissed off, but they will never know what happened to Eiger."

"Nathan, that would have been the case if you had not chosen to let the remaining crew on the freighter go free. Now there are survivors who will testify it was the demon warrior who attacked them and most assuredly killed a soon-to-be member of the royal clan. I have no doubt they will claim the wealth you took belonged to them as well. You will now be seen as the hostile aggressor, and the Murlak will hunt you till the end of time if that is what it takes."

As a rule, I tried to keep myself in an upbeat mood when it came to adversity. It was difficult at times, but I always gave it a try regardless. Since I was only one of the two Earthlings I knew of, who were out in the galaxy trying to change things for the better, it was a necessity. Having someone point out that another couple of hundred billion or so aliens were lining up to get a piece of me, pretty much ruined my optimistic outlook. One thing I knew for sure, the Murlak royal clan would learn the hard way: killing me is easier said than done.

The End

Made in the USA
San Bernardino, CA
23 January 2020